rewrite our stars

Samantha Fox

contents

1. Chapter 1 — 1
2. Chapter 2 — 13
3. Chapter 3 — 27
4. Chapter 4 — 38
5. Chapter 5 — 53
6. Chapter 6 — 70
7. Chapter 7 — 86
8. Chapter 8 — 103
9. Chapter 9 — 121
10. Chapter 10 — 138
11. Chapter 11 — 152
12. Chapter 12 — 170
13. Chapter 13 — 187
14. Chapter 14 — 205
15. Chapter 15 — 221
16. Chapter 16 — 242

17. Chapter 17   260

18. Chapter 18   278

19. Chapter 19   291

20. Chapter 20   312

21. Chapter 21   331

22. Chapter 22   347

23. Chapter 23   364

24. Chapter 24   381

25. Chapter 25   397

26. Epilogue   412

CHAPTER 1

T he late August sun beat down on my skin as I stood on my balcony, looking out at the vast amount of land that my parents owned. It was the kind of day where, if I had the choice, I'd relax by the pool with my sunglasses shading my eyes and my music on, enjoying myself as summer dwindled to an end.

However, that wasn't a possibility for me. I had responsibilities, and they weren't the kind that could be disregarded for a day of fun in the sun.

Sighing I was brought back to memories of when I was a little girl; when times were a whole lot simpler. Times when my mom would watch over me as I swam laps in the pool, or when my father would play with me in the backyard, throwing around the frisbee or teaching me how to perfect my dive.

Times had since changed though, because as my sister and I grew up, my mother and father started to mingle with the elite socialites of our town, and as their friends expected them to appear straight and narrow, our parents expectations of us grew to heights unimaginable.

In the eyes of our parents, if my sister or I messed up or embarrassed ourselves publicly it would reflect directly on them, and that was something they couldn't afford. They owned the highest dominating law firm in the state, and other firms, along with the press, were just looking for ways to knock them down.

We were supposed to be the daughters that succeeded in school, participated in events within the community, and most importantly, stayed in line.

That all went down hill when my sister and I both made the biggest mistakes of our lives within the same year.

My sister was only 16 years old, nearing the end of grade 10 when she was arrested for destruction of property and trespassing. She thought that it'd be a good idea to spray paint one of the towns boring signs, giving more life to the board. However, she wasn't careful enough, and even though our parents had immediately paid her bail, word quickly spread of her arrest.

A few short months later, during the summer before my freshman year of university, was when my mistake came to play. Going out and partying to celebrate graduating with your friends always seems like a good idea, but when you end up drunk and mistakenly sleeping with one of the most notorious players in the year, you have regrets.

That night I didn't just come home to disappointed parents as I nursed a killer hangover, I came home pregnant.

When I first found out I immediately considered abortion, adoption and every other option under the sun, but quickly realized that this was my mistake to deal with, finally deciding to keep the baby as my own.

Fast-forward three years and I was here, finally ready to move out from under the watchful eye of my parents, and I couldn't be more thrilled.

The sound of small thumping footsteps brought me out of my reflecting daze, as I turned around to see my three-year-old bundle of joy come skipping into my bedroom.

"Mommy!" she chirped happily, her blonde hair bouncing around her shoulders as she ran over to me in excitement, "My toys are all packed."

Smiling down at her, my heart beat with undeniable love for my daughter. Even though getting pregnant was one of the biggest mistakes of my life, I knew the very first moment I held my daughter in my arms that I would never regret giving her life.

"You are?" I asked in an overly happy voice, picking her up gently and resting her on my hip. "Well let's get the rest of your stuff packed before we get on the road."

She giggled, wrapping her tiny arms around my shoulder as I walked the two of us towards her room at the other end of the hall.

When my parents found out I was pregnant, one thing was for sure, they were furious. They didn't understand how I, their daughter who was destined to follow in their golden footsteps, had made such a careless, stupid mistake.

At first my parents had talked about disowning me as their colleagues quickly started to spread rumours about my pregnancy, however, when I informed them that I would support myself and my daughter to the best of my abilities, they simply nodded.

Since Abbie was born my parents more or less had left the two of us be. If I had a question about how to get her to stop crying, or how to change a diaper, I'd have to go to our housekeeper, Greta, for the answer. My mom and dad left the hallway that I lived on to Abbie and I, barely ever making an appearance unless it was completely necessary.

Pushing open the door to Abbie's room, I saw that my daughter had been telling the truth for the most part. All of the dolls and toys that she had were stuffed into a box in the left corner of her room, with only her small beloved teddy bear still laying untouched on the bed.

"Are you going to take Mr. Cuddles with you in the car Abbie?" I asked, tickling her side gently as I placed her down.

"Mhm," she giggled, running over to bed and squeezing her beloved bear tightly.

Looking around the room, I realized that for the first time in over three years, that it was almost completely empty. The walls were bare of the pictures and drawings that I had so often hung up, and her small dresser and closet were bare of clothing, having already been packed in the days previous.

"Let's take this box of toys down to the car, and then you can say goodbye to Greta while I come and pack up the rest." I said simply, trying not to confuse her with long complicated sentences.

She was smart for her age, but not that smart.

"Okay!" she said, agreeing immediately as she saw me pick up the box of toys and head towards the door, following me down the hallway and the staircase to the foyer.

Placing her toys on the car floor of the passengers seat, I walked back inside to hear Abbie talking to Greta in the kitchen.

"So I'm never gonna see you 'gain?" Abbie asked sadly, trying her best to talk in full sentences as I rounded the corner.

Greta, who was one of the nicest people I'd ever met, bent down with a sad smile on her face, brushing my daughter's hair out of her face. "You don't know that sweetie," she replied, "Maybe one day you'll come back and visit, or who knows, maybe I'll come out and visit you and your momma."

Having already noticed me, I smiled at Greta as I pointed upstairs, silently signaling that I would be grabbing the rest of my things. When she nodded understandingly, hugging my daughter close to her, my heart clenched as I gratefully smiled, turning around quietly.

Twenty minutes later, after taking one last look around the house to make sure I hadn't forgotten anything, I closed the trunk of my car, making sure it was secure before walking to where Greta and Abbie stood some ways up the driveway.

"Okay, we're all packed and ready to go." I stated, smiling sadly at Greta.

After my parents joined their social circle when I was still young, they started to give Greta the responsibility of looking after my sister and I while they were busy. The older we got, the more Greta was around and the less we saw of our parents. She was the person that made moving away from home the hardest.

Greta, who was holding Abbie's small hand in her own, pushed her towards me slightly before I picked her up, heading to the back seat of the car where her car seat sat.

"You've gone to the bathroom, right honey?" I asked sweetly, making sure I wasn't strapping in a little girl who would just have to stop for a potty break in less than 20 kilometers.

Her little head bounced up and down in a nod. "Yup." she replied proudly. "G'eta took me."

Smiling at her mispronunciation of Greta, I nodded, tucking Mr. Cuddles into her arm as I buckled her into the car seat. "Good girl."

Inching my way out of the back seat after I made sure she was strapped in tight, I closed the car door before turning back to Greta.

"Your parents would love to be here Zoe, it's just..." Greta trailed off, her smile showcasing sympathy.

"I know," I nodded, my emotions unmoved as I knew they really just couldn't be bothered. To them I was a disappointment, and until I did anything that they deemed exceptional, that's all I'd ever be to them. "They're busy."

Nodding sadly, Greta looked at me with love in her eyes. "I'm going to miss you honey," she said, stepping forward and hugging me, to which I immediately returned.

"I'll miss you too Greta."

Pulling back, it looked as though a tear or two were building in the corner of her eyes. "Remember to call whenever you need anything, and tell Emily I said hi."

"I will," I smiled, "Don't worry."

She nodded. "Now go, live your life."

"Goodbye Greta."

And with one wave as I retreated to my car, that was that.

Turning my key in the ignition, the engine came to life immediately, lighting up the dashboard and sending music through the speakers. As I put the car in drive and headed slowly down the driveway, I glanced in the rearview mirror to see Greta waving goodbye, my childhood house standing tall in the background.

The gates to the estate opened in front of me, and as I turned down the road, it was as if I was leaving my past behind me, heading towards a brighter future.

When I told my sister that I'd be driving down to LA, she thought I was crazy, even more so considering I was also dragging along a restless three year old. Even going as far as to offer to buy the two of us planes tickets, I knew that the most efficient way to get all of our baggage down to the house was by driving.

Plus, I wasn't that big of fan of planes.

Two hours in however, I was starting to wish that I'd taken Emily up on her offer as my butt was starting to numb and my hands were beginning to cramp from gripping the steering wheel for so long.

Glancing in my rear-view mirror to check on Abbie, I saw that she was still wide awake, which I found rather odd for a toddler her age, keeping herself busy talking and playing with Mr. Cuddles.

As we passed a sign notifying me of a rest stop a few minutes up the road, I partially turned my head back towards Abbie.

"Hey sweetie, we're going to stop in a few minutes." I stated with a smile. "We'll get some food and take a potty break, okay?"

"Okay momma." she chirped with a bright smile.

Nodding at her, I returned my full attention to the road in front of me... the straight, long road that seemed to run for hours.

Thankfully, the sign notifying the rest stop hadn't been lying, as just a few minutes later I was turning my signal light on and smoothly exiting the highway.

Pulling into a free parking space, I took the keys out of the ignition, turning around to smile at my daughter. "So, you ready for food little girl?" I asked, bringing my hand up to gently tickle her stomach, causing her to giggle and squirm in her car seat.

"Yeah momma," she replied through her fit of laughter, "Stop momma."

At her words, I retracted my hand, climbing out of the car before unclasping her seat and cradling her against my hipbone.

"Food now?" she asked, playing with the ends of my hair as I locked the car doors and headed into the rustic looking restaurant.

Looking down at her with love in my eyes, I laughed. "Yes Abbie, food now." I replied, opening the door to the sound of a welcoming bell above our heads.

"Yay!" she cheered, clapping her tiny hands together as we headed up to the counter to order

Fifteen minutes later I was sitting in a small booth, nestled in the corner of the restaurant with Abbie sitting on a booster chair beside me, almost halfway through her small serving of chicken fingers. Laughing down at her as I swallowed the last of my burger, I picked up a napkin from the middle of the table and gently cradled her chin in my free hand.

"Abbie sweetie, how did you manage to get sauce on your nose?" I asked with amusement, wiping her nose gently until it was clean.

She simply grinned at me before dipping another chicken strip in her mountain of sauce and biting off the end.

Sitting back and watching my daughter eat was something I never thought would bring me joy, but sitting here with her, watching as she almost completely destroyed her food, I was completely content with my life.

I could, however, do without the several hours of driving that was ahead of me, but hey, nobody could have a perfect life.

Speaking of the hours ahead of me, a familiar ringtone started to blast from my pocket, and pulling out my phone, I saw that Emily was calling me.

"Hey sis," I greeted as I accepted the call, "What's up?"

"Hey, I'm just on my lunch break." she informed me, sounding as if she was walking down the busy streets of LA. "I wanted to know where you guys are to make sure I'm home when you get there."

"We've only been driving for a little over two hours so we're still pretty far away." I replied, "We're eating lunch right now on a little restaurant off the highway, but probably in about ten or fifteen we'll be driving again. I'd say that we might get near LA around seven tonight but it might take a while to get through the traffic."

"Well it's a Friday night Zoe, what did you expect?" Emily laughed, her voice echoing through the phone.

"I expected the traffic, I'm not delusional, but I just chose a stupid day to move down to LA."

"True." she agreed as the two of us laughed, the sounds fading as she continued. "So you'll probably be here before eight then?"

Nodding my head for a second, I quickly realized that she couldn't see me. "Yea, that sounds about right." I replied, "Why what are you up to tonight?"

"Not that much since I work until four and then I think Dustin's just going to be coming over to hang out after that," she explained. "But don't worry, I've already persuaded him to help you move yours and Abbie's stuff into your rooms."

"You're the best Em." I said with a smile, resting back into the cushioned booth as I watched Abbie finish the last of what was on her small plate.

"I know."

I rolled my eyes at my sister's remark. "Anyways, Abbie's pretty much done eating so I'm going to take her to the bathroom before we hit the road again."

"Okay, tell that little cutie that I'll see her tonight."

I smiled at my sister's love for her niece. "I will," I agreed, "See you tonight."

"See you tonight, love you."

"Love you too."

Pressing the end call button as I brought the phone away from my ear, I looked down at Abbie. "Aunty Emily says that she's excited see you tonight." I said, bringing a napkin up to her face to wipe off the excess food that was visible.

Her grin grew two sizes as she heard her favourite (and only) aunt's name.

"Now, how about we head to the bathroom for a potty break before getting back in the car?" I asked happily in my motherly voice, picking her up from her booster seat and placing her on the ground beside the booth.

"Yea momma!" she cheered, overly excited about such a simple thing as she took off running with her small legs to the back of the restaurant where the bathrooms were located.

Shaking my head in amusement, I followed my daughter, as I was positive she did not have a clue where she was going.

Hours passed by as I drove down the long, winding highways on route to Los Angeles, California. An hour after leaving the restaurant was when Abbie had pretty much passed out in her car seat, leaving me to my thoughts as I turned the radio up slightly, taking the chance to listen to the music I enjoyed.

My butt had long since gone numb from sitting so long, and even when we stopped for a quick dinner before hitting L.A traffic, my legs took a couple of seconds to adapt to the sensation of not being cramped underneath a steering wheel.

As I hit the massive traffic lines coming in and out of Los Angeles, I realized that Emily truly wasn't joking when she mentioned the traffic was horrible. All I could see in front of me was cars moving bumper to bumper, the impatient drivers honking as the others just seemed used to the irregularly busy streets.

Finally, however, as I managed to pull out of the massive traffic pile up and onto a side street, the clock on the dash illuminated telling me that it had just passed eight 'o'clock. The end of summer sun was starting to lower on the horizon as my phone's automatic GPS told me to twist and turn on an abundance of side roads leading up to our destination.

Emily had lived in the area for a few years, but when I mentioned wanting to move out here as well, she immediately found a place for the two of us to share, making sure that it was still safe and practical for Abbie.

So far I'd only seen the small Skype tour she'd given me the month previous when she moved in, but it seemed like it'd be the perfect place to start over.

"Mommy," Abbie said, fully awake now after her elongated nap earlier in the day, "Are we there yet?"

Sighing in amusement, this was probably the thirtieth time I'd heard those words come from her mouth in the last three hours.

"No honey, but it'll only be a few more minutes." I responded calmly as the GPS instructed me to turn right on the next street.

It didn't take long for us to reach our destination from there, and before Abbie could utter the words 'are we there yet' once more, I pulled into the driveway of a small house in a calm, yet lively, neighbourhood.

Putting the car into park I looked back at my daughter, smiling at her in achievement. "We're here."

Leaving our luggage in the car, I quickly unbuckled Abbie from her car seat, picking her up and resting her on my hip as I walked up the driveway towards the house.

Reaching the front door, I brought my free hand up to knock, and not even fifteen seconds had passed before the door sporadically opened, revealing my little sister's ecstatic face.

"You made it!" she exclaimed, welcoming me into the foyer.

Taking a step into my new house, I felt like everything was finally falling into place. It was like nothing would suddenly come out of left field and blindside me; my life was on track, and it was a track I wanted to be on.

Looking around, I saw that Emily had already made herself at home, and it made me smile to think that, soon enough, I would too.

Turning back to see my sister, I saw her close the door and smile at me.

"Welcome to your new home sis."

CHAPTER 2

The night I arrived in LA was busier than expected. Even with Dustin's help, it still took the three of us at least half an hour to transfer everything out of my fully packed car and into the house.

By the time I had somewhat sorted the boxes into piles to later be unpacked I realized that it was well past ten 'o'clock, which came with Dustin bidding us adieu, promising to return tomorrow. Abbie had taken up a resting spot on the couch in the living room, but after some gentle maneuvers, and a bit of luck on my part, I had moved her into my room, settling her under the covers before kissing her forehead and wishing her a goodnight sleep.

Downstairs I found Emily without much trouble, following my sense of smell as I headed towards the kitchen. "Mhmm," I started, "What smells so good?"

Emily, who was previously facing the counter, looked over her shoulder with a smile on her face as she nodded to the cup she was mixing. "Hot chocolate," she replied, "Want one?"

Nodding in response, I opened two cupboards before finding where she had stored the mugs. "It smells just like the kind Greta used to make us when we were younger." I commented, sliding the empty mug over to her, willing her to work her magic.

"That's because it is," she replied as she started mixing the ingredients together, "Greta gave me the recipe one night when I called her after a break-up a few years back. She thought it'd help to cheer me up a bit."

"And did it? Help with the break-up?"

"A bit, if I remember correctly," she smiled in response; stirring in the heated milk she had on hand from her own drink. "That and time I guess. But hey, I met Dustin a couple months after that, so I can't complain about the way everything turned out."

Nodding as she finished up, the two of us moved to the living room, where although there were too many boxes littered around the floor, the room brought a sense of comfort that the kitchen was lacking. Tucking my legs up under my body, I smiled at Emily. "How are things with you and Dustin?" I asked, genuinely interested in what I'd missed being so far away from my sister. There were only so many things you could catch up on with the odd phone call. "By what I saw tonight I'd say that he's completely in love with you."

Emily's cheeks reddened slightly at my comment as she sipped at her hot chocolate, but the grin that soon followed told me that she felt the same way. "Things are good, I mean we've been together for almost two years so we're pretty much over the honeymoon stage, but once and a while he still does things that are adorably sweet. I love him and right now, I can see myself with him in the future."

A small awing noise escaped my lips as I listened to my love-struck sister. "Well if you're happy with him then I'm happy for you."

"Thanks," she mumbled, "But what about your love life? Did you leave a trail of broken hearts on your way down here?" Smiling grimly I shook my head, responding with a negative as I sipped at my hot chocolate. With a frown, Emily looked at me confusedly. "Well why not?"

"It's not that hard to explain Em, in fact, you can probably guess the answer." I started. "Sure there's been a few dates here and there over the past couple of years, but they never end up going anywhere because as soon as Abbie's name gets thrown into the mix it's game over. No unattached guy my age wants a girl with a three year old, hence no boyfriend."

"Well maybe you'll find somebody down here that'll want to get to know you! I mean, sure you have a daughter, but you're still a great person. You're smart, funny, and you like to have fun once in a while, and soon enough, somebody will see that."

"We'll see." I said, the side of my lips turning up at her excitement and loving honesty.

As the conversation took a turn away from our love lives, or more specifically my non-existent one, our hot chocolates were soon gone, the mugs left resting empty on the coffee table as the two of us sat there talking, catching up with each other's lives as the time ticked by. Somewhere between midnight and one 'o'clock in the morning was when the exhaustion finally settled in, the two of us deciding it was finally time for bed.

Heading back upstairs to my room, I walked in to see Abbie right where I left her, her blonde hair splayed out messily as she slept softly on one side of the bed. Sighing softly, I was glad that I decided to wear comfortable clothes for the ride down here, as I didn't have the energy to search through boxes for a pair of pajamas at this time of night. Walking to the other side of the bed, I pulled the covers up slightly, slipping underneath them as I cuddled up to Abbie.

I didn't bother to think about the fact that Abbie would more than likely move during the night and proceed to wake me up, or the fact that I'd probably be awoken much earlier than I'd like. I was just too tired, and it wasn't long after I closed my eyes that I sunk into a peaceful slumber.

Poking; soft and consistent poking was all I felt as I slowly seeped back into consciousness. "Wake up momma!" I heard Abbie chirp as her small hands continued to poke my arm.

Rolling over, I lazily opened my eyes, to see the blurred face of my daughter quickly come into focus. "Good morning baby girl," I said sleepily through a yawn.

"Morning momma!"

Hugging her tiny body close to me, laughter exploded from her as I playfully pulled the covers back up over both of our heads. "Did you have a good sleep?" I asked, tickling her stomach gently.

As she nodded and squirmed in my arms, it amazed me how much energy she had at this time in the morning. Judging by the way the sunlight was so brightly seeping in through the windows, my best guess was that it was around seven 'o'clock in the morning, and still, Abbie was acting as if she had just been given chocolate in the middle of the day.

"Hungry momma!" she chirped through her giggles.

"Oh," I said, stopping my tickling assault on my daughter as I raised an eyebrow, "Do you want breakfast?" When she smiled and nodded in response I sighed. "Okay, how about we make a deal? If you go the bathroom and then wash your hands like a good little girl, I'll meet you downstairs and then I'll make breakfast."

"Okay momma!" she replied excitedly, scurrying her way slowly out of the covers before sliding off the side of the bed and heading to the bathroom down the hall.

Leaning back onto my pillow, I flipped the covers off of me and sighed. Turning to my side I saw that the small clock on the bedside table read 7:05am, and with one last yawn, I stumbled out of bed and headed downstairs, as I was in desperate need of a cup of coffee.

Minutes later I was still going through multiple cupboards in search of where my sister kept the coffee when I heard small pattering footsteps coming towards me. Turning around I saw Abbie come in with her hands still dripping wet from having washed them.

"Did somebody forget to dry their hands again?" I asked jokingly, grabbing a paper towel as I walked up to her and dried her hands off. "So," I continued, picking her up on my hip before placing her in one of the chairs at the kitchen table, "Do you want peanut butter and jelly or cereal for breakfast?"

"Peanubu'er jelly!" she answered happily.

Smiling with amusement at her vocabulary, I nodded. "Peanut butter and jelly coming right up."

Minutes later I was placing a plate in front of Abbie that held a piece of peanut butter and jelly covered toast, as well as a glass of milk while I sat down with my own piece of toast. Just as we were about to start eating, Emily walked around the corner clad in a pair of pajamas.

"Good morning little princess." she said softly, kissing the side of Abbie's head before heading to the cupboards and pulling out a box of tea. "So," she continued, looking to me this time as she flipped the kettle on, "How'd you sleep?"

"Alright I guess," I shrugged. "I'm still tired from last night but that's probably because we stayed up till almost one 'o'clock in the morning, and then this little rascal woke me up about fifteen minutes ago. Why are you up so early though?"

"I work at eight 'o'clock," she replied easily. "What about you, what are your plans for the day?"

"Besides unpacking?" I asked jokingly, gesturing to some small boxes that had been brought into the kitchen the previous night. "I found a day care a few blocks away from the university, so I'm going to bring Abbie by there around lunch time, and then I'll probably just walk around the city for a bit, maybe look for a part-time job."

"A part-time job?" my sister repeated, scrunching up her eyebrows inquisitively.

"Yea, you know, a night or two a week." I replied, finishing off the toast I'd made for myself. "Maybe a couple of weekend shifts."

"Zoe," she started, however, she was interrupted as her kettle finished. Pausing to finish her tea, she brought her finished cup over to the table, taking the seat beside me. "Zoe, how are you expecting to finish your degree, take care of Abbie and still take on a part-time job?"

Sighing, I shook my head, plastering on a small, fake smile as I turned to Abbie, who seemed to pretty much be done with her breakfast. "Abbie honey, do you want to go watch cartoons for a bit?" I asked kindly, and when she nodded, I got up from my seat and brought her into the living room, quickly finding a children's channel before returning to the kitchen.

Picking up my plate, as well as Abbie's dirty dishes, I brought them to the sink and started washing them. "You know I'm not expecting you to pay for this house by yourself right?"

"I know that Zoe, but you have enough money to get you through the year..." she started.

"Don't you think I know that Emily?" I said angrily, turning around to look at her. "I've been working two jobs the past couple of years to save up and move down here, and even with that money, what happens when Abbie suddenly grows and needs new clothes? What happens if we suddenly have to pay for something unexpected?"

Silence floated between the two of us for a small amount of time before Emily mumbled something under her breath. Not able to understand her, I asked her to repeat herself.

"I said," she sighed before continuing softly, "What about the money mom and dad gave you when Abbie was born?"

My teeth clenched at the memory, one I wasn't so keen to remember. When Abbie was born my parents didn't care that they now had a granddaughter, no, they only cared that for all intents and purposes the two of us stay out of the public eye. They went as far as giving me more than $100,000 to follow their demands.

"No." I replied hotly. "I spent a small amount of that money the first year to purchase everything I needed for Abbie, but ever since I got my own job I haven't touched a cent of it. It's for when she grows up. I'm not touching that money ever again."

"Zoe," Emily started, her voice seeping with pity.

"No Emily, I'm not touching that money."

"I was actually going to say that that plate looks dry enough." she commented, nodding to the plate I was currently wiping down with a towel after washing it. I hadn't even realize I'd still been washing it.

"Oops," I replied embarrassedly, placing the plate down on the counter before picking up the other one.

"And I'm sorry," Emily continued, "You know, for bringing up our parents."

"It's okay," I admitted, exhaling as I attempted to get rid of the stress that had started to build up inside of me at the mention of our parents, "I just don't believe in using that money if I can find a way to make my own."

"Duly noted," Emily replied. "Just know that if you ever do need help, I'm always here for you."

"Thanks sis." I responded, and when she took a sip of her tea, something sparked my memory. "Oh, by the way, where do you keep the coffee? I tried looking for it before you got up but I couldn't find it anywhere."

"Shoot, I knew I forgot something." she mumbled under her breath.

"Come again?"

"Sorry Zoe, I totally forgot you drank coffee." she apologized. "I went to the grocery store and everything yesterday to get a few extra things, but since I haven't drank coffee in over a year I didn't even think about getting any."

"Don't worry about it," I said, waving it off as I put away the dishes I had just finished washing. "When I'm out with Abbie later today I'll pick up a coffee from somewhere in town."

"I'll remember to pick some up on the way home though," she said. "Speaking of which, I have to get ready and head to work."

"Okay, have a good day."

As she nodded, exiting the kitchen with her cup of tea in hand, I quickly followed, heading into the living room to see the show I had put on for Abbie was just ending. "So, who's ready to find your toothbrush and clothes in this pile of boxes?" I asked Abbie as I set to work opening what would surely be the first of many boxes to be unpacked that afternoon.

Just about five hours later, the day was already in full spin.

Once I had gotten myself and Abbie ready for the day, I set her up with a few of her toys that I'd been able to quickly find while I started unpacking the mound of boxes. For the two hours that followed I had mostly finished setting up the things in the kitchen and bathroom that had been packed away, but when it came to the things for mine and Abbie's rooms, I still had a lot to do.

Lunch came and went, and once I called the day care to make sure it was okay for Abbie and I to drop by, that's where we headed. All in all, the day care seemed fairly impressive; it was a short drive from the house, and from what I had seen online, my university was just a few blocks over.

"Abbie seems to be fitting right in," one of the women running the day care said as we spoke, nodding to where Abbie and a few other girls were playing with a set of dolls.

Smiling at the daughter making friends, I nodded. "Yea," I said warmly, "She does."

"So, you said Abbie was three years old?" the woman inquired.

I nodded. "Yes, she turned three in May."

"And are you looking for full-day care, or is it going to be just a few times a week?"

"Umm, I'm pretty sure it'll be everyday except for Thursdays." I replied. "My schedule is pretty packed because I have to take an extra class or two to graduate this year, but I managed to clear one day of the week."

She nodded, writing the information down on a form that I had already filled out with Abbie's health and general information. "So if you're looking for 8:00 to 4:00 care four days a week it'll be $160 a week, and she'll just need to bring her own lunch. Other than that she should have fun here, and we do try to teach a few basic concepts to them so they're at least a little prepared for when they start kindergarten."

Although the cost would definitely put a dent in my savings, I tried not to show my worry as I nodded. "Okay, that sounds good. I guess I'll just bring the money next Monday when I drop her off the first day."

"That's perfectly fine," she replied, standing up as she spoke. "It's actually time for me to take the kids outside for twenty minutes, would you mind if Abbie stayed and played for a while? You're welcome to look around the neighbourhood while she stays here if you want to get a feel of the city."

Thinking about it, I saw that Abbie looked to be enjoying herself with the children her age, and since she hadn't really been able to experience that back in our old town, I smiled. "Yea, alright." I agreed, walking over to my daughter while the other woman gathered up the rest of the children.

"Hey baby." I said softly, crouching down beside her as she turned to smile at me. "Are you having fun?"

"Yea mommy!" she chirped, showing me the doll in her hands. "She pw-etty!"

"Wow, did you dress her yourself?"

She nodded excitedly. "Yea and the o'her girls dwessed dolls too!"

"So you're having fun here?" I asked, to which she smiled widely and nodded.

"What do you think about playing outside with your new friends while I go look around town for a while?"

"Ou'side?" she mumbled, putting her doll back with the others as her eyes sparkled with excitement.

"Yea baby, there's a swing set and slide outside for you to play on."

"Okay!" she said, standing up quickly as she took my hand.

I walked with her to where the rest of the kids were standing, putting on their shoes to go outside. "I'll be back soon baby," I said, kissing the top of her head lightly as I helped her slide into her light up running shoes. "I love you."

"Love you." she smiled, waving goodbye as she ran with the other kids outside towards the play structure.

After being reassured that Abbie was in good hands for the next little while, I headed back out onto the streets. It was a beautiful sunny day in the city of Los Angeles, and although it was loud with a rush of cars and pedestrians, it was already starting to feel more like home than I thought it would.

Walking up a few blocks I arrived at a strip of stores that were perfect for window-shopping. Although I couldn't afford most of the items displayed, it was still nice to look at the flowing dresses and expensive shoes.

Just as I tore my gaze away from a beautiful black dress, a small shop across the street caught my attention. Corner Café looked as if it didn't belong on this street, with it's run down exterior and chalkboard advertising, but when I remembered that I hadn't been able to have my daily dose of caffeine this morning, my legs were already crossing the street.

A bell rung above me as I entered the café; a sweet aroma quickly filling my senses as I took a quick look around. There were numerous booths and tables taken up by people working or just catching up with friends, but the whole atmosphere seemed serene, as if walking into the building brought you away from the hustle and bustle of the city.

"Hi, can I get you anything?" a perky voice asked, and when I looked to my side, I saw a barista around my age smiling at me.

"Oh yea sorry," I replied, walking closer to the counter as I browsed the menu quickly. "Can I just get a coffee, 2 milk, 2 sugar, with a bit of vanilla in it?"

"Sure thing," the barista replied, punching my order into the till. "That's $2.25."

Pulling out a five-dollar bill, I received the change and an order number as I moved to the side to wait for my order. A minute later the same barista returned with my coffee in her hand. "Here you go," she said, handing me the coffee.

"Thank you," I replied gently, handing her back my order number as I sipped at the coffee. As the warmth hit my lips, my eyes latched onto a sign to the left of the register. "You guys are hiring?"

Realizing I was talking to her, the barista looked down to the sign and nodded. "Yea," she sighed, "My parents run this place and we used to have two other workers, but since summer is ending both of them cut back their hours and we need somebody to help part-time. Why are you interested?"

"That depends," I started, "Do you think that you'll parents will care that I'm only really available some nights and weekends?"

"That's actually when we need the help," she explained, "One of the workers that cut back is starting night school next week and the other one is getting married, so her and her fiancé want to spend the weekends planning details and everything. By the way, my name's Colette."

"Zoe."

"Well Zoe," Colette said, pulling out a piece of paper and a pen from under the counter, "Here's an application form. Just fill out everything you can and ask me if you have any questions."

"Thanks."

Offering her a smile, I took the form and headed to one of the only empty seats in the café. As I sipped at my coffee and filled out the form, I realized that most of the information they wanted was standard; name, address, experience, hours available, etc. Although I had to text Emily to confirm our address, I didn't take long before my coffee was almost drained and the form was completed.

Tossing out my garbage as I headed back up to the counter, I saw that Colette was just running a cloth over the counters. "Hey, thanks for the application."

"Not a problem," she smiled as she wiped her hands and took the application off my hands. "We haven't gotten many people in here wanting to apply, so I'll give this to my parents and hopefully we'll call you soon."

"Thanks Colette."

"Not a problem, have a good day."

As Colette went back to work, I realized that twenty minutes had already passed since I left Abbie at the day care, and their playtime was probably coming to an end. Turning around, I hadn't noticed the person coming up to the counter, bumping straight into them, dropping my purse as a few bits flew across the floor.

"Oh, sorry." I apologized, not bothering to look at who I had bumped into as I crouched down to pick up my purse, trying to grab the things that had fallen out.

"It's not a problem," a deep voice replied, reaching down beside me to hand me my sunglasses that had escaped my purse. "I think these are yours."

"Yea, thank..." I began, but as I looked up at him, I realized that I had bumped into an extremely attractive guy. Although he was wearing a baseball cap and sunglasses, he seemed to be a bit older than me. Dressed in a loose fitting muscle shirt and shorts, it wasn't hard to tell that he was certainly easy on the eyes. "Um...

thank you." I cleared my throat, taking my eyes off his clearly defined muscles as I stood up.

Judging by the small smirk that grew on his lips, I assumed he had caught me checking him out. "Like I said," he replied, moving his sunglasses up slightly as his green eyes shone with mischief, "Not a problem."

"Well, I'll just let you order." I said, backing away from the counter to avoid further embarrassment.

"You're not ordering?" he asked, raising an eyebrow as he readjusted his sunglasses to hide his eyes.

I shook my head. "I already finished, I was just talking to the barista about something."

"So, maybe I'll see you around." he stated, and although I couldn't see his eyes, by the grin the he was trying to conceal, I figured he was checking me out.

Rolling my eyes, I highly doubted there was a chance of that happening. "We'll see."

"Looking forward to it," he added as I turned towards the door, and as I shook my head in amusement, he turned to Colette to order, disregarding me as I exited the café.

Heading back down the street to pick up Abbie, I pushed the handsome stranger to the back of my mind. I had enough on my plate at the moment, and I really didn't need another distraction.

Plus, what were the odds that I'd end up bumping into him again in a city like LA, right?

CHAPTER 3

Arriving at the day care to pick up Abbie, I saw that she was sitting and talking with two of the young girls. It warmed my heart to see my daughter making friends, and when the woman who had been looking after her reassured me that Abbie had fit right in with the rest of the children, I knew that I'd function easier leaving her in their care.

The rest of the day flew by; it seemed, in a blur of chaos.

The boxes that remained packed up were the majority of our possessions, and it was a mission and a half to get everything laid out and sorted. Emily arrived home shortly after four thirty, Dustin in tow, and with their help I had been able to get somewhat organized, with everything but a couple of miscellaneous boxes still left unsorted.

Dinner had been a late and simple affair. The four of us decided to just order a few boxes of pizza to curb our hunger. It didn't take long for Abbie's bedtime to roll around once supper was finished, and since he had to work early, Dustin to headed home fairly early as well.

"So," Emily started as she entered the living room, having gone outside to say goodbye to Dustin as he left. "Are you heading to bed soon or are you going to stay awake for a little while?"

I had been sitting on the couch in the living room, scrolling through my phone as the television buzzed quietly in the background, but at the sound of her voice, I looked up towards her. "Umm, I can probably stay up for a while, why?" I replied after checking to see that it was only half past nine.

"I was thinking of putting a movie in," she said, "Do you want to watch anything specific?"

"Well considering most of my movies are still packed away in a box upstairs, I'd say that you can pick." I shrugged before sending her a pointed look. "Just no horror."

"Yea, I remember the last time I watched a horror movie with you," Emily snorted, heading over to the section beside the television that held her DVD's. "I'm pretty sure Greta had to come and make sure that we weren't being murdered at least five times that night - that's how bad your screams were."

"That was before Abbie was even born." I pointed out.

"And have your watched another scary movie since?" she asked, and when I simply looked down, a light and embarrassing blush covering my cheeks, she got her answer. "I rest my case."

"Whatever." I rolled my eyes, standing up. "I'm going go change into some pajamas. I'll be right back."

Heading upstairs, I first peeked into Abbie's room, which for the most part had been set up and organized before she had been put to bed. Smiling softly, I saw her small pink night-light brightening up the room as she lay sleeping in her bed. Shutting the door quietly, I quietly moved to my room, picking out a pair of pajamas from my dresser before moving in the direction of the bathroom.

Five minutes later I was changed, my hair messily pulled into a topknot, and my face free of make-up as I headed back down the stairs to see my sister sliding a movie into the DVD player.

"You picked a movie then?" I asked, hovering near the bottom of the staircase.

She turned around, nodding. "Yea, it's an action romance movie from last year that I never got along to watching."

"Okay. By the way, do you have any popcorn I can make before we start the movie?"

"Second cupboard on the right at the top." she replied. "I'm going to go change while you make the popcorn."

As she hurried up the stairs, I turned towards the kitchen and after following Emily's directions, I found the popcorn rested beside an unopened box of poptarts. Grabbing a bag, I ripped the package open, plopping it face down in the microwave, setting the timer before standing back.

The popcorn spun slowly in the microwave, and as the kernels started to pop and the previews for the movie could be heard through the hallway, it felt nice to know that this was becoming my home. I'd been here for just over 24 hours and I was already getting closer to my sister, meeting new people, and most importantly, I was living my life.

The timer on the microwave went off then, shaking me out of my thoughts as I poured the popped corn into a large bowl before heading into the living room.

"So, what exactly is this movie supposed to be about?" I asked, placing the bowl on the table as I situated myself on the couch.

Emily, who was now clad in a pair of pajamas similar to my own, held the remote in her hand as she flipped the light off and came to sit beside me. "I think it's mainly about a guy in the C.I.A that's a number one agent or something before he gets partnered with a girl for a huge assignment," she explained with a shrug. "I don't know, some of my friends said it was a good movie so I went out and bought it. Plus, the guy in it is mega hot."

"Well then it must be good." I said sarcastically.

"Exactly."

Laughing quietly, I grabbed the popcorn, placing it on the couch between Emily and I as the opening scene started to play. The action started right away with a sticky situation and a fight scene, and although the man playing the C.I.A agent was moving to fast to really see his face, I could definitely see what Emily was talking about. His fighting seemed effortless, which I knew was choreographed and practiced, but his black clothes hung tight on his body, showing off his every muscle as he moved and every flawless part of his body.

"Told you." I heard Emily whisper as the screen suddenly zoomed in on his arms as he sent a knock out punch to the guy he had been fighting.

Shaking my head, I said nothing as I grabbed another handful and popped it into my mouth.

Turning my attention back to the movie, I choked on my popcorn as the actors face came into focus. My eyes latched onto his face as I slowly zoned out of the world around me. His character was speaking but I wasn't processing the words that were coming out. Those lips that spoke were familiar, and although his hair was slightly longer on screen, I was almost positive I wasn't imagining this. When I looked at his eyes however, I knew I wasn't. Those eyes were the very same ones I had seen earlier today, and even though it had only been for a brief amount of time, I knew that this was the same guy that had bumped into me in the café.

"Zoe. Zoe. Zoe."

I was suddenly brought out of my shock as Emily held my arm, trying to get my attention. "Sorry, what?" I asked, coughing slightly as I tried to dislodge small pieces of popcorn that had gotten stuck my throat.

"My god Zoe, I was asking if you were okay after you choked, but it was as if you drifted off into your own world." she said worriedly, looking at me strangely.

"Oh yea, sorry." I said softly, looking back at the television to see his face again. "Umm... Emily, do you know who that is?"

As I pointed at the screen, Emily scrunched up her eyebrows in confusion. "It's Ryan Adams why?" she asked.

"I think I've seen him before."

"You probably have," she shrugged. "He was in a couple of big movies this year. I think this one was actually one of the first ones he was in..."

She trailed off as I shook my head. "You're not understanding," I stated softly, taking a breath before speaking. "I saw him today when I was in town."

I could see my words processing in her mind, the cogs turning as she stayed silent for a few seconds. "Wait really?" she asked, and when I nodded her excitement grew tenfold. "Oh my god Zoe! You met Ryan Adams? When was this? What was he like? Was he as good looking in person?"

Laughing at her, I cut off her spew of questions with some answers. "It wasn't like I knew it was him at the time, actually, I've never really heard of him before."

"Where have you been living the past year? Under a rock?" she said, cutting me off. When I sent her a look, referring to the fact that yes, I'd basically been living in seclusion at our parent's house; she turned sheepish. "Oh, right."

"Anyways, I was talking to the barista at this place called Corner Café about getting a part-time job there," I started to explain, continuing on while ignoring the look that Emily sent me at the mention of a job, "And when I went to leave I bumped into him, dropping my purse in the process."

I went on to explain how our short meeting progressed, and although I didn't find anything about it that intriguing, my sister obviously did. She stayed relatively silent as I spoke, but as soon as I was done, she released a squeal of excitement.

"He was totally flirting with you Zoe! Oh my god this is so exciting!"

"He was not flirting with me." I replied adamantly, and although there was a small part of my brain that disagreed with my statement, I shook my head. "He's famous, he probably talks like that to everyone he meets. I mean, he has to keep up his public image right?"

"But you said he was in disguise Zoe. That means he wasn't trying to be seen in public," she stated.

"A hat and a pair of sunglasses isn't much of a disguise."

"Trust me, in LA, where there's a bunch of people around you at all time, a hat and a pair of sunglasses would be enough."

"Whatever," I said, "Let's just drop it. It's not like I'm going to be bumping into him again any time soon."

"You never know Zoe," Emily said with a smile, her excitement now considerably reserved. "Stranger things have happened."

Rolling my eyes, I chose not to reply as I focused my attention back to the movie. It felt strange to know that the guy I had been attracted to, even for a brief moment, was famous. As I watched Ryan Adam's character play a world-class spy, I was intrigued, but I honestly had no idea what I would do if I ever ran into him again.

That week passed in a blink of an eye, and before I knew it August turned into September and I was getting ready to begin my last year of university. Three years ago I had decided to pursue an English degree, but when first year was over, although I still loved English, I transferred into my local journalism program. Most of my credits had transferred over, but now, as I entered my last year at a new university, I knew that I had to work hard if I wanted to earn my degree by the end of the year.

Writing was something I had always been passionate about. I was the girl in high school that almost always had her head stuck in a book, was editor of the school newspaper, and didn't bother to care what anybody thought of me when I was simply being true to myself. Now, as I was on the verge of entering a career that I had only dreamed of, I wanted everything to be as smooth as possible.

Dropping Abbie off at daycare the first morning was certainly hard, as I was so used to just leaving her in Greta's care. It was a little unsettling leaving her with people I had only met once, but with a bit of reassurance I passed Abbie her princess lunch box, kissed her on the forehead, and promised to be back that afternoon.

When I transferred my credits over to UCLA I had endless con-versations with a career advisor, and now I had an appointment with her before my first lecture, just to make sure everything was set for me to walk across the stage at the end of the year.

Arriving on campus minutes later, I immediately noticed that it was a lot nicer than my last school, but it was also quite a lot bigger. Even with a map it took me a while to find the administration office, which was where I was told to meet my career advisor. When I finally located the building, I walked in only to be greeted by receptionist.

"Hi, can I help you with anything?" she asked.

"Umm, yea..." I trailed, pulling my bag's strap higher on my shoulder as I walked up to the desk. "I'm supposed to be meeting with Tentley Penrose at 8:30."

The receptionist nodded, typing something into the computer. "I'll just tell her you're here, you can take a seat while you wait." she said, gesturing to the seats behind me as she picked up the phone.

Taking one of the empty seats, I reached into my bag to pick up my phone, only to see that I had a message from Emily.

[Good luck today! Hope it's not too stressful :)]

Smiling, I texted her back quickly before I heard my name. "Zoe Hamilton?"

Looking up I saw a woman smiling at me. "Yes," I said, standing up.

"Follow me, we can talk in my office."

Although she only looked to be ten years older than me, as I followed her I couldn't help but be slightly intimidated by her confidence and the way she presented herself so professionally.

"So, how are you adjusting to living in Los Angeles so far?" she asked as I sat down across for her, her desk the only thing separating the two of us.

I sighed, glad that she appeared to be as nice as she seemed to be through the phone. "I guess I'm doing pretty good." I replied. "I'm all unpacked and I found my daughter Abbie a daycare that she seems to like, so hopefully everything else will work out."

"That's good," she smiled, before pulling up something on her computer. "So you're here today because you need to fit a few more classes into your year, correct?"

I nodded. "Yes, I only switched into journalism my second year, so although I'm mostly caught up, I still need a bit of help to make sure I fulfill all the requirements for my degree by the end of the year."

"Well by the looks of your transcripts, your grades clearly show that you know how to work hard, so I don't think you'll have a problem with an extra course or two. You'll also be required to complete an eight week placement next semester to receive your degree."

Nodding, I listened and offered suggestions as she, very kindly, helped me prepare for my last year. She went over the general layout of the campus, where and when my most important classes were, and gave me a few suggestions about who to contact now in regards to the placement I had to complete by the end of the year.

It was approaching nine 'o'clock when I finished in her office, and after thanking her, I headed back out to class, hoping to find the building where my nine thirty lecture was without much trouble.

The day passed relatively quickly, most of my lectures consisting of a short introduction about the course, what was expected of us, and the timeline that the semester would follow. My journalism lab started off with an assignment right away, as I had to write a one page piece about an event that had happen in my life over the past year, which for me was an easy choice: moving out to LA.

It was clear, even after my first day, that my schedule for the next couple of months would be quite hectic, but I knew that there was a future at the end of it all; one that I desperately wanted.

Walking towards the front of campus after my last lecture of the day, I felt my phone go off in my pocket only to see that an unknown number was calling me. Thinking it was a telemarketer,

I answered it to tell them to take me off their call list, but instead, I was met with a semi-familiar voice.

"Hello? Zoe?"

"Yes, who is this?" I asked confusedly.

"It's Colette, from Corner Café."

"Oh, hi Colette."

"Hey, I was calling to ask if you had any free time this afternoon to come in and pick up some paper work and stuff?" she asked.

"Paper work?"

"Yea, and you'll need to pick up your apron before your first day."

"Wait," I said, halting my steps as I reached the edge of campus, "You're saying I got the job?"

"Of course you did," she replied happily. "I told you that not many other people had applied, didn't I? Plus, I put in a good word with my parents and they didn't see any reason why we shouldn't hire you."

"Wow, thank you." I replied gratefully, pulling my phone away from my ear for a second, checking the time to see that it was only a bit after 3:00. "And actually, I have almost an hour before I have to pick up Abbie. Do you think I can drop by now?"

"Yea that should be fine. It doesn't get too busy until four or five, so I should have a bit of time to talk to you."

"Okay, I'll head over there now." I said, crossing the street as the sign signaled for me to walk. "Thanks Colette."

"No problem," she replied, "I'll see you soon."

It didn't take as long as I thought to get to Corner Café, a fifteen minute walk at most, and when I pulled open the door, the bell sounding above me, I saw Colette behind the counter as she finished serving the only person in line.

"Hey," I greeted as I walked up to the counter.

Colette smiled at me. "Hey Zoe," she said before pulling out a few forms from underneath the counter. "My parents just wanted you to pick these up before the end of the week." she explained, passing me what seemed like five or six forms held together with a paperclip. "Your schedule for next week is in there, but it starts on Saturday and goes until next Friday. I think there's a few safety forms that you'll have to fill out, then there's just an information page that says that you have to bring a void check in so that my parents can directly deposit your pay checks into your bank account, and a couple of other things that you can read over later."

"Okay," I nodded, "That sounds easy enough."

"They actually wanted to meet you today, but they aren't going to be back for an hour or so when it starts to get a bit busier."

"I'm sure I'll meet them when I start working."

Colette nodded. "Yea, I think your first shift is sometime Saturday morning according to your schedule, and they'll definitely be around at that time."

"Sounds good," I said with a smile. "I guess I'll see you Saturday then."

Just as I was about to turn and leave, Colette called me back. "Wait, you're probably going to want this," she said, tossing me a small brown paper bag.

Opening it up curiously, I realized that it was a black apron with the café's logo printed on the front, along with a small metallic name tag.

"Welcome to Corner Café."

CHAPTER 4

I t didn't take long for a routine to form.

On the days that I had classes I would wake up relatively early with Abbie, giving me enough time to make breakfast for the two of us, and Emily on occasion, before getting the two of us ready. I'd leave the house just after Emily, first heading in the direction to drop Abbie off at day care, and then switching course to campus.

The UCLA campus was huge, and even after my first week I still didn't know exactly where all my classes were. I was taking six lecture courses and a lab this term, and even though my schedule seemed full, it wasn't something I minded. Going off how the classes were so far, I enjoyed most of them as they greatly prepared me for next year when I'd be out in the real world.

Thursdays, however, were a different story.

I had managed to clear my schedule for Thursdays with only one goal in mind; spend quality time with my daughter. So when Thursday rolled around, I was gifted with not only a lie in, but also a day full of cartoons, dolls, and laughs with my little princess. I had laid out all her toys that had just been stuffed in the corner, letting her place them where she chose, and by the time lunch rolled around, we met up with Emily in town at a small diner.

The day had been success; a relaxed day spent with my daughter, and the thought of it becoming a weekly occurrence put a smile on my face.

It was in a blink of an eye that my first week in Los Angeles had come and gone, and now, as I awoke Saturday morning, I was left to get ready my first shift at Corner Café.

Just as Colette had mentioned, my first shift was scheduled from ten to four so that the café wasn't extremely busy while I was still getting used to everything. After having gotten up around eight, thanks to an energetic three year old, I had busied myself with breakfast and tiding up a bit before getting ready.

When I had texted Colette to ask what type of clothes I should wear she simply said casual. With that in my mind I had pulled on a pair of black leggings and a white scoop neck t-shirt, dusting on a minimal amount of make-up so that I looked somewhat presentable.

Checking the time to see that it was almost 9:30, I quickly turned to the mirror, pulling my brown hair into a tamed ponytail on the top of my head. "This'll have to do," I thought as I grabbed my handbag, tossing in both my apron and nametag, along with the papers I had signed and a few other miscellaneous items before heading downstairs to see Emily and Abbie sitting on the couch watching a cartoon.

Emily, who must've heard me coming down the stairs, turned around and smiled at me. "Well, somebody looks ready to go to work," she said, nudging Abbie. "What do you think Abbie, how does your mom look?"

Abbie's small innocent eyes turned to look at me as I walked over to her. "You look pwetty momma!" she said, smiling widely.

My heart squeezed at my daughter's words as I leant down to hug her, her small arms stretching to reach over my shoulders. "Thanks baby," I returned, pulling back to plant a small kiss on her forehead.

Abbie's attention quickly returned to the television as Emily told her to sit tight, following me to the door.

"Are you sure you're okay watching her for the day?" I asked cautiously. I knew she was my sister and that she loved her niece, but I didn't want it to feel like I was pushing her to watch Abbie when I had to work.

Emily nodded. "I'm sure," she replied, stepping forward to give me a quick hug. "You've got enough to worry about today, what with starting a new job, so stop worrying about Abbie. She'll be happy spending some quality time with her favourite aunt."

"You're her only aunt."

"Favourite, only, same thing."

Laughing, I smiled, thankful to have been given at least one family member that I didn't despise. "Thank you, thank you, thank you." I repeated, pulling on a pair of black running shoes.

"No thanks needed," Emily replied, "Now go, before you're late."

I couldn't help myself as I thanked her once more before heading out the door and down the street, on route to my new job at Corner Café.

Twenty minutes later, after having walked down the crowded downtown streets of Los Angeles, I opened the front door to the café and was hit with the sweet smell of freshly brewed coffee and mouth-watering treats.

"Hey, you're early." Colette said, having noticed me from behind the counter as she worked on a customers order.

"Not that early." I pointed out, gesturing to the clock that showed the time as five to ten.

Passing the coffee she had just made to the customer, she gestured for me to come behind the counter. "So, are you ready for today?" Colette asked, abandoning the cashier as she led me to the back of the café.

"Nervous," I admitted, "But I think I'll be okay. Isn't somebody supposed to watch the front?"

"My parents know I'm showing you around, and if a customer comes they'll just ring the bell on the counter," she replied, waving off my question as we walked through another door into a room that seemed to be a small break room

"Now, through here are a few lockers where you can leave your things. When you're on your break you can either come chill out in here or head out for something to eat, just remember to clock in and out on time, which reminds me..." she trailed, motioning to a small pin pad near the door. "You're pin number is 0040, so just punch that number in and click enter when you need to, which is at the beginning and end of every shift, along with every break you take."

Nodding in understanding, she motioned me forward to punch in. When the pin pad lit up, accepting the number I had punched in, Colette spoke. "Now, seeing as your punched in for work, just throw your apron and nametag on and meet me up front; I'll give you a basic run down of the place."

Following her instructions, I pulled the apron on over my clothes, letting it sit comfortably as I tied the middle around my stomach. After pinning my nametag onto my shirt, I grabbed the paperwork I'd filled out, stuffed my bag into an empty locker, and headed out to see where Colette had gone off.

"Hey, do you want me to put these anywhere?" I asked, looking down at the papers in my hand as I reentered the chatter at front of the restaurant. Looking up, I saw Colette talking to a woman I assumed was her mother while her father finished taking an order. "Oh, hello."

"Hi, you must be Zoe. I'm Angela and that's my husband Adam," her mom said, holding her hand out as I stepped forward and shook it.

"It's good to meet you."

"Hopefully Colette here will be able to show you the ropes," she said, gesturing to her daughter, "And welcome to the team."

"Well thank you for hiring me." I replied gratefully, smiling as I passed her the papers I still held onto. "And I think these are for you."

"Thank you," she said as her husband finished with the orders.

Although Adam didn't appear as extroverted as his wife did, he still shook my hand and introduced himself, welcoming me to the café before he retreated to the back of the café.

"We'll be in the back if you need any help out here honey," Angela said, directing her words towards Colette before turning to me once more. "I hope you find yourself liking it here, and if Colette isn't clear about anything, I'm always happy to help."

"Mom," Colette complained, rolling her eyes at her mother's teasing words.

"Oh hush up and get to training." she replied, wishing us luck as she followed the path to the back of the café that her husband had taken.

"So, those are my parents," Colette started, "And as you can see, my mom still seems to think it's cool to try and embarrass me."

I cracked a smile, as I could tell that, even with the teasing from both sides, her and her mom had a great relationship. "I like them, they seem cool," I shrugged. "Plus, they're probably a lot better than my parents."

My guess was that she heard something in my tone or saw something in my eyes, but whatever the reason, she let the comment about my parents drop, choosing instead to start showing me around.

While no new customers entered the café, Colette took the opportunity to show me the back of the café. "So you won't exactly be working back here, unless we're in dire need of help, but this is where everything gets made before it's set up out front." she explained, nodding to the multiple ovens, cooling trays, and ingredients splayed out over the vast amount of counter space. "My mom and dad run this for the most part, but in the mornings we get two workers in here to prepare most things and make sure that everything's set up for the day."

Nodding along, I took in what Colette was saying as she directed me around the room. It didn't take long for the tour to move back to the main area of the café.

"Now where you'll mostly be working is behind the counter," she started, knocking on the hardwood counter. "You'll start off taking orders, packaging the pastries, and cleaning up the main area, but eventually you'll have shifts where it's strictly making drinks so if you learn as you go it'll be easier in the end."

Her tips and tricks continued as she showed me the multiple machines they had equipped the café with, trying to briefly explain what each one did and what drinks were made with each one. The coffee machines were, luckily, simple to understand as they simply brewed fresh blends of their own coffee every half hour or whenever they were running low.

When it came to learning the till, there wasn't much that surprised me. I had worked a few customer service jobs in the past, and although each till varied, they generally had the same layout. The only thing slightly confusing about there's was that, with all the different variations and add-ons available for drinks, they had quite a few buttons. The touchscreen looked intimidating to say the least, but when Colette promised me that it wasn't actually as confusing as it seemed to be, I breathed easier.

As Colette finished her spiel, the ringing of a familiar bell, signaling a customer, was heard throughout the building. Looking up, I saw two middle-aged women entering the café and heading towards the counter.

Glancing at Colette nervously, I wasn't reassured in the slightest as I saw a cheshire grin on her face. Raising her eyebrows, she nodded towards the till.

"Looks like it's your time to shine." she teased, standing beside me as the pair of women approached.

Taking a deep breath, I put a smile on my face as I tried to push my nerves aside. "Hi, welcome to Corner Café, what can I get for you two ladies today?"

Luckily, the first couple of orders I took were simple coffees and pastries and after locating the correct buttons, all I had to do was punch them in before accepting the cash and handing back change. However, when the more complicated orders started coming in around lunchtime, Colette took over, letting me watch as she pressed multiple buttons just to punch in one drink.

It would definitely take a while to get used to, that was for sure.

By the time my lunch break rolled around, Colette, who informed me that I was allowed free food during a shift, punched my order of a small sandwich and drink into the till while I went around the back to clock out for twenty minutes. When my break was over I happily took a step back from the counter, heading instead for the main area of the café where I cleaned up the various messes' customers had left behind.

All in all, as the clock ticked forward and my shift started to wind down, I found myself enjoying my day. Sure, I might not have picked up the till right away, and I might not have been born to be a barista, but I wasn't horrible and that was a good thing.

"So, one more hour until you're done," Colette commented as she wiped down one of the coffee machines, "How are you liking it so far?"

"I think once I get everything down it'll be easier, but I'm liking it." I replied as I heard the bell by the door go off again, "Thanks for helping me get the job."

"No problem, I like working with someone around my age instead of being the only young one around here," she replied, her voice dropping as she nodded to the other side of the counter. "Customer."

"Welcome to the Corner Café," I greeted before looking up at the customer, and let me tell you; I was shocked when I did.

There, standing right in front of me, was Ryan Adams.

Not surprisingly, he was once again wearing a pair of sunglasses and a baseball cap. What made my breath catch, however, was the tight white t-shirt that was adorning the top half of his body, giving me a perfect view of his sculpted muscles.

Clearing my throat, quickly tearing my eyes away from his body, I looked up to his face. "Umm, what can I get for you?"

When he didn't respond immediately I had a feeling that he was staring at me, and with the sunglasses completely shielding his eyes, I wasn't sure if that was a good thing or a bad thing.

"I said," I cleared my throat, speaking quite timidly, "What can I..."

I didn't get to finish my question again though, as Ryan's voice cut me off. "You're that girl from last weekend," he pointed out.

Shit.

It didn't seem as though he wanted me to reply as he continued, his deep voice incredibly sexy as he spoke. "When did you start working here?"

His question wasn't meant to be rude, but more curious as, I assumed, his eyes stayed trained on me.

"Umm... today's my first day." I replied hesitantly, drumming my fingers nervously against the edges of the cash register.

My heart skipped a beat when a small smile grew on his lips as he pulled his glass up to rest on his head. "I told you I'd see you around," he commented, "So, do you have a break soon, or..."

His question trailed off as he looked at me expectantly. "I don 't... I umm,"

Colette, with a smirk on her face, cut off my embarrassing stuttering early. "Actually, since you're working six hours, you still have a twenty minute break to take," she pointed out.

"Great," Ryan said, dropping his sunglasses back to hide his face. "Do you want to sit down and talk?"

Looking between him and Colette, who had an expectant grin on her face, I sighed. "Sure," I replied softly, "Let me just take your order and I'll bring it out to you."

"Don't worry about it, I'll get the order while you go clock out," Colette said, butting in as she nudged me sideways with her hip.

Rolling my eyes with amusement, I turned and headed to the back, clocking out quickly before coming back out to the front to see that Ryan had taken a seat in one of the back booths.

"Zoe, here's the drink you're looking for," Colette said teasingly as I approached her, handing me the cup that was seemingly Ryan's.

"You are so going to get it," I whispered, taking the cup with a smile as I headed over to where Ryan had taken a seat.

"Your drink," I stated softly, sliding into the other side of the booth slowly. I noticed that he had taken his sunglasses off, placing them on the table next to a chocolate chip muffin.

"Thanks Zoe," he said smiling, pushing the chocolate chip muffin towards me slightly, "For you."

"I never told you my name," I pointed out, raising an eyebrow at him.

He nodded to my chest. "Nametag."

"Oh, right," I mumbled, "And thanks by the way, for the muffin."

His lips lifted up slightly at my nervousness. "No problem," he replied, "But I probably should tell you that I didn't pay for it. Colette over there told me that she punched it in as part of your break meal."

Letting loose a short laugh, I was surprised that he was admitting that. "Still, thanks." I said, popping a piece of it into my mouth.

"I'm Ryan by the way."

"I know," I replied, only noticing my mistake when he raised an eyebrow in amusement. "I mean, uh..."

"You know who I am?"

"Yeah," I admitted sheepishly, "I mean at first I didn't, but my sister and I were watching a movie last weekend and I recognized you, so, yeah."

"Oh really, which movie?"

"Umm... the spy one that's like a year old," I explained, not really sure of what the movie was actually called.

"You mean Agent Prector?" he asked, and assuming that was the title I nodded. When a smirk appeared on his face however, I suddenly wished I hadn't. "So what, were you so distracted by my muscles and my abilities that you couldn't even remember the name of the movie?"

"Get over yourself," I replied with an eye roll, hoping that he couldn't see the blush rising on my neck at his slightly true statement.

I could tell, as his eyes briefly dropped to my neck, that he had noticed my blush, but I was thankful that he didn't press on the subject. "So," he started, taking a drink from his coffee before continuing, "Why did you decide to start working here? It wasn't just so you could start stalking me at my favourite coffee shop, was it?"

"This is your favourite coffee shop?" I asked, rolling off his teasing accusation.

He nodded with a smile. "With all the expensive stores around here, no paparazzi ever really come around this café, hence, I don't need much of a disguise to come here without a body guard," he explained. "But, you never answered my question."

"No surprisingly enough, you weren't the reason I got a job here," I replied in amusement. "I actually just moved here, and when I came in last week I saw that they were hiring here, so, I applied."

"You just moved here?" he asked, and I nodded. "Where'd you move from?"

"I lived near the border of Arizona and New Mexico, and hour or so east of Flagstaff, Arizona." I explained, not wanting to give too much of my past away.

"So, you cheer for the Diamondbacks and the Coyotes I'm assuming?"

"When I was younger I did," I replied, smiling as a few memories of my dad taking my sister and I to games flashed through my mind.

"You don't anymore?" he asked, his eyebrows crunching in confusion.

I shrugged. "Eventually I stopped going to games and following the seasons. I still enjoy watching a game here and there, I'm just not a die hard fan like I was when I was little."

He nodded, and maybe he could tell I was omitting things, like how my dad suddenly had no time to bring his daughters to games, and how my mother didn't want me acting like such a tomboy, but he veered off the subject. "And you just decided to move to Los Angeles?"

"Well my sister's lived here for a couple of years, and I just needed a change," I replied. "I helped my sister find a new house, transferred universities, and now voilà, here I am."

"So now you go to..."

"UCLA for journalism," I finished, earning a hearty laugh from Ryan. "What?" I asked with a smile.

"Nothing," he replied, shaking his head. "It's just funny how the first girl I've met in a long time that doesn't freak out about me being an actor is studying to be part of the people who I despise."

Suddenly seeing the humour in the situation, I let loose a laugh. "What? Are you scared?" I asked teasingly.

"Not really," he responded simply, "You don't seem like the type of person who spills people's secrets."

Smiling softly, I replied. "That's because I'm not. I'm more interested in political and national news than what's new in Hollywood. No offense."

"Non-taken," he said. "But, since your break is almost over, I still have one very important question to ask you."

His eyes met mine, and with the serious look they held, I didn't know if I wanted to hear what he was about to say. "And what is that?" I asked softly as I squirmed slightly in my seat.

He was silent for a second; staring at me intensely, before his exterior cracked and a smile appeared. "What's your favourite colour?"

Laughing as the words processed in my head, my whole body relaxed as I realized it was nothing serious. "That's your question?" I asked with amusement as I stopped laughing, and when he nodded, my smile grew. "Purple."

"Really?"

"Really," I affirmed.

Just as I was about to continue I heard the bell by the door go off, and when I took a glance, I was surprised to see Emily with a smiling Abbie in her arms. I didn't have to say anything as Emily's eyes swept the café, catching mine briefly as she smiled.

"There you are," she said as she walked over, "What are you doing back here? Slacking off already?"

I assumed that she hadn't seen Ryan yet, so as I stood up, I walked slightly away from the table as I reached out to grab Abbie from her hold. "I'm just finishing up my break," I replied before turning and poking Abbie lightly on the nose, "And how are you doing little princess?"

She giggled in my arms. "I hungry, Aunty Emily pwomised me food."

"And you couldn't have waited until I finished my shift?" I asked, directing my question at Emily.

"We were getting bored at home, and Abbie was missing you so I decided to treat her. It's not like you're hiding anything from me," she shrugged, but that was the exact moment that Ryan stood up from where he'd been sitting in the booth. Emily definitely took notice of this as her eyes widened. "Or maybe you are."

A sheepish smile appeared on my face as Ryan took a step towards us, his sunglasses now back on his face as he held out his hand to Emily. "Hey, I'm Ryan."

Emily's eyebrows shot to the roof in surprise, and I realized that she definitely remembered our conversation about me meeting him. I saw as she tried to contain her excitement, holding out her hand to shake Ryan's. "Emily, I'm this one's younger sister," she greeted, however, when she smirked at me, a glint in her eye, a glint of worry passed through me.

And for good reason it seemed.

"So you're the guy that Zoe mentioned."

I wished, at that moment, that the world would swallow me whole as I scowled at my sister, only to see Ryan turning to me with a grin plastered on his face. "You've mentioned me?"

"I told you I recognized you when we watched a movie together last week." I mumbled as I felt my cheeks heat up in embarrassment.

"You sure you weren't gossiping about how hot you thought I was when I bumped into you?"

"I'm sure," I snapped quickly, sending a glare at my sister as I realized I only had one minute left of my break. "Anyways, my break's over so I have to get back to work."

"Yeah, I had better get going to," Ryan mentioned, nodding towards the door as he picked up his empty coffee mug and my leftovers from the table, tossing them into the nearby trash. "It was good meeting you Emily, and I'll see you around Zoe."

He smiled at me, which I returned as he turned and headed out the front door.

"You are so spilling everything after you're done your shift," Emily pressed as she took Abbie back off me and stood her on the ground, clasping Abbie's small hand within her own.

"Yea, yea," I blushed, shooing them towards where Colette was taking an order. "Just go order. I'll be done in a half an hour or so."

Heading right for the back room to clock back in, I leaned against the cold wall and blew out a breath that I hadn't realized I was holding.

'Since when did my life get so interesting?' I thought, shaking my head as I headed back to work.

CHAPTER 5

Emily was not one to let things go.

Not even two minutes after my shift ended she began throwing question after question at me. 'What were you doing with him?', 'Why didn't you tell me?', 'Please tell me you got his number.'

More than once on the walk home I had tried to explain that I was just talking to Ryan on my break, nothing more, and that she didn't really need to read any more into it.

She was adamant however, that I was withholding details. It was when I told her, for quite possibly the fifth time, that nothing more than a friendship would emerge from this situation that she finally let the subject drop, although I did expect to hear about it again sooner or later.

My shift the following day was less eventful, and with no sudden appearance from Ryan, I was left to act as though nothing strange had happened the day previous. Despite the odd smirk or teasing comment thrown my way by Colette, it was an alright day, and it seemed that the more comfortable I got working behind the counter, the more I was picking up. By the end of my second shift I had successfully figured out where a majority of the buttons on the till rested, as well as successfully made a few drinks with little to no assistance.

As Sunday came to an end and the new week began, school really started up. The first week was a teaser of what the semester would bring, and as I went to bed Wednesday night feeling utterly exhausted from the three assignments I had stayed up to finish, I figured it would only get worse. Seeing that it was almost two in the morning as I closed my eyes, I fell asleep calmly, knowing that Thursday would come with a day off; a day to spend with Abbie.

"Momma," I heard Abbie's voice whine from upstairs the next afternoon as I sat in the living room studying for a test scheduled for the following day.

Looking down at my open books, I sighed, abandoning the notes I had been taking. "Coming Abbie," I replied loudly, standing up from my place on the sofa as I quickly headed upstairs, peeking into Abbie's bedroom where I had left her to play. "What is it baby?"

My eyes latched onto her small body, leaning next to her dresser, as she tried to reach on top of it. "Necklace," she stated simply.

Shaking my head with amusement, I walked over to where she was still attempting to reach, picking up the small ice cream necklace I had bought her for her third birthday. "Now why do you need this?" I asked, crouching down in front of her as I dangled it the chain in the air.

"Polly needs a necklace," she replied, smiling widely as she picked up the doll that had been resting by her feet.

"Well," I started, unclasping the chain before reaching behind Abbie's neck, "I think Polly looks beautiful just the way she is, but you my dearie, would look amazing with this necklace on."

I rested my hands by her sides as she brought her small ones up to feel the necklace that now hung loosely around her neck.

"Do I look pwetty now momma?" she asked, looking down at the necklace with a smile.

"You look very pretty Abbie," I replied with a soft smile, poking her nose gently as she a high-pitched giggle escaped my little girl. "So, are you hungry?"

"Hungry?" she asked, her small head tilting sideways slightly in confusion.

I nodded, standing up slowly. "Yeah, I was thinking about making some grilled cheese sandwiches for lunch, how does that sound?"

A toothy grin appeared on her face as I mentioned one of her favourite meals. "Gwilled cheese!" she exclaimed excitedly, grabbing onto my hand as she attempted to pull me into the hallway.

Laughing as I moved along behind her, I picked her up, settling her on my hip as we made our way down the stairs. "After lunch what do you want to do?" I asked her, sitting her down in a chair as I started on the grilled cheese. "Do you want to watch a movie?" I continued, to which she thought about it before shaking her head. "Hmm... how about a trip to the park?"

"Park?" Abbie repeated, stumbling slightly on the pronunciation as her eyes shone with excitement.

I nodded, smiling in response. "Yeah, we can walk around, play on the swings and the slide..." I trailed.

"Yay!" Abbie replied, cutting me off with a yelp as she clapped her small hands together in happiness.

That's how, half an hour later, we found ourselves walking down the side streets of Los Angeles, on track to a park I'd seen near the university.

"I'm gonna go on the swing and the slide and pick flowers and..." Abbie listed off as she skipped merrily beside me.

"You're going to do all that baby girl?" I asked with wonder, my mom voice coming out as I looked down at my daughter, who was nodding her head. "Well then, we'd better get there fast."

Pushing her ahead slightly as I let go of her hand, I let her run a bit in front of me as I quickened my pace the tiniest amount to keep up with her. Five minutes later the cement beneath our feet had turned to sand as I helped Abbie sit up on one of the free swings.

"Do you need a push?"

Abbie, although she tried to pump her feet, wasn't really going anywhere when I asked if she needed help. She nodded, looking a little put out that she couldn't swing by herself.

Crouching down in front of her, I took her ankles gently and slowly started moving the swing. "Remember to move your legs back when you're moving back and move them forward when you're going forward." I said slowly, moving her legs as I explained the motions to her. I stayed pushing her for a couple of minutes stepping back only when I saw her slowly starting to understand the motions herself.

"Look, I'm doing it!" she cheered ecstatically, and although she wasn't moving nearly as fast or going as high as the other children, my heart beat with affections I watched her.

"Yeah, you are."

I stood watching her for about five minutes before she asked for me to continue pushing her. Seeing her have fun was enough for me to stay, and as the time passed, follow her around to the different structures the park had. When the slide was free minutes later, I watched from the ground as she slowly climbed up the stairs before sitting herself down at the top and smiling freely as she slid down quickly.

The laughter and playfulness continued for a little more than a half an hour before Abbie grew tired of the playground.

"So, what do you want to do now?" I asked as we headed for the grassy area of the park. When we came to an area that wasn't all that occupied, I stopped and crouched down, shaking the sand off her clothes as I tried to clean her up a bit.

"I dunno," she replied, her small face scrunching up in confusion.

"What about..." I started, but before I could continue, a dog's barking cut me off. Confused, I looked around to see a man walking through the park with a small dog, a very familiar looking man.

"Puppy!" Abbie cheered as she noticed the dog coming towards us, making me laugh as Ryan stopped next to us, letting Abbie pet his dog.

"Hey, I thought I recognized you," Ryan said.

"Well Mr. Hollywood," I greeted teasingly, standing up as I did so, "What were you going to do if I wasn't who you though I was."

"Apologize and walk the other way before they recognized who I am," he replied sheepishly, to which I replied with a light laugh. "But yeah, shouldn't you have class or something?"

I shook my head. "No class on Thursdays."

"Really? And how'd you manage to swing that?"

"I packed the other four days full," I shrugged. "Thursdays are for me and Abbie."

At the mention of Abbie, Ryan looked down at her as she continued to pet and play with his dog. "And I'm assuming this little cutie is Abbie," he stated, and when I nodded, he crouched down and smiled at her. "Hi Abbie, my name's Ryan."

"Hi!" she chirped, looking between Ryan and I as she smiled. "Are you my momma's fwiend?"

"Momma?" Ryan repeated questioningly, raising an eyebrow as he looked up to me for confirmation. When I nodded slightly, I didn't miss something flash through his eyes, before he focused his attention back on Abbie. "Yeah Abbie, I'm friends with your momma."

"Cool, so what's you puppy's name?" she asked.

He let loose a laugh, rubbing his dog's head playfully. "This is Rocky, and he seems to like you."

"I like him too."

Letting Abbie and Rocky play a little more, Ryan stood up, looking straight at me as I stood there nervously. "So, you have a daughter?"

There was something off to his tone, as though he was trying to mask how he really felt. "Yeah," I replied nervously.

He nodded. "And her father?"

I shook my head slowly, a sad smile on my face. "Bailed the minute I told him," I said, making sure to keep my voice quiet enough so that Abbie wouldn't hear. She understood that her father wasn't in the picture, but I'd rather her not know anything about him until she was old enough to understand it.

"Dick," Ryan mumbled angrily under his breath, making a burst of laughter escape from within me.

"You can say that again."

"Well," he started, "The guy's missing out on a cute kid."

When a smile appeared on my face at his comment, he smiled back in return, noticing that he had cheered me up. Instead of replying I looked around, quickly noticing that there were quite a lot of people walking through the park, also picking up on the fact that Ryan currently didn't have much of a disguise on.

"So you're actually walking through Los Angeles without any sunglasses on," I spoke, stating the obvious.

He rolled his eyes. "I still have a hat on," he pointed out, "Plus, I doubt these people are looking to spot me on their walk through the park."

"Well you never know," I replied teasingly, "What, does an A-list Hollywood actor not need a bodyguard when he goes out to walk his dog?"

"Actually," he raised an eyebrow with a smirk, nodding to the left, "He's right over there."

Sure enough, when I turned my head to the left I spotted a man that seemed slightly out of place. He wore sunglasses, a black t-shirt, and had his bulging muscles on display as he leant up against a tree, keeping himself to the shade.

"Oh."

"Yeah."

Looking back at Ryan, I was able to pick up on the slight dis-appointment in his voice, but I didn't think it was my place to be prying into his life.

"Well, I was thinking about taking Abbie out for ice cream before we headed home," I started, but when Abbie heard both her name and the words 'ice cream', she stared up at me with wide eyes and bright smile.

"We're getting ice cream?" she asked excitedly.

"Do you want to?" I returned, looking down at her as she nodded her head quickly. "Then I guess we are."

"Yay!" she cheered, abandoning Rocky as she launched herself at my legs, hugging them tightly. "Thanks momma!"

"No problem sweetie," I smiled, as I picked her up and rested her on my hip before returning my attention to Ryan. "You're welcome to join us."

"With a dog? And the big guy over there watching my every move? I don't think that'll go very well," he said, shrugging it of.

His eyes however, betrayed his true emotions. He didn't want to reject my offer, but obviously felt he couldn't sit out and eat ice cream like a normal person.

Biting my lip, I looked down at Abbie, who was still smiling with the thought of ice cream on her mind before looking back at Ryan. Before I could say anything though, Ryan spoke.

"It's okay Zoe," he stated, the side of his mouth tilting upwards, "Have fun, and I'll see you around."

I wasn't given the chance to reply, as seconds later he was walking past me, leaving me standing there shocked, and Abbie confused with the situation. Taking a deep breath, I spun around quickly.

"Wait," I said, and he immediately halted his steps, turning back to face me. "I have some ice cream at my house, and I'm sure Abbie wouldn't mind eating there instead of at a parlour. Plus, it's free and my house is dog friendly."

"You know, you don't have to do this."

"Do what?" I asked, worrying that I was doing something wrong.

He cracked a smile as he and Rocky walked back over to us. "Be so nice all the time," he commented, "Especially to someone that you barely know."

"Oh umm..." I stuttered, not sure of what to make of his words.

"I didn't mean that to be a bad thing," he pointed out in a rush. "I guess it's just refreshing to meet somebody that thinks of me as an actual person rather than an actor."

I bit my lip, trying to keep a smile from emerging at his compliment.

"And if you're sincerely offering," he continued slowly, "I wouldn't object to some free ice cream."

I laughed at his words, smiling up at him as I bounced Abbie slightly on my hip. "What do you think Abbie, should we let Ryan and Rocky come over for ice cream?"

At the mention of Rocky coming over, she smiled. "Yeah, then I can play with him some more."

"I think my daughter is getting quite attached to your dog," I commented, nodding down to Rocky, who was currently sniffing the grass beside Ryan's feet, "And she doesn't seem to mind you either, so the offer's open."

A smile grew on Ryan's face as his gaze turned to Abbie's for a few seconds before turning back to me. "I'll just go talk to Chad real quick," he said, before jogging over to his bodyguard, Rocky following behind him with the leash.

"So, you really don't mind Ryan coming over?" I asked Abbie quietly, looking down at her curiously.

She shook her head. "He seems nice," she explained simply.

"Yeah, he does," I replied under my breath as my gaze travelled to where Ryan stood, under the shade of a bunch of trees as he spoke to his bodyguard.

I didn't know what he told him, or how the whole bodyguard situation worked, but less than a minute later Ryan and Rocky were heading back towards us as Chad made his way towards the exit of the park.

"Ready to go?" he asked, stopping a few feet in front of me.

Nodding, I tilted my head towards the exit. "Yeah, let's go."

It wasn't until the three of us were halfway home that I realized that Ryan's bodyguard was following us. I thought I'd seen him leave the park after talking to Ryan, and up until that moment, I hadn't seen a glimpse of him again, thinking he had gone off duty.

"So does mister tall and buff always follow you around?" I asked quietly, taking a glance over my shoulder to see his figure almost a block away from us.

Ryan chuckled in response, noticing the wariness I had with the situation. "Most of the time," he replied, before shrugging and sticking his hands deep in his jean pockets. Abbie, after begging and pleading for a few minutes, had been given the privilege of walking Rocky, and the two were situated a few steps in front of us. "I know it's a little bit weird," he trailed, "But my agent insists that if I'm going places with a lot of people, especially out in LA, that I should bring a bodyguard with me."

"It's not what I'd call weird," I offered.

"Oh trust me, it's weird," he returned, cracking a small smile.

"Umm, is he coming in?" I asked apprehensively as we reached the street I lived on.

Ryan shook his head. "Don't worry, he's actually heading back to my place once he sees I'm not out in the open any more. He'll be back eventually with my car so I don't have to walk back through LA."

Nodding in understanding, I felt a little bad for his bodyguard. I understood that it was the guy's job, but I figured that Ryan didn't live that close to my suburban neighbourhood, so he was in for quite a walk.

"Well," I said as Abbie, who was still a few steps in front of me, turned onto our lawn with Rocky, "This is it."

"Nice house," he said as I picked my key out of my pocket and unlocked the front door, ushering the three of us in as Rocky's leash was returned to Ryan. "Is it okay for me to let him off the leash?"

I looked down at Rocky, who seemed pretty mellow as I kicked my shoes to the side. "I don't know," I replied, raising an eyebrow at Ryan, "Is he housetrained?"

Ryan nodded, smiling down at me as I bent down to help Abbie with her shoes. "He's good."

"Then he's welcome to roam free," I replied, petting Rocky gently as Ryan unhooked his leash, leaving him with his collar as he encouraged him to move further into the house.

"Are we still having ice cream?" Abbie asked, hopeful for the right answer.

I smiled at her. "Of course we are sweetie," I replied. "Just go wash your hands in the kitchen and I'll be there in a second."

She didn't need any further encouragement as a wide smile spread across her face, and without another word, her little legs turned around and headed quickly into the kitchen, Rocky following after her.

"So, you share this place with your sister?" Ryan asked as he stepped into the living room with me, stopping briefly to take a look around.

"Yeah. Emily and I were close growing up, but she moved down here when she was finished high school, and when I mentioned wanting to move out, we thought it'd be nice to share a place for a while."

"I wish I still lived with my brother," Ryan commented as his eyes travelled around the room, only stopping when he noticed the books that I had left out earlier this afternoon. "Studying hard?"

I ducked my head embarrassedly, rushing over to the couch to gather my things. Not speaking, I stuffed the loose papers in the front of my binder, but was surprised when my textbook was picked up.

"Media Culture: A Handbook to New Aged Journalism," he read, listing off the title of the book before quickly flipping through it. He handed over soon enough, raising an amused eyebrow as he did. "Are you sure you're not studying to out my private life to the public?"

His question seemed to ease my worries. I knew I had told him that I was studying for journalism, but I didn't fully know if he was comfortable hanging around me because of it. He seemed, however, quite relaxed at the moment, and if could dismiss it, then I would to.

"Studying for a test tomorrow actually," I replied as I took the textbook, along with my things that had been lying around and moved them onto a free shelf.

"Did you want to study?" he asked hesitantly. "I mean I can leave if you need me to, it's not that big of a deal. I'll just get Rocky and we'll go."

I shook my head, the sides of my mouth tilting upwards at his rambling. "Don't worry about it," I said sincerely, Ryan's shoulders and posture relaxing as I turned to head into the kitchen. "I'm going to be studying a lot tonight after Abbie's in bed anyways, plus, the test isn't worth that much of my grade."

"Oh, okay."

I went to reply as I entered the kitchen alongside Ryan, but as I did, my eyes widened at the scene before me. There, standing on a chair that she had leant up against the fridge, was Abbie, reaching her hands into the freezer in search of the ice cream. Ryan started laughing as I quickly stepped up to Abbie, picking her up from her place on the chair and putting her feet back on the ground.

"Don't do that Abbie," I stated worriedly, my motherly instincts kicking in as I ran my eyes over her to make sure she was okay. "That's dangerous sweetie, you could've gotten hurt."

"I just wanted the ice cream," she said, her bottom lip jutting out in sadness.

"Well, you've certainly got one ambitious daughter" Ryan said, amusement still clear in his voice as he walked up to the freezer, pulling out a tub of cookies and cream as he knelt down beside me, facing Abbie. "Is this what you were looking for?" he asked her, shaking the tub in his hand.

Abbie's mood went from sadness to happiness in less than a minute as her eyes glowed in excitement and she nodded her head.

"Then you're going to have to apologize to your mom first, she was worried about you." he stated, surprising me as he tossed the ice cream my way and stood up.

Abbie glanced down to the ice cream quickly before looking back up at me. "I'm sorry momma," she pouted, "I just wanted the ice cream."

My heart clenched at the apologetic look she was giving me, and either she was developing one strong puppy dog face or she was truly sorry. I sighed. "I know sweetie," I said, hugging her to my side as I lifted her up to one of the dining room chairs, "Just promise me that you won't do anything dangerous like that again."

"I pwomise," she replied, her eyes looking up at me hopefully.

"Good," I nodded, cracking a smile. "Now, who wants some ice cream?"

"Are you sure eating all of that ice cream fits into your Hollywood lifestyle?" I asked teasingly.

The ice cream, which was unsurprisingly delicious, had pretty much been emptied as both Abbie and Ryan pigged out on the desert, while I kept to a reasonable amount in fear of getting a brain freeze. Once the ice cream had been finished and I had cleaned up Abbie's face, as she had somehow managed to look as though she'd grown an ice cream beard, she went off to play with Rocky, leaving me alone with Ryan. Him and I were currently lounging on the couch, simply talking to each other as the time passed by.

He rolled his eyes. "Oh come on, I didn't eat that much."

"The nearly empty tub of ice cream begs to differ."

"Then I guess it's a good thing I'm not really working right now, so there's no real reason for me not to eat a tub of ice cream," he countered, extending his arm across the back of the couch. With his arm now resting there, his hand was dangerously close to where my head was settled.

I tried not to focus on that as I replied. "What do you mean you're not working right now?"

"Well I finished filming a movie a little over a month ago, and at least for the next few months I don't have any big projects scheduled," he explained. "I mean I have a few interviews and public appearances over the next few weeks, and I signed on for a movie that starts filming in the new year, so that script should be sent my way soon, but I shouldn't really have much press stuff until December when the movie comes out."

"Mmm... sounds nice being a big ticket movie star," I commented, closing my eyes as I jokingly tried to picture it. "No tests to study for, no side jobs that you need to pay the bills, you get time off when you want it."

"It's not always that great," he pointed out, and I don't know if it was purposeful or accidental, but his fingers slowly started to twirl the ends of my hair that were splayed out near his hand. "I mean yeah, after high school I never really had to hold down a part-time job or anything, but I still had to work to be where I am. I was constantly turned down for parts and I had my agent hounding me constantly to be better and get in shape. It wasn't until probably two years ago that I actually got a leading role when he laid off a bit and just handled my meetings and appearances instead of how I lived my life. Plus, being in the public eye isn't always a good thing when you want a private life."

Listening to him talk, I realized that, other than the few times I'd spoken to him, I really didn't know much about him. Ryan seemed like he had his life together at the moment, but as he spoke, I figured that he must have gone through a lot to get to where he is. "It must be tough sometimes," I responded, absentmindedly playing with the couch cushion, "Being in the spotlight I mean."

"Sometimes," he replied vaguely, lifting the side of his mouth into a small smile, "But other times it has its perks."

I thought I saw something meaningful flash across his face, but as I opened my mouth to respond, I heard the front door open and two familiar voices waft into the house. Turning my head quickly to the clock on the wall, I saw that time had flown by and it was approaching four thirty, meaning that Emily and Dustin were already done work.

"Since when did we get a dog?" I heard Emily ask worriedly, as Rocky started barking. Emily stepped into the living room, Dustin right behind her as they rounded the corner, but as she noticed that I was not alone, she stopped abruptly. "Oh, hello."

"Hey," Ryan greeted in reply, sitting up a bit as he raised his hand that had been entangled in my hair for a small wave. "Emily right?"

She nodded, looking at me with wide eyes before shaking herself out of her shocked trance. "So I'm guessing the dog belongs to you," she commented as Rocky ran into the living room, Abbie not far behind.

"You'd be right with that guess," he replied, rubbing his dog's ears as he came to sit by his feet.

"Dude, you're Ryan Adams," Dustin commented, looking star struck as he stared at Ryan.

"Oh right," I said, standing up as I gestured between the two of them. "Dustin, meet my friend Ryan. Ryan, meet Emily's boyfriend Dustin."

"Good to meet you man," Ryan said, standing up beside me.

Dustin, who seemed to have been shaken out of his star struck state, nodded. "You too."

"I actually should get going though," Ryan stated, taking a look at his phone before smiling down at me. "Thanks for having me over."

"I'll walk you out."

As I led him towards the entryway, Dustin and Emily walked further into the house while Abbie and Rocky scrambled behind us.

"Are you leaving?" Abbie asked with a pouty smile, leaning down to wrap her arms around Rocky. I smiled lightly at the sight, wrapping the cardigan I was wearing tighter around my stomach as I watched Ryan crouch down to her level.

"Yeah sweetie, I've got to go," he replied, clipping Rocky's leash onto his collar as he spoke, "But I'm sure I'll see you and your mommy again."

"Okay!" she cheered at his words, "Bye Ryan!"

He chuckled lightly. "Bye sweetie," he returned with a smile before Abbie turned and headed into the living room where I could hear her talking with Emily and Dustin.

"Weren't you waiting for your bodyguard to come back with your car?" I asked. "I thought you didn't want to walk home."

"Why, you don't want me to leave?" he replied teasingly, to which I rolled my eyes. "Actually he texted me a while ago telling me he was here."

My eyes widened slightly. "Why didn't you just tell me? You could've left if you wanted to."

He shrugged. "I didn't want to," he replied, smiling as he saw a dust of pink colour my cheeks, turning as he opened the door. "I'll see you around Zoe."

"Yeah, see you around," I responded, just loud enough for him to hear it as he closed the door behind him.

"Well, well, well," Emily said teasingly as I walked back into the living room to see her bouncing Abbie up and down on her knee. "Did you have fun on your ice cream date?" she asked, and when I raised an eyebrow, wondering how she knew that, she tickled Abbie's sides. "This little monster spilled the beans."

"What I can't have friends?" I asked, deciding not to comment as I breezed past them and headed into the kitchen to start on dinner.

"Not ones who are that hot!" she fired back, making me laugh as I shook my head.

Ryan Adams had snuck up on me. He was a mystery that I had yet to solve, and as I set to work on dinner for the four of us, I wasn't sure if I wanted to or not.

CHAPTER 6

I didn't see much of Ryan after the day he visited for ice cream; in fact, almost a month went by and I saw very little of him. It wasn't because of the lack of trying though.

As September passed quickly and October came upon us, our schedules just seemed to clash. My school work really started to pile up, Colette and her parents were slowly getting me used to how they ran their cafe, and with midterms rolling up, I didn't have much free time on my hands other than the days I left dedicated to Abbie.

Ryan, on the other hand, had a full schedule for an entirely different reason. The interviews and guest appearances he had scheduled toward the end of September had been crazy, and when we did talk, he'd fill me in on the shenanigans I missed by not tuning into the local media. I was hearing first hand what it meant to be a true Hollywood star, and what I'd learned over the passed few weeks was that he was well acquainted with the fame, but somehow, once a week he'd still find time to stroll into the café and talk with me over my break.

Something about those few cherished minutes made him seem normal to me; like he wasn't the object of millions of girls fantasies across the world, but just a normal guy talking to a normal girl.

Those minutes came and went though, and as I found myself drifting towards the middle of October, I also found myself working more frequent hours at Corner Café.

"Hazelnut cappuccino with two espresso shots and extra vanilla," Colette called out from where she stood, manning the cash register as I stood in as the barista.

"On it," I replied, placing a medium cup under one of the coffee machines, punching in the cappuccino as I added the hazelnut and vanilla flavouring.

It hadn't taken me long, a couple of weeks at most, to get the hang of the different machines that lined the counters, and after a fair few failed attempts, I knew how to make most of the drinks on the menu.

Waiting for the coffee to stop dripping, I quickly added the espresso shots before capping the drink and calling out the order. "Have a nice day," I smiled, handing the drink to the woman that stepped up as I heard Colette call out the next order.

It was just after one in the afternoon on the second weekend of October, and although people could've been at home cozying up to their fireplaces or seeking more than a quick drink for lunch, Corner Café had been going crazy for the past hour, the line looking as though it was never ending.

"Chocolate and vanilla mocha with a shot of peppermint and extra milk," Colette hollered a few orders later, making me crack a smile as I started a drink.

"Hey, that's basically the same as..." I started, turning to talk to Colette before catching the eye of a familiar face that stood on the opposite side of the counter, "Ryan's normal order." I finished, sending him a quick smile as I finished his drink, spraying a little extra whip cream on the top before capping it.

"Thanks," he smiled as I handed him his signature drink.

"What are you doing here?" I asked, "I thought you had that thing today."

'That thing' happened to be an interview with some well-known talk show host, but just in case one of the many people in the café overheard me, I expressed my curiosity vaguely as I waited for a reply.

"That thing, as you so eloquently put it, was this morning and I actually finished it about a half an hour ago," he explained, and when I actually took a look at him, I could see what he was talking about. On top of his normal disguise of a baseball cap and sunglasses, he had on a pair of form fitting khakis and a button down shirt, looking more dressy than casual as he stood in the café.

"And what, you decided to come straight here?" I asked raising an eyebrow as I set to work on the next order Colette called out.

"Well I did text you when I was done, but when you didn't reply I remembered you said you were working this morning," he said, "So yea, I decided that a delicious mocha made by a gorgeous barista was just what I needed."

With my hair tied up in a frizzy ponytail on the top of my head, along with my coffee covered apron and slightly sweaty skin, I doubted I looked anything close to gorgeous at that very moment. Nonetheless, his comment still made a slight colour frost across my cheeks.

"Just so you know, I already used my break earlier," I pointed out, "And I'm not off for almost another two hours."

I quickly handed out two coffees to the women waiting patiently beside Ryan, wishing them a good day before listening to Ryan's reply. "And your point being?" he asked.

I sent him a flat look over my shoulder as I mixed a hot chocolate together. "That if you have a point, you better get to it quick."

He rolled his eyes. "The last time I talked to you, I'm pretty sure I remember you mentioning something about your last midterm being yesterday," he specified, "And me being the amazing friend that I am, thought you'd want to celebrate a little."

It was true, that although I had another round of midterms in November, for the next few weeks the only things taking up my time would be piles of assignments with no extra studying required. At the thought of celebration, I was honestly touched that he thought of something so sweet, but knowing that I really couldn't go out and have fun like a normal university student put a slight damper on things.

"That's really sweet Ryan," I trailed, and judging by the lack of conviction I spoke with, Ryan was able to tell right away that something was wrong.

"But..."

"But," I continued sheepishly, "I kind of already made plans with a three year old."

"Oh," he responded, sounding somewhat put down.

"Sorry," I apologized. "It's just that with being swamped with midterms and having to work I haven't gotten a lot of time with her, so I promised a proper Disney marathon after I finished work."

"It's fine Zoe, I get that you're a mom above everything else," he replied understandingly, making a small smile appear on my face. That's the one thing that most of my friends hadn't understood back home when they asked me to hang out. I couldn't just drop everything and go out, and with Abbie at home, nine out of ten times I found myself wanting to stay home with her. "However, there wouldn't, by any chance, happen to be room for one more at this Disney party?"

My eyes widened slightly at his question, and when I looked him over in my stunned state, I realized that he looked fidgety and nervous, as though he didn't know how his question would be received.

After spending several seconds looking like a fish out of water, my mouth repeatedly opening and closing with shock, I shook myself out of it. "Why, do you know anybody who's interested?" I asked.

He chuckled lightly, although I could still sense the nervousness emitting off of him as I passed a few more customers their drinks. "I might know somebody."

"Oh will you two stop flirting already," Colette called out before rattling off another order.

I immediately felt my face turn beet red at her comment, but when I noticed a pink tinge to Ryan's cheeks, I felt somewhat better knowing it wasn't only me who had been embarrassed.

Clearing my throat, I started on the next order as I looked up to face Ryan. "Anyways, umm... yeah, you're welcome to come over tonight."

"Really?" he asked, and when I nodded shyly at the small flickers of happiness I saw in his eyes, he smiled widely. "I can just meet you here once you're done your shift if you want," he offered.

"Yeah," I said with a smile, "Sure, that'd be good."

"I guess I'll see you later then."

"See you," I replied, raising my hand in a small wave before he turned, heading through the café door and onto the busy street.

"Well, well, well," Colette started, turning to face me as a customer used the debit machine, "Looks like somebody's in for a good night."

Her wiggling eyebrows and suggestive look was enough to deepen my blush, as it hadn't really faded completely in the first place. "Oh shut up," I mumbled embarrassingly.

"By the way, I need a coffee with a double espresso," she rattled off, amusement still clear in her voice.

"Coming right up," I replied brightly, mocking her amusement as I placed a medium cup under the machine and waited for the espresso shots to pour.

Taking a quick glance at the clock on the wall, as well as the ever-growing line on the other side of the counter, I sighed, knowing that the next hour and a half would be a torturous wait.

Although the minutes didn't breeze by, I didn't find the remainder of my shift as bad as I thought it'd be. Colette, who was quite intrigued by the nature of my relationship with Ryan, kept her teasing comments to a minimum, and with the multitude of customers, I was left with little time to spare Ryan a second thought.

The line of customers only started to thin around quarter to three, so when I finally got around to clearing the tables and wiping down the dining areas, my shift was nearing its end.

Leaning over the one of the last tables to be cleared, I sprayed the top before running a cloth over the top.

"You missed a spot."

Rolling my eyes at the remark, I looked over my shoulder to see Ryan adorned with a new set of clothes, sunglasses, his baseball cap, and a grin on his face. "Funny," I replied, finishing off the table before turning around to face him.

"I thought so."

Smiling, I shook my head in amusement before gesturing to the few tables I had left to clean. "Anyways, I have a couple tables left to clean before I clock out," I said, "I shouldn't be too long."

"Take your time," he grinned, "I was enjoying the view anyways."

"Hey!" I laughed, hitting his arm with the dirty cloth before going back to work. "You're a complete dork."

He shrugged, clearly amused by my reaction, but he didn't comment. Instead, he took a seat at one of the tables I had already cleaned and pulled out his phone, waiting patiently as I finished work.

Fifteen minutes later I was grabbing my bag from my locker, done for the day, only to jump as I noticed Colette waiting behind me. "Oh god," I said startled, "Next time make a noise or something."

"So, what's with you and Ryan?" she asked, wiggling her eyebrows with a smile on her face. "He's been coming here a lot more since you started working here."

Narrowing my eyes at her jokingly, I replied. "Nothing's going on," I shrugged. "We get along and we're friends... that's it."

"Okay, okay, I believe you," she said, putting her hands up in mock surrender, "For now."

Rolling my eyes, I headed towards the door. "Bye Colette," I called out, waving my hand above my head as I made my way back into the front of the store, vaguely acknowledging her goodbye as the door closed behind me.

"I still can't believe you agreed to this," I told Ryan as we made our way through the streets of LA, "Actually, I can't believe you volunteered for this."

"What?" he rebutted, "You don't think I'm excited for a Disney marathon?"

"Are you?"

"I'll have you know that I loved Disney movies when I was a kid."

"Let me guess, Snow White was your favourite right?" I asked jokingly.

"I mean the dwarfs were definitely amusing," he continued teasingly, but shook his head seconds later. "But no, it was actually Peter Pan. I used to pretend I was one of the lost boys, never having to grow up and just have a lifetime worth of fun."

I smiled at his honesty, picturing a five year old Ryan running around with neighbourhood kids. "I can totally see that," I commented, "But just so you're aware, Abbie's more fond of the Disney princesses then a boy flying around in tights."

"I figured, but she's cute, so I can deal with it," he cracked a smile. "Plus, I still get to spend time with you, which was what I was planning to do today anyways."

He spoke calmly, as if his words weren't sweet and unexpected, and although I let my mouth turn up into a smile, I managed to keep an impending blush down as I continued the conversation. The rest of the walk went without a lull or awkward moment, which I was glad of, and without even realizing it over twenty minutes had passed and we were approaching my front door.

"I'm home," I announced as I stepped through into the entryway, holding the door open for Ryan to step in before closing it behind me. Taking off my shoes, I heard a pitter patter of footsteps growing louder, and before long, Abbie's excited face came into eyesight.

"Momma!" she cheered happily, running up to me with her arms wide, wrapping them gently around my legs in a hug.

"Hey sweetie, did you have fun today with Emily and Dustin?" I asked, bending down to kiss her forehead.

She nodded. "They coloured with me, let me watch TV and made me gwilled cheese." she explained happily, slurring some words together as she did. Before I could reply however, she turned her attention to Ryan, her eyes widening as she realized somebody else was here. "Ryan!" she exclaimed, "What are you doing here?"

Already having ditched his 'disguise', Ryan smiled down at Abbie. "Well, your mom invited me over. She mentioned something about watching Disney movies after supper and I couldn't pass that up," he replied. "Plus, I missed seeing your cute face."

Abbie's eyes grew excited when Ryan mentioned the Disney movies I had promised her early this morning. "Did you bwing Wocky with you?"

"Rocky?" he asked, raising an eyebrow questioningly at her pronunciation, and when she nodded in anticipation, he shook his head slowly. "Sorry Abbie, Rocky's actually back at my house relaxing," he started, continuing quickly when he saw her smile disappear, "But he told me to tell you he misses you."

"He does?" she asked skeptically.

Ryan nodded. "Yeah, and I promise that I'll bring him over soon to see you."

"Okay," she nodded, taking the explanation without a second thought before she grabbed my hand, pulling me into the house.

"Hey Zoe?" I heard Emily's voice strain from the kitchen.

"Yeah?"

Heading towards the kitchen, I waited for her reply. "I know you said that you'd cook dinner tonight, but Dustin and I were thinking about going out with some friends." she explained, her back turned to me as I entered the kitchen. My footsteps must have registered in her ears as she turned around about to continue. She stopped short though, obviously noticing that I wasn't alone as Ryan entered the room right behind me. "Well, I was going to ask you if you'd be okay with just Abbie tonight, but I see you already have another guest."

Her tone was teasing and light as she nodded to Ryan, who smiled at her in response. "Hey Emily," he greeted, before turning to Dustin, who had been standing by the fridge watching the exchange. "And Dustin, right?"

Dustin, who had somewhat mellowed out to the idea of me being friends with Ryan, simply nodded, offering him a smile before I spoke.

"You don't have to ask me if you want to go out on a Saturday night Emily, I'm not mom remember," I replied, sticking my tongue out childishly before continuing. "I'll be fine with just Abbie and Ryan tonight, go have fun."

"You're the best Zoe," she said, coming around the table to give me a hug, "And hopefully you'll have a fun night too," she continued teasingly, whispering her last words into my ear as she let go and headed upstairs, Dustin not far behind.

Her words caused a soft blush appear across my face, and when I looked to Ryan, who was standing not that far away from me, I saw the vague outline of a smirk dancing across his lips, telling me that he'd definitely heard what my sister had said.

"Sorry about my sister," I said quickly, nervously running my hand through my hair.

He shook his head in amusement. "It's fine," he replied. "But what was that she said about you making dinner?"

"Well I was planning on making a pasta bake tonight," I started before Ryan cut me off.

"That sounds pretty good."

"Really?" I asked nervously, not used to cooking for people other than Abbie and Emily. "Because if it'd be easier we could just order a takeout."

"If it was my choice, I'm actually quite interested to see what you can cook," he stated. "Plus, I have take-out way too often."

"What, do you not have a fancy home chef or something?" I asked jokingly.

"Surprisingly no," he replied in mock shock. "I mean I can cook, but it's not always the best option when you're cooking for one, so takeout is usually easier."

I nodded in understanding. "So is chicken penne alfredo good with you, or?"

Ryan smiled down at me. "Sounds good to me."

Dinner didn't end up taking as long to prepare as I expected.

The pasta and chicken took less than twenty minutes to cook, and once the sauce was mixed and heated, I tossed everything together before sprinkling a thin layer of cheese over the top, sticking it into the oven. I had a good ten minutes before the cheese was fully melted, so after putting the dirty dishes in the sink and going over the counter tops with a damp rag, I headed into the living room to see what Ryan and Abbie had gotten up to.

I thought that maybe Abbie would've conned him into playing with her dolls or watching a television show, but what I saw when I stepped into the next room surprised me.

"Umm... what's going on here?" I asked.

Ryan was seated on the floor in front of the couch with Abbie on his lap, and they were discussing the best Disney films while my entire Disney collection was laid out in front of them.

At the sound of my voice, Ryan turned his head to look over his shoulder, a sheepish smile growing on his face. "Sorry," he apologized, "Abbie wanted to look at all the Disney films, and before I knew it, they were all over the ground."

"Momma, I wanna watch Lion King and Awiel," Abbie stated before leaning over and holding up cases for both DVDs.

"You want to watch both eh?" I asked, walking over to her and grabbing both cases while she nodded. "Well if you head into the kitchen and get ready for dinner, maybe we'll have enough time for both."

Her eyes sparkled at my words as she quickly stumbled off of Ryan's lap. "Okay," she smiled excitedly, heading rather fast into the kitchen.

"I can clean all this up," Ryan offered guiltily as he stood up, gesturing to the remaining twenty or so DVDs that covered my living room floor.

I shook my head. "Don't worry about it," I said. "Dinner's pretty much ready and we can deal with this mess after we're done eating."

"Oh yeah," he stated, his eyes lighting up in amusement, "It's time for me to find out if you're cooking abilities are any good."

"Well hopefully you find them up to par, because that's the only thing we have to eat," I replied teasingly as he followed me into the kitchen.

And it turned out that my cooking was good enough. After making sure that both Abbie and I had had enough to eat, Ryan happily took seconds and thirds, finishing off the remaining food without a complaint.

Once dinner was finished I quickly cleaned up, refusing Ryan's adamant pleas to help, instead asking him to take Abbie into the living room and set up one of the movies, trusting him not to break the DVD player like Abbie had in the past.

Telling myself that I'd do the dishes later tonight, I let them soak in a bit of water as I cleaned the table off before heading into the living room.

"So, what movie is up first?" I asked, rubbing my hands together in anticipation as I walked into the living room, only to see that, along with the Little Mermaid playing on the television screen, all the DVDs had been put back in stacks on the TV stand. "You know you could've just shoved them all to the side for now."

Ryan shrugged, picking up the remote to pause the movie at the beginning as the three of us got settled on the couch. "It wasn't that big a deal," he replied, "And I got that little cutie to help, right Abbie?"

Abbie, who had plopped herself onto my lap after I settled myself on the couch, nodded enthusiastically. "I cleaned momma!"

"Good for you sweetie," I replied, tickling her sides gently as she squirmed on top of me before looking over to Ryan, "And thanks."

"No problem," he replied simply, nodding to the lamp beside him that was currently lighting up the entirety of the room. "Off or on?"

"Off," Abbie replied hurriedly, and when I nodded as well, the lights went down and the movie started up.

"Let's get this movie night started."

And started it got.

For the hour and a half that followed the three of us watched intently as Ariel was given legs, lost her voice, met and fell in love with Prince Eric, and finally defeated Ursula. As the movie played Abbie looked completely entranced, and even though I knew for a fact that she'd seen this movie many times, it seemed like she was watching it for the first time.

"So, the Lion King is next?" I asked as the credits started to roll and I tapped Abbie's leg, gently pushing her to the side as I got up and switched the disks.

"Yeah!" Abbie exclaimed before she scampered off the couch and headed up the stairs.

Ryan glanced to the stairs in confusion before turning to me. "Where'd she go?"

"Oh she'll be back," I replied, "She has a Simba stuffed animal that she likes to play with when she watches this movie."

"And how many times have you watched this movie?" he asked with an eyebrow raised in amusement.

"Since she was born... too many," I laughed.

Sure enough, not even a minute later the title screen for the movie appeared on the screen and Abbie came barreling into the room with her stuffed Simba in her hands.

As time went on and the movie played out, I found myself tearing up at Mufasa's tragic death scene, enjoying the movie I'd seen one too many times, and laughing as Abbie got Ryan to sing along to Hakuna Matata.

"Do we have time for another movie?" Abbie pleaded as the Lion King finished, but looking at the clock, I knew that her bedtime had already passed.

"It's already passed eight 'o'clock sweetie," I replied, shaking my head slightly. "You still have to take a bath before bed. I promise that we'll watch another movie tomorrow if you still want to."

"Okay momma," she said, hugging her stuffed animal to her chest as I picked her up. "Is Ryan gonna be here tomorrow?"

"Umm... if your mom doesn't mind, I might drop by for a bit." Ryan replied, moving anxiously where he sat.

"We'll see," I told Abbie, not going to force him to come by if he had already made plans. "You're welcome to just hang around here for a bit while I put this little one to bed. I shouldn't be more than twenty minutes," I continued, directing my words towards Ryan.

He nodded, relaxing back into the couch as I headed upstairs to take care of Abbie. After a quick bath, a good brush of her teeth and a change of clothes, I tucked my now warn-out daughter under her covers, kissing her forehead as her head sunk into the pillows.

"You know if you're busy tomorrow you don't actually have to come over," I informed him as I walked back into the living room about twenty minutes later. "I'll just tell Abbie that you couldn't make it."

Ryan, who looked to have stayed pretty chilled on the couch, tucked his phone away and turned to smile at me as I took a seat next to him. "Actually, I don't actually have much to do tomorrow, so if you don't mind, I can pop by for a while," he replied.

"Sounds good, just shoot me a text when you leave," I smiled before changing the subject. "So, was this what you had in mind this morning when you said you wanted to celebrate the end of my midterms?"

"Not exactly," he admitted with amusement, "But hey, I enjoyed myself."

"I could tell, I mean the notes you hit while singing were spot on," I teased.

"Hey, I'm an actor, I never said I was a singer," he replied, finding amusement in the situation as well. "And I actually wanted to hang out with you tonight so I could talk to you about something."

Suddenly confused, I urged him to continue. "Okay, what?"

"Okay, well my cousin, he's about my age, is getting married next weekend," he stated, but I didn't quite catch what he was getting at. "Anyways, I RSVP'd a long time ago, but he called me last week wanting to know if I was bringing anyone before finalizing the seating chart. Obviously I'm not dating anyone, but I thought I'd ask you if you wanted to come before I got back to him."

I was shell-shocked as he finished his explanation. He wanted me to be his plus one to his cousin's wedding? "Me... what?" I asked, my words stumbling as I tried to comprehend the situation.

He smiled nervously at me. "Yeah, I thought it'd be fun," he continued. "I mean you don't have to if you don't want to, it was just a thought."

After a few more seconds of silence, I managed to shake myself out of shock. "Well, umm, is it in town or?"

He shook his head. "It's actually in Bakersfield, so about two hours away," he explained. "I was originally planning on leaving Saturday morning before the wedding and coming home Sunday morning, but if you want to come we'll come back Saturday night."

"Would I be able to get back to you tomorrow?" I asked fidgety. "If I talk to Emily about watching Abbie for the day, then yeah, I think I'd be okay with going."

Ryan's persona suddenly turned from one of nerves to one of happiness. "Really?"

I nodded shyly, biting my lip.

"Great," he chirped a little overexcitedly, making both him and I burst out in a fit of laughter.

The rest of the night was simply the two of us talking, joking around and just getting to know each other better, and without even realizing it; I slipped into bed later that evening with a permanent smile etched across my face.

CHAPTER 7

"It's not that big of a deal." I insisted.

Today was Saturday, the day of Ryan's cousin's wedding, and after asking a rather excited Emily if she minded babysitting Abbie for the day, one quick phone call was all it took for my name to be added to the guest list.

"Not that big of a deal?" Emily repeated incredulously. I was currently finishing up my makeup while Emily sat on my bed, but as she replied, I turned around to face her with a shrug. "Okay, let's forget for a second that he's one of the most sought after guys on the planet right now; let's talk about the fact that you're going out on a date with the hottest guy I've ever laid eyes on."

"Nobody said anything about it being a date," I mumbled nervously, turning back around to conceal the heat that greeted my cheeks.

"Come on Zoe, I can see you blushing," she pushed, coming over to stand beside me. "Just talk to me."

I sighed. "Honestly," I started, looking up at her expectant face, "I don't know if I want it to be a date."

"But why?"

"Because he shouldn't have to be tied down to a girl like me," I admitted quietly. "Ryan's one of the nicest guys I've ever met, and even when he found out about Abbie, he just said that her dad was a dick for leaving and then went on as if nothing happened. I mean, I have a kid, and it's not like I've been dating much in the past few years, so why would he want to be with me?"

"Zoe," Emily started, placing her hands on my shoulders in comfort, forcing my eyes up to meet hers, "You're being too hard on yourself. I know you haven't had the best luck with guys in the past, but if Ryan, who's constantly surrounded with supermodels and gorgeous actresses, wants to get to know you, then you're obviously doing something right."

A small smile graced my face at her words. "That still doesn't mean it's a date," I pointed out, standing up to grab my handbag from the corner of my room.

"Well, you look pretty good for somebody whose not going on a date," Emily said, smiling at me in encouragement.

Taking a quick peek in the mirror hanging on my closet door, I smiled at my reflection. Not wanting to show up to the wedding in rags, I had pulled on a long sleeved peach dress from my closet that had two slits running down the majority of the arms. I hadn't worn it since I started university, but when I saw it hanging at the back of my closet earlier in the week, I knew it'd be perfect for today. On top of the dress, I'd curled my hair so that it rested loose against my shoulder, as well as thrown on a few pieces of jewelry and done my makeup.

"It's a wedding," I rolled my eyes, "I'm supposed to dress up a bit." However, her words suddenly threw my nerves into a frenzy. "Why? Do I look like I'm trying too hard?"

Emily shook her head. "Don't worry about it Zoe, you look great," she reassured me before her smile turned into a smirk, "And I'm sure Ryan will think so too."

A blush came across my cheeks again, however I didn't reply, simply giving my sister a shy smile before walking into the hallway towards Abbie's room. Standing in her doorway, I saw her playing with a handful of her toys next to her bed.

"Knock, knock," I said out loud as I brought my hand up against her door a few times, smiling down at her as her head popped up in my direction. "How's my little angel doing?"

"Hi momma," she smiled, holding up the doll in her hands as I walked over to her, "I'm dwessing Angie up for a wedding."

"Oh yeah," I asked curiously, "Who's getting married?"

"Billy and Molly," Abbie replied easily, pointing to two of her teddy bears that she had already dressed up. "I'll be at a wedding today too, like you."

I smiled down at her as my heart squeezed gently. I wish I could be taking Abbie today, but I didn't want Ryan's family to have to deal with another new face on top of mine, and on top of that, one of a three year old. "I'm sorry you can't come with me today," I stated, pulling her closer to me as I wrapped my arms around me. "Are you going to be okay staying with Aunty Emily today?"

I was reassured, as she pulled back slightly from my arms and nodded. "It's okay momma."

"Zoe, stop worrying, it's fine that you're going out today," Emily said, suddenly appearing in the doorway as she smiled at Abbie. "Plus, me and Abbie are going to have an awesome day today, right sweetie?"

A smile grew on Abbie's face as she stood up and ran over to Emily. "EEEEEHHH!" she squealed in excitement. I stood up smiling, feeling immensely glad that I had two people in my life that I could always make me smile.

"Well, it looks like she's going to be in good hands," I said, nodding to Abbie as I sent a silent thank you to Emily for taking care of her for the day.

"You look pwetty momma," Abbie suddenly said, and as I looked at the grin on her face, I smiled.

"Thanks baby girl," I replied, and as the words slipped out of my mouth, the doorbell rang, sounding throughout the house.

"And soon somebody else will be telling her the same thing," Emily stated cheekily, winking at me as she quickly headed down-stairs, Abbie still in her arms.

Glancing at the clock on Abbie's bedside table, I saw that it was already twelve 'o'clock, the time that Ryan mentioned he'd be picking me up. Taking a deep breath to calm my nerves, I let it out as I slowly made my way downstairs, double-checking my handbag first to make sure I hadn't forgotten anything.

Walking down the stairs, I could hear Emily and Ryan talking in the entryway, and when I rounded the corner, my eyes imme-diately latched onto Ryan. To say he didn't look amazing would be an outright lie. He had on a pair of maroon dress pants that matched his tie, a white dress shirt, and grey jacket buttoned up to top it off.

I could feel Ryan's eyes on me as my own made their way down his body, but my train of thought was interrupted as Emily suddenly spoke up.

"Well, I hope you guys have fun today," she said, a smirk on her face as her eyes flickered between the two of us. "And Ryan, you better make sure she comes home with a smile on her face."

"I'll try," he replied, shooting a smile my way as Emily nodded in approval before stepping back into the living room, leaving Ryan and I to ourselves.

"Hey," I mumbled, not knowing what else to say as I broke the silence that had surrounded us.

"Hey," he repeated, smiling down at me as he took a step closer to me. "In case it wasn't already obvious, you look absolutely stunning."

I smiled shyly, feeling my nerves start to act up and my palms start to sweat as, unsurprisingly, a blush appeared on my cheeks. "Thanks, and you look pretty good too."

His smile widened at my compliment. "Thanks," he accepted, before nodding to the door behind him. "So, are you all good to head out? The ceremony starts at three and it's just over a two hour drive."

Nodding, I tried to push my growing nerves down as an apprehensive smile blossomed on my face. "Yeah, let's go."

I didn't realize how long this car journey would truly be, but as I sat in the passengers seat of Ryan's car, which happened to be one of the nicest cars I'd ever laid eyes on, I found myself continuously glancing at the clock on the center console, my anxiety about the day growing as each minute passed.

"So," I started nervously, speaking for the first time in over half an hour as Ryan turned down the radio to listen, "Exactly how many people are going to be there today?"

Turning his head to me briefly, he kept his eyes on the road as he shot me a reassuring smile. "I think there's about a hundred or so," he replied. "Our family is relatively big, but considering he has quite a few friends, and then adding in his fiancée's friends and family, the venue will probably be pretty packed."

His reply didn't help my nerves in the slightest. "And how many people know that you'll be coming?"

"Well my family obviously," he teased, smirking my way before continuing, "And then most of Mark's friends know that he's my cousin, but I'm guessing that most of the bride's side doesn't know."

"And in case you were wondering, I'm pretty sure Mark's the only one that knows I'm bringing somebody," he added as an afterthought.

"Great," I muttered under my breath, ducking my head as I nervously played with the hem of my dress.

"Hey," Ryan stated, surprising me as he reached over the center console and intertwined one of his hands with mine, "Don't be nervous. My family isn't going to care that you're coming, and I promise you'll have fun."

I sent a smile his way, squeezing his hand in comfort as my nerves started to settle. "Thanks."

The rest of the trip went without much of a hitch. About an hour onto the highway Ryan turned off on one of the exits to stop at a convenience store, picking up a boatload of snacks for the remainder of the ride. As the radio played quietly in the background, Ryan told me a little bit about his family that would be there today. His dad was an accountant while his mother stayed at home most of the time, and both of them volunteered a lot in their community. His little brother Dean, on the other hand, was in his senior year of high school and was the captain of the varsity basketball team.

As we passed the city limit of Bakersfield, my nerves suddenly made a reappearance. I knew absolutely nobody except for Ryan, and even with his reassurance, I still couldn't shake the feeling that this was a bad idea.

"So," I cleared my throat, "Is the wedding at a church or...?"

He shook his head as we hit a red light. "Neither of their families are super religious, so they rented out a venue and got the minister to officiate there," he replied. "I think the wedding is in one part of the venue and then the reception is in another part."

I nodded my head. "Okay," I mumbled.

By the time we pulled up to the venue I was wringing my hands nervously. According to Ryan the ceremony started at three, and with it being two thirty now, a few guests were pondering around the front of the venue in the fresh air.

I hadn't even realized that Ryan had parked the car, let alone gotten out and walked all the way around to my side until my door opened, making me jump in my seat.

"Are you ready?" Ryan asked, offering me a hand as he held the car door open for me.

Taking a deep breath, I unclasped my seatbelt. "Yeah," I replied, trying to sound confident as I accepted his hand and climbed out of the car.

It was obvious that my confidence was forced as my voice shook slightly and Ryan looked down at me with an encouraging smile on his face. "I know you agreed to coming, but if at any point you feel uncomfortable or want to leave just tell me and we'll head home early. I really don't mind."

I squeezed his hand that was still in mine as we slowly made our way across the parking lot. "I agreed to come Ryan," I replied quietly, "I think I can survive a few hours."

I was well aware of the eyes on us as we headed into the venue, but was surprised when Ryan suddenly pulled me to a stop, turning me slightly to face him. "Still," he started, "I know this isn't exactly an ideal situation."

"I'm used to a couple of stares Ryan, I'm a young mother for Christ sakes," I reminded him.

He smiled down at me softly, but as he opened his mouth to reply someone else's voice overpowered his own.

"Ryan, there you are!" a middle-aged woman said as she walked towards the two of us, "I was afraid there'd be too much traffic and you wouldn't get here in time."

Looking her way, I noticed the similarities between her and Ryan. Although hers was greying slightly, they had the same colour of hair and their eyes were the same shade of green. It was obvious that the woman stopping beside us was his mother.

"Hey mom," Ryan greeted with a wide smile, confirming my thoughts as he moved away from me slightly to wrap his arms around her in a hug. "And nope, we left just after twelve and the highways weren't that bad," he continued, stepping back beside me. "Mom, this is Zoe. Zoe, this is my mom."

"Nice to meet you Mrs. Adams," I said, smiling nervously as I reached my hand out to shake hers.

His mom let loose a cheery laugh as she completely ignored my outstretched hand and wrapped me up in a quick hug. Although I was surprised, I returned the quick hug and felt my nerves slowly start to dissipate, realizing that his family was a lot nicer than I anticipated. "Oh call me Sophie dear," she suggested, pulling back to smile at the two of us. "And Ryan, couldn't you have told me you were bringing a date?"

"It's not a date," he shook his head, although I could see the outline of a smile still gracing his face as I glanced his way.

His mom's eyes suddenly travelled to our hands, which were still intertwined. The two of us quickly pulled our hands away, a blush rising on my face as his mom shot us both a secretive grin. "Sure," she said sarcastically, obviously not believing a word her son had said. "Anyways, your dad and brother are already in there saving us seats, so we'll just have to make room for you sweet pea."

She walked off ahead of us, and as the two of us followed I really got to see how beautiful the venue looked. The room where the ceremony was being held was absolutely breathtaking. There were two sections of chair that lined either side of the room with small bouquets of sunflowers and white roses hanging at the end of each row. There were drapes hung strategically around the room, giving the perfect amount of light to the room, as well as small candles burning in lanterns up at the front of the room. Light yellow petals covered the aisle that led up to a beautiful vine-covered arch with fairy lights strung elegantly around it.

"Wow, this is gorgeous," I voiced, my eyes wandering around the room.

"Well Mark's fiancée hired one of the best wedding planners they could afford," he informed me as his mom came to a stop in front of us, heading into a row of chairs where two other men were currently seated.

That must be his dad and little brother.

"Brad, this is Zoe. She came with Ryan," his mom gushed as she sat down beside her husband, gesturing to the two of us as we took our seats beside her.

His dad's eyes latched onto me, and unlike his wife, he held out a hand to me. "Nice to meet you Zoe," he greeted smiling at me as I shook his hand before looking proudly at Ryan. "You didn't tell me you were bringing your girlfriend son."

"Yeah, and what are you doing with a guy like Ryan?" his little brother butted in, smirking at his older brother.

"She's not my girlfriend you little shit," Ryan replied teasingly as he reached over to punch his brother in the arm. "Zoe's just a friend."

"Okay, okay you two, none of that today," his mom said, breaking up the quarrel between her sons before it really got started. "Sorry about them Zoe."

I laughed lightly. "Don't worry about it."

As Ryan caught up with his family, I sat there comfortably as I observed the four of them. Sitting there made it seem like Ryan was just a normal guy, not a star-studded actor or a Hollywood hotshot, and when he tried to include me in as much of the conversation as he could, I felt at ease, wondering why I was so worried about today in the first place.

The ceremony was breathtakingly captivating.

I had always been a fan of weddings growing up, so when the conversations around us slowly simmered down, and the music started to play, my interests were sparked. Standing up along with the rest of the guests, I glanced to the front of the church to see the groom, Ryan's cousin, standing up there nervously as the wedding party slowly started to proceed down the aisle.

When the bride finally started to process down the aisle on the arm of her father, I smiled softly; looking back up to the front to see that Ryan's cousin's nerves had disappeared. He was smiling proudly at the woman he loved, not ashamed to be up there in front of everybody waiting to say 'I do'.

The couple wrote their own vows, including cute personal promises that I could only smile at, and by the time he wrapped her up in his arms to give her their first kiss as husband and wife, I felt tears building up in my eyes at the magic of it all.

When it was all over and the bridal party went off to take pictures, the rest of us headed towards the ballroom where the reception was taking place. Keeping to the theme that the couple had chosen, the room was decorated in a rustic-yet stylish fall fashion, putting me in awe with the effort they had put into the decorations.

"Do you want something to drink?" Ryan asked as we headed towards the table we were seated at.

I looked up at him as I placed my handbag on a chair. "Umm... if they have any lemonade that'd be nice," I responded, not really in the mood for anything stronger.

He nodded, making sure I was good to stick with his family for a few minutes before he headed over to the bar.

"So Zoe," Ryan's mom started as I sat down with them, "When did you meet our son?"

"Oh, well I umm, actually bumped into him at this café in LA, but I didn't know who he was at the time," I admitted shyly as his mom smiled at me. "And then when I got a job there we just saw each other often and we became friends."

I saw his mom nod in acceptance before continuing. "So you work at this café then?" she asked sweetly, seeming genuinely curious about me.

"Yeah," I nodded, "I work there part-time and then I'm finishing up my last year at UCLA."

"Oh, what are you studying?"

"Journalism."

Dean, his little brother, laughed at my reply. "So you're studying journalism and you're friends with my brother?" he asked, obviously seeing the humour in the situation.

I shrugged, holding back a smirk. "I see it as a funny coincidence."

The rest of his family laughed as well, Dean smirking at me. "Well if you ever need any embarrassing stories about Ryan, just let me know."

I grinned, shaking my head in amusement as Ryan reappeared, placing both our drinks on the table before shoving his brother sideways, taking a seat in the free seat between the two of us. "Don't listen to anything this little twerp tells you," Ryan grinned, "Most of it isn't even true anyways."

"Well it's a good thing he didn't let anything slip yet, eh?" I asked, smirking slightly before picking up the lemonade he'd placed in front of me. "And thanks for the drink."

He shrugged, "No problem."

Ryan's dad suddenly swept him up in a conversation about his latest movie, and as time went on and the room slowly started to fill up, I got more and more comfortable sitting there with his family. His aunt and uncle, as well as one of his cousins joined our table a little while after, and minus the awkward introduction, everything went swimmingly.

"And for the first time, I'd like everyone to give a warm hand as I announce the wonderful Mr. and Mrs. Mark Adams!" the announcer pronounced about an hour after the ceremony as the two made their way happily into the room, cheers erupting all around.

"Thank you so much for coming and celebrating this special day with us," Mark said, talking into a microphone as him and his new wife stood happily at the front of the room. "We appreciate each and every one of you, and without you guys, me and my beautiful wife here might not be where we are right now."

"Now, we know you guys are all getting antsy, so we're officially opening buffet table, and you're all welcome to eat whenever you'd like," his wife said, making a lot of the guests cheer as they stepped down, making a bee-line to the food themselves.

Table by table, guests slowly started to line up behind the couple, eager for food as the smell wafted its way throughout the entire room. An hour or so later when most of the food was finished and everybody was up and socializing, Ryan's cousin appeared behind us.

Ryan jumped slightly at the sound of his cousin's voice, but as he turned around to see Mark, and not another star struck fan, he relaxed. "Hey sorry, I thought it was another group of people wanting a picture or something," Ryan said. It was true, quite a few people that were friends with the bride, who had no idea he'd be in attendance, had come up to him over the last hour requesting an autograph or a photo.

"Congratulations man; never thought I'd see the day you finally settled down."

"Thanks," Mark smiled, glancing back to look at his wife who was talking with other friends across the room, "And neither did I, but I just couldn't let her get away from me."

I smiled at the love and devotion in his voice. "That's so sweet," I gushed, before ducking my head embarrassedly as the two guys looked down at me with identical smiles on their faces.

"And I'm guessing this is the girl you told me about," Mark grinned, winking quickly at his cousin. "I'm Mark by the way, but I'm sure this lug already told you that."

"Zoe," I greeted, shaking his hand nervously.

"Well it's nice to meet you Zoe, but I actually have to get back to my wife, so I'll see you guys later," Mark stated, saying goodbye quickly before heading across the room.

After another couple minutes passed, slowly but surely guests started to surround the dance floor, where the two of us were standing, as Mark and his wife made their way over as well.

"Please, could we have everybody gather around as the Mr. and Mrs. have their first dance as husband and wife," the announcer said as the pair stepped onto the dance floor.

I stood on the side next to Ryan, a soft smile on my face as I watched the couple slowly start to sway to 'I Don't Dance' by Lee Brice. It was as if the two of them were in their own little world as they danced, whispering in each other's ears and smiling at one another as the song came to an end.

The song switched to another slow song as the pair continued to dance, but as other couples slowly started to trickle onto the dance floor, the slow songs continued.

"That's so cute," I said quietly, nodding to an elderly man who pulled his wife onto the dance floor, looking as though they were still just as in love as they were when the two of them were married.

Ryan obviously heard me, and before I knew it, a smirk grew on his face and his hand intertwined with my own, pulling me out of the crowd and onto the dance floor.

My eyes widened as I was dragged into his arms. "What are you doing?" I asked incredulously, looking at all the people standing around watching us.

"I'm just enjoying myself," he smiled down at me, wrapping his arms loosely around my waist.

"You know I can't really dance," I admitted shyly, a blush rising to my face as I brought my hands up to rest around his neck.

"Then follow my lead," he smirked as we slowly started to sway to the rhythm of the music.

I wouldn't say dancing with Ryan was awkward, in fact, it felt kind of nice to be able to let go and enjoy myself. Song after song, as couples slowly started to trickle off the floor in exchange for others, we stayed together, getting more and more comfortable as the time went on. It felt as though the two of us were dancing for the rest of the night. Sure, we'd take breaks now and then to refuel or grab a drink of water, but it didn't take long for us to return to the dance floor.

As the end of the night was upon us, I felt my heart beating a little faster as we danced. Ryan's eyes didn't stray from my own, and even though my mind was telling me that I shouldn't be enjoying this as much as I was, my heart was not protesting one bit. We were so close together that there was barely an inch of space between the two of us, and as I rested my head on his shoulder, I felt as if this was where I wanted to stay for the rest of the night.

That wasn't possible however, as time was working against us.

When the hands on the clock passed nine, I knew that the experience was ending when Ryan pulled away from me and nodded to where his parents were chatting with some of his relatives. "We should say goodbye to them before we head out," he suggested and I nodded in agreement, following him off the dance floor.

"Oh, are you guys finally done then?" his mom asked as we approached the table, a small but satisfied smile resting on her face.

"Yeah," Ryan replied, ignoring the look that his mom was sending him as he continued, "But me and Zoe actually have to get going if we're going to make it home tonight."

"I thought you were only leaving tomorrow morning?"

Ryan shook his head. "Sorry, but Zoe's got to be back tonight," he explained, yet I felt a little bad that I was taking Ryan away from his family, forcing him to drive home early.

"Oh okay," his mom said, taking the explanation, the smile never left her face. "It was nice to meet you dear, and hopefully we'll get to see you again."

"It was nice to meet you guys too," I replied, smiling as I spoke to his mom and dad.

"Where did Dean get to?" Ryan asked curiously.

"You looking for me bro?" Dean said, suddenly appearing next to him. "You guys leaving?"

Ryan nodded, throwing his arm around his little brother in a loose headlock. Dean honestly looked pretty similar to Ryan, with the obvious differences of height and muscle mass, and looking at the two of them, it made me grateful that I had a sister to lean on.

"Yeah, we're heading out. Text me when you start missing me," Ryan told Dean teasingly.

"Come see one of my games soon if you're not too busy with you're big Hollywood career," Dean threw back, but the love and bond between the brothers was obvious.

"I'll try," Ryan replied, and once I threw out a quick goodbye to his brother, he led me out to the parking lot.

The drive home seemed to take less time than the drive there, but that might have been the wave of exhaustion that suddenly washed over me. Sitting in the passengers seat, I was looking out the window and into the sky, admiring the clear night and the shining stars, but gradually everything went black.

"Zoe. Zoe," I heard quietly, my name being repeated as I tried to remember where I was. Opening my eyes, I saw that Ryan was crouched beside me, having already parked outside my house, now shaking my shoulder gently to awaken me. "Hey sleepyhead."

"Sorry about falling asleep," I apologized, slowly stretching out in my seat.

He shook his head. "Don't worry about it," he replied. "It's almost midnight so it's not a surprise you fell asleep, plus, we were dancing for a while tonight."

"Yeah," I smiled softly as Ryan helped me out of the car. "Thanks for inviting me tonight, I had a lot of fun, and your family's really nice."

"Well, I'm glad you enjoyed yourself," he smiled down at me. I saw a sign of something flick through his gaze, but before I could figure out what that was, it was gone. "I guess I'll see you later in the week."

I nodded. "Definitely. Have a good night Ryan."

"Goodnight."

We parted ways, me heading up the driveway as he stood outside his car, watching me until I was safely inside my house, waving one last time to him before closing the door behind me.

The lights were off throughout the house, and assuming Emily had already gone to bed, I headed upstairs as well, knowing that she'd be up early tomorrow wanting to know how my night had gone.

I changed out of my dress quickly, taking off my makeup, and by the time my head hit the pillow I was already falling asleep.

CHAPTER 8

"**Z**oe, Zoe, Zoe."

I rolled over groggily in bed as my name continually dragged me out of my dream, bringing me back into reality all too soon. Cracking my eyes open, I saw that only a hint of light was making its way through my blinds before I turned to see a fully awake Emily at the foot of my bed. "What time is it?" I groaned.

"Half past six," Emily chirped happily.

Rolling over to greet my pillows once more, I let out another groan. "Why are you up so early?" I asked, mumbling the question into the pillow. "Abbie doesn't even get up this early," I continued, lowering my voice with hopes that my daughter didn't suddenly wake up.

I rolled back over, opening my eyes slightly to see my sister shrug. "I fell asleep early last night, Abbie tired me out," she explained, but she didn't seem at all fussed about it as, even at this time in the morning, excitement and anticipation radiated off of her. "Plus," she continued happily, "I want to hear everything about yesterday."

"Couldn't you have waited a few hours?" I asked, pushing myself into a sitting position, "You know, until the sun was actually up."

She shook her head, the smile not leaving her face. "But then you'll be too busy with Abbie or homework to actually talk," she reasoned, making herself comfortable at the foot of my bed, "And I want details."

The persistence in her voice told me that, with her here, I didn't have a chance of falling back asleep. "What do you want to know?" I sighed, concealing a yawn as I wiped the sleep from my eyes.

"Well how was it?" she asked, not giving me the chance to reply as she continued with quesitons. "Was is weird meeting his family? How were they? How was the ride there? Did you have fun? What was it like having Ryan as a date?"

After the initial shock of curiosity, my lips turned up into a smile as I thought back to the day before. "It was good actually," I admitted shyly, playing with the blankets that were splayed out around my waist. The cheshire smile that spread across Emily's face at my response wordlessly begged me to continue. "It took a bit longer than I thought to actually get there, but we weren't late or anything. His family was really nice when I met them, and Ryan seemed to joke around with his brother a lot."

"Wait, that guy has a brother?" she asked, cutting me off.

I laughed. "Yeah Em, and he's seventeen." I stated teasingly, watching her face drop slightly before I continued. "Anyways, the wedding was gorgeous and his cousin seemed so in love with his wife, it was so sweet."

I went on to describe the little things, like how the ceremony had gone and what their first dance was. I told her how Ryan's family seemed really loving and caring, basically the total opposite of what ours was at the moment, and how good the food had been.

"Wow," she commented as I finished my explanation, and although she stayed quiet for a few seconds, a smirk eventually found its way onto her face. "So, did you catch the bouquet?" she asked, wiggling her eyebrows suggestively.

"No," I blushed, ducking my head so I was no longer looking directly at her.

"Oh come on Zoe, you can't tell me that nothing happened yesterday," she persisted, climbing further up the bed as she took a seat beside me. "When he showed up at the door he looked like a million bucks, and he looked totally into you." The blush on my cheeks deepened, spreading down my neck. "You've got to give me something here."

"Like what?" I asked, not having done this whole boy-gossip thing in a long time. In fact, the last time I'd really talked about a guy with my sister was when I went to her, confused and terrified, after I found out I was pregnant with Abbie.

"I don't know," she shrugged, "How about you admit you found him extremely attractive when you saw him yesterday afternoon?"

"Well that's not that hard," I admitted, "I mean he looked beyond handsome, and he was easily the hottest guy that showed up yesterday."

"And..." Emily egged me on, willing me to keep talking.

"And I guess it was a little surreal to be honest. A bunch of the bride's friends that didn't know he'd be there came up to him all night and it was like he didn't even notice them," I stated incredulously. "Some of these girls could've easily passed for models Emily, that's how gorgeous they looked."

"But he stayed with you," Emily said softly, not needing me to finish my story. It was true, he'd rejected the offers he'd gotten to dance, and he hardly left my side the entire night.

"Yeah," I admitted quietly, still in awe of the situation.

"Zoe, you just have to realize that you're on a whole other level to those girls," Emily explained. "Girls flock to Ryan because of his success and his looks, but you got to know the guy behind the one pictured in countless magazines, and I think that counts for a whole lot more than just a pretty face."

Warmth spread through me at her reassurance as I leaned over and rested my head on her shoulder. "Thanks Em."

"No problem," she replied off-handedly as the two of us just sat there, leaning on each other as the sun continued its slow ascent into the sky. "So, was there a goodnight kiss?" she asked cheekily, filling the silence that had surrounded us over the past couple of minutes.

Picking up a spare pillow from the bed, I brought it up to hit her face jokingly, leaving her with a look of surprise as my cheeks coloured once again. "No," I affirmed, my voice slightly shaky as my train of thought leaped to the possibility of kissing Ryan.

"But you wanted to," Emily teased, noting my blush as she nudged my side.

Just as I was about to deny her claim, spurting some sort of bold-faced lie to my sister, tiny footsteps suddenly registered in my ears. As I turned my head, I saw Abbie standing in the doorway, one of her teddy bears clutched in her arms as she looked at me with tired eyes.

"Good morning momma," she greeted, the sleepiness quickly rushing out of her body as she noticed I was already awake, and after taking a quick glance to the clock on my bedside table, it appeared I had been for almost an hour now.

Had I really been talking to Emily for that long?

"Morning sweetie," I smiled as she came over, crawling up onto the bed while settling herself comfortably in between the two of us. "Did you sleep okay?"

She nodded, looking between the two of us with a look of curiosity on her face. "What you doing?" she asked.

"Your mommy and I were just talking," Emily replied, grinning at me before looking back down to Abbie. "She was telling me all about her day yesterday."

Narrowing my eyes at my sister, I didn't get a chance to say much before Abbie turned and smiled at me. "Did you have fun with Ryan?" she asked happily, letting her teddy bear fall onto her lap as she looked up at me expectantly.

Emily snorted, letting me know that her mind jumped straight to something a three year old did not need to know about. Choosing to ignore her, I combed through Abbie's hair gently. "Yeah sweetie, momma had fun."

And that was the advantage of talking to a three year old, because even though I'd barely said anything, Abbie seemed happy with my reply, not going any further as she started to tell me all about the day her and Emily had had the day before.

The three of us sat in bed just talking for a while, but when Abbie's stomach growled with hunger half an hour later, both Emily and I laughed. "Is somebody a little hungry?" I asked, tickling her stomach lightly as she let loose a giggle.

She nodded. "Yeah momma," she chirped, her giggles continuing until my hand left her stomach.

"Well then, how about we all get out of bed and get dressed," I suggested, "And then the three of us can go out and eat breakfast."

"I'm in," Emily agreed, not giving it a second thought before she picked up Abbie and sat her gently on her lap, "And what about you little girl, do you want to go out to eat breakfast?"

"We get pancakes?" Abbie asked innocently, tilting her head to the side as she looked to me for a response.

I nodded, smiling down at her. "Sure sweetie, you can get pancakes."

The smile that graced her face was huge as she squealed with delight.

"Now go get dressed," I said, picking her up from Emily's lap as I slid out from under the covers, placing her on her feet beside the bed, "Because the quicker you do, the quicker you'll get your food."

No more words were needed as she scurried her way out of the room, dragging her teddy bear behind her and I didn't blame her. Truth be told, I was almost as excited for breakfast as Abbie.

Less than thirty minutes later the three of us were dressed, hungry, and heading out the front door.

"Do you know any good breakfast places?" I asked Emily, the three of us walking without a destination as we turned off our street towards the more commercialized part of the neighbour-hood. The sun was shining brightly, forecasting gorgeous weather for this mid-October day, not one cloud visible in the sky above.

Emily shook her head in amusement. "Couldn't use your head before your stomach?" she asked teasingly, a sheepish expression emerging on my face in response. "Don't worry about it," she continued, steering us onto a side street. "About two blocks from here there's a few small stores. Dustin takes me to this 24-hour diner there sometimes, and the food's really good."

"Do they have p-a-n-c-a-k-e-s?" I asked, spelling out the word as to not over excite Abbie. Her small hand had been twisted with mine from the moment we stepped out the door, and as I smiled down at her, she stopped humming the Disney tune she had stuck in her head to grin up at me.

Emily laughed at my question, finding clear amusement in my spelling as she nodded. "They definitely have them."

Nodding, I let her lead us the rest of the way, which as it turned out, wasn't that far at all. It wasn't even ten minutes later the three of us turned onto an unfamiliar road, noisy pedestrians and bright store fronts engulfing us.

"It's a Sunday morning, why is this place so busy?" I asked, tightening my hold slightly on Abbie's hand as we headed down the sidewalk.

Emily laughed. "This isn't even busy Zoe," she stated as we past a small flower shop that was already full of life. "Try coming here during the week around supper time, it's packed."

"How did you find this place?" I asked, taking the chance to look around a bit. On top of the flower shop, we passed a fair few specialty shops, food vendors, and convenience stores before hitting a crosswalk.

"It wasn't that hard," she shrugged as we stood with the other early morning risers, waiting for the lights to change, "This place is actually pretty popular for the people who aren't rolling around the city with money. Plus, the gallery I work at is about two streets away, so I'm around here a lot."

The light switched, stopping the oncoming cars as we hurried to cross the road. "You really need to show me around more one day," I said, "I've barely seen anything other than the university or the café."

"It's a deal," she replied, smiling at me.

As we rounded yet another corner, with a promise from Emily that we were only a street away from the diner, a small commotion had started a few steps in front of us. Ten or so girls, ranging from teenagers to middle-aged women were crowding around a cart set out in front of a store. "What's going on?"

"No clue," Emily replied curiously, "It's just a convenience store."

As we got closer it was easier to see that the group was surrounding a magazine stand that had been set up outside the store. Most of them seem outraged as they all huddled together, taking up most of the sidewalk as they flipped through one of the copies on display.

"When did he get a girlfriend?"

"What does she have that I don't?"

"Why her?"

I still didn't understand what all the fuss was about as I went to steer Abbie and I around them. "Umm... Zoe," Emily said, and when I glanced back to see that she had snagged a copy of the magazine, I stopped, looking at her curiously. "I think I know what they're all obsessing about," she continued, lowering her voice as her concern seeped through.

More confused then ever, I didn't get a chance to ask her what she was talking about as she showed me the magazine. It was as if time stopped for a second, freezing me in the moment as a chill of worry ran down my spine. I stood there, wide-eyed and without a clue as my eyes trailed over the story that graced the front cover.

'Ryan Adams... Off The Market?'

There, on the front cover, was an enlarged picture of the two of us dancing at the wedding the night before.

"What the... fudge?" I exclaimed, wanting to swear but thinking better of it as I looked down at the confusion plastered across my daughters face. I was speechless. Although the picture wasn't the clearest, you could clearly make out Ryan's face as he smiled down at me, thinking he was free of paparazzi for the night.

"I mean, at least you can't tell it's you," Emily offered quietly, making sure the group of gossiping girls couldn't overhear our conversation.

And she was right. The way the picture had been taken was so that my back was towards the camera, but that still didn't mean they didn't know who I was.

"Can we just get out of here?" I muttered, ducking my head as I turned to head down the street.

Without a reply, it wasn't two seconds later that Emily fell into step beside me not uttering a word. Thoughts about the magazine, my life, and of course Ryan, were flowing through my head at lightening speed. With every step I took I felt my heartbeat increase little by little, my nerves causing my inner worries to grow and stem to unruly places.

"Are you okay momma?" Abbie asked, her hand squeezing mine as she looked up at me worriedly.

Taking in my surroundings, I grasped onto the world around me once more, realizing that through my moments of panic I had still managed to steer myself into the diner Emily had spoken about.

My heartbeat was slowing down again, the new environment kicking my nerves down a few pegs as I shakily tipped my mouth into a smile. "I'll be fine," I breathed out.

"Your mom just has to use the bathroom, so how about we go get a table while we wait for her," Emily stepped in, watching as Abbie nodded. She shot me a worried look as Abbie started to drag her towards a free booth. "Go cool down, we'll be fine," she reassured me quietly, sending me an encouraging smile before following her overly excited niece.

Turning to see a sign pointing me in the direction of the restrooms, I followed the arrows, pushing open the door with a cartoon skirt on it, slipping inside before locking the door behind me. I didn't notice the fact that the place was relatively clean for being open to the public as I gripped the sides of the sink tightly, taking deep breaths as I attempted to calm myself down.

It was minutes later when my grip loosened that I opened my eyes, which had clenched shut, and looked at myself in the mirror. Nothing jumped out as extraordinary to me. I had brown hair that hadn't even been brushed today before I threw it into a topknot, plain facial features and average clothes. I wasn't anything special, so I couldn't understand why I was fatedly deemed good enough to appear on a cover of a magazine with Ryan Adams.

When my train of thought came to a halt and I brought my pulse back down to normality, I noticed that my skin had paled, cringing at the mess that looked back at me.

Heading back to meet with Emily and Abbie, I quickly located the rustic red booth that the two had slid into, taking my own seat beside my daughter as I sat across from Emily. "So, have you guys ordered yet?" I asked, scanning the menu in front of me.

"Are you okay?" Emily mouthed at me, her eyes scanning me quickly as I nodded, silently signaling her to let it drop. Staring for a second, she must have seen that I'd truly calmed down as she responded. "Nope, we were waiting for you."

Nodding in understanding, I looked back down at the menu, deliberating over a few things before my eyes caught a specialty breakfast sandwich in the top right corner. When the waitress came to take our orders, the three of us spoke in turn, an excited grin on Abbie's face as she excitedly told her that she wanted lots of pancakes with maple syrup. The waitress grinned back at her, writing down our orders with the promise that they'd be ready shortly.

The drinks came a few minutes later as Abbie was showing me the colour that Emily had painted her nails, which was a bright purple.

"Oh, did you choose the colour?" I asked, eyes wide in curiosity as I looked at her nails, smiling as the waitress headed back to serve another table.

Abbie smiled widely. "Yeah, it's my favowite," she exclaimed.

"Is it now?" I asked with amusement, knowing that her favourite colour changed almost daily. Sometimes it was blue, sometimes it was pink, and today, it seemed to be purple.

"Yup," she replied with confidence, picking up a crayon that the waitress had brought over to draw on a scrap piece of paper.

"So, with the risk of you panicking again," Emily drawled, taking a sip of her water, "That picture sure looked cute," she continued, referencing the picture on the front of the magazine. A blush blossomed on the apples of my cheeks as I thought back to it. I wasn't a fan of public displays of affection, and even though it'd just been a picture of the two of us dancing, it didn't mean it wasn't embarrassing.

Her grin grew slowly as she continued to talk; leaving me wishing that I'd wore my hair down so that I'd be able to cover my face. "His sculpted arms wrapped around you as you danced, the smile he had when he looked down at you, I mean, that picture pretty much depicted a fairytale," she stated wistfully, an underlying teasing air to her voice.

"Like a princess?" Abbie asked wide-eyed.

Emily laughed, beaming at Abbie. "Yeah, your mommy was dancing like a princess, and Ryan was her prince," she teased, poking her niece on the nose as Abbie let loose a giggle.

"I wike Ryan," she stated as she went back to her colouring.

Emily grinned at the statement while my blush deepened, not needing my daughter to get involved in my non-existent love life. However, just as she opened her mouth to continue teasing me, my cell phone awoke, blasting a familiar jingle.

Pulling it out of my pocket, a puzzled look on my face as I wondered who would be calling me this early on a Sunday morning. My eyes widened as I read the name flashing across the screen, suddenly thinking I knew exactly what this call was about.

Biting my lip nervously, I pressed the green button all while ignoring Emily's questioning gaze, accepting the call as I brought the phone up to my ear. "Umm... hi."

"Zoe, thank god you picked up," Ryan said hurriedly, sounding slightly stressed as he continued. "I didn't wake you up did I?"

"No, no," I quickly denied, "I've been up for a few hours actually."

"Oh, okay," he said. "Well I, umm, I have something I need to talk to you about, so do you maybe want to come over? I mean, it's not life or death, but it's important if you're free."

"I know about the magazine Ryan," I murmured quietly, hoping my voice was loud enough to carry through the receiver. It was definitely loud enough for Emily to pick up on, her eyes widening as Ryan's name slipped through my lips.

"What?" Ryan asked, stupefied at my reply.

"Yeah, I'm out for breakfast with Emily and Abbie," I revealed, picking at the napkin laid out in front of me. "On our way over here we passed a group of girls obsessing over it, and well, I kind of saw the cover."

"Well then," he paused, "Are you busy later, like after you're done with breakfast? I just want to talk to you about all this, and I'd rather not do it over the phone."

"I don't know," I trailed, my nerves acting up once more.

"Emily and Abbie are welcome to come to," Ryan pushed gently, "Plus, Rocky misses the little one."

Seeing the waitress approaching our table with our meals, and Emily's keen grin across from me, I sighed. "Okay," I breathed out, "Okay."

Even though the food was delicious, I couldn't fully enjoy it with Ryan's phone call running through my mind. He'd said he wanted to talk, but about what? Was he embarrassed to be seen with me?

Did he blame me for the picture? I just didn't know, and that's what was truly killing me.

Shortly after hanging up, Ryan had texted me his address, adding that a cab would probably be our best bet at getting there if we'd not taken the car, which we hadn't. Before long the food had been eaten, the bill had been paid, and we were back out on the streets of LA waiting for a cab that we'd ordered.

Despite the fact that I had no idea how to get to the address Ryan had texted me, when the cab pulled up minutes later, it seemed as though the driver did. Rattling it off as he typed it into his navigator, we were off, the three of us squished into the backseat of the rather small yellow cab.

Glancing out the window, I slowly noticed the traffic start to die down, the craziness of town dying down as we headed out towards the edges of the city where the houses were bigger and air was cleaner.

As the cab driver gradually came to a stop, parking outside a house that was equal in size to my parents, I doubled checked the address, making sure we were in the right place before paying the driver as the three of us tumbled out of the cab.

"I'm surprised he doesn't have a gate," Emily commented as we headed up the driveway, glancing my way as I narrowed my eyes at her. "What? He's famous. I just assumed he'd have a gate so that paparazzi can't get on the property."

I rolled my eyes. "It's still trespassing even if he doesn't have a gate," I pointed out.

"Still."

Shaking my head, I decided not to disagree further as we reached the door, Abbie reaching her tiny hand up to hit the doorbell - a mere five times. Laughing at her eagerness, I gently pulled her arm away from the button as she went to press the bell again. "I think he'll hear it sweetie," I said, smothering my laughs.

Through the door I could clearly hear a repetitive chiming, still ringing in result of Abbie's button assault, but the sound of a small dog barking and footsteps coming closer was enough for Abbie to grin widely, turning to face the door just as it was pulled open.

Ryan stood there, dressed in sweatpants and a simple t-shirt, and although I'd mostly seen him in his work attire or more casual clothing, the thought that he looked better in his loungewear definitely sailed across my mind. He opened the door wider as he saw the three of us, ushering us in. "Hey guys," he greeted, smiling guiltily at us as we shed our shoes and he closed the door behind us. "Sorry about ruining whatever plans you guys had, I just needed to talk to you," he finished, addressing me specifically as he went on.

Before I can say anything, Emily waved her hand in dismissal. "Don't worry about it," she responded, "If whatever you have to talk about will calm Zoe's nerves, then I'm all for it. Plus, I've never been to a famous person's house before."

Ryan let loose an airy laugh. "Well feel free to look around," he returned amusedly, "It seems as though Abbie already has."

At the sound of her name, she looked up from where she'd been sitting comfortably, on the ground with a rather playful Rocky. "Hi Ryan," she chirped, petting Rocky's belly as the dog rolled over, "Rocky's fun."

"He's been missing you," Ryan said, earning a smile from her before she went back to playing with the dog. "Why don't you head into the other room? There's a whole bunch of dog toys that you can look through."

"Okay," she replied happily, standing up, moving quickly into the other room, Rocky following not far behind her.

"I'll go watch them," Emily offered, "Leave you two to whatever you have to talk about. Just come find me when you're done." Not leaving us the chance to respond, she followed the path that Abbie had.

"So..." I drawled nervously, "Hi."

"Hey," Ryan replied, the sides of his mouth turning up. He stuffed his hands into his pockets, shrugging his shoulders as he nodded to the side. "Do you want to go talk downstairs?"

"Sure," I mumbled, following him as he led the way.

Although his house seemed extravagant from the outside, and I expected the inside to look posh and well kept like my parents had been, it surprised me. There weren't any fancy bookshelves or unnecessary trinkets littering the shelves, just a few pictures of his family hanging on the walls and common household furniture placed in different rooms. "Nice house," I commented, willing myself not to laugh at the slight mess of the kitchen as we passed through it. It was kind of reassuring that he wasn't trying to portray himself as perfect, the dirty dishes piled up on his counters attesting to that.

"Thanks," he replied as we left the kitchen, opening a door that revealed a staircase. "It's a little too big for just me, but there's room for guests and stuff, so I can't complain."

With the flick of a light switch he lit up the room below us, taking the stairs one at a time as we headed down. The room was actually quite big, two couches taking up a majority of the room, lined up in front of a flat screen that was big enough to be considered a small movie screen. I also took notice of the dartboard hanging on the wall and the pool table standing on the other side of the room.

"You said you saw the magazine right?" Ryan started, getting right to it as he sat down on the couch, me right beside him.

I nodded shyly. "Umm, yeah," I replied, not sure what I supposed to say. "Why, you haven't?"

Ryan shook his head. "I don't usually read magazines," he said, "Most of the stories are embellished or completely made up; I just don't see the point."

"How'd you find out about it then?" I asked curiously.

"My mom called me and woke me up, right before I called you actually," he replied, raking a hand nervously through his hair. "She said that there were a bunch of reporters waiting outside the hotel I was supposed to be staying at, and that somebody had leaked a few photos of the two of us from yesterday. I called my manager right after that and he told me about the magazine."

I was about to ask if his family was fine when his cell phone rang. "Speaking of her," Ryan smiled, pressing the call button as he turned on speakerphone, "Hey mom."

"Oh Ryan are you okay?" she asked frantically. "Your manager just texted me about the magazine. I'm so sorry that happened to you. Do you know who leaked the photo? Have you talked to Zoe yet, how's she doing?"

Ryan signaled for me to talk, telling me it was okay. "Hi Sophie," I greeted timidly, biting my lip as I didn't know what else to say. It was sweet that she was worried about me, considering I'd only met her yesterday.

"Zoe darling," Sophie stated happily, "I'd ask how you're handling this but if you're with my son then you must be at least okay right?" she continued, causing a blush to grow on my cheeks, travelling down my neck at her words.

Ryan cleared his throat. "Mom," he said warningly.

"Oh hush," she dismissed, "But since you can't tell it's you in the photo and your name's not in the magazine, I'd say your fine Zoe.

Just don't worry about anything that my son tries to say to scare you."

"Thanks," I laughed lightly, partially at her words and partially because Ryan was groaning in response next to me.

"But do you know who leaked the photo son?"

Ryan shook his head, stopping when he realized that his mom couldn't actually see him. "No clue, but my best guess is one of Mark's wife's friends," he replied. "There's nothing I can really do anyways, I just have to stay out of the spotlight for a few days until it dies down. Plus, I don't have anything lined up for the next week or so, so I should be fine once it blows over."

"I just wanted to make sure you were alright because we're about to head home," his mom said gently, "And I hope we'll see each other again Zoe."

"Yeah, me too."

"But I have to go, so stay safe you two," she advised before ending the call.

"Are you mad?" I asked, voicing my thoughts to break the silence.

"Mad?" he repeated, looking at me as though I'd lost my plot. "Why would I be mad?"

"I don't know," I mumbled, "You only got pictured because you were with me, and I didn't know if you were okay with it, or if you were embarrassed or anything."

"I'm not embarrassed to be photographed with you Zoe," he denied fiercely. "I wouldn't have invited you out in the first place if I was," he continued, "But I'm used to be photographed and having my pictures in the paper, it's a part of my job. I wanted to talk to you to make sure you were okay with everything."

"Well I freaked out a bit when I saw it this morning," I stated blankly. "How did they even rush it to print that fast?"

Ryan shrugged. "The press works in mysterious ways. Sometimes it's best if I just ignore it, you know, not ask any questions."

"And you're sure that it'll all blow over soon?" I asked timidly.

"Not 100% sure," he admitted honestly, moving closer to me as he noticed my insecurities coming through. His arm came down around my shoulder, pulling me to him in a comforting gesture. "But hopefully it will, and in the mean time, I promise you have nothing to worry about."

My shoulders relaxed slightly as I nodded. "Okay," I muttered as I leant further into him, accepting the comfort he was offering. His hand slowly started to rub my arm reassuringly as we sat there, no more words to say.

The only thing I could hope for was for him to be right; hopefully I had nothing to worry about.

CHAPTER 9

In the days that followed the release of the magazine there was a constant anxiety circling the back of my mind. Whenever I'd step foot in public, whether it be for class, for work, or for groceries, it was as if I was waiting for somebody to recognize me. It was irrational, I knew, since both my name and face were concealed, but I still couldn't help thinking that somebody would recognize me.

Once a few days had passed without incident, and with constant reassurance from both Ryan and Emily, it seemed as though the truth had finally stuck. Ryan had been right; nobody knew who I was and nobody knew that I was the one with him in the picture – I had nothing to worry about.

With worries no longer plaguing my thoughts, it felt as though the rest of October passed by in a flash. I went to class, I did my assignments, I spent time with my daughter, and, in what felt like no time at all, it was Halloween.

"So, have anything fun planned for tonight?" Colette asked as she came back from her break to see me washing down the back counters of the café.

It was a Wednesday afternoon and, for the most part, Corner Café hadn't seen much business after the daily lunch rush. I'd finished classes early for the day, a few of my lectures having been cancelled or postponed, and with the free time I'd been given, I'd picked up a last minute shift after agreeing with Emily that she'd pick up Abbie from daycare.

"I have a three year old at home Colette," I replied, reminding her as I finished up my cleaning, "By the time I get home she'll be dressed up in her costume, waiting at the door to go trick or treating."

"Well I guess that rules out you coming to a party with me tonight then?"

Having not heard the bell ring to signify a new customer, I jumped, releasing a small yelp as I turned to see Ryan standing on the other side of the counter. A smirk started to appear on his lips at my reaction, but an eyebrow was also raised, awaiting my reply.

While his picture with me on the front of the magazine had caused quite a frenzy with his fans, he had taken his own advice, staying in the shadows as he let it blow over. That being said, with him laying low over the past couple of weeks, his visits to the café had been few and far between.

Dropping the rag I'd been using, I brought a hand up to my chest, waiting for my heart to stop its rapid beating. "God, you scared me," I stated, calming my breathing before fully registering his question. "And oh, umm, yea sorry," I replied sheepishly, "I don't really have time for parties much these days."

"It's fine," he shook his head, a smile still gracing his face, "I figured you'd be going out with Abbie tonight, I just thought I'd give it a shot," he shrugged.

"She's just too cool to attend your big Hollywood parties," Colette teased as Ryan stepped up to the cash, shaking his head in amusement as he recited his usual order.

"Yeah, maybe she is," he replied softly, loud enough for me to catch it and send a small smile his way as I set to work on his usual drink.

Colette turned to me once his order had been punched through. "Actually, I was wondering if you were doing anything to celebrate your birthday," she restating her previous question. "After all, you only turn twenty two once."

"I have the day off, which is lucky I guess," I replied, but more or less shrugged off her question as I finished up Ryan's drink, "I never really celebrate my birthday that much anyways."

Ryan, having caught on to what the two of us were talking about, looked at me with a puzzled expression as I handed him his drink. "It's your birthday?" he asked, his eyebrows scrunched together curiously.

"Not today, but tomorrow, yeah," I replied, shifting uncomfortably while shooting a small glare Colette's way. She simply shrugged, not looking all that apologetic as she headed to the back to help out.

My birthday wasn't something that I really celebrated, not since before Abbie was born. It never bothered me though. The most I'd get was a card left out from my parents and a nice breakfast cooked from Greta back home, and truthfully, I didn't need anything special. To me, it was just another day to get crossed off on my calendar.

"And you aren't celebrating?" he pushed further, but I knew it was just his general curiosity.

I sighed and shook my head. "It's not that big of a deal," I persisted, "I'm just not someone who throws a party every year."

As I looked into his eyes, I saw something flash through them, as though his mind was starting to spin with ideas. "And don't you think that just because you're famous you won't get punched if you throw me a party," I continued.

"I'd pay to see that happen," Colette threw in teasingly, coming back through the kitchen doors with a plate of pastries for the display cases.

Redness tinged my cheeks as I realized that if she'd been able to hear our conversation from the back, the only other people in the café at the moment, an elderly couple who sat conversing in a booth near the back, would have been able to as well.

"The thought didn't even cross my mind," Ryan expressed, a humour to his voice that shot a nervous tingle down my spine.

"Sure it didn't," I rolled my eyes, my embarrassment fading as I took a few steps back, finishing the cleaning I had started before his arrival.

"So you're definitely busy for the night, right?" Ryan stepped up, moving along the counter to where I was standing.

"Yes," I trailed, a small smile playing on my lips as I looked up at him, "But if you're in the mood to skip your fancy party and come trick or treating with us instead, the offer's open," I stated jokingly.

"Good to know," he smiled, bringing his drink up to his lips.

Just as I was about to continue the conversation, I turned my head to see a few new customers strolling into the café.

"Well, I guess I'd better go," Ryan said, shading his face from the new customers, as he pulled out a pair of sunglasses from his pockets and slipped them on. "Have fun tonight."

"You too," I nodded, saying a quick goodbye before I slipped back into work mode, starting up the order that Colette was punching in.

Three hours later I was running late.

I'd promised Emily that I'd be home by 5:30, but as my phone flashed telling me that it was already 5:40, I quickened my pace, still having a few blocks to go.

The café had been hit with an unexpected rush at five 'o'clock, just as I was about to finish my cleaning and clock out, so I'd stayed behind a few minutes to help out. Those few minutes had somehow turned into almost a half an hour, and when the line started to dwindle down to its usual size, it'd been Colette who'd pushed me to leave, saying that she'd be able to handle it.

Now, pretty much running up the driveway, I burst through the door. "Sorry I'm late," I called out, breathing heavily as I dropped my bag near the door, heading into the kitchen.

Rounding the corner I saw Emily and Abbie sitting at the table, each digging into a bowl of macaroni and cheese. Abbie turned to face me, a grin on her face as she stuffed another spoonful of food into her mouth. "Hi momma," she chirped, speaking through her mouthful of food, "Aunty Emily made cheesy pasta."

"I can see that," I said, grabbing a napkin from the center of the table to wipe the mess off her face, "But remember what I said before sweetie; don't talk with you mouth full."

Her hand came up to cover her mouth, but I could still see her grinning as she nodded.

"Don't worry, I made sure there was enough for you," Emily stated, gesturing to the stove where the leftover food was sitting.

"Thanks," I smiled, grabbing a bowl from the cupboard before finishing off the macaroni and cheese. "Are you and Dustin still going out tonight?" I asked, sitting down with my food across from her.

She nodded, having finished up her food as she stood up to put her dishes in the sink. "Yeah, one of his friends is having a house party and we're going to head over there for a bit," she explained, "He should be here around six."

"A party?" I inquired, raising an eyebrow in amusement, "On a Wednesday?"

She smirked. "Don't worry, I know I'm working tomorrow morning."

"Hey, I'm not the boss of you," I replied with hilarity, "Go out and have fun."

"Oh I will," Emily nodded happily, smiling as she finished cleaning off the counters. "I'm heading upstairs to change, call for me if Dustin gets here."

"You got it," I said as she left the room, shoveling a rather large spoonful of cheesy goodness into my mouth. A few bites in I felt a tugging on my shirt, only to look to my side to see Abbie trying to get my attention. Once again, her mouth was full of cheese sauce, but her bowl was empty. "What is it sweetie?"

"Is it time to go get candy yet?" she asked sweetly, excitement shining in her eyes as I cleaned off the mess she'd made.

"Well you have to put your costume on first sweetie, so why don't you go tug it on while I finish up in here."

She nodded excessively, giggling as she more or less launched herself off of her chair and out of the kitchen, her little feet pattering up the stairs as she headed to her bedroom.

It didn't take long for me to finish my dinner and clean up the rest of the kitchen, and a mere ten minutes later I was heading upstairs to see how Abbie was getting on with her costume. "Knock, knock," I voiced as I stood in the doorway to her room, "How's the costume coming along?"

I tried not to laugh as I looked down at Abbie to see that, although she'd tried, the dress she was wearing was on backwards.

"It's not working momma," she complained, attempting to figure out what was wrong with it as she looked in the mirror.

"Here, let me," I offered, concealing my laughter as I walked over and sorted out her dress. "There," I said, smiling at her as I turned her to face the mirror, "All you had to do was turn the dress around."

Abbie grinned as she saw herself in the mirror. "I'm a pwincess momma!" she cheered as she picked up the bottom her dress and started spinning with glee.

"Whoa there my little princess," I expressed, picking her up before she got too dizzy, "You don't want to hurt yourself before you go trick or treating do you?" She shook her head. "So, how about we go downstairs and find that tiara I bought you? Then you'll look like a real princess."

She cheered giddily, clapping her hands as I laughed at her excitement, carrying her down the stairs on my hip.

I'd remembered where I put the tiara when I had purchased it the other day. It was cheap and a piece of plastic, but when I spotted it grocery shopping, I knew that Abbie would love it, so I'd thrown it in the cart. Placing Abbie down on the couch, making sure not to wrinkle her dress, I walked over to the television stand and pulled out the plastic bag I'd hidden behind it.

"So, what do you think?"

I pulled the tiara out of the bag, and even though it was clearly not real, Abbie's face lit up like a Christmas tree. "It's so pwetty!" she said happily, and I smiled, placing it softly on her head.

"There, now you look like a real princess."

As Abbie swung her feet off the side of the couch, visibly happy about her costume, the doorbell rang. Just as I was about to stand up to answer the door, I caught the sound of footsteps barreling down the stairs. "I've got it," Emily called, and I shrugged it off, assuming it was Dustin at the door.

Looking back down at Abbie, I placed my hands gently on her knees and smiled. "Are you ready to go trick or treating?"

"Yeah," she cheered happily.

"Well how about you go grab that pillowcase I laid out in the kitchen while I go set up the candy outside for other kids," I suggested, and although she might not have fully understood me, she agreed, wiggling herself off the couch before turning towards the kitchen.

"Zoe," Emily called out, "I think this trick or treater is looking for you."

I stood up, confused as I headed to the doorway to see what Emily was on about. "What are you talking about?" I asked, "Who would be at the door..." I trailed off as I rounded the corner into the entryway.

Standing there was Ryan Adams, dressed up in a full pirate costume.

I stood there shocked, wondering what to say, but before I could utter a sound, I saw Emily smirk as Dustin's car pulled into the driveway.

"Well, that's my ride," Emily stated, slipping on a pair of shoes and picking up her bag from the counter. "Have fun tonight," she continued, looking between the two of us in amusement before heading out the door.

"What are you doing here?" I asked, breaking the seconds of silence that had passed.

He opened his mouth to reply, but just as the smallest of sounds passed through his lips, Abbie came running around the corner, waving her pillowcase around her head.

"I found the bag momma," she said, grinning up at me as though it was her greatest achievement. It didn't take her long however, to notice that we weren't alone. "Ryan!" she chirped, looking up at him happily, "What are you doing here?"

"Your mom invited me to go trick or treating with you," he replied, crouching down to poke Abbie gently on the nose, "Is that okay with you?"

"You're coming out to get candy?" she asked, scrunching her face up. Noticing her face, he nodded slowly, the both of us waiting hesitantly for her reaction. "Yay," she cheered, a moronic smile spreading across her face as she more or less jumped with joy. "But why are you dressed up as a pirate?"

"I would also like to know the answer to that," I asserted, a smirk playing on my lips as he stood up from his crouched position.

He shrugged. "It's one of the only costumes they had last minute."

I raised an eyebrow at his reply. "I thought you were going to a party tonight," I stated, "Wouldn't you have needed a costume for that?"

"Contrary to popular belief, a party on Halloween isn't necessarily a costume party," he responded teasingly, making me roll my eyes. "But I since you oh-so-graciously invited me out tonight, I figured I'd dress up a bit."

"Are you sure you didn't just choose it because the pirate hat and eye patch keep your face hidden?" I asked, nodding to the two things currently resting on top of his head.

Pulling the eye patch down to cover his left eye, I saw the outline of a smirk appear on his lips. "That may have been a contributing factor."

"You should've been a king Ryan," Abbie pointed out, "Cause I'm a pwincess and then momma could be the queen."

Ryan's eyes lit up with mischief at my daughter's suggestion, looking towards me for a response. Meanwhile, I stood there, stunned speechless for a second as a small blush made it's way to my cheeks, shocked that my daughter had unknowingly just married Ryan and I in her mind.

"Aren't we supposed to leaving?" I asked, steering the topic of conversation in a different direction as I shook the bowl of candy that Emily had left, opening the door and placing it, along with a note on the front porch. "I mean, you don't want people to run out of candy, do you?"

Luckily, as I mentioned the word 'candy' Abbie quickly forgot what she'd suggested, and instead cheered, but I knew from the way Ryan was looking at me, amusement in his eyes, that he'd picked up on my diversion tactics.

With Abbie at my side, grabbing my hand as I stood outside, I turned back to look at Ryan. "Aren't you going to walk the plank captain?" I asked teasingly.

Ryan smirked. "Aye aye captain," he winked, closing the door behind him.

"Now let's go get candy," Abbie shrieked, pulling my hand as she hurried the both of us down the driveway, Ryan following closely behind us.

Trick or treating was interesting to say the least.

Walking around the neighbourhood, it seemed as though every kid under the age of thirteen was out on a hunt for candy. Ryan, however, seemed to be the only adult who chose to wear a costume. I found it highly amusing when other parents would look at him funny, muttering under their breaths about how weird or sweet he was to dress up, as I somewhat agreed.

Somewhere towards the middle of the night Ryan had convinced both Abbie and I, after a lot of hesitation, to go through a haunted house that a neighbour had set up in their garage. It didn't end up being all that scary; just a lot of fake blood, cobwebs, and disturbing pictures.

That was, until the end.

Just when we thought it was over, the owner of the house, dressed in a bloodied scarecrow costume, jumped out at us. Abbie and I had both shrieked in fear, her more than me as I had to calm her down gently, explaining that he was simply wearing a scary costume. She seemed to understand, her fear quickly disappearing as the man handed her some candy, apologizing for scaring her.

Sooner or later the streetlights flickered on as the sun started to dim, and Abbie had collected a full pillowcase of candy.

"Can you carry my candy?" Abbie asked, yawning as she trudged along beside the two of us.

I chuckled, taking the pillowcase off her hands as I rubbed her head gently. "Don't worry sweetie, we'll be home soon," I promised.

"But I'm tired now," she whined, getting agitated with the amount of walking she'd done so far tonight. And to be fair, we'd spent more than two hours going from house to house, her adrenaline seemingly dwindling towards the end of it.

I looked down at the pillowcase in my hand, and even though it was heavy, tried to calculate if I'd be able to carry her the rest of the way as well. Before I could speak though, Ryan stopped and dipped down in front Abbie.

"Do you want a piggyback ride home?" he asked gently. She nodded, a small and tired smile growing on her lips as she raised her arms up above her head.

"Up, up!"

Ryan laughed as he turned around, letting my little monster jump on his back, making sure he had a good grip on her before he stood up again. "You okay all the way up there?" he asked jokingly as Abbie's small arms rested loosely around his neck.

"Mhm," she mumbled, her head falling lightly onto his shoulder.

He turned to face me, raising an eyebrow at my stunned expression. "What?" he asked wondrously, readjusting my daughter on his back.

I smiled softly at him, shaking my head. "Nothing."

Ryan still looked at me strangely for a second, trying to get inside my head. It was clear he couldn't find what he was looking for, as he shook his head, accepting my reply as we turned onto my street.

Ten minutes later Abbie was pretty much asleep on his back as I unlocked the front door, grabbing the, now empty, candy bowl from the porch, and bringing it inside. Dropping her full bag of candy at the bottom of the staircase, I turned back to Ryan. "Pass me the sleepy critter," I said, holding out my arms. He gently shrugged Abbie off his back, positioning her in his arms before passing her off to me. "I'll just go put her to bed," I stated, hoisting her up onto my hip as she mumbled, "You're welcome to stick around though, I'll just be a couple of minutes."

True to my word, it seemed that Abbie really was exhausted. It took me no longer than five minutes to strip off her costume, gently pull on her pajamas, and tuck her softly into bed. With the exhaustion she already held, it seemed as though the minute her head hit her pillow she was out like a light.

Shutting the light off and closing the door, I headed back downstairs where I'd left Ryan to wait. "Sorry about that," I apologized, finding him seated on the sofa in the living room.

"Don't worry about it," he replied, standing up from where he'd previously been.

"Oh, are you leaving?"

"Why, did you not want me to?"

"Well, I was just going to pop a movie in," I replied. "You're welcome to stay and watch."

"What kind of movie?" he asked, raising an eyebrow. I shrugged. A smirk grew on his face. "What about a horror movie?"

"Horror?" I repeated nervously, glancing at the DVD case that I knew held some of Emily's horror movies.

"Yeah, you know, get into the Halloween spirit," he teased, picking up on my hesitation. "Why, are you scared?"

"No," I denied hurriedly, "But if you want to watch a scary movie, you have to choose it."

"Deal," he grinned.

I nodded, gesturing to where the movies were kept before heading into the kitchen to make a bowl of popcorn. As the microwave clocked ticked down, I sat propped against the counter with clenched hands. If I was being honest, horror movies weren't my forte, and I was a bundle of nerves wondering which movie he'd pick.

As I headed into the living room minutes later, popcorn in hand, I saw Ryan getting comfortable on the couch as the previews for a movie flashed on the screen. He'd shed the accessories that accompanied his costume, leaving him in a flowing striped top and a pair of ripped black pants.

"Do you mind getting the light?" he asked, turning his head to smile at me as I set the bowl on the table.

I nodded, walking over to flip the switch before taking a seat beside him. "So," I fidgeted nervously, "What are we watching?"

"You'll see," he replied with a smirk, resting his arm along the back of the couch.

I was determined to not jump at the movie, but as the first scene rolled through, I was already shaking in my seat. By the time we reached the last scene of the movie my body was more or less pressed up against Ryan's side, my face hidden in his chest as I gazed quickly back at the screen

It turned out to be a bad idea, because as the movie came to a close, a demon popped out of nowhere, terrorizing the people that hadn't yet died.

"Fuck," I muttered, squeezing my eyes shut as I clenched my hands around Ryan's thigh.

"Okay, okay," Ryan seethed, gripping my hands before I drew blood, "Loosen the grip a bit."

"This is all your fault," I declared, bringing my head up as I heard the credits start to roll.

He held his hands up in a mock surrender. "Hey, you agreed to the movie," he stated, "You could've just told me you were scared."

"I'm not scared," I huffed under my breath.

He raised an eyebrow. "Oh, really?" he asked sarcastically, "You sure have a good grip for somebody who wasn't scared."

"Shut up," I mumbled embarrassedly.

"So, how about another movie?" he asked, clapping his hands together excitedly. I looked at him as though he was crazy. There was no way I was sitting through another horror movie if I planned to get any sleep tonight. He laughed at my reaction. "I meant something that's not scary."

"Oh, sure."

"Any preference?" he asked, pushing himself up to change the DVD.

"There's some comedies stacked down there if you want," I replied, "It doesn't really matter to me."

He ended up choosing a case at random, pulling out a 1980's dramatic comedy that I hadn't seen in a while. As the movie progressed I found myself sinking back into the comfort of Ryan's arms, a blanket lay out on top of us as the chilly evening air blew in through the open windows.

"Hey Ryan," I started; having lost most of my interest in the movie by the time an hour had passed.

"Yeah?"

I looked up from where I'd been resting my head to see two curious orbs gazing down at me. "Why did you show up here tonight?" I finally asked, getting a question, which had been circling my thoughts since he turned up this evening, off my mind.

"What?" he blanked.

I pushed myself up slightly, looking him in the eyes as I continued. "What made you decide to come here tonight? I mean, you showed up at the café looking excited to go to this party, but then you never went."

"I wasn't all that excited for the party to be honest," he confessed, "I just thought it'd be cool to take you. You know, introduce you to some other famous people in the area, but you couldn't, so why would I?"

"Umm... because you were the one invited?" I offered, still not understanding his train of thought.

"And you invited me trick or treating tonight, did you not?" he threw back, and I realized his words were true. Even though I'd meant it as a joke, I did tell him that he was welcome to come. "Plus," he added, digging his hand into his pocket, "I thought I'd give you this."

"What..." I trailed as he pulled out a thin rectangular box and held it out to me.

"You said it was your birthday tomorrow right? So consider it an early birthday present."

"But you only found out a few hours ago," I replied shakily, "You didn't need to get me anything."

He brought up a hand to rub the back of his neck nervously. "I actually bought it a few weeks ago," he confessed. "I thought it'd look nice on you at the wedding, but then I sort of forgot about it. So technically, it's just a gift that's two weeks overdue."

I nervously took the box from his hand, cracking it open to see the most gorgeous gold chain with a small emerald pendant. I gulped, running my fingers over it gently as I realized the gem was real.

"Ryan," I said breathlessly, looking up at him through my eyelashes, "This is too much."

"Don't worry about the price Zoe," he insisted in a voice that nobody would be able to resist. "May I?" he asked, plucking the necklace out of its box. I nodded pushing my hair to one side as his hands came around my neck and clasped the necklace, letting it fall down the curve of my neck. "See, it looks perfect."

I sat there stunned, picking up the pendant with two fingers as I admired it. "Thank you," I breathed out.

I looked up to see Ryan, a soft smile playing on his lips. "Your welcome."

A matching grin slowly appeared on my face, and just as I was about to speak, I heard the sound of jingling keys before the front door opened.

"You know you forgot to lock the door again Zoe," I heard Emily's voice carry, her footsteps becoming louder as she followed the sound the television was emitting. "Oh," she paused as she stepped foot into the living room, noticing that I wasn't the only one here, "So that's who's car is parked across the street."

"Yeah..." I trailed, looking slowly between Ryan and Emily as I inched my way out of his arms.

"I'm guessing you guys had a good night then?" she asked, dropping her keys on the ledge next to her with a smirk.

Thinking back, I realized that this was one of the better nights I'd had in a while. It'd been relaxing, I got to spend time with Abbie knowing that I didn't have to wake up for school in the morning, and it certainly had been full or surprises.

"Yeah," I smiled, playing with my pendant gently as I looked up at Emily, "I guess you could say that."

Chapter 10

"Are you sure about this?"

Emily was currently sitting in a plush chair at the hair salon, and from where I was standing behind her, I could see her hands clenching the arm rests firmly, the tips of her fingers turning white as she did so.

She shut her eyes, taking a deep breath before releasing it slowly. "I'm sure."

A few days ago I had mentioned to Emily that I was planning to get a haircut soon, as I was in desperate need of a short trim, and asked if she knew any good hair salons. It turned out that not only did she not know of any hair salons, she had also made the split second decision to dye her naturally brown hair a rich, deep purple.

I was shocked at first, but after being shown numerous pictures of the hairstyle that she wanted, I conceded, that although it was out of the box, the style actually fit her creative personality.

The next thing I knew the two of us were scouring the Internet for the closest hair salon, which happened to be on the top floor of the local mall, and booking our appointments.

I had already had my hair trimmed and was quite happy with the way it'd turned out. The hair stylist hadn't done much, only taken a few inches off the ends, but it already looked a lot healthier than it had been.

"I can't believe you're actually doing it," Colette noted, bouncing Abbie up and down on her knee as they sat on one of the free chairs. Her parents had given her the weekend off, and I thought it wouldn't hurt inviting her along on our 'girls days out'. "If I ever have the urge to dye my hair, I always wimp out at the last minute."

"Not helping," Emily said tightly, her teeth clenched as her shoulders tensed.

"Sorry," Colette apologized sheepishly, turning her attention to Abbie as she held out her phone, introducing the three year old to a few games to pass the time.

Turning back to Emily, I put my hands on her shoulders to ease some of the tension. "You know you don't have to do this right?"

"But I want to," she replied softly, wringing her hands together in front of her, "My nerves are just all over the place."

Before I could ask her anything further the hair stylist returned from the back, looking happy to see Emily seated in her chair. "So," she started, looking down at Emily with a kind smile on her face, "Are we ready to get started?"

Awaiting her reply, I saw Emily nod her head slightly, taking a deep breath as she replied. "Let's do this."

Twenty minutes later her hair was washed and trimmed as the stylist mixed the hair dye in a small jar. Pulling on a pair of gloves, the hair stylist dipped the end of her brush in the dye, picking up a small chunk of Emily's hair before lathering it from root to tip in the purplish substance.

"Well, there's no going back now," I stated, offering her an encouraging smile as I sat next to Colette and Abbie, watching and waiting for Emily's hair to be finished.

Emily smiled tentatively back at me through the mirror, breathing calmly as another piece of her brown hair was covered in dye.

"Don't worry darling," the hair stylist said encouragingly, "This colour is going to look absolutely gorgeous on you, just you wait."

"Let's hope so," Emily muttered, "But how about you guys try to get my mind off it."

"Umm... okay," I replied hesitantly, glancing to see if Colette had any ideas. With a shake of her head, I tried to scrounge up anything that I could. "How's your job going at the art gallery? Anything exciting happening?"

Emily rolled her eyes at my useless attempt at making conversation. "It's fine, but nothing's really exciting there unless new pieces come in," she replied. "What about you; how's your job?"

Her tone was teasing, as though she knew something that I didn't. "Good," I trailed, raising an eyebrow wondering where this was going, "Why?"

"You're the one who brought the topic up in the first place," she pointed out.

"She's right you know," Colette added in, joining the conversation as Abbie immersed herself into a matching game on her phone.

"Anyways, you're saying the café's just good?" Emily repeated teasingly. I nodded warily, confused as to what she was thinking. "What, has your boy toy not been dropping by to see you enough?"

And there it was. She'd brought the conversation around to somehow focus on Ryan and I, like she'd done numerous times over the past few weeks.

"Oh trust me, he's been stopping by," Colette cut in, a smirk growing on her lips. "Almost every day she's working he's there ordering a drink or waiting for her to go on break." Emily's eyes widened at this information. "He even drops by when she's not even there, trying to play it off like he's just in the mood for a coffee, but I still see his eyes searching the store for hints of our little Zoe."

I threw a glare towards Colette. "Shut up," I mumbled embarrassedly, "He doesn't come that often."

"Oh yes he does."

"I still can't believe neither of you have made a move yet," Emily stated, and when she saw my reflection through the mirror, she continued, "And don't even try to say that you don't want something more from him."

"We're friends," I mumbled non-convincingly as my cheeks started to colour.

"Friends don't buy each other necklaces like that," Emily pointed out, referring to the green emerald that was currently hung around my neck. "And I know for a fact you haven't taken that thing off since he gave it to you."

"Wait, wait, wait," Colette said, looking between the two of us before she focused her gaze on the pendant, "Ryan bought you that for your birthday?"

"She didn't tell you?"

"I just thought it was something that she'd found in her things and decided to start wearing. A family heirloom or something."

"Like our parents would give us something that valuable," Emily snorted in disbelief before a smug-like smile blossomed on her lips. "All I know is that I came home on Halloween to see her and Ryan cuddled up on the sofa, a rectangular box resting on the coffee table, and that emerald necklace hanging from her neck."

"I wish I had a guy like that," Colette sighed wistfully as she stared at the pendant that I now held between my fingertips.

I shifted uncomfortably in my chair. "He's not my guy."

"Honey, if he gave you a necklace like that, there's something going on," the hair stylist pointed out, having been eavesdropping on our conversation as she finished up a section of Emily's hair. "He may not be your guy, but he sure doesn't sound like just a friend."

"She's right you know," Emily added on, as the last of her hair was stripped of its natural colour. "I've seen you guys together, and even if you don't see it, there's times when he looks at you like your some kind of miracle."

"He really does," Colette added in.

Emily nodded, staring at me knowingly. "Just be ready, because sooner or later one of you guys are going to make a move, and then there's no going back."

As the hair stylist finished up the last strand of hair, directing Emily towards the sinks and chairs at the back of the salon, and Colette and Abbie got into a heated debate about game was the best, I sat back, taking in what Emily had said.

I fully acknowledged that my feelings for Ryan were slowly blossoming into something more. How could they not? He was sweet, kind, handsome, funny, and didn't seem to mind playing with Abbie when opportunities arose.

The only thing that was holding me back from doing something about it was my own insecurities. Besides what people kept telling me, I honestly had no idea if Ryan had feelings for me, and it was scary – falling for someone always was. I just didn't know if I had the courage to put my heart on the line if there was a chance I'd end up with a broken heart.

"So, any regrets?" I asked, turning to Emily as the four of us walked side-by-side out of the hair salon.

It seemed as though her mind was elsewhere as she held her phone in her hand, ignoring the people and stores we passed, playing and admiring her new hair-do. She'd had a bit chopped off, her hair now falling a few inches past her shoulder, and the colour truly looked amazing. It wasn't too bright and it wasn't too dull – it was just right.

"No," Emily replied after a pregnant pause, shaking her head as a smile bloomed on her face, "I actually regret not getting it done sooner."

"I'm guessing you like it then," Colette, who stood on the other side of Emily, said, nodding to the newly purpled hair. Emily nodded, running her fingers through her hair. "What about you Abbie?" she continued, looking down at the toddler who had her hand wrapped within mine. "Do you like your aunt's new hair?"

Abbie, who seemed to have gained a new liking for Colette over the past hour or so, grinned back at her. "It's purple!" she exclaimed happily.

"Yes it is," Colette nodded, smiling back at Emily. "Well, I think she approves."

Emily laughed, seemingly amused with her niece's reaction. When her laughter dwindled down to a smile, her eyes slowly started to wander, finally taking in the stores as we passed them.

As a result, the next hour or so was spent going in and out of several stores, trying on different clothes and shoes, and just enjoying the day. Both Emily and Colette appeared to be going all out on this girls' day, while I had only purchased a summer dress for myself and a cute bracelet for Abbie.

"I'm hungry," Abbie whined an hour later as we exited the sixth shop, pulling gently on my hand to get my attention. "Can we eat lunch now?"

I laughed at her moaning. "What do you say guys, are we ready for lunch?" I asked the other two teasingly, knowing that a stop for food was way over due. Abbie whipped her head around quickly, sporting wide eyes and a jutted lip as she looked up at Colette and Emily with hope.

The two of them shared a glance of amusement before smiling down at a jittery Abbie.

"I was actually thinking about checking out that store over there," Emily trailed, gesturing to a small boutique a few stores down. The sides of Abbie's mouth turned downwards, not picking up on the sarcasm. "But, I guess we can squeeze in a trip to the food court before that."

The life sprung back into Abbie's face, a broad grin emerging as she jumped for joy. "Yay!" she chirped, pulling me forward eagerly. "Come on."

The three of us laughed as Abbie continued to scurry her tiny feet in front of me, never letting go of my hand as she zigzagged through the multitude of other shoppers. As we reached the edge of the food court, she gave me an extra little tug, bringing me off balance slightly as I bumped into someone walking past us.

"Oh, I'm so sorry," I apologized as I realized what had happened, taking notice of the two bags that had fallen out of the person's hand.

"It's not a problem," a male voice replied - a slightly familiar male voice. Looking up at whom I'd hit, I came face to face with Dean Adams, Ryan's little brother. "Oh hey," he greeted in recognition, "Zoe right?"

I nodded. "Yeah, how've you been?"

"Oh you know, surviving my senior year the best I can," he replied jokingly. I smiled, knowing that he was probably doing more than just surviving. From what I remembered, Ryan had said he was quite popular, as well as smart, and had already earned a basketball scholarship for the following year. "And who's this?" he continued as he bent down to pick up the bags he'd dropped.

I'd remembered that I hadn't mentioned Abbie when I met Ryan's family, and now, as Abbie cozied up to the side of my leg, I felt a tad nervous about how the information would be taken. I placed my hand on her shoulder, smiling softly. "This is my daughter Abbie."

At the word daughter Dean's eyes widened, looking back and forth between Abbie and I, taking in the information. Seconds later he let out a low whistle. "Well damn," he said rubbing the back of his neck slowly, "I thought you and my brother were..."

I shook my head, keeping my blush at bay. "No, sorry."

"It's just, with the way he talked about you recently..."

"He's talked about me?" I asked incredulously, the words slipping through my lips before I could stop them.

Dean held a calculating look in his eye as he noticed the blush of embarrassment diffuse down my neck. I saw the exact moment understanding crossed his eyes as a knowing smirk appeared on his lips. "Ah, I see," he voiced as if he'd just come across a solution to world peace, "Her father's not in the picture, is he?"

"No, he's definitely not," Emily cut in, sending a sideways smirk my way before addressing Dean once again. "Hey, I'm her sister Emily and this is our friend Colette."

"It's nice to meet you," he acknowledged before turning to Colette, "And I think I've met you before..."

Colette nodded. "My parents own Corner Café in the city," she explained. "I think I've seen you there a few times with your brother."

"That'd make sense," he said, clicking his tongue as he remembered. "Speaking of my brother, I was actually heading to meet Ryan for something to eat. Do you guys want to join?"

"Your brother's here?" I asked in disbelief.

"Yes..." Dean replied, his smirk reappearing, "I stayed over at his house last night and told him I needed to pick up some things from the mall, so he came with. "

"I'm sure he'd love to see you," he teased as an afterthought.

"What, is he wearing a ski mask or something?" Emily asked jokingly, somewhat voicing my thoughts. How could someone as famous as him be in this mall and not have already caused a commotion?

Dean shook his head, seemingly relaxed about the issue. "Actually, people don't usually look twice at him."

"Really?" the three of us voiced skeptically, Abbie keeping quiet as she merely listened to our conversation.

"Look how many people are in this mall right now," Dean replied, gesturing around him as numerous people passed by, "If anybody recognizes him they'd have to be looking pretty hard. Usually he just wears a hat, puts a pair of sunglasses on, and has his bodyguard follow us at a distance. Plus, a lot of the people that are born and raised here don't tend to scour the city for celebrities in their free time."

He spoke as if he knew exactly what he was talking about, but I figured that since he'd grown up in LA with an actor as a brother, he probably did.

"What do you say Abbie?" I asked, crouching down to her eye level. "Do you want to eat lunch with Ryan and his brother?"

Her eyes shone with recognition and happiness at Ryan's name, nevertheless, her face scrunched up with confusion as she glanced up at Dean. "You're Ryan's brother?" she asked, making Dean nod. "But you don't look like him."

It was true to an extent. While the two didn't look alike now, Ryan having grown into himself height and muscle wise, their similar facial features proved that Dean would more than likely grow to look very much like his brother in the next few years.

"Yeah, but I'm the more attractive brother," Dean winked at me.

"Come on hot shot," I replied, rolling my eyes as I grabbed Abbie's hand, "Lead the way."

"Look who I bumped into," Dean announced, shaking his head with mock disgrace as we approached the table where his brother sat, "Dropped my bags and everything." I rolled my eyes at his verbal nonsense.

"Hey," Ryan greeted, a mask of surprise washing over his face, "What are you guys doing here?"

"Shopping," I replied simply, "Plus, Emily wanted a new hairstyle."

An understanding smile appeared as his gaze dropped to the bags in our hands. "I can see that," he said before taking in Emily's new do, "And it looks good Em."

"Thanks," she grinned, bringing a hand up to comb through the ends of her hair.

Abbie wiggled her small hand out my grip, skipping her way over to Ryan with wide arms. "Hi," she chirped, squirming her way up onto his lap with a cheshire smile.

"Hi there," Ryan returned sweetly, poking her sides gently, "Did you get to buy any new toys today?"

"No," she frowned, shaking her head slightly before a smile appeared once more, "But I picked out a pwetty bracelet," she continued, pointing to the small bag that I was holding which held her purchase.

"I'm sure it looks very pretty," Ryan grinned, "But how about after we eat, I take you to the toy store to pick something out?"

"Really?" Abbie cried, eyes wide as she bounced on his lap with excitement.

"Yep," he replied happily, before wincing my way with apologetic eyes, "That is, if it's okay with your mom."

Both Ryan and Abbie were looking at me, but I couldn't get one word passed my lips, as I stood there, shocked still – and I wasn't the only one. Both Emily and Colette were sporting identical looks of fascination, making it seem like Ryan had just offered to buy them each a new sports car, while Dean, well, he was almost the opposite.

His eyes were trained on his brother and my daughter, a calculating manner to them as though he was trying to put together the last pieces of a jigsaw puzzle. As his gaze turned to me, I saw the exact moment when understanding crossed his brain, not a clue as to what he was thinking, as a knowing smile graced his lips.

Focusing back on the situation at hand, I felt bad saying yes. I wanted Ryan and Abbie to bond, but I didn't want him to think that he had to buy her things that I might not be able to afford. However, I knew that with the way that she was staring up at me, I didn't have the heart to deny her this small grain of happiness.

"Sure," I forced out as it felt like my heart lodged itself into my throat. Abbie let out an excited whoop noise, smiling broadly as she glanced happily between Ryan and I. I needed a moment to process this, the fact that not only did he seem interested in getting closer to me, but my daughter as well. It was all a bit too much for me at that moment, and to me, volunteering to go and get everyone's food seemed like the best option.

Luckily, everybody seemed okay with burgers and fries. After putting in the rather large order, I wasn't sure if I was happy or not when Dean walked up behind me, tapping me on the shoulder.

"Sorry," he quickly apologized when he realized he'd made me jump, having not seen him approach, "Just wondering if you're going to need any help with all the food?"

Looking at the two trays that the people behind the counter were currently stacking full with my order, I sighed, nodding at Dean. "Yeah, if that's all right."

"It's what I'm here for," he declared, making me raise an eyebrow in disbelief, calling a silent bullshit on his statement. He chuckled at my reaction, "You know, you're pretty smart Zoe," he stated, dipping his hands deep into his pockets. His expression turned from one full of amusement to one of full seriousness. "Honestly, it's clear I don't know much about what's going on between you and my brother, but rest assured, he's a good guy."

I laughed lightly under my breath, trying to ease some of the tension from my body. "Did Ryan send you over here to wingman for him?"

"Nope, he didn't need to ask," he grinned, "And even though I might not be the best person to be giving you this advice, trust me, Ryan probably just needs a little encouragement to make a move."

He spoke as if he knew something I didn't, as I hadn't the slightest clue as to what he was talking about. Before I could ask anything further the order was up and Dean picked up one of the trays, waltzing back to the table with an unnerving glint in his eyes. I didn't dwell on it, but by the time everybody was sat down comfortably and enjoying the food, it became fairly apparent to me as to what Dean's intentions were.

"So, Ryan," Dean started halfway through his burger, my eyes flicking between the brothers as he continued, "Did you tell Zoe about my basketball game next Friday?"

Dean looked somewhat smug as his brother choked slightly on the food in his mouth, taking a drink of his soda before replying. "No," he coughed nervously, "I, uh, didn't get the chance yet."

My eyebrows were scrunched in confusion as I looked to Dean. "What game?"

"My team made the state championships," he replied proudly, greeted with congratulations from both Emily and Colette. "The games' at my school next Friday, and Ryan mentioned wanting to take you if you were up for it."

Glancing to my left, I saw Ryan sending a glare across the table at his little brother. "Really?" I asked shyly.

"Umm, yeah," Ryan admitted, looking to me tensely. "I know you finish classes a little late Fridays, and sometimes you work, so I wasn't sure if you'd be able to."

"She's free," Colette jumped in with a wide smile, staring between the two of us encouragingly. Emily wasn't much better, wiggling her eyebrows suggestively as she hid her grin behind the burger she was biting into.

Before I could reply, Abbie popped into the conversation as she looked at Dean curiously. "What's bas'etball?" she asked. I smiled to myself, knowing she was trying as she stumbled over her words slightly.

"Well Abbie, it's a sport I play with my friends where we have to shoot a ball into a hoop," he explained simply, smiling as Abbie tilted her head to the side.

"Is it fun?"

"Oh," Dean smiled widely, "It's tons of fun."

"Can I come?" she asked eagerly, seeming generally interested as she stared up at Ryan and me with wonder.

Looking to Ryan, I saw a smile grace his lips as he nodded his head slightly, in turn, making me smile.

"I guess it sounds like a plan," I replied softly, making Abbie clap her hands cheerfully. She quickly went back to devouring the fries still left in her kids' meal, as I gazed at Ryan, a shy smile growing at the way he was looking at me.

It was like he was happy, surprised, and amazed all at once.

"Fantastic," Dean said wickedly, looking as though he'd just pulled off the greatest magic trick of all time, grinning across the table before turning his attention back to his food.

Shaking my head, I ducked my head as I realized Ryan's seventeen-year-old brother had just set the two of us up. The more prominent thought that was circling my mind though, was whether or not this was meant to be a date.

CHAPTER 11

As my last class finished up on Friday, the professor adamantly reminding us that our second midterm was fast approaching, I walked out of the room feeling utterly relieved. The weekend could not have come at a better time. I'd had six assignments due over the last four days, and even though I had a full day without classes, I still ended up spending my day off surrounded by textbooks in full-on work mode.

I was in desperate need for a break, and tonight was going to give me that.

Tonight would be awkward to say the least. Even though Dean had been the one to set it up, the feeling that it was a date was definitely dancing around my mind. Albeit, it was a date with a three-year-old chaperone; but it was a date nonetheless.

I had half been expecting a phone call from Ryan sometime throughout the day, telling me that he'd wanted to cancel, but as the hours trailed on, my phone stayed silent and my nerves gradually settled.

Breathing in the fresh LA air as I followed a crowd off campus, I pulled my sweater tighter around my shoulders. It was already the middle of November, and even though it sometimes felt like the temperature would never drop, a much needed breeze blew gently as I headed across the street.

Turning and following the familiar path to Abbie's daycare, my train of thought circled one particular track, and every stop seemed to link back to Ryan. What was he doing? Was he as nervous as I was for tonight? Was he excited? Every question seemed to have a variety of answers, but I knew which ones stuck out as the ones I wanted to be true.

Time passed quickly as my thoughts swept me off my feet, and minutes later I was walking into the daycare. Expecting the kids to be running around and playing like they normally were, I was thoroughly surprised to see them seated in the middle of the room, not making a sound.

'Well, there's my answer,' I thought to myself, smiling as I rested my back against the wall, quietly observing the sight in front of me.

Ryan sat on a chair in front of all the children, a book in his hand as he grinned animatedly at his young crowd. "The moon lit up the sky as Nellie looked up at it from her window," he read, enthusiasm clear in his voice as he flipped the page of the picture book.

Other parents slowly started to trickle in, flabbergasted to see Ryan Adams sitting there reading to their children. I'm sure it wasn't everyday that they found themselves in the midst an A-list actor.

A smile stretched across my face as Ryan finished the story, a happy ending causing the children to cheer and applaud. Finally taking notice of the other people in the room, I saw Ryan's gaze sweep over the handful of parents before his eyes locked on mine; a small, sexy smile growing as the kids in front of him scattered themselves across the room.

Before my instincts kicked in and caused a blush to dust my cheeks, I averted my gaze as Abbie came skipping happily towards me, arms wide in excitement. "Did you see it momma?" she squealed as I dropped my school bag, wrapping my arms around her in a hug and situating her comfortably on my hip. "Ryan came in and played with us at playtime, and then he read us a book!"

"He did?" I asked in amazement. She nodded. "That's pretty great of him, isn't it? Did you say thank you?"

Her mouth popped open in shock, telling me that, no, she hadn't thanked him, but was sorry she'd forgotten. Her head whipped around to where Ryan had been talking to the leader of the daycare, wiggling herself down off my hip before scurrying over to Ryan. Smiling to myself, I saw her tug the side of his jeans, grabbing his attention before starting to speak. I could hear her enthusiastically thanking him like I'd told her to, but before I knew it, they were both grinning at each other as she grabbed his hand and tugged him in my direction.

"Hey," he greeted, the side of his mouth tilting up enticingly.

I played with the hem of my sweater, suddenly very aware of the curious eyes of the other parents. "Hey," I returned shyly, "What are you doing here?"

He smiled sheepishly. "Well, the three of us are still going to Dean's game tonight, right?" he asked, raising an eyebrow at me.

"Doesn't the game only start at seven?" I asked, confused, suddenly thinking I'd gotten the time wrong, as it was only half past four.

He nodded. "Yeah, but I thought that maybe we could grab a bite to eat first," he trailed, rubbing the back of his neck nervously. "My car's parked around the corner, we could walk into town and then drive to the game?"

"Oh, I want to!" Abbie cheered, jumping up and down eagerly. "Can we get hotdogs momma?"

"I don't know," I trailed, looking back up at Ryan with a smile, "Do you know any good hotdog stands?"

He grinned back at me. "Just a few, but they're a little bit of a walk," he replied before crouching down to Abbie's level. "What do you say Abbie? You think you can handle walking for a bit?"

Abbie nodded, eyes wide as Ryan tempted her with one of her favourite foods.

I laughed. "Hotdogs it is then," I replied happily. The truth was, although I didn't eat it often, I really could never turn down junk food – it tasted too good to give up.

Cheers of excitement emerged from Abbie's mouth as Ryan offered to help her grab her bag.

Watching the two of them walk off to the other side of the room, I noticed that, although most of the other kids had left already, a few had yet to be picked up as Diane, one of the leaders of the daycare, and the one I saw most frequently, came over to talk to me.

"Ryan Adams huh?" she asked, a small smirk playing on her face, but not delving any deeper into the topic. "Abbie seems to get along great with him."

"Yeah, she really likes him," I replied, admiring the way that Ryan helped her reach her bag as she struggled on her tiptoes.

"Well it looks like you've found yourself a keeper," she smiled gently, as she watched the same scene I was. "Just remember that he's welcome back any time. The kids seemed to love him."

I nodded shyly, ducking my head as I picked up my bag, a blush slowly spreading across my cheeks. "Noted," I muttered, saying a quick goodbye as Abbie and Ryan headed towards the door, both beckoning me to hurry as I followed the two of them out the door.

The 'little' walk to the hotdog stand turned out to be not so little. It seemed like we were going nowhere after twenty minutes of dodging the busy Friday crowds as Abbie easily coaxed Ryan into giving her a piggyback ride, grumbling that her feet were starting to hurt.

Finally, forty minutes after leaving the daycare's parking lot, we'd come to a marketplace set up around a park ground.

"What is this place?" I asked, looking around in awe at the stalls and booths that were just as lively as the rest of the city.

Ryan smiled, having already adorned his signature hat and sunglasses as he took a look around. "The North Market," he replied, "My parents used to take Dean and I here a lot when we first moved out here, but that," he stopped, nodding off towards his left, "Would be the reason why we're here."

Following his gaze, my eyes locked onto one stall in particular, and it seemed to be one of the busiest ones. Steam and smoke bellowed from the back of the stall where the barbeque sat, mixing with the smells of the surrounding stalls. "These better be some top notch hotdogs," I smirked as we headed over to join the long queue.

"Trust me," he grinned back, "They're definitely worth it."

It took us a few minutes to move up enough steps so that the menu was visible, but even with the extra time I couldn't decide what I wanted when the three of us were called up to order. In the end I'd just gone with their original hotdog, ordering one for me and one for Abbie, while Ryan ordered one of the specialty dogs. I'd also tried to convince him to let me pay for my own food, but that conversation didn't last too long when he simply handed the man running the stall enough change to cover both our orders.

My eyes widened slightly when our order number was called and they passed us our food. "You sure you'll be able to eat all of that?" I asked, amazed as I watched Ryan help Abbie cover the top of her hotdog with mustard and ketchup. The hotdogs we'd been given were, in fact, huge, and if I didn't think I would be able to finish mine, I wondered how my three-year-old would manage.

"Mhm," she nodded greedily, stuffing the end of hers into her tiny mouth. I looked down at her, holding in a laugh as I picked up a pile of extra napkins, knowing I'd definitely need them as her chin was already covered in ketchup.

Walking away from the condiment stand, we looked around for a spot to sit. Luckily enough, it didn't take us long to find a free bench near the edge of the chaos, sitting down promptly to enjoy our meal.

Abbie barely made it halfway through her hotdog, complaining that she was too full to eat another bite. She did, however, take immediate interest in the baby ducks that were swimming in the pond a few feet in front of us. With out even having to ask, she looked up at me with wide doe eyes and I smiled, nodding as she shrieked, skipping off with happiness.

"So," I started, shifting towards Ryan a little more, tucking my knees underneath my body, "Does your body guard know you're out in public like this?"

My teasing tone made him crack a grin as he shook his head. "He thinks I went to my parents house for dinner before Dean's game," he replied cheekily.

"Do you usually lie to him like that?" I laughed, taking another bite of my hotdog. Despite the size, it was one of the best hotdogs I'd ever tasted.

He shrugged. "Sometimes when I want a bit of privacy, sure," he answered honestly. "Chad's a great guy and everything, but he works for my manager, not for me, so sometimes he can be a bit overbearing with the security and stuff."

"Have you talked to him about it, or even your manager?" I asked awkwardly, not really knowing how the whole 'famous' thing worked. Glancing to see Abbie still safely playing near the edge of the pond, I looked back to Ryan, waiting for his reply.

"Chad's cool about a lot of things, that's why when he is around he usually stays in the shadows," he explained. "My manager, on the other hand, thinks that every time I step outside I need to be watched. He doesn't realize that not everybody in the city is out to spot celebrities. I usually don't get noticed when I'm like this, I just have to watch out when I have a movie coming out or I'm in the spotlight."

"Why don't you just find a new manager?"

Ryan shrugged. "Besides being overbearing when it comes to publicity, he's actually a good manager," he reasoned.

I shook my head. "Doesn't it get hard, not having a lot of privacy?"

"Sometimes," he offered, "But I can't imagine ever doing anything else. I just see myself as lucky; not everybody finds a job that they love."

It was strange, hearing him talk so much about the other part of his life. It was true that he'd never tried to hide the fact that he was famous, at least from me. Sometimes it just felt like there was just an invisible wall between us, blocking me from seeing him for what he truly was; an actor.

Smiling as our conversation slowly veered onto a different track, I was glad that I'd gotten a tiny snippet into his stardom. We talked easily about what we'd been up to the last few weeks, how my classes were going, and a funny interview he'd recently had for a magazine.

I didn't even realize the time was flying by until Ryan brought it to my attention. "Oh wow, we'd better get going," he said in a rush, picking up the garbage we'd placed on the bench beside us. "It'll take us a while to get back to my car and the game starts in about an hour and a half."

Calling Abbie in from where she'd started playing with another little girl, I saw the small mud stains she'd picked up as she ran back, grinning widely with damp and dirty hands.

"We might need to stop back at my place quickly," I stated with amusement, as Ryan looked at me curiously. "It seems that someone had a bit too much fun."

When his eyes landed on Abbie, an understanding grin crossed his face. "Well, I guess we'd better hurry then," he said, not even bothering to wipe Abbie's hands clean before he crouched down in front of her, "Hop on."

Shaking my head at the two of them, I waited for Ryan to get Abbie situated on his back, getting slightly dirty in the process, before the three of us began the long walk back through the city.

More than an hour later, after a five-minute stop off at the house to change Abbie's shirt, Ryan was pulling his car into a parking space at the edge of a high school parking lot.

"Aren't you going to need those?" I frowned, looking at him curiously as he took off his sunglasses and hat, leaving them on the center console.

He shook his head. "I've been to some of Dean's games before and I'm pretty sure the whole school knows he's my brother," he explained. "It's not that big of a deal."

"But what about..." I trailed worriedly, abruptly cut off as Ryan's hand covered my mouth lightly.

"Zoe," he started sincerely, looking me in the eyes as the edges of his lips tilted upwards. And just with that simple movement, I could already feel the tension dissipating from my body. "Don't worry about it, it'll all be fine," he continued, moving his hand away as he spoke. "The worst thing that'll happen is a few people asking me for my autograph, so trust me, okay."

"Okay."

Seeming happy with my answer, Ryan nodded, taking the keys out of the ignition and opening his door. "Now come on, we don't want to be late."

Walking into the gym I was stunned. For a high school basketball game everything seemed so intense. Upbeat music was blaring from the speakers while both teams ran through warm-ups; the stands full of friends, family, and onlookers ready for the game.

Looking down as Abbie squeezed my hand, I was slightly worried that she'd find the gym too hectic, but the expression of awe on her face as she gazed around the gym told me that she was fine. Turning my gaze towards the court, I tried to spot Dean, which was a bit harder than I expected, as about thirty guys, all about the same height, were continuously moving, shooting and stretching.

Dean finally caught my eye, wearing the same white and orange jersey as the rest of his team as he passed the ball to a teammate before jogging over towards us. "Hey," he greeted with a smile, "You guys made it."

"We told you we would," I nodded.

"Hi Dean," Abbie chirped, buzzing with excitement.

Dean smiled down at her. "Hey sweetie, are you ready to see my team win?" he asked confidently. She nodded. "Great, just make sure to cheer when one of my teammates gets the ball in the net."

"Okay!"

Dean laughed, looking to his brother as he nodded towards the middle of the bleachers. "Mom and dad are already sitting in the stands if you want to find them," he said, turning his attention back to the court as his coach called him. "I've got to get back to warm-ups, but hopefully I'll be able to see you guys after the game."

"Good luck kid," Ryan said, smiling proudly at his brother before he turned and jogged back onto the court.

"Your parents are here?" I asked, looking down at Abbie nervously.

Ryan, who was leading us towards where his parents were presumably seated, looked back at me and immediately picked up on my nerves. "Hey, don't worry about them," he smiled encouragingly, "I told them a few days ago that you had a daughter and they didn't seem to mind."

Still not fully comfortable with the situation, I nodded, squeezing Abbie's hand, a little less stressed that his parents at least knew she existed.

It didn't take long for Ryan to find his parents amidst the crowd, mostly due to the fact that his mom waved the three of us down as soon as she spotted us.

"I'm so glad you guys could make it," Sophie, Ryan's mom, said as the three of us sat down in the free spot next to them. Ryan took a seat next to her, Abbie beside him, with me on the end. "It's good to see you again."

"You too," I replied, smiling shakily as I saw her eyes drop to Abbie.

"And you must be Abbie," she spoke softly; looking down at her as though she was the cutest thing she'd ever seen.

"Abbie, this is my mom, Sophie, and my dad, Brad." Ryan smiled, introducing the three of them.

"You're Ryan's parents?" she asked curiously, and when they both nodded, she grinned at the both of them. "Hi!"

Sophie laughed at my daughter's cheerfulness, and even Ryan's dad was smiling down at her, cracking a grin as his wife handed her a noisemaker to cheer on her son's team. My heart clenched at the thoughtful gesture as it became abundantly clear that every member of the Adam's had a soft spot for children.

"I told you everything would be fine," Ryan mouthed to me as Abbie climbed up on his lap to continue talking with his mom.

A soft smile drew slowly on my lips as my nerves flew free. "Thank you," I mouthed back, sliding closer to him as a few people squeezed past us on their way to their seats. I noticed, looking back down at the court, that although the opposing team was huddled at their bench, Dean's team seemed to have disappeared. "Where'd the team go?" I asked Ryan.

"Never been to a basketball game before?" he smirked. I rolled my eyes, shoving his shoulder as he chuckled. "They just went to the locker-room to talk before the game starts. Don't worry, they'll be back out when the buzzer sounds."

Sure enough, about ten minutes later when a loud buzzer sounded, Dean's team came running through the gym doors energetically, feeding the crowds enthusiasm for the game as everybody was soon up on their feet with cheer.

It didn't take long for the game to start once both teams were settled on their benches. The starters took to the court and I instantly spotted Dean standing next to one of the refs, wearing a look of concentration and the number 8 on his back.

The whistle went, the ball was thrown into the air, and Dean's teamed earned first possession as him and one of his teammates quickly passed the ball to each other and scored the first two points of the game.

Abbie was enjoying herself as her and Ryan's mom cheered every time the ball went threw the hoop for our team, and although I was truly having fun, I just didn't have the energy that they seemed to.

Watching both teams play against each other, it made perfect sense for them to be competing against one another for the championship. Both teams had solid defense, offensive plays that left the opposing team puzzled, and were making shots that looked close to impossible.

By the time the buzzer went, signaling the end of the first quarter, our team was losing by a mere six points. However, when the second quarter started and the clock ticked down from eight minutes to zero, they came back with a new aggression and power, finishing off with a three point lead going into the second half.

"So, high schools don't happen to have half-time shows, do they?" I asked jokingly.

Ryan looked at me, amusement spreading across his face as he shook his head. "Unfortunately no," he chuckled. "But they do have something," he continued, nodding up to jumbotron at the end of the gym.

Surprisingly enough, the score of the game had been moved to the bottom corner of the screen as it now displayed two giant words, delicately displayed and handwritten in pink.

Kiss Cam

"A kiss cam?" I asked, "The school let's them do that?"

Ryan shrugged. "Well they don't have a cheerleading squad and they retired their mascot outfit a few years back," he explained. "They need something to keep the crowd awake, plus, it's amusing sometimes."

Looking down to see the guy with the camera filming couples as the crowd egged them on to lock lips, I shook my head. "You find strange things amusing."

"What's weird about a few teenagers being pressured into kissing on camera?" he asked, although I was positive he knew what I was talking about from that sentence alone.

"Umm... everything."

"I'll let you know, Dean happened to have his first kiss on the kiss cam in freshman year, and he didn't seem to mind one bit."

"Really?" I laughed, "His first kiss?"

Ryan nodded, concealing a laugh himself. "Yep," he replied, "I was sitting right beside him at a varsity game he wanted to come and watch. He ended up kissing the girl that was sitting next to him. Her father didn't look all that happy with him after that."

My laughter continued, trying to imagine what the girl's father must've thought about the random boy who was kissing his daughter. "Oh my god, that's..." I trailed, wiping my eyes to keep my tears at bay. When I re-opened my eyes however, Ryan's amusement had completely washed away, replaced with an irritated aura. "Ryan?" I asked cautiously, "What's wrong?"

I became all too aware of my surroundings in that moment. The people sitting around us were starting to whisper and cheer, having noticed that Ryan Adams was in the building. It kicked in, however, that not only were people around us cheering, but almost the entire gym.

"That kid is going to get it," I thought I heard Ryan mumble under his breath, clenching his fists in his lap as he took a few deep breaths.

Looking around the gym, all eyes were on us, but only as I glanced up at the jumbotron did I realize why.

There, on the giant kiss cam screen, was Ryan and I.

Gulping, nerves shot out through my body as my hands clammed up and my cheeks turned pink. "I... what... I," I stuttered, not able to form a sentence as I looked to Ryan for reassurance.

I could see his parents faces as they sat there awkwardly next to us, but for some reason, they looked more amused than uncomfortable, and Abbie, well she was now sitting on the other side of Ryan with wide and expectant eyes.

All I wanted to do in that moment, as everybody around us started to chant, begging for us to kiss, was disappear – hide underneath an invisibility cloak and fade from people's sight.

This wasn't going to happen, and looking up at Ryan, I prayed for him to do something, anything, to take the attention off of us. And sure, it'd be awkward getting rejected in front of all these people, but at least it'd be the right thing to do.

As Ryan's eyes met mine, I saw a similar discomfort and un-easiness, but as he brought his hand up, seemingly to signal the camera and crowd that there, in fact, wasn't going to be a kiss, he surprised me.

Instead, his hand came up to softly cup the side of my cheek, and before I could even process what was happening, he was lean-ing in, his eyes turning apologetic before they closed completely as his lips softly met my own.

It was a light pressure at first, my eyes widening at the sudden contact before they slowly fluttered close, our surroundings fad-ing from my sight and my brain. One of my hands slipped up to grab the side of his shirt, bunching the material within my fingers as I tentatively began to move my lips with his.

I didn't know if my response was the one he wanted, but as his lips turned up into a smile underneath my own, I felt the signifi-cant flutter of butterflies come alive in the pit of my stomach.

Slightly encouraged by his reaction, I increased the pressure slightly, moving my lips in sync with Ryan's. It was over all too fast though. I heard the quick hitch of his breath just seconds before distance wove it's way between us, reality coming crashing down around us.

I had just kissed Ryan and it was abundantly clear that we were not alone.

Cheers, boos, and all things alike were hitting my ears as my mind suddenly became a jumbled mess. It felt as though everybody's eyes were on us as the kiss cam screen faded from the jumbotron, the buzzer sounding as both teams emerged from opposite sides of the gym.

The second half started in a flash, a blur of plays and points as I tried to pay attention to the court. Yet, it didn't matter how hard I tried. Ryan was still sitting beside me, my mind reeling with flashes of the kiss we'd shared, and I couldn't seem to keep myself focused on the game.

In the end I was at least aware that when the final buzzer sounded it was our team that held the lead. Standing up with the majority of the crowd, I cheered as they were presented with the trophy, watching proudly as Dean hoisted it up into the air with his teammates.

The music came back on in celebration, blasting throughout the gymnasium as everyone slowly left their seats to find friends to celebrate with.

"I'm going to go find Dean before we head out," Ryan stated, as he stood up from his seat. "I'll be right back."

As Ryan disappeared from my view, Abbie crawled along the bench until she was sitting on my lap with a wide smile plastered on her face. "You kissed Ryan momma!" Abbie chirped happily, making me duck my head in embarrassment, glancing to where Ryan's parents still sat.

"It seems she did," Sophie cut in sneakily, the vague outline of a smirk visible as her husband got up, heading towards where Ryan and Dean were talking near the edge of the court. "I thought the two of you weren't dating."

I bit my lip as she looked at me with knowing eyes, a blush slowly spreading across my cheeks. "We're not," I admitted, although, with the airy undertone, it didn't sound all that convincing.

Understanding crossed her eyes and she nodded. "Well, I know my son," she smiled, gesturing to where Ryan was talking with Dean and his dad, "Just give him a chance darling. I'm sure you'll find what you're looking for."

I smiled tentatively at her, not knowing what else I could say as she walked off to join the rest of her family. As she reached them, I saw Ryan address her quickly before turning and walking towards me.

"Ready to go?" he asked.

Nodding, the three of us headed out into the chilly November air, the moon and streetlights illuminating the ground. The parking lot was slowly being emptied of other cars, people from the opposing team sulking while friends and families from Dean's team were celebrating.

The ride home was awkward, although Ryan seemed fairly calm as he drove the familiar route to my house. Meanwhile, I was in the passenger seat, my leg bouncing nervously as the music coming from the radio failed to level the tension. Abbie kept the ride bearable at least, talking about the game in such an animated way that I knew by the time I got her to bed tonight she'd already be drained of energy.

When Ryan pulled into my driveway, cutting the engine, it was as if the awkwardness came back at full force. Despite my protests, Abbie unbuckled herself immediately, pushing open her door before running towards the front door.

"Umm... thanks for the drive home," I said, playing with the end of my sweater.

He smiled. "No problem."

Seconds of silence followed, a disheartening feeling filling my body knowing that he wasn't going to bring up the kiss tonight. I forced a smile onto my lips, nodding as I went to open my door. I froze, however, when I felt a hand land on my shoulder.

"Zoe, wait," Ryan stammered out nervously.

I turned to him slowly, biting my lip as anticipation built in the pit of my stomach. "Yes?" I asked softly, urging him to continue.

"I was, well, I was wondering," he began as he lowered his eyes, taking a deep breath. I didn't know whose nerves were acting up more in that moment, but as he looked up again, his eyes shining with sincerity and hope, my breath caught in the back of my throat. "Do you want to go out to dinner tomorrow?"

He stared at me carefully, watching his question process, looking as though he was genuinely nervous that I'd say no. "Really?" I asked, biting my lip as to conceal the grin that threatened to appear.

"Yeah," he breathed out.

"Then yeah," I smiled, "I'd really like that."

His eyes widened, as though he could hardly believe what he was hearing. "Actually?"

I giggled, nodding my head. "Just call me tomorrow," I stated, feeling bold as I leaned over the center console and placed my lips lightly on his cheek. Pulling back with a smile on my face, I saw his cheeks flush the lightest of pinks. "Goodnight."

"Goodnight," he returned as I finally stepped out of the car, turning to wave at him as I reached my front door.

Stepping inside, I was able to let out a breath that I hadn't realized I'd been holding. Leaning back against the door, my lips tugged up into a smile. I could hear Abbie describing the game to Emily in the next room, giggling as she told my sister about Ryan kissing me.

I didn't matter though, because in that moment I was happy – truly happy.

CHAPTER 12

1 ^{0:43}

Biting my lip nervously, I turned back to the mirror that stood in front of me, wondering if I'd gone a little overboard as I applied a final coat of mascara. Placing the plastic tube back into my make-up bag, my eyes scanned the outfit I'd chosen. I was wearing a long sleeved black shirt that tucked into a navy and white skirt, and I'd curled my hair loosely, letting fall freely past my shoulders.

I didn't look bad, I just felt like I looked a little too put together for a lunch date.

It had taken me only a few minutes after walking through the door the night before to realize that, in the heat of the moment, I had completely forgotten about the shift I had later today at the café. I'd texted him immediately, apologizing profusely while telling him that there was no way I would be able miss another one of my usual shifts this week, but it didn't seem to bother him. It somewhat surprised me that he just simply asked if I was free in the afternoon instead, and since I didn't start until 3:00, I didn't hesitate in saying yes.

And now, knowing that he'd be here in less than fifteen minutes, my nerves were starting to act up again.

"Well, well, don't you look fancy," I heard Emily say teasingly as I looked over my shoulder to find her leaning against my bedroom door, a smirk ever so present on her face.

"You don't think it's too much?" I asked indecisively, running my fingers through my hair.

"He's taking you out for lunch right?" she asked. I nodded. "Then no. It's a first date; you can dress up a bit if you want to."

"Sorry," I apologized sheepishly, flattening out my skirt, giving my antsy hands something to do. "I'm just nervous," I continued, taking a seat on the edge of my bed.

"No need to apologize," Emily said shaking her head, taking a seat beside me. "And why are you nervous, its just Ryan."

I wound my hands together, ducking my head as I stared down at my lap. "Because its Ryan," I tried to explain. "I mean, I haven't been on a real date in a long time, and having Abbie, it makes it hard to date. I don't know, I just, I'm really starting to like him and I don't want anything to go wrong."

I blushed as the words left my lips, only looking up when I felt Emily inch closer and wrap one of her arms around my shoulders in support. "Sometimes things go wrong, but that's just what makes the relationship real," she voiced honestly. "And I wouldn't worry too much about the date; you guys get along great, and I'd be surprised if you didn't come home with a smile on your face."

My lips tugged up into a smile. "Aren't I supposed to be the older sister?" I asked jokingly, lightening the mood, "You know, giving you advice on relationships and everything, not the other way around."

Emily laughed. "If we were just talking about life, I'd definitely say you know more," she said, "But when it comes to relationships, you and I both know that I've had my fair share of ups and downs."

I laughed lightly along with her, realizing that what she was saying was true. I had never been in a serious relationship. There was one guy that I went on a few dates with in high school, but it'd only last a few weeks at most before we'd drifted apart, and besides the one night stand that led to Abbie being born, I'd only been on a handful of dates since then.

Looking back on it though, I wouldn't change the way my life had gone, because if I did, I might not have ended up where I am; nervously awaiting for Ryan to pick me up for our first date.

"So," she started, raising an eyebrow questioningly as a smile appeared on her face, "Do you know where he's taking you?"

I shook my head as I smiled, shyly playing with the end of my skirt. "He didn't say," I replied, "But thank you so much for agreeing to watch Abbie. I know I kind of sprung it on you."

"Don't worry about it," she shrugged off, "I told you I'm fine with watching her while you're working, so what's a few more hours."

I released a breath, relaxing slightly at how accepting and calm she seemed about it. "Still, thanks."

"No problem," she smiled as the sound of tiny footsteps grew louder and louder. "Speaking of the little princess."

Abbie appeared seconds later, smiling widely as she entered my bedroom and made her way happily towards the two of us. "Momma, momma!" she cheered excitedly, dangling something in her right hand.

"What do you have there sweetie?" I asked, looking at her hand curiously as she reached up and placed both hands on my lap.

"It's a bracelet I made with Gweta," she explained, looking up at me with a wide grin. At the mention of Greta's name, I made a mental note to call her soon, as it'd been about two weeks since we'd last spoken. "You should wear it so Ryan thinks you look pwetty."

Looking at the bracelet she was handing to me, I somewhat recognized the brightly coloured beads and strings from one of the kits I'd bought her a while ago as a gift, and although it wasn't really something meant to wear, the elated look on Abbie's face was impossible to say no to.

Sliding off the small silver bangles I'd put on minutes before, I stretched out the colourful bracelet slightly, rolling it up over my hand to let it rest on my wrist. "Thanks darling," I smiled. It didn't matter that it wasn't the nicest piece of jewelry I owned or that it didn't match my outfit. My daughter had made me the bracelet, and honestly, the smile on her face was enough to make my heart clench with copious amounts of love.

If it was possible, her grin grew as she pushed herself up onto the bed, wiggling herself between Emily and I. "You're welcome," she replied happily, twisting the beads on my bracelet.

"Hey sweetie," I started softly, waiting to continue until she looked up at me, her eyes doe-eyed and curious. "Are you okay with me going out with Ryan, you know, on a date?"

I held my breath as I waited for her to reply, knowing that if she really wasn't okay with it, no matter how young she was, I knew I wouldn't go through with it.

She came first, and she always would.

I was able to relax, as it didn't take her long to nod, her un-ruly blonde hair bobbing up and down. "It's okay momma," she beamed. "I like Ryan, and he makes you happy, and Aunty Emily said that if you guys kiss more maybe you guys will get married."

The word marriage caused an unfamiliar and uneasy feeling to come alive in the pit of my stomach; this was a first date for Pete's sake. Marriage wasn't anywhere in the near future.

I raised my head to look at Emily, who had a small smirk on her face as she looked at me with amusement, shrugging her shoulders in a dismissing manner. "Aunty Emily told you that, huh?" I asked, looking between Abbie and Emily.

"Mhm," Abbie nodded, smiling up at me innocently. "And I think you and Ryan should kiss more 'cause you smile more around him."

Her words made my heart beat a tad faster, and although I knew she partially had no idea what she was talking about, I also knew that maybe I should give her a bit more credit for her observation skills.

I laughed lightly, pulling her closer to me in a side hug that, at the moment, was just what I needed.

The moment didn't last that long however, as the sound of the doorbell ringing snapped my nerves right back into place.

"Speaking of Ryan," Emily trailed delightedly, pulling Abbie up onto her lap, "Are you going to get that, or should I?"

I took in a deep breath, releasing it slowly before standing up, smoothing out my outfit. "I'm going," I said, turning to her as I bit my lip nervously. "Are you sure I look okay?"

She chuckled. "You look great Zoe," she replied encouragingly, "Now go have fun."

Taking the stairs a little quicker than usual, I paused as I reached the door, taking a final breath to try and calm my nerves before turning the doorknob. Opening the door, I saw Ryan waiting patiently on the front steps as a gentle breeze made its way past me and into the house. He was decked out in a pair of dark jeans and a grey button down short sleeve while his hair was slightly messier than usual — as though he'd been running his fingers through it constantly.

A subtle blush covered my cheeks as I drew my eyes away from his body, only to realize that his eyes were looking over my outfit in approval. "Hey," I greeted shyly, watching Ryan's eyes snap up to my face, a sheepish smile on his face.

"Hey," he replied, bringing his hands out from behind his back to reveal a beautiful bouquet of flowers.

I hadn't even noticed he'd been hiding something, so I was sure that my face held the look of surprise as I pulled the bouquet into my chest. It was as if, with just one whiff of the fresh flowers in my hand, all the nerves slowly seeped from my body. "You bought me flowers?" I asked softly, admiring the sunflowers and lilies before looking up at him through my eyelashes.

He shrugged his shoulders as he stepped into the entryway. "I saw them on the way over here. I thought you'd like them."

"Well thank you, that's really sweet," I said as I touched the pedals of one of the sunflowers, "I'm just going to find a vase for these quickly and then we can head out."

"There's no rush," he smiled, digging his hands into his pockets.

I nodded heading into the kitchen in search of a vase, but came up short after flipping through a few cupboards, deciding that a large water jug would have to do. Turning the water tap off, I set the jug on the counter and placed the flowers inside. Smiling at the display, I turned around to head back out to the entryway to meet Ryan, only to be surprised to see him resting contently at the entrance to the kitchen. "Oh sorry," I said, "I didn't hear you follow me in here."

"It's fine," he dismissed. Standing up straight, he nodded back towards the entryway, "You ready to go?"

I nodded, anxious but excited to see what this afternoon had in store.

"So, are you going to tell me where we're headed?"

We'd been driving through town for almost twenty minutes, having settled into a comfortable silence as the songs from the radio filled our ears, and although I'd pestered him as he'd pulled out of my driveway, he had yet to tell me anything about this date other than we were headed for lunch.

He flicked his eyes towards me for a second, turning the volume of the radio down before focusing his sights back onto the road. "I've told you already," he grinned broadly, "We're headed to lunch."

I rolled my eyes. "Then please tell me we're almost there."

"Why? Getting a little impatient?" Ryan asked amusingly. In response I said nothing, shrugging my shoulders as I looked out the passenger's window to try and settle the blush that crept up my neck. Seconds later I felt a hand fall on top of mine, squeezing gently before retracting itself back to the steering wheel. I tore my gaze away from the road to see that his grin had transformed into a small, reassuring smile. "Don't worry, we're only a few blocks away."

The song on the radio didn't even have time to finish and Ryan was already pulling his car into an underground parking garage. Finding a free space deemed itself a difficult task for a Saturday afternoon, but once Ryan spotted one, he pulled in quickly, cutting the engine before climbing out of the car.

I made a move to follow him, pausing for only a second to pick up my purse that I'd grabbed on my way out the door. As I went to open the door, it flew open without my help, leaving Ryan standing there with an eyebrow raised as he offered me a hand. "Are you going to get out, or are you going to sit in the car all afternoon?" he asked jokingly, grinning as I rolled my eyes at him and placed my hand in his.

"So, no sunglasses today?" I asked curiously looking up at him as he led us through the busy LA streets.

I caught a few people glance our way as he led me down a fairly vacant side street. "I was wondering when you'd finally realize," he replied, squeezing my hand.

"Aren't you worried about getting noticed?"

He shrugged. "It's crossed my mind," he replied, his lips twitching upwards, "But I'm not embarrassed to be seen with you, so I thought I'd give being me a shot."

A warm feeling coursed through my veins, but before I could reply he stopped, bringing my attention to the quaint restaurant we were standing in front of.

"By the way," he started, pulling me back slightly as I bumped into his chest. He ducked his head so that his breath blew warm against my ear. "You look beautiful," he continued, whispering in my ear before nudging me forward and into the restaurant.

As the door closed behind us and I was greeted with the delicious aromas within the restaurant, I knew that my cheeks were flushing pink at his compliment. Although the hostess seemed a little stunned to see Ryan, she happily led us to a secluded booth near the back of the restaurant, handing us our menus before returning to the front to greet other guests.

"So, how did you find this place?" I asked, glancing across the table at him as I flipped open my menu.

My eyes caught the way his shoulders stiffened and he kept his gaze solely focused on his menu as he replied – as though he wanted to hide the colour that dusted the apples of his cheeks. "I found it online," he coughed out, making it blatantly obvious that he was lying.

"Okay," I drawled, watching him relax and shoot me a smile as he realized I wasn't going to push him for the truth.

I hadn't even finished reading over the whole menu before the waitress came over and took our drink orders, giving us only a few minutes to decide on our orders before she returned with our drinks. My eyes dragged over everything once more, and with the variety of options that the restaurant offered, it was hard for me to decide. However, when the waitress finished scribbling down Ryan's order and turned to me, I went with the classic chicken wrap and garden salad.

As I reached forward to bring my glass of water closer to me, Ryan's hand moved across the table, stopping as he fiddled with the beads on the bracelet Abbie had given me. "Cute bracelet," he said cheekily, "Though it's a bit brighter than the rest of your outfit."

I laughed, taking a sip of my drink before replying. "Abbie gave it to me this morning. She said that if I wore it, it'd make me prettier."

"Well she certainly was onto something," he grinned, letting go of the bracelet as he turned my hand over, delicately intertwining his fingers with mine. "Did she make it at daycare?"

I shook my head, trying not to get distracted by the patterns he was drawing on the outside of my thumb. "I bought her a bracelet making kit for her birthday, so I guess her and Greta got around to using it a few times before we moved down here," I explained.

"Who's Greta?"

I hesitated for a second, knowing that, up until now, I'd more or less avoided saying too much about my family. "She's the one who took care of Emily and I growing up," I started. "My parents got really busy with work when I was around ten years old, so Greta, who was just our housekeeper up until then, got more involved in our lives. She'd make us breakfast, take us out to play, and put us to bed at night."

"And what, your parents weren't around?"

I struggled to find the right words to say. Never, even to my closest friends in high school, had I fully disclosed everything about my home life, but for some reason, it felt completely right to come clean to him.

"They were when I was younger," I trailed, seeing a curious expression on Ryan's face, "But when their company started to get bigger they were around less. They spent a lot of time at events with their clients and colleagues, and a lot of the time they were away on business trips, but they still expected Emily and I to be perfect."

"So what happen they found out-"

"About Abbie?" I finished, raising an eyebrow as I saw him grasping for what to say. He nodded carefully. "It's okay," I shrugged, "Their reaction at first was pretty normal; they were shocked that I'd been so careless, but they got a lot madder when I told them I wanted to keep her. I'd considered abortion and adoption when I found out, but I couldn't go through with either. When I told them that, it more or less felt as though they just cut me out of their lives."

"They gave me money when Abbie was born so I could support her and still get an education, but they never really wanted to see her. I think Abbie's only properly met them about ten times since she was born, and that's usually just to drop off birthday or Christmas presents."

"So Abbie doesn't even know her own grandparents?" he asked with a frown.

I shook my head sadly. "They never wanted to get to know her," I said. "I think they felt like I embarrassed them by becoming a single mother so young."

"That's nothing to be embarrassed of," Ryan said reassuringly, squeezing my hand gently. "Abbie's a gorgeous little girl, and she's lucky to have you as a mom."

"Thanks," I breathed out a bit quieter, feeling the butterflies come alive in my stomach.

For the first time I'd finally told someone besides my family about my life and, despite my fears, they hadn't run in the other direction. Ryan had stayed, and he genuinely seemed to understand. I wanted to say so much more; but I couldn't find the words. Before I could think of anything though, the waitress arrived with our food.

The conversation seemed to take a less serious turn as we started eating. We talked about Abbie a bit more, my job, what we both liked to do in our spare time, and he explained a bit more about what his schedule was over the next couple of weeks. He told me that he had a few photo-shoots and interviews, as well as a bunch of meetings for a fundraising event he had gotten involved with. There wasn't a single awkward silence.. Talking with him felt like second nature to me, and while that should of scared me, considering I'd only known him for a short amount of time, it didn't.

After our meals were finished, he surprised me by ordering a slice of strawberry cheesecake for the two of us to share.

I grinned to myself as the waitress returned with the dessert, not giving me a second glance as she smiled widely at Ryan and told him not to hesitate to call her back to the table if he had any problems. She was clearly trying to get noticed by a celebrity, and when I took a look around us, I realized that quite a few other girls were also eyeing Ryan from their seats.

"What?" Ryan asked curiously, handing me a clean fork as he moved the cheesecake to the middle of the table.

Taking a small piece off the end, I grinned. "Nothing," I shrugged with amusement, "I was just wondering if you're aware of all the attention you seem to be getting?"

His eyes shifted as he took a bite of cheesecake, taking in the tables around us. There was a group of girls near the back of the restaurant that were whispering and kept glancing this way, as well as several other guests surrounding us that were hoping to catch Ryan's attention.

"What jealous?" he asked, turning back to me with an eyebrow raised.

I shook my head. "I just find it funny that even when you're out like a normal person, people still find you interesting."

"What? And you don't?" he teased.

"Well, you've managed to keep my attention this long," I returned, my lips twitching upwards.

"And I tend to keep it a little while longer," he smiled, making my heart beat a little faster as I returned his smile.

It didn't take long for our slice of cheesecake to disappear, and with that, our time at the restaurant dwindled down. When the check came I told Ryan that I didn't mind splitting the bill. Hushing up my protests, Ryan paid for the food before ushering me out of the restaurant.

"So, when do you need to be at work?" Ryan asked as we stepped back out onto the streets.

"What time is it?"

"Half past twelve."

"I work at three, so I have a good two hours before I need to be home, why?"

"Do you want to explore a little bit?" he asked, nodding down the road.

I saw the hopefulness in his eyes as he waited for me to respond. "Let's do it," I smiled, taking his hand in mine.

It didn't take long to realize that this part of town seemed fairly familiar to Ryan as he took a few turns on impulse, leading us to the entrance of a rather large family park.

We'd spent a lot of time just talking as we strolled around the park, and in my mind, the day had been absolutely perfect so far. I was kicking myself for being so nervous about it, because as the two of us took a seat under a tree, my head falling comfortably down onto his shoulder, I felt content.

The time seemed to get away from us as we sat watching the people who passed us by, and we ended up having to run part of the way to the garage where the car was parked.

"Thanks for lunch," I said, turning to smile at him as he pulled up in front of my house a while later, "I had fun."

"Me too," he agreed.

And that's when the air turned awkward for the first time that afternoon.

I wasn't brave enough to make a move, and from where I was sitting, watching Ryan grasp the steering wheel tightly, I felt a hint of sorrow knowing that maybe, he wasn't either.

"I guess I'll see you later," I offered.

"Yeah, later," he nodded nervously.

Sighing, I turned and slipped out of the car, making my way up the driveway. I was second guessing myself, I knew, wondering if this date had actually not been as great as I thought it'd been.

"Wait," I heard Ryan say loudly.

I froze for only a moment before I turned to see him walking around the front of his car and right towards me. In seconds he was standing right in front of me.

"I forgot something."

I felt his fingers land softly on the skin of my wrist and slowly roam up my arm, leaving goose bumps as they went. When his hand reached just below my chin, it stopped, hovering there as I let loose the breath I'd been holding. "What?" I asked quietly, looking him in the eyes as I waited for his reply.

His eyes bore into mine for what felt like forever, but was realistically only a second or two. My breathing sped up as he came closer; too close.

Without another word his lips slanted on top of mine and, embarrassingly enough, a soft moan escaped my lips at the feel of them. When he didn't pull away immediately I felt myself responding as though it was second nature, and in the moment, it felt like it was.

His lips were soft and slow at first, but as I ran my hand over his shirt slowly, reaching up to cup his cheek, the pace quickened and I could feel both my heart and his beating uncontrollably. His tongue darted out quickly, parting my lips for one sweet second before he pulled back altogether, eyes closed and breathing hard.

"That," he said, replying to my earlier question, pecking my lips once more before resting his head on mine.

Opening my eyes slowly, a grin formed on my face. "Oh, that." I said, biting my lip.

Ryan chuckled, his breath fanning my face. "Yeah," he said slow-ly, his eyes darting between my eyes and my lips as he brought his hand up to sweep a piece of stray hair behind my ear. "So, do you work tomorrow?"

I nodded. "In the morning."

"How about a dinner date this time then?" he asked. "You and Abbie can come over and we can all watch a movie together."

The fact that his offer included Abbie made me like him even more, if that was even possible in that instant. "I think we'd both really like that."

"Great," he grinned, pausing for a second as he played with a few strands of my hair. "Are you sure you don't need a ride to work?"

I shook my head. "I'm good," I replied, reaching up on my tiptoes to plant one final kiss on his lips before stepping back from his hold. "I'll see you tomorrow."

"See you tomorrow," he replied, standing close to still in my driveway until I reached my door. Turning back to smile at him, I headed inside and closed the door behind me.

Knowing that I didn't have much time before my shift started at the café, I wasn't left with time to walk around with a dopey smile as I rushed upstairs, hoping that I didn't run into Emily before I could change and leave again.

"Oh come on, that's it?" Colette asked much later that evening as we sat on the couch in my living room, whining as I finished telling both her and Emily about my date, "There has to be more," she persisted.

I laughed at her reaction, shaking my head.

When I'd arrived at work earlier, Colette had mercilessly tried to pester me for details about my date, but knowing that she'd already been invited over for a girls night, I refused, making her wait patiently until now to hear the story.

"Sorry, nothing more," I replied, "Why, what were you expecting?"

"I don't know," she huffed, "Maybe an extravagant helicopter ride around the city or a hot make-out session in the back seat of the limo." At that, both Emily and I laughed. "What? It could've happened."

"Who exactly did you think I was going out with... the king of England?" I asked jokingly.

"No, you were going out with Ryan Adams," Emily pointed out.

"So?"

"So... he's one of the most sought after celebrities right now," Emily continued. "He no doubt would've had enough money to do something over the top, so it just seems a bit strange to us that he did what any other guy would've done for a first date."

"He's just a normal guy," I said, ducking my head as I picked at the bottom of my pyjama shirt.

"To you, yes, but to us, sometimes we need that extra reminder," Colette said, smiling as I looked back up at the two of them.

"But, since he's just a normal guy," Emily started teasingly, "You wouldn't mind telling us more about that kiss, right?"

My cheeks burned red at the mention of the kiss as every moment came rushing back to me. "It was good," I offered shyly.

"Oh come on," they both fussed.

"What do you want me to say?" I asked incredulously. "You want me to say that I felt like I was floating on clouds when he kissed me, or that fireworks were going off in every corner of my mind?"

"Yes," they agreed as I realized what I'd just said.

I saw their eyes sparkling with interest, but to me, it just didn't feel right to share anymore. Those moments were between Ryan and I, and that, I decided, was where they were to be kept. Blushing profusely, I stood up from the couch, suggesting they choose a movie to put on as I headed into the kitchen to calm myself.

Taking a few deep breaths, I decided to throw a bag of popcorn into the microwave, hoping that by the time it was done I'd be able to re-join my friends without any more questions.

Just as the timer on the microwave was ticking down towards zero, my phone, which I'd left on the counter, beeped and I saw it was a message from Ryan.

I'll see you tomorrow, Goodnight xx

I smiled as my eyes focused on the two x's at the tail end of the text. As I pressed send on a short goodnight message of my own, the timer on the popcorn went off.

Pouring the steaming kernels into a bowl, I headed back into the living room hoping for a quiet and relaxing night. But really, what were the odds of that?

CHAPTER 13

Since the day of our first date it was plain to see that something had shifted between Ryan and I. Maybe it was that we were finally accepting our feelings, or maybe it was because the two of us just seemed to be more at ease with one another, but whatever the reason, the chemistry between us was flowing, and it didn't seem like it was slowing down anytime soon.

From the time I'd stepped into his house the following night, where he'd greeted me with a smile and a quick, yet amorous kiss, it felt as though I was living in a fairytale. Ryan was the knight in shining armor and I was the girl that, somehow, managed to catch his attention.

The way he treated me as the days passed was surprising, but not at all unwelcomed. Whenever we were around each other, it was as though he always found a way to touch me, and even if all I felt was the light pressure of his hand resting against the small of my back, it was the feeling of comfort that I found myself constantly craving. And although the attention and companionship would take some getting used to, what really made me smile was seeing him interact with my small, three-year-old bundle of joy.

It was clear to anyone that Abbie absolutely adored Ryan. Every time the two of them were together it made my heart beat twice as fast. There weren't many people in my life that truly accepted Abbie, and the fact that Ryan did made happiness surge through my veins.

As the days passed, a pattern started to develop. I'd more often than not wake up to a text on my phone from Ryan, and throughout the day, while I was in class or finishing up at work, we'd talk whenever the two of us could find the time. But when school was out or work was finished, it seemed as though Ryan was always there, and I didn't mind one bit.

The two of us hadn't talked much about what we were, if we were together or if I was his girlfriend, but in the moments that we had completely to ourselves, those things didn't seem to matter.

We were just us; happy, content, and enjoying our time together.

Time was whizzing by, and as the month of November came to a close, I was all too aware if how close my finals were. I'd booked off a fair amount of time from work over the next few weeks so that I could focus purely on studying in my free time, but with one final shift before my time off, I trudged out of the building along with my other classmates, knowing that I had to be at the café in less than an hour.

As a few of my classmates turned to head in the direction of the library, wanting to get a jump on studying, I kept straight, ducking my head as I got lost in crowd of students heading off campus.

Feeling my phone buzz in my pocket, I pulled it out and looked down, causing students to swerve around me as I stopped to read the text.

'Look to your right x'

Seeing that it was Ryan who'd sent the message, I lifted my head in curiosity. Through the sea of students, I didn't know exactly what I was supposed to be looking for, but as I spied a familiar car parked on the side of the curb about a hundred feet away, it all clicked.

Tucking my phone back into my pocket, I zigged and zagged my way through the mass of students, noticing that although the windows were tinted, multiple heads were turning towards Ryan's car with curiosity.

As I came within a few feet of the car, the passengers' window rolled down, revealing a smiling Ryan resting in the drivers seat. His sunglasses were on, only mildly guarding his appearance, as he leaned over the center console.

I smiled, shaking my head in amusement. "What are you doing here?" I asked curiously, though the reason didn't really matter to me. I was just happy to see him.

"Is it against the law to come and pick you up?" he asked cheekily.

"No," I rolled my eyes, leaning slightly against the car, looking through the window with a small smile on my face. "But you know I have to be at work in half an hour; I can't just not show up."

"Who said anything about skipping work?" he asked, raising an eyebrow as the outline of a smirk appeared on his face. "I'm just here so you don't have to drag that bag of books all the way to the café." Hearing the ding that unlocked the doors, Ryan nodded towards the passenger's seat. "Get in."

Trying not to pay attention to the inquisitive gazes of other students looking my way, I swiftly opened the door and slid into the empty seat. "You know this wasn't necessary right?" I asked, dropping my bag to my feet as I pulled my seatbelt on.

"Sure," he shrugged before flashing me a grin and starting the car, rolling the window up as he did, "But I wanted to see you."

"You saw me last night."

Even though I hadn't had classes the day before, I'd spent a good chunk of the day surrounded by my laptop and textbooks, studying for my upcoming exams. Ryan had come over in the afternoon to play with Abbie, as he had had the day off and wanted to come and help out. He also surprised me by cooking dinner and helping me study after my daughter was safely tucked up in bed.

"But that was last night, this is today," he pointed out, leaning over to peck my lips, pulling back before I even had a chance to reply. "How do you feel about ice cream?"

My forehead wrinkled slightly as he pulled the car away from the curb. "Isn't it a bit cold for ice cream?"

"Zoe, Zoe, Zoe," Ryan shook his head, a smile still very apparent on his face, "You have so much to learn."

That's how, less than half an hour later and after taking one of the longest routes I could've ever imagined, I walked through the door of the café with my bag thrown over one shoulder and a half eaten ice cream cone in my hand.

Colette raised her eyebrow at me as she handed a coffee over the counter to a customer. Her eyes were amused and her smile knowing. "Don't say it," I mumbled, ducking my head as I passed the short line of customers and headed for the back room, leaving her to deal with the orders until my shift started.

"Here you go," I smiled at the customer, handing her drink over the counter, "Have a nice day."

Dusting my hands off on the front of my apron as the customer smiled and took a seat at an empty table, I was finally free to take a breather. The dinner rush had been unusually busy, and with eight 'o'clock quickly approaching, we'd had almost three hours of non-stop orders.

Turning to see if Colette wanted anything done before I cleaned up and clocked out, I saw that she was already looking at me. She was leaning back against the counter, arms crossed across her chest as she sent me a look of amusement.

"What?" I asked warily, picking up a clean rag from underneath the counter to start wiping things down.

Although she'd become one of my closest friends over the past couple of months, as her calculating gaze held mine, I couldn't help but feel slightly uncomfortable. "Oh nothing," she shrugged, although the smirk on her face was telling me the exact opposite. "I was just wondering if your boyfriend is going to be stopping by soon to pick you up?"

Heat spread across my cheeks. "He's having dinner with his parents tonight," I explained faintly, shaking my head, "And I'm fine walking home by myself."

"And he's not my boyfriend," I added, dismissing the idea timidly.

"Not your boyfriend?" Colette repeated, not believing me for a second as she rolled her eyes. "And what world are you living in that Ryan Adams, the guy that basically worships the ground you walk on, isn't your boyfriend?"

"I mean, umm," I started, stumbling over my words as I looked at the few customers that remained in the café. I didn't want any of them overhearing this conversation, and when I saw that they all were otherwise occupied, I nervously turned back to Colette. "We haven't really talked about that yet."

"Seriously?" she asked in disbelief, to which I nodded slowly. "Well how long have you guys been, you know, seeing each other?"

The two of us had now abandoned the cleaning as we stood behind the counter waiting for the customers to trickle out of the café. "He took me out to lunch almost three weeks ago," I replied, biting my lip nervously.

"And you haven't had that conversation yet?"

"No..." I trailed off, suddenly unsure of myself. Up until now, it hadn't crossed my mind to make things official with Ryan. Our relationship was progressing slowly, and it seemed to be working.

Colette clicked her tongue against her teeth. "Well," she started, "What do you want?"

And that one simple question was all it took to create a whirl-wind of chaos within my mind.

I didn't have an answer for her then, as all of a sudden, I wasn't so sure what I wanted. After cleaning up quickly and clocking out, it seemed as though I was operating almost robotically as I walked home and tucked Abbie into bed. Even hours later, lying in my bed with my eyes wide-open, thoughts of our flourishing relationship were still circling around my head.

The thing was, I'd never been in a real relationship. In high school I focused more on studying than being popular and having friends, and after the disastrous night that gave me Abbie, I'd only been on a handful of dates. They were few and far between, and none of the guys had interested me in the slightest, especially after seeing the way they reacted when I brought up the subject of having a daughter so young.

Then there was Ryan.

He'd sparked my interest from the very first time I'd bumped into him at the café, and after realizing whom he was, my instincts seemed to be right. It was the small things that, although I didn't notice at the time, made my feelings grow. When he'd smile at me after a long shift at work, how he didn't seem to mind, yet fully accepted the fact that Abbie was the biggest part of my life, and how, despite his fame, wasn't above hanging around a plain-Jane girl like me.

Although I knew the chemistry we had was hurdling down the path of a relationship, I liked the way things were right now. Things were easy; they were simple and fun, and I didn't want anything to change, especially if, for some reason, things didn't end up going like I hoped.

It seemed as though I was awake for hours, tossing and turning just like the thoughts in my head, but I must've fallen asleep eventually, as hours later, with rays of sunlight seeping into my room, a rather rambunctious three year old woke me up, bouncing up and down on my bed.

"Momma, momma!" I heard, as I was slowly brought back into the world of the living, "Wake up momma."

Groaning slightly, I brought my arms out from under the covers, circling them quickly around Abbie's torso, pulling her towards me in a hug. She giggled as I opened my eyes and smiled at her. "Good morning," I said groggily, "How did you sleep?"

"Good, but it's time to wake up," she said, wiggling around in my arms as she pulled at the covers that still covered me, keeping me snuggled up in the comfort of my bed.

"I am awake sweetie," I said, yawning as I pulled myself into a sitting position. As I turned my head to see how early it was, my eyes nearly bugged out of my head when I saw that it was almost eleven 'o'clock.

How was it possible I'd slept this late?

Slightly more awake now, I looked down at Abbie, who had climbed beside me in bed, but saw that she was already dressed, and her hair had been pulled into two adorable braided pigtails.

"Why didn't you wake me up earlier?" I asked, hopping up off the bed as she followed. I couldn't remember the last time that I slept past eight, as juggling school, work and a toddler made it difficult to not be a morning person.

Abbie just shrugged, not seeing anything wrong with the situation. "Auntie Emily said you were tired, but now she said you have to get up."

Still confused, I guided Abbie along with me as I headed downstairs, on the lookout for my sister.

"Ahhh, you're finally up," Emily commented, turning her head over her shoulder as I entered the kitchen. From what I could tell, she was hard at work making bacon and eggs, and it smelt absolutely delicious. She looked down at Abbie as she came around me, climbing into her usual seat at the table. "I see you succeeded in waking the beast," she said teasingly.

Abbie giggled and nodded as I subconsciously brought my hand up to my hair, feeling a mess of knots and curls. Pulling my bed head into a quick ponytail, I walked across the room towards the fridge. Grabbing the carton of orange juice from the fridge, I took two glasses out of the cupboard. "Did you want any?" I asked, turning to Emily. When she nodded, I grabbed a third glass.

"So, why didn't you wake me up this morning?"

Emily looked at me as though the answer was obvious, but with the curious look on my face, she must've realized that I just wasn't catching on. She looked hesitantly at Abbie before turning back to me seeming somewhat concerned. "Zoe," she started quietly, "You seemed so out of it last night when you came home, and when I woke up to get a snack last night, I could hear you tossing and turning."

My eyes widened slightly as she spoke, as I hadn't realized my mood had been so evident. "I..." I said briefly, my voice staggering as I tried to figure out what to say.

She shook her head as a small, sympathetic smile graced her lips. "We'll talk later," she mouthed, before turning towards Abbie. "Now, who wants some food?"

When breakfast was over, or should I say lunch, I set up the television in the living room for Abbie, switching the channel to Disney Jr. before heading back into the kitchen to help Emily clean up.

"So, what happened last night?"

"It's nothing really," I said. Though I tried to make myself sound convincing, the flat look that Emily was giving me was telling me that she clearly wasn't buying any of it. "It's just something Colette said last night, that's all," I started, walking over to place a pile of dirty dishes into the sink before leaning back against the countertops.

"And...?"

Sighing, my shoulders sagged slightly as I crossed my arms nervously over my chest. "I guess it's nothing bad, she just mentioned something about Ryan and me."

"Which was...?" she egged me on.

"She wanted to know if 'my boyfriend' was picking me up last night, but when I said he wasn't actually my boyfriend, she started asking me why and what was going on," I tried to explain.

"Wait, he's not your boyfriend?" she asked, eyebrows furred as a mask of confusion spread across her face.

"Umm, no."

"Okay," she trailed slowly, "So what are you two then?"

"That's what been bothering me because I don't know!" I exclaimed, running my fingers through my hair. "Up until now I hadn't really thought about it. I feel happy when I'm around him and whenever I see him I feel like smiling, but it hadn't occurred to me to actually make it official. I've never been in a relationship, and I feel like if we go down that road, if we make this thing between us real, that something is going to go wrong or everything's just going to crumble." I explained, laying all my fears and insecurities on the table.

"You're scared," Emily said simply,

"I'm terrified," I agreed, letting loose a long, slow breath.

An encouraging smile graced my sister's lips as she walked over to me. "Even if I could give you all the answers, which I can't, I'd still say that the best thing for you to do is talk to Ryan," she advised. "You never know, maybe he's feeling the same mixed emotions as you are, and that's why the conversation's never come up."

"But what if he's not?" I asked timidly.

"If he really cares about you, which anyone can see that he does, he'll listen to what you have to say," she replied. "Oh, and I'd advise talking to him soon, or you'll end up driving yourself crazy," she added teasingly.

I cracked a smile as I shoved her gently in the side. "He's coming over tonight for dinner," I stated shyly, "I'll talk to him then."

"Good," she nodded, seeming satisfied with my choice, "Just don't chicken out."

"I won't," I replied determinedly, rolling my eyes, but as she turned her back to me to focus back on the dishes, I whispered it again under my breath, wondering how many times I'd have to repeat it before I truly started to believe it.

Studying for my upcoming finals proved to be a sufficient distraction.

With my head stuck in my books, my mind had little to no time to drift to the jumble of thoughts at the back of my mind. Keeping my focus set firmly on the piles of notes and textbooks laid out around me, it seemed like no time at all had passed when the doorbell sounded, startling me out of my studying trance.

Dustin, who Emily had invited over earlier, was already here and helping my sister out in the kitchen. Although her intentions had been good, stating that if there were another guy around, maybe I'd feel more at ease during dinner, her logic was slightly flawed. It did in fact, make me less stressed knowing the conversation over dinner wouldn't strictly be between Ryan and myself, however, I didn't, for one second, think Dustin would do me the honour of answering the door.

I shifted some of my notes to the side, standing up from the spot I'd been seated in for the past few hours, as I headed to answer the door. It wasn't until I opened it that I noticed an overly excited Abbie had been following closely behind.

"Ryan!" she exclaimed as he came into view, hurdling herself at his legs with open arms.

He crouched down, chuckling at her excitement as he picked her up, adjusting her comfortably onto his hip. "Hey there kid, what have you been up to today?"

As Abbie concentrated on telling him about the artwork she'd made earlier this afternoon, I took a second to calm myself down. With Ryan standing there in a pair of plain black jeans and a loose fitted flannel over his top, he somehow managed to look just as attractive as he would have in a suit. I could feel my heart beating faster from a mix of affection and nerves as Colette and Emily's words made there way out of the corners of my mind.

'You're scared.'

'You haven't had that conversation yet?'

'What do you want?'

'Just talk to him.'

"Zoe."

I snapped out of my thoughts as Ryan said my name, only to see him standing much closer to me than before; a frown and a worried expression pasted across his face.

"Where's Abbie?" I asked, noticing that she'd disappeared without me noticing.

"She went to get those paintings to show me," he explained, lifting his hand up to tuck a stray piece of hair behind my ear, though his expression didn't change. "Now are you okay? You were spacing out."

I took a deep breath. 'This is it,' I thought. I could tell him what's been on my mind and then it'd be over and done with.

Just as I opened my mouth, my worries about to jump from the tip of my tongue, Abbie came scurrying back into the entryway, waving two, still slightly damp, paintings in her hands. As she grabbed Ryan's attention, I exhaled slowly, realizing the moment was over and I'd lost my resolve.

While Abbie explained to Ryan what each of her paintings were, he looked back up at me, the same worried expression as before sitting on his face.

"I'm fine," I mouthed, forcing a smile.

"You sure?" he mouthed back, to which I nodded. He still looked unsure as Abbie finished her explanation and he turned to her with a smile. "Those are really good Abbie," he said, making her smile widen in gratitude, "But you know where they'd look even better?"

"Where?"

He brought his hands up to tickle her sides gently as he smiled. "On the fridge for everyone to see."

Abbie's eyes were shining with excitement as she turned to me, silently asking if that was okay. The side of my mouth tilted upwards as I nodded my head in the direction of the kitchen. "Go see if Aunty Emily can find some spare magnets," I said, causing an elated cheer to escape her lips as she quickly made her way towards the kitchen.

Standing up, Ryan looked at me with curiosity in his eyes. "Are you sure you're okay?"

I sighed, turning to head back into the living room where I'd left my mess of notes. "I'm fine," I replied, "I'm just a little stressed studying for finals."

The lie slipped through my lips easily enough, and as Ryan caught my hand, turning me around to face him, I could see in his eyes that he'd bought it, at least for the time being.

"Do you want any more help studying?" he asked, smiling down at me as his arms looped around my waist. "I've been known to write some killer revision notes."

I laughed at how serious his offer seemed, but shook my head. "Not right now," I replied, "What I think I really need is to just put my notes away for the night."

"Well, my offer still stands until you're finished with exams," he said softly, trailing one of his hands up my arm as his face inched towards mine.

My gaze flickered from his eyes to his mouth. "That's good to know," I replied in a hush voice before his lips connected with mine.

As we kissed, I couldn't help but think my worries were displaced and I truly had nothing to worry about. However, as the night lingered on, I felt myself sinking into a deep sense of paranoia. Any little thing Ryan would do, whether it was offer to help in the kitchen, kiss me quickly as we passed, or play with Abbie as dinner was being served, had me questioning if he was in this for the long haul or if this whole thing was just a short-term fling for him.

It was amazing how much an ounce of paranoia could mess with your brain.

Emily had attempted to encourage me throughout the night, telling me that I really was crazy if I didn't think Ryan's intentions were pure, but every time I'd pump myself up to talk to him and clear everything up, I found myself chickening out.

Needless to say I'd managed to avoid talking to him for the majority of the night, and I knew he was starting to catch on to my not-so-subtle avoidance tactics.

Dinner, for all intents and purposes was good. The food Emily and Dustin had made was delicious, and there were no awkward lulls in conversation with everybody sitting around the table happily. As I sat across from Ryan, I could feel his eyes constantly flickering to me as I talked with Emily about a new exhibit opening at her work, and as everyone's plates cleared off, I knew I didn't have it in me to keep ignoring the guy I was fast falling for.

"Hey Emily," Ryan started minutes later, walking into the kitchen where my sister and I were cleaning up, "Would you mind if I stole Zoe away for a bit?"

"Don't worry about it, I'll finish cleaning up," she smiled in response before turning to send me a pointed look.

Wiping my damp hands on the back of my pants, I followed Ryan as he turned and headed into the living room, only to see Abbie and Dustin still sitting at the kitchen table talking about how daycare was going.

"Hey Abbie, Ryan and I are going out for a quick walk," I started, but before I could say that we'd be back soon, she had already cut me off.

"Can I come?" she asked happily, and with a quick glance to Ryan, I knew neither he nor I could say no to her adorably excited face.

"Go grab your coat," I sighed, nodding towards the entryway as she squealed in excitement.

Once I'd thrown on a sweater and helped tie up the laces on Abbie's shoes, the three of us clambered quickly out the door. "So, where are we going?" Abbie asked, slipping one of her hands into mine and the other into Ryan's as we headed down the road, no destination in particular in mind.

"What about the park?" Ryan suggested after a few seconds of silence, raising his eyebrow at me as Abbie nodded her head in agreement.

I smiled softly. "The park's good."

The sun had already started to set and the streetlights illuminated the sidewalk as we walked the rest of the way with just the sounds of nature to keep us company. As soon as the park came into view, Abbie let loose an excited squeal, letting go of both of our hands as she made a bee-line for on of the slides.

Watching her happily playing put a smile on my face, but it didn't last long as I heard Ryan's low and concerned voice behind me.

"Zoe," he started, walking up beside me so we were both facing the playground as our hands brushed up against one another, "You've been acting weird since I walked in the door earlier."

I sighed, sagging my head as I closed my eyes. "Ryan," I said slowly, knowing there was no way out of this conversation now. Besides Abbie, we were more or less alone in this park, and it didn't seem as though Ryan was going anywhere soon.

Before I could get another word out, Ryan stepped out in front of me, bringing his hand up to cup my chin as he tilted my head up to meet my eyes. "Is there something you're not telling me? Is something wrong?"

His worry laced between his words made me feel awful, as thought my silence was chipping off pieces of his heart, but with his thumb rubbing softly on my neck and his eyes piercing deeply into mine, I couldn't find the words to answer him.

"Zoe?"

"What are we?" I blurted out, only to realize my mistake once it was too late. Ryan's eyes widened at my question and my heart was hammering in my chest. "Oh wow," I continued embarrassedly, a blush spreading quickly across my cheeks, "I'm sorry, I didn't mean to ask that."

Ducking my head, I attempted to maneuver my way around him, but his hold on me didn't loosen, in fact, his arms circled my waist to keep me in place. "Where is this coming from?" he asked softly, having more than likely pieced together my puzzled thoughts.

"It's just, yesterday Colette said something to me and," I started, not really knowing how to go on; not knowing how to put my feelings into words so that he'd understand.

His eyebrows scrunched in confusion, though he stayed silent, waiting for me to continue.

"She asked about us being a couple," I confessed, looking up at him nervously as I continued. "I told her that we haven't really talked about us being, well, an us, and she was just surprised. I don't really have all that much experience with relationships, and I guess I've just been worried that if we did talk about it, you wouldn't feel the same way about me as I feel about you."

I'd done it. I'd laid my feelings out on the table, and now, as I held my breath waiting for him to say respond, I could feel my heart beating rapidly with anticipation.

He brought both hands up to cup my neck softly. "I need you to listen to what I say next, and listen carefully because I'm only going to say this once," he spelled out. "When you didn't recognize me the first time we met, I was shocked, but I was also intrigued. Over the last few years I've met a lot of people who want to get close to me because my job puts me in the spotlight, but it didn't take long to realize that you weren't one of those people. You were real, and were interested in getting to know the real me, not the guy that everybody sees in the movies. When we first started hanging out, I didn't know if you were looking at me as a friend or something more, but after the basketball game, it all just kind of fell into place for me."

"You're one of the most thoughtful, kind, smart, caring, and beautiful people I've ever met, and this isn't just some fling for me. I want to be with you, and spend every day hoping that you'll never come to your senses and realize that you could do so much better than me. I want for you to be my girlfriend. I want for you to be able to come to me with any insecurities or problems you're having, knowing that I'll be there to listen, and I want to be the one you call when you've had a bad day knowing that I'll always try and find a way cheer you up."

And with that, all my doubts and worries that had built up over the last twenty-four hours flew out the window.

There were tears building up in my eyes as he finished talking and my heart was beating erratically as I tried to find the words to reply.

Instead, not knowing what to say, I grabbed at the front of his shirt, pushing myself up to plant my lips firmly on top of his. Through this kiss I tried to convey everything that I could; that I wanted the same things he did, and maybe even more.

He understood me. He made me feel like I could be completely myself.

As I parted my lips and his tongue slipped through the opening, an involuntary moan escaped. This only seemed to encourage him as his hands slowly trailed down my sides, gripping my hips as he pulled me impossibly close, leaving a trail of heat and desire anywhere he touched.

When my head started to whirl with elation, I pulled back, breathless and smiling.

"Feeling better?" Ryan asked breathlessly, a touch of a smile on his lips as he pushed a few stray strands of hair back behind my ear.

I bit my lip lightly, attempting to conceal the grin that threatened to appear as I nodded, wrapping my arms around his waist and pulling him into a hug. My head rested softly on his chest as his arms wrapped themselves tightly around me. My eyes latched on to Abbie as I saw her sitting at the bottom of the slide, all playing forgone, as she smiled giddily watching Ryan and I.

Just as I was about to call out to her, a sudden flash startled Ryan and I apart. And as the sound of a camera shutter hit my ears, I realized that this night, that could have been spectacular, was headed straight for disaster.

CHAPTER 14

After being with Ryan the past few weeks, I'd been slowly starting to accept the fact that, while I might not be completely ready for it, I knew that sooner or later the two of us would be photographed together. We weren't exactly trying to keep our relationship a secret, and once that picture of us had surfaced after his cousin's wedding, I figured it was inevitable.

Just not right now. Not in this moment.

SNAP

I felt like a deer in the headlights as the camera continued to flash mere meters away from us, but as Ryan's arms wove their way around me, attempting to shield me from view, I snapped out of it.

"Abbie!" I yelled frantically, pushing myself away from Ryan as I headed quickly in her direction. I could hear Ryan following close behind, yelling something I couldn't quite comprehend, because in that moment, I really didn't care about much other than getting my daughter out of here.

My heart clenched painfully as I reached where she was sitting on the play structure, knees curled up to her chest, wide eyes, and a frightened look plastered across her face. "It's okay sweetie,"

I said softly, bringing my arms around her tightly in a means of comfort, "It'll be alright."

I almost forgot Ryan had followed me until he appeared behind me, wrapping an arm around my shoulder protectively. "Come on," Ryan said smoothly, his face holding a stern and serious expression, "We'd better get out of here." Silently asking me if he could take Abbie, I nodded, watching as he gently picked her up and rested her on his hip, muttering quietly to her that everything was going to be fine.

"The guy ran off," he started again, nodding in the direction of a car park, "But we should get going before he decides to come back." As his eyes met mine once more, I saw in them the words he refused to say.

If the photographer comes back, he won't be alone.

Nodding, it was as if my mind suddenly flipped its switch from manual to automatic, giving me absolutely no control over my actions. In fact, I'd spent the better part of the journey home coiled nervously against Ryan's side as he guided us swiftly through my neighbourhood streets without fail. It became apparent that, as I cast my gaze back over my shoulder every few steps, I was letting the paranoia of being followed sink in.

It came as a surprise to me, when Ryan steered us into a driveway, that we had managed to make it back to my house in record time, and all without being followed. As the three of us burst through the front door, closing and locking it behind us, my mind slowly started to register what had happened within the span of the last fifteen minutes.

There was a flash, followed by yelling and crying as the paparazzi managed to ruin one of the best moments of my life.

My eyes snapped towards my daughter, who still looked scared out of her mind as she clung tightly onto Ryan's shirt, tears slowly dripping down her face. Ryan sent me a sympathetic look as he shifted her in his arms, nodding for me to take her.

"Abbie sweetie," I spoke quietly, holding in my arms gently, "Everything's alright now. It's okay." As her tears slowed down and her sniffles began, I wanted nothing more than to be able to put a smile on her face.

"But you were scared momma," she whimpered, wrapping her arms around my neck tighter. My heart lodged in my throat as I realized that she wasn't crying for herself, but rather because she was scared for me.

"Oh sweetie," I sighed, rubbing my hand affectionately through her hair for comfort, "Don't worry about me, I'm fine."

Shuffling in the living room caught my attention as I heard Emily getting up and walking towards us. "So, how was your walk?" Her voice chipper as her footsteps became louder. "Did you have a good...?" Taking in the scene in front of her, her smile wavered and her eyes flashed with worry. "What happened?"

The panic of not knowing seeped into her voice, but before I could reassure her that everything was fine, Ryan spoke up. "We may have a slight problem."

Emily's eyes flicked from Ryan to me as she raised an eyebrow hesitantly. "What kind of problem?"

I grimaced, looking to Ryan for support as he placed his hand on the base of my back; however, I saw uncertainty clouding in his eyes. "Maybe we should go sit down," I mumbled under my breath, leading the two of them into the living room, only to see Dustin lounging on the couch.

And then I told them.

I explained how we'd gone to the park and, after thinking that nobody was around, had gotten caught by the paparazzi, who'd disappeared with the picture before we rushed home safely. Ryan helped fill in the gaps, recounting the details I couldn't quite remember, and as our story came to a close, I sat bouncing Abbie on my knee, waiting for a reaction.

"And you just let him get away?" Emily asked incredulously.

Before I could answer, a soft tugging at my hair stole my attention. "Can I go play upstairs?" Abbie asked softly. Having had time to settle down, she seemed to be back to her usual playful self as she looked up at me with wishful eyes, waiting for me to reply.

"Sure sweetie."

As an excited giggle passed through her lips, I let her down off my lap, watching as she readily hurried her way up the stairs before turning back to Emily.

"And yeah, what did you expect us to do Emily?" I replied.

"I don't know, but you could've done something!"

"If we would've waited to see if he came back, he probably wouldn't have come alone," Ryan reasoned, extending his arm that previously lay behind me on the couch so that it wrapped securely around my shoulder, pulling me into his warm embrace.

Emily's eyes shifted between Ryan and I. "But aren't you worried?" she asked, an overflowing amount of concern coating her words.

I bit my lip, knowing the consequences of what could happen as a result of those pictures, although I had truly had no idea what could be done about them.

"Honey," I heard Dustin mutter towards his worried girlfriend, "Why don't we leave them be for a while?"

As Emily reluctantly agreed with him, standing up to give us a bit of privacy, I sent Dustin a small, yet grateful smile, watching as he nodded in return before following his girlfriend into the kitchen.

Turning to Ryan, I looked up at him, trying to decipher what was going on inside his head, but all I could see was a sea of worry and guilt within his deep blue eyes. This wasn't a reassuring revelation as my heart began to beat faster, uncertainty about our situation flooding my mind.

I ducked my head, letting some of my hair fall down to cover my face, my eyes studying my hands that were clasped together anxiously in my lap.

"I should go," Ryan said, breaking the silence that surrounded us.

The sound of his voice, so detached and emotionless, caused me to shutter as I dared to meet his eyes.

"What?" I asked, my voice cracking as I waited to hear the words once again, hoping that I'd somehow heard them wrong the first time.

"I said I should go," he repeated, his voice wavering this time as he made a move to stand, his eyes fixated on the front door.

I couldn't let him leave though.

"Wait," I croaked out, my voice too filled with emotion to stay steady. His movements halted as I reached out to place my hand on top of his. "Don't go."

Ryan turned back to me, and as I saw the worry and guilt once again in his eyes, I knew that I still had a chance to fix this. A small chance, but a chance none the less. He sighed, turning his palm over to meet mine, intertwining our fingers tightly. "I shouldn't have come back here with you. It's not safe for me to be here right now."

"What are you talking about?"

Messing his hair up as he ran his free hand through it, frustration radiated off of him. "The people who want those photos are only around because of me. I took you and Abbie to the park because I was worried something was bothering you, and all that got me was more to worry about." He exhaled heavily, shaking his head.

"I should've been more careful, I should've tried to stop him, I just..."

"Hey, hey, hey, you did nothing wrong," I spoke softly; trying to reassure him that he'd done more than enough. Bringing my hand up, my thumb softly touched his chin as my fingers splayed gently across his cheek. "It wasn't your fault that some people just don't understand the meaning of the word privacy."

"But..."

"No buts," I shook my head, "I've known for a while that getting photographed with you was a possibility and I've come to terms with it. I want to be with you, and not just the guy that sits here with me acting like a normal person. I want to be with the guy whose face is on thousands of screens and graces the covers of magazines. The guy who is so successful because he works hard for what he loves."

"Zoe," he said gently, cracking a small smile as he leant into my touch, "I have to go."

My insides crumbled as his words felt like a shot to my heart. "What?" My voice was tight as I struggled not to fall apart in front of him.

"Not that I don't want to stay," he rushed to continue, seeing quickly that I'd misunderstood his words. "It's just that if we were followed, by any chance, I don't want those people to know where you live," he explained. "My car's still outside and if anyone comes looking around the neighbourhood, they'll recognize it."

"I need to go."

"Then let me come with you," I suggested quietly. "I don't want you to leave."

His eyes softened. "You have Abbie to think about," he replied. "She's going to need you tonight, and that's okay."

"What if she came with us?" It seemed as though my question shocked him, as his jaw unhinged and his eyes bugged out. "Umm, Ryan?" I started again, "Did you hear what I said?"

"Yeah, I just," he stammered, pausing to take a breath before he continued. "You would really be okay with that?"

A small smile played on my lips. "Yeah, I mean she's really been missing Rocky, and it's almost her bedtime anyway so she'll be tired as soon as we get there, and..."

Ryan cut off my nervous rambling, leaning in to steal a quick kiss off my lips, effectively cutting me off.

"In that case, I think I'd like that, if it really is okay with you," he said as he pulled back, a smile gracing his face.

I bit my lip, trying to contain the grin that threatened to appear. "It's okay with me."

Half an hour later Abbie and I were sitting in his car, on the way to his house. After explaining the situation to Emily and packing up a few necessities, like clothes and a toothbrush, I'd moved Abbie's car seat to the backseat of Ryan's car before we were off.

While Abbie was content humming along to the music flowing quietly from the speakers, I sat fidgeting in the passenger's seat, watching as Ryan every so often glanced in the rearview mirror. From what I could tell, we hadn't been followed, but that didn't stop Ryan from taking plenty of side roads on the way to his house. I couldn't even break the awkwardness, as I didn't know what to say. I felt a little weird knowing that I'd actually be staying at his house tonight, because even though I'd been over there multiple times, I'd never stayed the night.

Before I had enough time to worry about where Abbie and I would sleep, Ryan finally turned onto an all too familiar road, pulling into his driveway before killing the engine. Not many words were said as we climbed out of the car, Ryan grabbing the bag I'd packed while I helped Abbie out of her car seat before heading straight inside.

As the door opened and the lights flickered on automatically, the barking started up and a broad grin lit up Abbie's features as Rocky rounded the corner, scurrying playfully around our feet.

"Hey there buddy," Ryan chuckled, leaning down to pet Rocky for a few seconds, "Miss me?"

A loud, pronounced bark was all he got as a reply before Abbie let her excitement take over and sat down next to Rocky, pulling him onto her lap as he looked up at her with wide, playful eyes.

"Can I pway with him before bed?" Abbie asked, her eyes sparkling.

Ryan looked to me first, raising an eyebrow. I shrugged in response, knowing she still had a bit of time to kill before her bedtime. "Sure Abbie, you know where the toys are" Ryan replied, smiling down at her as he nodded to the other room, "Try to tire him out before bed."

She let out an excited squeal. "Come on Rocky!" she said as she stood up, watching as the dog followed her as she scuttled her way out of sight.

"So... did you want to put a movie on?" Ryan asked, pushing his hands deep in his pockets, shoulders hunched, as he waited for my reply.

I bit my lip to conceal the laugh that threatened to escape. It was amusing to see him looking so unsure of himself, whereas I was used to seeing him so confident and comfortable, especially in his own house.

"Sure," I smiled, watching as some of the tenseness in his shoulders dissipated. "What do you want to watch?"

"It doesn't matter to me," he shrugged, "Just put whatever on and I'll be down in a few, I'm just going to put your bag upstairs."

I nodded, standing up on my tiptoes to plant a kiss on his cheek. I saw the vague outline of a smile grace his lips as I stepped back, turning towards the hallway that led downstairs.

Stepping down off the last step, I headed straight for his movie collection. From all the times that I've been over here, I'd come to realize that even though he owned an extensive DVD collection, he didn't own any of his own movies. I'd once asked him about it and he'd just explained that, after experiencing all the work that was behind each film, watching it back just didn't do it justice.

After picking out a comedy that I vaguely remembered watching a few years back, I popped it into the DVD player, letting the trailers run through as I made myself comfy on the couch. Despite what had transpired tonight, as I sat relaxing in Ryan's lounge, I couldn't help but feel at ease. Since I'd met him, there hadn't been many moments where being around Ryan made me feel uncomfortable, which may have been the reason why, although I could've very well stayed home tonight, I'd chosen to seek comfort here.

Completely content, I turned as the sound of footsteps hit my ears, watching Ryan as he flicked the lights off before plopping down beside me on the couch. Curling my legs up underneath me, I fit my head into the crook of his neck as his arm wove its way around my shoulders.

"What movie did you pick?" he asked quietly, watching as the last of the trailers faded from the screen.

I leaned my head back slightly, looking up at him. "You'll see," I smiled, before snuggling back into a comfortable position.

The movie was just as funny as I remembered, and as I sat there laughing with Ryan, the time seemed to get away from us. After what felt like no time at all, I shifted away from Ryan, turning my head towards the stairs at the pitter-patter of tiny footsteps.

"Abbie," I started, glancing to the clock on the wall to see that it was much later than I'd assumed. As she walked over to me, rubbing her eyes tiredly with the back of her hands, I continued. "Where'd Rocky go?"

"He's sleeping," she yawned, leaning against the couch. "Momma, I'm tired."

I saw Ryan lean forward out of the corner of my eye, pausing the movie. "All that playing tired you out, eh?" he asked as Abbie shifted her tired eyes towards him, nodding her head slowly. "I'll tell you what; you and your momma can sleep in my bed tonight, and when you wake up tomorrow morning, I'll make you guys pancakes for breakfast."

Despite being tired, excitement still sparkled in her eyes. "With chocolate chips?"

Ryan nodded, a proud smile on his face. "With chocolate chips," he confirmed.

"Okay," Abbie said, releasing a huge yawn as I stood up. Picking her up, I placed her securely on my hip before turning back to Ryan. "Goodnight Ryan," she muttered quietly, resting her head against my shoulder.

"Goodnight Abbie."

"I'll be back down in a little bit," I said softly.

"Take you time."

And I did. Walking upstairs, I pushed open the door to Ryan's room to see the bag I'd packed lying on top of his duvet. Grabbing the essentials, I helped Abbie change into her pajamas before brushing her teeth and pulling her wild blonde hair into a ponytail at the back of her head. Normally it would've required a short bedtime story to get her brain to wind down and her eyes to droop low, but as I tucked her into Ryan's queen size bed, no story was required. Within minutes her breathing had leveled out and her eyelids drew shut.

Leaning over her, I placed a small kiss on the top of her head, gently rearranging the covers before retreating from the room.

Venturing back downstairs, I stopped short as I came across Ryan. Now in the kitchen, his back was facing me as he stirred two mugs that sat next to one another on the counter. He must have heard my footsteps, as he looked over his shoulder, a faint smile on his lips as he took me in. "Hey," he said, his voice soft and sultry.

"Hey." I eyed the mugs on the counter carefully as the sweet smell of chocolate hit my nose. "What happened to watching the movie?"

"The movie's still on," he admitted. "I just thought that after the day you've had, some homemade hot chocolate wouldn't hurt."

My heart warmed at his gesture. "Thanks," I replied, taking the mug he held out to me. Cradling the warmth between my hands, I brought the murky, chocolate liquid up to my lips and took a sip, releasing a sigh as I swallowed. "This is exactly what I needed."

Taking the mugs of hot chocolate back downstairs, we settled back into the couch as the movie started up once again.

"So, did Abbie have any trouble getting to sleep?" Ryan asked, turning to face me with a curious look. "I know sometimes kids don't like sleeping in a bed that's not their own."

"And where did you hear that?" Pink dusted across his cheeks as he brought his mug up to his lips, mumbling a reply into his drink. My eyes grew amused at his embarrassment. "What was that?"

He sighed. "I may have read it online."

Even though his reply was mumbled, I was able to pick up on his words without any difficulty.

A bubble of laughter escaped my lips before I bit my lip, concealing my smile as I saw his eyebrows rise. "Abbie's fine. She was already half-asleep when I tucked her in," I explained. "Thanks, by the way, for offering your room. You didn't need to do that."

"It's fine." He shook his head, cracking a smile. "Besides, Abbie deserves the best, and my bed is the comfiest one in the house."

"Still," I paused, "Where are you going to sleep?"

Ryan waved off my comment. "There's two spare rooms upstairs, plus the couch in the den upstairs is pretty comfy."

Rolling my eyes, I sat my mug steadily on the coffee table before leaning forward and pressing my lips against his softly. It wasn't a long kiss, but there wasn't much else I could've said to show him how much I appreciated him. Pulling back slightly, I could still feel his warm breath fanning my lips. "Thank you."

From this close, I could see as his eyes darkened, his gaze locking me in place. Unable to help myself, my hands trailed up his chest to wind around his neck, my fingers sliding their way into his hair as my eyes fluttered shut.

Desire buzzed through me as I felt him draw closer, and as his lips finally met my own, it was as though the scenes that surrounded us faded into nothingness. His arms drew me closer to him so that our bodies were flush against one another, so that I could feel his heart beating faster through his chest and he could feel mine.

As our lips moved against one another, slowly and without hesitation, his tongue swiped across my bottom lip, delving into my mouth passionately as I met his enthusiasm with my own. Feeling cramped in our current position, I slowly leaned backwards, not once breaking the kiss as my hands trailed around to the front of Ryan's shirt, clenching the fabric between my fingers as I pulled him down on top of me.

Ryan's hands started to venture downwards. He trailed them slowly over my shoulders, across my ribs, and just above my hips before pushing the fabric of my shirt a tad higher, exposing the skin underneath as his fingers splayed out. Everywhere he touched seemed to spark a reaction from me, a pool of heat and desire building in the pit of my stomach.

It was when my legs wove their way around his waist, and his hands slowly started to inch upwards, that his mouth left mine.

My eyes were still closed and my breathing shallow as I felt his head dip, his mouth brushing the skin below my ear. "We should stop."

Not fully coherent, I was too focused on the man that was currently sucking softly on my shoulder. His teeth lightly nipped at the skin and the slickness and warmth of his tongue quickly followed. "Mhmmm," I murmured incoherently.

He chuckled, which sounded like a melody as I lay there beneath him, wanting nothing more than continue what we were doing. I knew that if we did however, we might not be able to stop.

Pulling away from my shoulder, he dropped one last kiss on my lips before hoisting himself up onto his arms so that he hovered me. Slowly opening my eyes, I traced my tongue slowly across my own lips, watching as Ryan's eyes zeroed in on the movement.

"Well isn't that a shame," I said, my voice barely audible, yet filled with lust.

"What?" Ryan's eyes searched my face curiously, waiting for a response.

My lips tilted upwards as I nodded towards the television, where the credits of the movie were scrolling up the screen. "We missed the movie," I replied in amusement.

Ryan's eyes shone with happiness as a smile graced his face. "I wasn't even paying much attention to the movie anyways," he spoke, bringing a hand up, his thumb caressing my cheek.

I could feel the heat creep up my neck, a pink tint appearing on my skin as Ryan ducked his head, bringing his lips back down onto my own.

▯▯

Opening my eyes, I felt slightly disoriented as I was met with darkness. Rolling over in the bed, I saw that Abbie was still sleeping soundly beside me, but for some reason, despite the hour, my body appeared to be wide-awake.

Rolling out of the bed, I was careful not to wake Abbie. Setting my sights on the kitchen, I headed downstairs, only to glance and see that, according to the wall clock near the stairs, it was just after six in the morning.

Stepping down onto the landing, a frown creased my forehead as I noticed the lights in the kitchen were on. Guilt swam in the pit of my stomach as I turned my head, focusing on the couch. There was a pillow and a few blankets thrown over it, as though Ryan had slept there throughout the night after giving up his own bed to Abbie and I. Although the couch didn't look especially uncomfortable, the fact that it seemed to be, at the least, a few inches shorter than Ryan, had me regretting accepting his generosity.

Turning my feet towards the kitchen, I figured that's where I'd find Ryan. And I did, but he wasn't alone.

The man that stood across from Ryan seemed like a professional and was dressed for business, despite the early hour. His eyebrows rose as he noticed me enter the kitchen, his eyes studying me for a few seconds before turning back to Ryan. "So, I'm assuming this is Zoe?"

As his gaze returned to me, I suddenly felt self-conscious, standing there in just my pajamas. I tugged at the bottom of Ryan's sweatshirt, wishing that the fabric spontaneously grew a few inches to cover my shorts and legs.

"Zoe, this is my manager, Travis." Ryan sighed stressfully, waving a hand between the two of us. "Travis, this is my girlfriend, Zoe."

"Nice to meet you," he greeted, to which I nodded in reply. "But I'd better get going considering I have a meeting in less than an hour. Remember what I told you." He looked pointedly at Ryan after his last comment, leaving me slightly confused as Travis walked passed me, heading for the exit.

When the front door slammed shut behind him, Ryan looked towards me, worry in his eyes. "Did we wake you up?"

I yawned, shaking my head. "Don't worry about it, I woke up on my own," I explained. "Why was your manager here so early anyways?"

Ryan shook his head, stepping closer to me before his head landed on my shoulder. "He was just being his usual self, not wanting me in public without Chad following me around 24/7," he grumbled. "He called and woke me up about two minutes before he walked through the door."

"I'm guessing this is about the photographer?" I asked softly, resting my hands on his hips.

"Yeah," he sighed, moving his head so that his forehead rested against mine. "But I do have some good news."

"Really?"

He cracked a smile. "Travis tracked down the guy in the park. Apparently he was trying to sell our photo to a local magazine, but Travis was able to intercept it and pay him off before he could."

I raised an eyebrow, my forehead crinkling as I did so. "And that's a good thing?" I asked hesitantly.

"Isn't it?" He frowned. "I thought you wanted to keep our relationship away from the public."

I bit my lip. "I mean I do, but..." I trailed, not being able to find the words to explain.

There was no debating on whether or not I wanted to be with him, I knew I did, but I was also aware of the price that came with it. I would have to give up my privacy, as well as step completely into a world that I was currently overlooking from the sidelines. I didn't know what the consequences of my choice would be, but for him, I thought it just might be worth it.

It was as if Ryan could see the inner workings of my mind, as if he knew exactly what I was thinking. His concentrated gaze suddenly widened and his frown disappeared, a soft smile taking its place.

"I get it," he said softly, bringing his hand up to brush through my hair. My unruly, bedhead ridden hair. "Let's just see how this goes, and we'll deal with the obstacles as they come."

His lips came down to capture mine briefly, and even with the lightest of pressures, his lips were intoxicating. The threat of morning breath circled the back of my mind, but I couldn't fight past the fire that he lit within me. He pulled away after a moment or two, his eyes bright, roaming my face intently.

"I wouldn't have it any other way."

CHAPTER 15

Scribbling down the remainder of the conclusion, I flipped over the pages I'd already written. Twirling my pen nervously through my fingers, I glanced up at the wall. The hands of the clock were ticking slowly, telling me that I still had another ten minutes before I'd have to hand in my paper.

The stress that had built up over the past couple of hours, and over the past few weeks of studying, slowly started to dissipate as I re-read what I'd manage to write. I made sure to re-write the run-on sentences, fix the spelling mistakes I'd made in a rush to get my ideas onto the paper, and double-checked that my thesis and introduction were clear, as well as supported throughout my paper.

Erasing one last mistake I leaned back in my chair, sighing in relief as the timer at the front of the classroom went off. Looking around, I saw some of my classmates struggling to write down one more sentence while others just looked relived to be done.

At the front of the room, our professor stood up. "Your time for the exam is now over," she said, eyeing the one or two students that were still writing. "Please drop your booklets in the basket on the desk on your way out. Hopefully you all make the most of your holidays, and I'll see you next semester."

Tossing my pen into my bag, I pulled on my jacket and hoisted my bag up over my shoulder. Making my way to the front, I dropped my booklet into the bin, wishing my professor a merry Christmas before following the hoard of students out of the class-room.

A lot of my classmates seemed to be talking with one another, asking each other how they thought they did and how they wrote their paper, but as I stepped out into the quad, I found myself perfectly content. After weeks of studying and non-stop stress, I was finally able to take a breath, take my head out of my books, and relax.

Wrapping my jacket around me tighter as I strode through campus, I turned my head slightly; trying to avoid the brunt of the winds that seemed all too keen on sweeping my hair up to block my line of sight. Although it wasn't necessarily cold, the temperature had taken a significant dive into the single digits, bringing a troop of fierce winds along as backup.

Knowing it was just after three when my exam ended, I changed my direction, weaving through the rest of the students so desperate to get off campus now that the holidays had arrived and set a course towards one of the campus cafes. I'd decided that after all the work I'd put into school over the past couple of weeks, a delicious hot chocolate was a reward too appealing to pass up.

Ten minutes later I made my way off campus, en route to Abbie's day care with a warm cup cradled between my hands. The walk wasn't far, but it did give me enough time to finish my drink and toss the cup in the garbage outside the day care, knowing Abbie inevitably would've asked why I didn't grab one for her as well.

Walking inside, I hovered around the entryway as Diane dismissed the kids from the circle they sat in on the carpet, telling them to go and play. I smiled as I saw Abbie talking with two girls about her age, the three of them headed straight for the boxes of dolls that were stacked towards the back.

"Hey," Diane greeted, appearing next to me. "Are you here to pick up Abbie?"

I smiled sheepishly and nodded. "Sorry, I know I'm a little early..."

"Oh nonsense," she waved me off, turning towards the play area, "Abbie!"

At the sound of her name, my daughter's head popped up curiously, her blonde hair falling messily around her face. Noticing me standing there, her eyes gleamed with excitement and happiness. "Mommy!" Abbie exclaimed loudly as she skipped to my side, throwing her arms around my legs tightly. "You're here early."

I nodded with smile, leaning down to kiss the top of her head before smoothing down her hair. "I am," I affirmed, "But I don't mind waiting if you want to finish playing with your friends."

She peeked back at the girls she'd been playing with, seeing them still happily playing with the dolls, before turning back to me and shaking her head. "I can pway with dolls at home," she said.

I chuckled lightly. "Okay sweetie, why don't you go get your lunch bag and then we'll leave. Maybe you'll even be able to catch Emily before she has to leave for the night."

Tonight, on top of being the start of my holidays, also happened to be a big night for my little sister. The gallery that she worked at was holding a gala viewing tonight in celebration of the end of the year, and even though she was given the day off, she had to be there before five to set up. A lot of big names would be there tonight with hopes of buying local pieces, and I was nervous just to be on the guest list - I couldn't fathom how she would be able to keep calm all night as one of the hosts.

Bouncing with excitement, Abbie nodded, heading towards her cubby where her lunch and jacket were stored.

"She really is such a sweet young girl Zoe," Diane said.

A smile on my face as I watched her struggle into her jacket, I nodded. "She is."

"We'll definitely miss her around here over the break," she admitted, "But I'm sure she'd much rather be at home with you."

"You never know," I quipped, "She does seem to like it here." Abbie came waddling over then, her princess lunch bag in one hand as she struggled to zip up the front of her jacket. "You ready to go sweet pea?" I asked, crouching down to help her with her zipper before bopping her on the nose quickly.

"Yup," she replied. "Bye Mrs. Diane. Merry Chris'mas!"

"Merry Christmas to you too Abbie," Diane said softly before turning back to me. "I should get back to the kids. I hope you guys have a good holiday."

"You too Diane," I responded happily as she headed towards a group of boys that seemed happy to be building a tower with blocks, even if they were a couple of additions away from a toppling castle.

After a long enough walk, the two of us arrived home and hurried through the door only to see a rather nervous looking Emily pacing the living room. She'd already gotten ready for the night, having curled her hair, put on a bit of make-up, and changed into a black cocktail dress.

"Hey Em," I said tentatively, "Is everything alright?"

She stopped pacing as she noticed the two of us standing there. "Yeah," she admitted slowly, taking a deep breath as she ran a hand through her perfectly curled hair. "I'm just a little worked up about tonight. It's like the only time my nerves act up is when I know I'm helping to host a gala."

"I'm sure you'll do great tonight," I said encouragingly, "Plus, Ryan, Dustin, and I will be there. I'm sure if you ever need a break, one of us will be around to help calm you nerves."

"Thanks," she replied, the corners of her mouth lifting up into a thankful grin.

"Yeah Aunty Emily, you'll do gweat!" Abbie pitched in enthusiastically.

"Awe thanks sweetie." Emily crouched down in front of Abbie, wrapping her arms around her in a loose hug. "It's too bad you're not coming tonight because then I'd be able to have you as a sidekick all night."

Abbie pulled back from her aunt slightly, tilting her head curiously. "Why can't I come again?" Abbie asked glumly.

"Oh Abbie," she sighed, "You're not old enough to come tonight. But don't worry, just because you're not going out, doesn't mean you're not going to have fun here."

Her words seemed to lift Abbie's spirits a bit. When I'd first told her that she'd have to stay home while the rest of us went out tonight she didn't take it well. However, after a lot of reassurance and a couple of extra desserts, she seemed to have understood.

Dustin had asked his little sister if she was busy for the night, as she supposedly babysat a lot of the kids in their neighbourhood over the years, and after having her over a few days ago to meet Abbie, I felt good enough to leave my daughter in her care for a few hours tonight.

"Well," Emily stood up; glancing back at the clock "I'd better head out soon if I'm going to get there on time. Sara said that she'd be here before seven, so you should have time to make dinner and get ready before then, and the address to the gallery is on a sticky note taped to the fridge."

I nodded, wishing her good luck one last time before she headed out the door. Hearing the slam that signified she was gone, I sighed, looking down at Abbie with a curious smile on my face.

"Now, what would you like for dinner?"

Hours later I was in my room, finishing up my hair as one of the last loose curls fell from the curling iron, delicately framing my face along with the others. I'd long since left Abbie to her toys in her room, hoping that the distraction would give me enough time to properly get ready.

Just as I unplugged the curling iron, the doorbell went, making me jump slightly. I looked down at what I was currently wearing – a fluffy purple bathrobe with nothing but my knickers underneath – and shook my head, scurrying from my room in hopes that my boyfriend wasn't on the other side of the door.

Luckily, after looking through the peephole, I saw Sara, Dustin's little sister, standing on the other side of the door. Opening the door, I held it open just enough for her to get through, making sure I was fairly hidden.

"Hey, sorry," I said sheepishly, closing the door before pulling my robe tighter around myself, "I'm still in the middle of getting ready."

She shed her coat and shoes, looking over her shoulder at me as she replied. "Don't worry about it," she waved off, "I'm a little bit early anyways."

"Abbie's just up in her room playing," I explained, leading her up the stairs. "Abbie," I called, standing in the entryway of her room as she turned, switching her attention from the various dolls she'd laid out across the floor to me, "Sara's here."

"Hi Sara!" she chirped, holding up the doll that'd been laying in her lap, "Do you wanna play with me?"

"Sure sweetie," Sara smiled.

"Are you sure you're okay with watching her tonight?" I asked quietly as she went to move towards Abbie. Although I knew from Dustin that she was trustworthy, there was always that sliver of doubt I had before leaving her with someone new. "I mean, if you had plans that you had to cancel or..."

"It's okay Zoe, the two of us will be fine," she replied reassuringly. "Just go finish getting ready and make sure to have a good time tonight."

Returning to my room, I eyed the outfit that I'd laid out on my bed with caution, suddenly having seconds thoughts about my dress choice. I'd never been to a black tie event before and I didn't exactly know what the appropriate attire was. I didn't have an extravagant amount of money to spend on an evening gown that I'd probably never wear again after tonight, so when I'd gone shopping with Emily, I'd picked up one of the first dresses I'd found that managed to stay within my price range while still holding an ounce of formal elegance. It was a long sleeve black dress that fell to about the middle of my thigh with a high neckline and a drooping back. Silver beading covered the majority of the back, as well as the shoulders and the ends of the sleeves.

Mulling it over for a fair few seconds, I decided that it wasn't going to get any better and slipped it on, slipping on a pair of silver heels Emily had let me borrow. I left my makeup simple — a grey smoky eye with the addition of a bit of blush and a nude lipstick that tied the look together.

As I finished cleaning up a bit, I quickly ordered a taxi to the house before throwing a few essentials into a small clutch, the doorbell sounding loudly as I did so.

"I've got it Zoe," Sara said loudly, allowing me to finish up as I heard her and Abbie bustle down the stairs, letting Ryan in.

Casting a brief glance at myself in the mirror, a smile slipped onto my face. It was amazing what a few hours could do for ones appearance.

Heading down the stairs, my movements faltered slightly when I caught sight of Ryan talking to Sara and Abbie in the foyer. I'd seen him a few times in dress clothes when he dropped by after work, and even slightly more dressed up at his cousin's wedding, but this was different. He was wearing a newly pressed suit that fit him perfectly, and although I hadn't told him what my dress looked like, I had a Emily had let it slip, as the silver tie hanging perfectly on top of his white dress shirt matched the beading on my dress.

As his eyes shifted up towards me, I forced my legs into motion, shakily moving the rest of the way down the stairs. I took notice as his eyes followed every movement I made, not stopping until I stood a few feet in front of him, a light flush of pink dusting the apples of my cheeks. His eyes trailed up and down my body slowly, taking in my outfit as I took the time to admire his own. A warm smile graced his lips as our eyes met and the butterflies inside me fluttered around mercilessly.

"You look beautiful Zoe," he said softly, leaning down to press a gentle kiss against my cheek. "But don't think that dress isn't sexy as hell," he spoke roughly as an after thought, his voice quiet enough for only me to hear before he pulled back, leaving my reply lodged in the back of my throat.

"You don't look too bad yourself," I stammered out quietly, a throaty chuckle emanating from him in reply.

"Why thank you," he winked.

"What do you think Abbie? Does you mom look pretty?" Sara cut in, breaking the spell that I seemed to be under as the two of us turned towards where her and Abbie were still standing, a noticeable smirk playing on Sara's lips.

"Yeah, you look pwetty momma!" she agreed eagerly, a toothy smile growing on her face.

"Thanks sweetie," I laughed, crouching down to bring my arms around her, "Have a good time with Sara tonight, and be a good girl alright."

"Don't worry Zoe," Sara spoke up, "Abbie and I are going to have a great night, aren't we little one?"

"Yeah!"

I sent a grateful look to Sara. "Thanks again for babysitting," I said appreciatively as I heard a car horn beep a few times. "And that'll be the cab. I left my cell number on the fridge with a few simple reminders so call if anything goes wrong, and hopefully we'll be back before midnight."

"Got it," she nodded, keeping her hand on Abbie's shoulder, "Now go have fun."

Ryan took this opportunity to offer me his arm, making me smile as I looped my hand through the crook of his elbow. I forewent my coat, knowing that it would just be an inconvenience later in the evening. As we headed down the driveway to the cab, I let go of Ryan's arm, rushing the rest of the way to the cab to avoid the chilly evening winds.

Bringing my foot up to climb into the cab, I heard a soft whistle from behind me. Glancing back curiously, I saw Ryan staring intently at the back of my dress. "Damn," he shook his head, grinning wolfishly as he caught up to me. Leaning down, he pressed his lips to mine passionately, not giving me time to respond before he pulled away. "You're too damn beautiful for your own good," he commented, his voice laced with lust as his hand trailed down the exposed skin of my back where goose bumps were quickly starting to form.

And they weren't from the cold.

When his hand trailed lower, sweeping over the material of my dress, I felt a light pain on my ass before he started nudging me into the cab. Looking up to see a smirk on his face, I bit my lip, foregoing a reply as I ducked my head, settling into the back seat of the cab where Ryan quickly joined me.

Throughout the ride the two of us somehow managed to keep a fairly civil conversation, despite the slightly steamer thoughts that were circling the back of my mind. I told him how my exams had gone and about my vague plans for the remainder of my holidays, but he took up most of the conversation, telling me about a few of the interviews he'd had earlier in the day and the new script he'd been given to look over.

When the driver pulled up at the venue almost half an hour later, I pulled out a couple of twenties from my clutch and thrust them his way before Ryan could say anything.

"You know I could've paid for the cab, right?" Ryan asked as we headed inside, his arm securely around my shoulders in an attempt to guard me from the cold, "Or better yet, I could've driven us here."

"Shh..." I said, turning to face him once we were safely inside the gallery, "I invited you tonight so I'll pay for the cab. Plus, I'm sure they have something to drink around here, so I didn't want to take the chance of either of us driving."

No sooner had I finished my sentence than a waiter with a tray of champagne filled flutes walked up to us, offering us each a drink. Nodding in appreciation, we each took our glasses, me raising mine in the air. "To being done exams and to an awesome night," I toasted.

"And to us," Ryan added.

"And to us," I repeated softly, knocking the side of my glass with his in a cheers before taking a sip, letting the bubbly liquid slide quickly down my throat.

It seemed as though we weren't the only ones taking advantage of the free drinks, as most people we passed as we walked around the gallery were holding their own drinks, keeping in time with their own conversations.

It was strange being out so publicly with Ryan by my side, especially since not many of the surrounding guests bared him a second glance, but I assumed that with the wealthy statuses that most of the people held, they weren't unfamiliar with being in the presence of someone famous. The women who did spare him a second glance however, didn't seem to be interested in him for his fame, but were merely staring at him with pure, unaltered lust in their eyes. My insides sang with pride and joy though, when I felt his hand squeeze my hip, because he chose to be here with me and not one of them.

When we settled into a corner near a rather abstract painting, I finally got a chance to take in the room. The gallery was an open-concept building, and besides the main desk at the front, no other furniture was present, just the numerous paintings and sketches that filled the walls with life. The room was also decorated sophisticatedly for the night; white and black streamers stretched from the chandelier on the ceiling to every corner of the room, those colours seemingly the theme for the night.

"Did you want to get something to eat?" Ryan ducked his head, speaking into my ear as to be heard over the soft melodic music that was playing in the background.

"You think they have chocolate?" I asked cheekily, causing him to crack a smile.

"We'll just have to find out, won't we?"

It turns out that on top of all the fancy finger foods, the gala was serving chocolate – and quite a lot of it. The two of us had shared a plate, each of us taking a handful of sweets for ourselves before retreating from the food table giddily, as though hording all of the sweets would get us kicked out.

"So, what do you think of this one?" Ryan asked a while later. We'd since finished of our sweets, though we'd grabbed another drink before beginning to peruse the art like the rest of the partygoers.

"Well, I think that the way artist used his brush so delicately and aggressively at the same time really says something about the piece," I said, talking in an exaggerated posh accent as I waved my hands over several different lines that the artist had clearly tried to highlight. "The whole thing just tells a magnificent story."

Noticing that I was simply taking the mick out of the painting, Ryan raised an eyebrow, playing along. "And what story would that be?" he asked in amusement as he took a sip from his glass.

"You know..." I trailed, failing to keep up my charade as I laughed, shaking my head. "I don't know," I admitted, looking back at the piece. It was really simple compared to some of the other works displayed around it, but when I looked at it, all I saw were a couple of black lines – all different sizes – taking up space on an otherwise blank canvas. "I mean on some level I'm sure he's an artistic genius and someone here will probably pay a lot of money for this painting, but to me it just looks like he gave his brush to a seven year old and told the kid to practice painting."

Ryan snorted at my description, forcing a sheepish smile onto my face. "At least we're on the same page," he replied, making me laugh along with him as he leaned closer to me, placing his lips against my temple for a few seconds before pulling back. "But maybe we should move on, because the people beside you looks like they want to have us thrown out of here for laughing."

Whipping my head to the side, I saw that there was indeed a group of older woman looking at the two of us in distaste, obviously having overheard what I'd just said.

I ducked my head embarrassedly into Ryan's chest, feeling him vibrate with silent laughter as he led us through the crowd, stopping in front of one of the more modern pieces in the gallery. And although it wasn't drawing many people in, in my opinion, it was one of the nicer ones displayed tonight.

"Now this is a nice painting," I pointed out. The painting in question was a modern painting of a street corner in the city. The silhouettes of people were painted dully in black while the buildings around them were vibrantly painted in colour, suggesting that the real life of the city was the city itself, not the people that walked the streets. Before I could voice any more of my opinions, Emily popped up beside the pair of us.

"Hey guys," she greeted overexcitedly, almost as though she was nervous. "Are you guys having fun?"

Ryan nodded with a smirk. "Oh yeah, only a few people here wish we were statues."

"Wait, what?" she asked, a frown of confusion causing her forehead to crinkle.

I shook my head. "Don't worry about it, some people just heard us talking about one of the paintings," I explained, changing the subject before she could question us further. "What about you? How's your night going, and where's Dustin?"

"He's over talking to my boss about something," she started, "And I think everything's going well. I've made a few sales so far to some regulars I see at the gallery, but other than that nothing special. Have you guys liked anything so far?"

"Umm, not really," I admitted sheepishly. "I mean, you know me, I don't really understand most of these fancy abstract paintings. But this one, actually, I quite liked..." I trailed off, turning to show her the painting, but she cut me off before I could.

"Oh, well I'm sure there are other paintings like this one in the gallery. Come on, I'll help you find a few," Emily suggested hurriedly, attempting to guide us away from the painting that I'd found so intriguing.

"Wait, I want to see if I know the person that painted this," I pulled back, trying to locate the artists name on the plaque underneath the piece despite Emily's protests. She quieted down when she saw I'd found it, but what I found, I definitely wasn't expecting. Swiveling my head back around, my eyes were wide in surprise as Emily face held a guilty expression. "Emily... why is your name on that painting?"

"Surprise?" she offered as a reply, shrugging her shoulder slowly with a small smile.

A wide smile spread across my face as I leaped forward and wrapped my arms around my sister tightly. "Why didn't you tell me?" I asked excitedly.

"I mean it's not that big of a deal..."

"Emily," I started, placing my hands on her shoulders, "It's a huge deal! Your work is hanging in a gallery and it's up for sale! Why aren't you more excited about this?"

Finally, I saw the first glimpse of a smile grace my little sister's lips. "I am excited," she admitted quietly, "But look around, it's not like everybody here is lining up to buy my work."

"It's still a big step Em, and I'm so proud of you," I said, hugging her again in congratulations. "And if somebody doesn't buy it tonight, that just means that more people will get to see your painting."

"Thanks," she smiled.

Another waiter came by then, followed closely by Dustin, as he exchanged Ryan and I's empty glasses with full ones, handing two more to Emily and Dustin.

"To Emily," I toasted, swishing the bubbling liquid lightly around the bottom of the flute before holding it up in the center of our small circle, "Who's on her way to living her dreams as an artist."

Emily ducked her head, leaning into Dustin's shoulder as she shyly lifted her glass. Ryan and Dustin lifted their glasses as well.

"To Emily."

Time passed and the gala started to wind down. Sold stickers were slowly posted on the side of paintings that were lucky enough to have been bought, and when I'd walked past Emily's painting the last time, I'd been ecstatic to see a small green sold sticker next to it.

Before Ryan and I headed out I'd stopped Emily, congratulating her once more on the sale of her painting as she finished closing yet another sale with an older couple. They seemed even more impressed by her as they learned she was not only working at the gallery, but also interested in art as a career, asking to see some of her other pieces at another time.

The night had truly been all about my sister, and I couldn't have been more proud.

"So, please tell me again why you thought walking home was a good idea?" Ryan asked, seemingly amused as the two of us turned off the street the gallery was on.

I shrugged, feeling the sizable amount of weight Ryan's jacket held as it rested around my shoulders. "I don't know," I admitted, swinging our intertwined hands gently between us, "I just thought it'd be nice to see some of the Christmas light displays."

I also may have been a little bit intoxicated when I'd suggested it. Oops.

"Yeah, but don't you think it'd be better to do this when it's not approaching midnight and when it's not about to rain?"

"It's not going to rain," I dismissed, shaking my head.

"Are you sure?" he asked, holding up his free hand with a smirk, "Because I'm pretty sure I just felt a few raindrops."

"I'm sure."

It seemed as though the champagne was clouding my common sense and judgment, as just a few blocks up, Ryan and I found ourselves jogging under the front awnings of random stores and cafes in an attempt to stay out of the rain.

"Okay," I breathed out, pulling him to a stop beneath one of the larger awnings that I could see on the street. Pushing my, now wet, hair out of my face, I shook my head. "Maybe you were onto something when you said it was going to rain."

"Oh you think?" he quipped smartly, although the smile on his face told me that he wasn't mad, but instead found the situation rather hilarious. Pulling his phone out from his pants pockets, he looked at me. "Now, can I please call a cab before we ruin our clothes even more?"

Nodding, I leaned back against the side of the building, pulling Ryan's damp jacket tighter around my waist in hopes of gaining some warmth.

When the cab pulled up in front of the building a few minutes later, the driver looked highly entertained to see the two of us dripping wet and shivering as we climbed into the back of his car. The traffic had long since let up so the ride home was quick, and I paid no mind as Ryan gave the driver a generous tip while I scampered my way up the driveway, unlocking the door as fast as I possibly could to escape the downpour that had started.

Still dripping wet, I slipped off Ryan's jacket and my heels before heading towards the living room. Sara was sitting comfortably on the couch, flipping through miscellaneous channels, but as she heard my footsteps, she glanced over, only to widen her eyes and unhinge her jaw in surprise.

"What happen to you guys?" she asked at last, her eyes flicking between myself and Ryan, who now stood behind me. I figured the two of us must have looked a sight, that is, if the amusement sparkling in her eyes was anything to go by.

"Before it started raining, someone decided that walking home would be a good idea," Ryan commented sarcastically, causing me to huff, mumbling an incoherent reply under my breath. "Let's just say that it wasn't the best idea."

I sighed, pushing my damp hair back out of my face. "Sorry we're late Sara," I apologized, rummaging through my clutch to find a few bills that didn't look as though they'd accidentally been run through a washing machine. Handing them to her, I continued. "I know you're probably tired from watching Abbie all night."

"That's okay," she shook her head, "Abbie and I actually watched a movie after you guys left, and it didn't take her long to fall asleep after that. Besides, it seems as though you guys are the ones who should be tired after the night you've had."

Yawning in response, I finally allowed the exhaustion to wash over me. Any effects of the alcohol I'd consumed had worn off in the rain, leaving nothing but dreariness behind. Sara took notice of this, doing her best to quickly gather her things before heading out with no more than a goodnight.

"Well, I'm beat," I pronounced lazily, another yawn escaping my mouth as I did so.

The corner of his lips twitched. "I never would've guessed."

Hitting the side of his stomach playfully, a smile grew on my face that mirrored his own. "Oh shush." I nodded up the stairs. "Did you want to come upstairs? I'm sure I have something that might fit you so you can change out of your suit."

"You sure this isn't just a way to get me out of my pants and take advantage of me?" he commented triumphantly, following me up the stairs with a grin.

Ignoring him, I simply sprinted ahead up the stairs, hoping that he didn't see the flush of pink that I felt crawling up my neck as I grabbed a pair of flannel pajamas and headed into the bathroom.

Risking a glance in the mirror, I cringed at the reflection staring back at me. My once curled hair had gone limp and frizzy in aid of the rain, and if that wasn't enough, the majority of the makeup around my eyes was now dry, having already trailed down my cheeks, staining my skin. Grabbing my face wash, I did my best to remove any evidence of makeup, feeling a bit fresher as I twisted my hair out of my face and into a braid.

"So... where is this clothes you're supposed to be lending me?" Ryan asked, his voice travelling through the crack in the door, as I hadn't shut the bathroom door fully.

"Just a second," I called back, my teeth chattering slightly as I slipped out of my wet dress, pulling on the warm and comfortable pajamas as a replacement.

Walking out of the bathroom, I saw Ryan looking at one of the pictures on my bedside table. It was a picture that Greta had taken of Abbie and I last year on Christmas morning.

"This is cute," he said softly, holding up the frame in his hands.

"Thanks," I returned, turning towards my closet to scrounge up something for him to wear.

"So, you know that Christmas is next week..." he trailed as I looked over my shoulder, raising an eyebrow at him.

"Ryan, I have a three year old; I'm well aware that Christmas is next week."

"Well..." he started, "If you're not doing anything after lunch that day, I was thinking, well actually my mom suggested it, but anyways," he rambled on, causing my forehead to crease with confusion as he took a deep breath. "Would you and Abbie want to have Christmas dinner with me and my family?"

"You want to have Christmas together?" I bit my lip, my heart feeling as though it was fluttering in my chest.

"If you want to."

"I'd loved to." His shoulders relaxed and his lips tilted upwards, wearing a grin that matched my own.

Catching the large sweatpants and extra large t-shirt I threw his way, it took me a bit by surprise when he undid his damp dress shirt, slipping it off in the middle of my bedroom. My eyes widened at his actions, and as hard as I'd been trying not to stare when the white fabric was sticking to the muscles of his stomach, it was almost impossible for me to pull my eyes away when he was completely shirtless.

I knew that my ogling wasn't going unnoticed, the vague outline of a smirk appearing on Ryan's lips as he pulled my large t-shirt over his head, obstructing the view that had caused my heart to lodge itself in my throat.

Crack.

I froze suddenly, knowing exactly what had made the sound.

I just didn't think I'd have to deal with it tonight.

Thunderstorms weren't exactly uncommon, but it didn't help that, since I'd been young, I'd never really been comfortable with the sounds that came along with them.

"Zoe."

Ryan's voice seemed to fall on deaf ears as I tried to get my breathing under control. The thunder sounded again, louder this time, making the task at hand ten times as hard as my body started to shake with fear.

"Zoe."

From what I could make out with closed eyes, his voice was more frantic this time, sensing that something was deeply wrong. I didn't take notice of him slipping on his sweatpants before he hurried towards me, wrapping his arms around me tightly in a comforting hug. Pressing my face into his chest, the familiarity of his embrace seemed to calm my racing heart. It took a few minutes of him murmuring in my ear for my breathing to even out, the lingering scent of his cologne helping just a smidge.

When I stopped shaking and I felt an ounce of control seep back into my body, I pulled back slightly, a frown on my face as I looked up at Ryan, ashamed.

"Sorry," I muttered, "Thunderstorms and me just don't mix."

My confession didn't seem to defer him in the slightest, one of his hands leaving my waist as it trailed up my arm, landing softly on my cheek. "Are you alright?" he asked, concern swimming in his eyes with a voice just above a whisper.

"Yeah," I breathed out, nodding slowly. Biting my lip as another crack of thunder hit my ears, I continued. "But do you think you could umm, stay for a while, until I fall asleep?"

"Always."

As Ryan made a move to flip the lights off, I crawled underneath the covers, finding a comfortable position before Ryan crawled on top of the blankets beside me. Although it was dark and the storm continued to roar outside my window, him laying here beside me did wonders in calming my jitters.

His arm managed to worm it's way around me, pulling me closer to him, giving me the safety blanket that I so desperately needed.

"Distract me," I yawned, snuggling further into his hold, desperately trying to ignore the sounds of the storm.

"Once upon a time in a land far, far away," he started gently, making me laugh as I felt myself beginning to relax, "There was a princess that took everyone's breath away with a mere glimpse. She was the picture of beauty and she didn't even realize it."

It wasn't long before I found myself drifting off, the smooth sound of Ryan's voice lulling me to sleep.

CHAPTER 16

"Momma."

It was early, that much was evident, as the sound of someone calling for my attention broke through my sleepy haze. The muffled sound may have been perfectly easy to ignore however, as I heard the sound again, I knew only one person who had this much persistence and energy this early in the morning.

"Momma, wake up!"

More effort was put into forcing my eyes open than need be, my vision slipping back into focus after a near-sleepless night. I'd stayed up well past two in the morning, feeling a little too festive as I wrapped the remainder of Abbie's presents and organized the living room for when she woke up.

I just didn't anticipate it being this early.

Abbie's eyes widened as she realized I was no longer asleep, a wide smile not far behind as she began bouncing in excitement on the side of my bed. "Momma, it's Christmas," she squealed, rousing me further from sleep, "We need to go see if Santa was here!"

Christmas morning seemed to knock any tiredness lingering in children's brains gone; the excitement of jolly old Saint Nick and the promise of new toys too much for them to even think about crawling back into bed.

I laughed tiredly as she struggled to pull the covers from me in the Christmas pajamas I'd slipped her into the night. "Momma's up sweetie." Pulling myself into a sitting position, my arms came around her small body, bringing her in for a hug. "Merry Christmas."

"Merry Christmas."

Wiggling out of my hold, she jumped out of the bed and waited, impatiently tapping her foot as I swung my legs out from underneath the covers. "Come on then," I yawned, stretching my arms above my head, "Let's go see what Santa's left you."

Abbie's Christmas joy couldn't be contained. Squealing in response before leaving the room in a rush, she headed downstairs to see what was waiting for her under the Christmas tree. Trailing behind her, I shook my head in silent laughter as my eyes caught the time.

6:02

Entering the living room, I smiled, watching Abbie crawl around the base of the Christmas tree, eyeing all the newly wrapped presents to see which ones had her name scrawled on the tag.

"Santa left me two gifts momma, and a s'ocking!" Her eyes sparkling as she turned to see the table, where a messed up plate of cookies laid. "And he ate his food!"

"It looks like he did," I grinned, walking over to clean up the small mess I'd made a few hours earlier. "I'll just put this in the kitchen," I said, picking up the plate and half empty glass of milk, "And then you can start opening your presents."

She nodded excitedly, climbing up onto the couch as I turned, heading towards the kitchen. What did surprise my though, was seeing Emily already awake, leaning against the counter as she waited for the coffee maker to finish dripping.

"Hey, did Abbie wake you up?" I winced, dropping the dirty dishes into the sink, setting a mental reminder for myself to wash them later.

Emily shook her head. "Dustin's coming to get me just after nine, so I figured we'd do Christmas early," she responded, filling up two mugs with coffee, sliding one towards me after filling it with milk and a generous helping of sugar.

I gave her a grateful smile, tilting the warm cup of liquid energy to my lips to take a sip. "Just promise me you didn't buy my daughter more stuff than I did," I commented cheekily as we made our way back to where Abbie was patiently waiting to open her gifts.

"Not a chance," she smirked, lowering her voice before she continued, "I don't fancy playing the role of Santa Claus for at least another few years."

Shaking my head, her remark went without a reply as I took a seat next to Abbie. "Did you want to open the presents in your stocking first?" I asked Abbie, who smiled widely, nodding her head as she sat down in front of it.

Wrapping paper started to decorate the floor in seconds as she began the unwrapping process. Her stocking wasn't full of much; just a bunch of cheap toys I'd picked up from the dollar store. By the time she was done there was a pile of play-doh, colouring books, and art supplies next to her empty stocking, along with a horde of chocolate.

"Can I open the big ones now?" Abbie asked, turning to me with comically wide eyes and a puppy dog pout.

She sprung up from her seat as I nodded, wrapping her arms around the present that was quite a bit bigger than her before ripping at the paper. Not able to contain her excitement as she unveiled her present, a high-pitched squeal escaped her lips. "A doll house!" She dropped to her knees again, quickly unwrapping Santa's other gift, which was, to no surprise, another doll.

Those presents seemed to exhaust all of her attention, as she sat for a good couple minutes inspecting the box of the doll house while cradling her new doll in her lap.

"Abbie," Emily said, catching my daughter's attention, "Do you want to open the rest of your gifts now?"

"There's more?"

Emily stood up from her chair. "Mhm," she replied, sorting through the gifts underneath the tree until there were two separate piles in front of her. "These," she pointed to one stack, "Are from me, and these," she gestured to the other pile, "Are from your mom."

Hyper as ever, she chose the present closest to her first, ripping off the paper as best as she could to reveal an art set I knew she'd been wanting for a while now.

When all was said and done, Abbie had done quite well for herself. While Emily had bought her a My Little Pony board game, as well as a pair of winter pajamas, I'd mostly stuck to clothes, figuring she'd need them in the new year when she started to grow again.

Discarded wrapping paper and bows were cluttered around her as I let her dip into her newly acquired chocolate supply. Freezing with half a piece of chocolate hanging out of her mouth, she stood up in a hurry, looking shocked and flustered. "Oh no, I forgot your pwesents," she said in a rush, bounding back up the stairs before either Emily or myself could say anything.

"She got us presents?" Emily asked, bewildered at the thought as I shrugged my shoulders. To my knowledge I didn't know of any presents and I had no idea what my little angel had planned.

She came bouncing down the stairs again a few seconds later, a smile now on her face as she held two pieces of paper in her hands. "I made you cards," she said, stating the obvious as she handed us each a folded piece of paper. She'd drawn the three of us together on the front of each of them, but where mine had a Christmas tree scribbled in the background, Emily's had a bunch of presents piled together.

Opening the inside, I saw that she'd tried her best to write Merry Christmas Mommy, and while she'd missed a couple of letters, the gesture still put a smile on my face. "This is really thoughtful Abbie, thank you."

Pulling her close, Emily joined in on the hug not long after, thanking her as well for her card.

A few minutes passed, and when I finished setting Abbie up at the table with a bowl of cereal and her new doll, I turned to Emily. "Do you want your presents now?"

She grinned in response. "You mean you actually got me something this year?"

It was true. We hadn't lived together last year and since she didn't come home for Christmas, I'd simply sent her a Christmas card with a gift card inside to one of her favourite restaurants. We normally didn't exchange gifts, the last time being when we lived under the same roof back home, but this year, I didn't feel right not to get her anything.

I rolled my eyes. "Of course I did."

Grabbing the gifts from underneath the tree, I passed her the first two, watching as she opened a book that she'd said she wanted to read and a set of new paints. Biting my lip as she thanked me, I passed over her final present nervously. "Now I don't know if you'll actually like it, but I saw you looking at it that day in the store, and, yeah."

Sending me a curious glance, she continued unwrapping the present until she pulled it from its box. Her eyes were wide as she looked up at me. "You went back for it?" she asked in awe, holding the short floral dress I'd bought on a whim up against her body. "Thank you," she smiled, wrapping her arms around me.

I let out the breath I'd been holding. "So you like it?"

She nodded. "I love it. I might even wear it today," she told me as she pulled two of her own presents from under the tree. "And these are for you."

I smiled gratefully, opening the larger one first, only to see a cardboard box full of assorted chocolates and sweets. "You're just trying to fatten me up, aren't you?"

Her own grin grew on her face as she shrugged innocently. "Maybe."

I laughed, pushing the box onto the coffee table before unwrapping the other present. It was significantly smaller than the box of chocolate, but as I pulled back the wrapping paper to reveal a velvet box only fit to hold jewelry, it made sense. I held my breath as I flipped the clasp open, a little bit relieved to see that there was no extravagant diamonds in the box. Instead, a small bracelet sat tucked in between the fabric, the word sister engraved on a charm that hung from one side. "Thank you," I said as I ran my hand over the charm, "It's beautiful."

"It's not much," she responded, "But I didn't want to go over-board."

"No," I shook my head, pulling her in for a hug for what felt like the fifth time that morning, "It's perfect. Thank you."

She grinned, leaning back. "Merry Christmas Zoe."

"Merry Christmas."

"But are you sure it's not stupid?"

It was almost noon now as I held my phone between my shoulder and my cheek, leaning forward to glaze the last bit of mascara onto my lashes.

Dustin had been by hours ago, picking up Emily to take her to his family's Christmas brunch. On the way out he'd turned to where Abbie and I sat in the living room, tuning in to the television as a showing of Frosty the Snowman aired, and tossed us each a wrapped present. It wasn't much, but he'd gifted Abbie with a stuffed elephant while I received yet another box of chocolates before the two smoothly made their exit.

"Your gift for Ryan isn't stupid. I would know, I helped you pick it out," Colette replied, her voice travelling through the speaker.

I was jittery and nervous it seemed, as I tried to force a smile in front of the mirror. "But what if..."

"No what if's," she cut me off, "Ryan will love whatever present he gets just because it's from you. And if all else fails, you could always just sleep with him to make him happy."

"Colette!" I squeaked in surprise, heat flooding to my cheeks at her suggestion.

"What? It's a solid idea. Unless," she trailed, "Have you not yet?" My prolonged silence was enough of an answer for her as she let loose a low whistle. "Really?"

"No," I mumbled under my breath.

"Well I'm just saying, maybe it's something you should start thinking about," she quipped jokingly, causing a bubble of laughter to escape me. I heard someone calling Colette's name through the phone. "And that's my cue," she sighed, "I'll see you at work later in the week."

"Merry Christmas Colette," I wished, a smile on my face as she returned the sediment before hanging up.

Sliding the phone into my back pocket, I turned to face the mirror. After talking to Ryan earlier and learning that this dinner wasn't anything fancy, I'd thrown on one of my Christmas sweaters with a pair of dark jeans. Skipping into my room, Abbie made me look as though I was barely trying at all with her bright red dress, pigtails, and a festive pair of reindeer antlers. Carrying the presents she'd picked out for Rocky in her hands, she waddled towards me, looking up. "When's Ryan coming?"

"He'll be here soon sweetie," I patted her head, readjusting the antlers that were slowly slipping forward on her head as the doorbell rang. I smiled. "That'll be him, why don't you go answer the door."

Whether it was because of the extra sugar she'd consumed so far today or just because Christmas made her excited, she bounced back out of my room without so much as a nod to wish my boyfriend a Merry Christmas.

Dubbing my outfit good enough, I pulled the bag that contained wrapped presents for Ryan's family out from the back of my closet. I hadn't gone overboard, but since they'd been nice enough to invite me over, I'd gotten his parents and brother each a small gift. Double-checking that all of them were in there, I piled Ryan's presents on the top before heading downstairs.

"I didn't want Rocky to miss out on pwesents, so I got him a toy," I heard Abbie explaining to Ryan as I entered the living room, smiling as I saw her sitting on Ryan's lap. "I also got him treats so when you go home he can have them."

"I'm sure he'll love them," Ryan grinned, tickling her gently before his head swiveled around to face me. He was wearing a tight fitting wool sweater and a dark pair of jeans, and even when he wasn't all polished up, he still made my heart flip with a simple smile. "Hey, Merry Christmas."

"You too," I grinned, leaning down to peck his cheek lightly, making sure not to leave a lipstick mark as I pulled away. "Are you ready to go?"

The drive took longer than it should have, with everyone in the city out on the roads and on their way to meet their families. The three of us ended up spending almost an hour in the car, Disney tunes playing from the radio until Ryan pulled into a suburban area, just outside of the main city.

The neighbourhood was quiet and the house was modest, the roof decorated with hanging lights while store bought statues took up space on the front lawn.

"Are we here?" Abbie asked as Ryan parked his car behind his parent's.

Turning off the ignition, he smiled and nodded. "Yup," he replied, causing Abbie to squeal in excitement, "So, let's get inside."

"We're here," Ryan announced as the three of us stepped into the house, presents in hand.

His mother was the one that came rushing around the corner, an apron on her waist as she pulled her son into a hug. "Merry Christmas," she cheered, patting his sides as she pulled back, "Have you been eating properly, it's like you've lost weight."

Laughing, he leaned down, shaking his head as he kissed her cheek. "Merry Christmas mom."

"We'll just have to fatten you up with dinner, won't we?" she responded smartly, cracking a smile before she turned to me. "It's nice to see you again Zoe."

"You too Sophie," I replied, returning the hug that she stepped forward to give me.

"And I hear that this one," she nodded in her son's direction, a smirk on her face, "Finally worked up the courage to ask you to go out with him."

"Mom," Ryan groaned in embarrassment, though his smile didn't disappear as I laughed lightly.

Smiling sheepishly, I said, "Yeah."

"Well I think it's great he's finally found someone he can bring around," she said, making me smile as I saw Ryan roll his eyes beside me. She looked down at Abbie, adoration in her eyes. "Hi Abbie."

"Hi," she chirped, bouncing in her spot with a toothy grin on her face, "Merry Chris'mas."

"Merry Christmas sweetie," she laughed, nodding towards the living room. "Why don't the three of you get settled in the living room while I finish getting some of the food ready."

Ryan nodded as Abbie ran ahead, scurrying her way further into the house. "Sure mom," he said, intertwining his hand with mine as he pulled me in the direction Abbie had gone.

I smiled as I saw pictures in the hung up in the hallway of Ryan and Dean when they were younger. They were both smiling widely at the camera most of the time, except one picture near the end where they were both covered in mud. Ryan, looking as though he was going through his awkward phase, had a young Dean clinging to his leg and was looking down at him in annoyance.

Entering the living room, Sophie excused herself into the kitchen while I saw Abbie climbing up to sit beside Dean, who looked more than happy to make a little extra room between him and his dad. Like the rest of his family, Dean seemed to have taken quite a liking to my little girl, smiling down at her widely as she showed him her reindeer antlers.

"Hey son," Ryan's dad waved, noticing the two of us first, "And it's good to see you Zoe."

"So..." Dean trailed teasingly, raising an eyebrow suspiciously as his gaze flicked between his brother and I, "How's it going?"

Ryan's fingers slipped from mine as he walked over to his brother, who was still grinning, and wrapped an arm around his neck. Abbie was laughing whole-heartedly, where as I chuckled to myself, as he started to mess up his brother's hair. "Good, how about you?" Ryan asked, leaning down to plant a big kiss on Dean's cheek.

"Worse now that you're here," he threw back as Ryan let up, wiping the saliva off his cheek with a screwed up smile.

And that's when Sophie walked in, a platter of finger foods in her hands. "Now what's everybody so fussed up about?"

"Oh nothing," Ryan replied with a smirk, nodding to the empty love seat next to where I stood. I took a seat, only getting comfortable when Ryan sat down beside me. "Just saying hello."

"Sure..." his mom trailed, shaking her head in amusement. "So," she clapped, "Who's ready for presents?"

Abbie's eyes went wide. "More pwesents?"

Just as I was about to correct her, telling her that no, there weren't any more presents for her, Dean jumped in. "Yeah, just wait one second okay," he said, jumping up from his spot beside her, rushing into the next room over.

I turned to Ryan with accusing eyes. "They bought her a present?" I asked under my breath.

He smiled innocently. "It's from me too if that helps."

"Of course it is," I mumbled, biting my lip as I heard Dean's footsteps returning. When he rounded the corner however, my jaw just about unhinged and my eyes went wide.

"EEEP!" Abbie squealed in excitement, her eyes landing on her present. It was a bright purple Fisher Price car, seemingly just her size as she jumped in the driver's seat, not wanting to wait to test it.

"What?" Ryan shrugged, putting on a face of innocence as I turned to look at him. "It's just a present."

"A present that you guys really didn't need to get her."

"And you're telling me that bag of yours doesn't have at least one present for my family in it?" he asked, raising an eyebrow.

"I mean... yeah," I stammered, before shaking my head, "But that's not the same thing. They aren't as expensive as..."

Ryan's hand was suddenly on my lips, preventing me from continuing. "It is the same thing," he claimed, "And we all pitched in, so don't worry about it."

I sighed, letting the conversation drop as I saw the grin Abbie was still sporting, listening to Dean as he showed her how to work her new toy.

The rest of the presents weren't as good as Abbie's, at least in her opinion, as the two of us sat back and let the Adam's exchange presents with one another. After they finished I'd taken the three presents I'd gotten for them out from my bag, leaving Ryan's present to sit in the bottom of the bag until we exchanged them later. I'd gotten his mom a candle and his dad a box of chocolate, while Dean unwrapped a quirky t-shirt I'd found at the mall that had the words iron man scrawled across the front, along with a cartoon of an iron.

Returning their thanks, I was a little surprised when Dean threw a bag from Victoria's Secret my way, earning a glare from his brother before the two of us realized it was simply a few body sprays and lotions.

The afternoon passed quickly, conversation lively as Sophie went back and forth between the kitchen and the living room, allowing me to help out where I could.

When dinner was served shortly after five 'o'clock, the six of us gathered around the table to eat, Abbie being the first to pop open her Christmas cracker in excitement. Once we'd followed her lead, opening our own crackers, the paper crowns sat atop our heads as we laughed, joked, and ate. It was rare that I got to spend moments like this, with my parents being so tuned out of my life the last few years, and yet, I managed to feel just as home here with Ryan's family as I ever had.

The food was delicious and by the time everybody was finished, I felt like I could've fallen into a food comma after the extra portions I'd helped myself too. It didn't look like I was alone, because as we migrated to the living room, Dean was the first to collapse on one of the couches, stretching out as he groaned in protest. His dad put a movie on, knowing that dessert was a long time off for most of us, and as we all took our seats to watch Dr. Seuss's: How The Grinch Stole Christmas, I couldn't help but feel the comfort and warmth the day had brought.

'This is how a real Christmas with your family should feel,' I thought, snuggling further into Ryan's arms.

An hour after the movie had finished, Abbie was playing a game of go-fish with Dean on the ground while I sat back and watched, having already lost the first three games.

"Zoe honey, can you go see what's keeping Ryan?" Sophie asked from where her and her husband were relaxing on the next couch over.

Ryan had disappeared before the cards had even been brought out, and even though I'd noticed his absence, I hadn't thought to ask if something was wrong.

I nodded. "Sure," I replied, receiving a smile in reply as I headed towards the kitchen.

With no signs of him in the kitchen, I peeked around the corner, looking left and right down the halls before I caught notice of the back door, not properly shut. Making my way down the hall, I pulled my sweater down over my hands, crossing my arms as I stepped out onto the back porch.

"Hey."

Although my voice was soft, it was enough to catch Ryan's attention from his position up against the railing, his head turning over his shoulder to look at me. "Hey."

"Your mom was wondering where you got off to," I stated, nodding back to the door as I took a seat on an old wooden swing bench that was rested up against the house.

"And she sent you to come and find me?" he asked, the tips of his lips tilting upwards into a smile.

"I guess she figured you'd like it more if I was the one to come and wrangle your ass back inside."

He chuckled. "Well, she was right."

Coming to sit next to me, he pulled me into his side as I looked up at him. "So... what were you doing out here?"

"Just thinking," he replied, moving a piece of hair out of my face before elaborating. "I miss it here sometimes. When I lived here everything was just so simple. I grew up here. I wasn't some big Hollywood star that people wanted to get to know; I was just a scrawny kid that got teased because he liked drama and science and wasn't the best at sports."

"You liked science?" I asked curiously, having not known that about him.

"Yeah." He nodded. "Before I got into drama I used to be the kid that built wooden planes from those model kits and tried to do science experiments with some of my mom's fancy shampoo." I smiled at his confession. "I started to pursue acting as soon as high school was over, and went threw a lot of rejections before I booked my first role. I had one line as an extra of a movie, but I just remember being the happiest I'd ever been when I got that call. My parents were so happy for me." He shook his head, a small smile gracing his lips. "They've always been there to support me."

"And they always will be."

"Yeah," he trailed off, his gaze slipping to the vast backyard before coming back to me. "I just wish there were more days like this, you know?"

I smiled, nodding before leaning up slightly to press my lips lightly against his. "I do," I said softly, my voice just above a whisper as I pulled back.

Neither of us spoke for the next few minutes, reveling in the silence until I saw him reach his hand into his pants pocket, pulling out a small wrapped box. Holding it out to me, a nervous smile on his lips, he nodded down to it. "For you."

Biting my lip, I pulled the wrapping paper from the box, unveiling a velvet box that held two small emerald earrings. They matched perfectly with the necklace he'd bought me for my birthday. "These are beautiful," I stated with awe, running my thumb over them as they sparkled in the moonlight.

"Which is why I thought they were perfect for you."

My heart had flipped and turned many times before, but what I felt then was completely different. It was as if something had lit a fire in my stomach, the sparks igniting large enough to scorch my heart. It was an overwhelming wave of passion that I'd never experienced before, and although the feeling was foreign, it wasn't utterly unwelcome.

"I, umm, I'll be right back," I sputtered out, kissing his cheek quickly before heading back inside. It wasn't that I didn't know what to say, although that may have been a contributing factor, but now, as I gripped the earrings in my hand, I didn't know how Ryan would feel about my gift. It certainly wasn't as extravagant as emerald earrings, but hopefully, he'd at least appreciate the thought I'd put into it.

Slipping back into the living room, I tried to bypass the curious eyes of his family and Abbie as I snatched up the two boxes remaining in the bag I'd brought, being as quiet as I could. Despite my best efforts, I was certain that all eyes were on my back as I headed back out the way I'd come.

"Sorry about that," I said nervously, stepping out onto the back porch once again. Settling myself next to Ryan once again, I handed him the smaller of the two boxes first. "Here," I started, continuing to ramble nervously as he unwrapped it. "It's not much but I thought you could use a new pair, and I thought it'd be kind of a joke, with you always wearing them when we go out..."

I stopped as Ryan finished unwrapping the pair of sunglasses I'd bought him, trying to gage his reaction. "Do you like them?"

A chuckle escaped him as he pulled the glasses from their sleeve, slipping them on. "Do I look like a movie star yet?"

I let out an airy laugh as I realized he wasn't making fun of them, seemingly understanding the slight joke to the gift. "Totally," I grinned, passing him the remaining box that lay in my lap. "Now this is your main gift," I said, waiting anxiously for him to take it, "And you can tell me if you don't like them."

Ryan ripped open the wrapping paper, flipping open the flaps of the cardboard box that it covered to reveal two patterned dress shirts. I'd noticed, over the past few months that he'd been in my life, that although he dressed up quite frequently for interviews and press junkets, I'd never seen him wear more than plain, old dress shirts. I'd bought him one with small polka dots and one that was a red and navy floral print, but still, as I watched him take them out of the box, I wasn't quite sure if he'd like them.

He turned, raising an eyebrow at me. "I love them," he grinned, pulling me into a hug. Pushing any thoughts of rejection out of my mind, I broke out in a smile as I laid my head against his chest. "I'll be sure to wear one next time I have an interview."

"You really don't have to do that."

"But I want to," he counteracted swiftly, kissing the tip of my nose. "Now, why don't we get back to the living room? They're probably wondering what's taking us so long."

I nodded, waiting as Ryan packed his presents back into their boxes before intertwining my fingers with his as we headed back indoors. Entering the living room, we dropped our gifts back into the bag I'd brought before relaxing into one of the empty couches. Abbie was sitting in between Ryan's mom and dad, her eyes trained on the television as Rudolph the Red-Nosed Reindeer played.

"Where'd Dean go?" Ryan asked, looking to his parents as he noticed his little brother's sudden absence. They simply shrugged, not replying, although the amusement that shone in their eyes as they glanced towards us was enough to put me on edge. Ryan must've caught it to, as his eyes narrowed, staring at them accusingly. "What?"

A split second passed before Dean appeared behind our couch, popping out of nowhere to surprise both his brother and I. As I jumped however, my eyes caught onto the small green plant that he held in his hand, swinging it just above Ryan's head and mine.

Mistletoe.

Ryan brought his arm out to slap his brother's chest, one of the only places reachable from his current position on the couch. "You little brat," he laughed, not seeming that bothered by his brother's antics.

Dean shrugged, a smug grin on his face. "It's tradition."

My cheeks were already ablaze with heat as Ryan's eyes met mine, and it didn't even feel like a second had passed before his lips were on mine. It a sweet and innocent kiss, our lips slotted together perfectly as one of his hands cupped my chin, the other threading around my waist to pull me impossibly close.

I was almost positive that, somewhere in the distance, one of his family members had managed to catch a photo of the two of us, and even though I should've been embarrassed, I wasn't.

I guess that's what Christmas was really about; letting all your worries go as you spend time with the ones you love, no matter how chaotic it may be. And as I pulled back, resting my head comfortably in the crook of Ryan's neck, I didn't think there was a way to make this day any better.

CHAPTER 17

"**H**ow about this one?"

Stepping out of my en-suite, I smoothed out the bottom of the dress, biting my lip as I tried to gauge Emily's reaction.

It was New Year's Eve and Ryan had invited me out to an A-list nightclub that one of his friends owned.

To say I was nervous was an understatement. I'd never been one that enjoyed a night out all that often, let alone one that included the definite possibility of mingling amongst the higher class. The burning question of what to wear also posed a dilemma. I didn't want to stand out, but I also didn't want to be the only one not dressed to the nines. After asking Ryan about it, who'd been of no help, I'd gone to Emily for advice. Now, what felt like hours later, we were still in my room, going through all the dresses that the both of us owned.

Emily, who was sitting on my bed with a magazine in hand, looked up and smiled. "It's gorgeous Zoe, just like the last five you've tried on."

Turning towards the mirror I scrutinized the dress. It was form fitting, hugging all my curves, and stopped about mid thigh. The entirety of the dress was made of sequins, bar the sheer bits falling down the arms, and although it was a little flashy, I didn't think it looked all that bad. "You don't think it's a little..." I trailed, attempting and failing to bring the front of the dress up higher on my chest, "Risqué?"

"Trust me Zoe," she laughed, "No one is going to be complaining about a little bit of cleavage, especially not Ryan. Hell, I'd be impressed if he could keep his hands off of you at all in that dress."

My cheeks flushed a bright shade of crimson at what she was insinuating. "You think?"

Emily nodded, a smirk appearing on her lips. "Just be mindful that I don't want to see you guys stumbling through the door after midnight looking to tear each other's clothes off."

I didn't think that there was much she could say to make my blush any more prominent, but evidently there was, as I felt the heat from my cheeks trail down my neck. "Oh shut up," I mumbled, turning my back towards her in embarrassment as I mindlessly shuffled through some of my makeup.

"Hey, is that any way to thank the person taking care of your daughter tonight?"

Freezing in place for a moment, I slowly turned around, a sheepish smile on my face when I saw her eyebrow raised. "Have I said thank you for that yet?"

"Only about a hundred times."

"Really Emily, thank you," I repeated, my voice sincere as I smiled in appreciation.

When Ryan had asked me to go out tonight, I'd been very apprehensive about agreeing, as I knew that there was a slim chance that I would be able to find a babysitter for Abbie. However, when I brought the issue up with Emily, wondering if she knew anyone who could look after her other than Dustin's little sister, she surprised me by volunteering on the spot. I tried to object, not wanting to ruin her New Years plans, but she wasn't having it and was adamant that a night in with Dustin was all she needed for the night to be special.

A smile that mirrored mine appeared on her face as she waved me off. "Really, it's not a problem."

"I still feel bad..."

"Well don't," she cut me off. "Abbie will probably be asleep before you even leave tonight, so all you have to do is sit and wait until you're whisked off by your knight in shining armour to have a night that you'll never forget." Her eyes were twinkling with amusement as she continued, waving me back into my en-suite. "Now hurry up and get changed. You promised you were cooking dinner tonight, and it'd be a shame if anything happened to that dress before Ryan got to see you in it."

I shook my head and stifled a laugh, but turned and headed back into my en-suite without a reply.

Dinner ended up being quick and easy. I'd lightly seasoned a few chicken breasts before throwing them in the oven, and while they were cooking, I'd tossed together a simple vegetable stir-fry. It was healthy, it was simple, and it was delicious.

After the dishes had been done and the extra food put away, I'd left Abbie and Emily watching a children's program on the television as I headed upstairs for a shower. Stepping out of the bathroom minutes later, a towel wrapped around my body, I pulled out a lacy set of undergarments, slipping them on before I stepped into my dress.

Looking in the mirror now, I felt better about the dress. I appreciated the way it accentuated my body in all the right ways, and it wasn't all that flashy, which would make it easier for me to blend in with a crowd.

Not wanting to seem too formal, I'd opted to straighten my hair after drying it, leaving it to hang freely just below my shoulders. I then moved on to my makeup, keeping it as simple as I could before adding a dark berry shade of lipstick as a finishing touch.

"Momma."

Turning to see Abbie loitering in my doorway, I smiled softly as I noticed she'd already changed into a pair of princess pajamas and had a teddy hair tucked loosely under her arm.

"Yes?"

"Can you tuck me in?" she yawned, bringing a hand up to sleepily rub at her eyes. Looking at the clock, I saw that it was already after eight.

Where had the time gone?

"Of course," I replied quietly, grabbing her hand as I led her towards her bedroom, "Come on then."

Pushing open the door to her room Abbie's grip fell from my hand as she stumbled tiredly into her bed. Following behind her, I waited until she stopped wiggling around, her head lying comfortably on her pillow, before tucking her covers snuggly around her.

"You look pwetty," she mumbled quietly, her eyes shutting on their own accord, "I hope you have fun tonight."

"Thanks sweetie," I smiled, pushing some of her hair back from her face. Leaning down, I placed a soft kiss right above her temple. "Sweet dreams." Flicking her night-light on, I slowly backed out of the room as I heard her sound snores slowly start to fill the air.

Knowing that Ryan was due to pick me up any minute now, I scurried back to my room and packed my cell phone, ID, keys, and some cash into a small black purse. Emily and Dustin, who were cuddled together on the couch watching a movie, greeted me as I came downstairs, a pair of silver heels in my hand.

"So Abbie's asleep," I started, bending over to slip the shoes onto my feet, "And hopefully she won't wake up and cause you two too much trouble."

"Zoe," Emily spoke, her head turned towards me as she spoke, "Like I've said already, don't worry about it. We'll be fine. It's not like we haven't looked after her before."

"I just don't know how late I'll be home."

Emily cut off my rambling with a smirk. "If you even come home." The pink spots that blossomed on my cheeks were enough to make both her and Dustin chuckle. "Look, just forget about us and have fun tonight okay. You look too good to waste your night worrying."

"Thanks," I mumbled shyly, hearing a knock on the front door just as my blush finally subsided.

Emily grinned, nodding towards the front door. "Go on, your knight awaits."

Scrambling to the entryway, I pulled open the door to reveal Ryan, dressed in a burgundy dress shirt and a pair of black jeans.

"Hey, sorry for knocking. I would've rung the doorbell but I didn't want Abbie to..." he started, stepping inside as he spoke. His voice faltered as his eyes landed on me, his speech beginning to stutter. "Umm... oh wow, you look gorgeous."

His hand came up to move a few stray hairs away from my face, his thumb gently caressing my cheek as he did so. I leaned into his touch with a smile on my face. "Thanks," I said softly, my eyes leaving his for a moment as they trailed down his body, "You don't look too bad yourself."

A grin appeared on his lips before he closed the gap between us. His lips were soft but needy, and from just a few seconds of contact they were able to make my stomach tighten and toes curl.

I was the one who pulled back however, giggling as I brought my hand up to rub the purple tinge of lipstick from his lips. "Maybe you shouldn't have kissed me."

He didn't seem to find it a problem, as he leaned in once more to peck my lips again. "You mean like that?" he asked cheekily, raising an eyebrow.

"Just like that," I nodded, taking a peek in the mirror to my left to see that, surprisingly enough, my lipstick hadn't been smeared at all in the process.

"I'll let you in on a secret," he whispered, leaning closer so that his breathe fanned my ear as I felt the slight scratch of his stubble rub against my cheek. "It's going to take a lot more than a bit of lipstick to keep me from kissing you."

The sensual undertones of his voice were enough to make my cheeks flare up once more as I turned back towards him, my eyes meeting his own. I had no reply for him. My words were lodged in the back of my throat as the silence around us sparked with electricity.

He seemed to realize he'd somehow been able to render me speechless, the corners of his tilting up into a smile. He nodded towards the door. "Do you want to head out?"

"Yeah, that sounds good," I nodded, regaining my voice as the conversation steered away from the dangerous waters it'd been treading in previously.

Stepping outside with him, hand in hand as the door closed behind us, my eyes widened slightly at what I saw in front of me. Instead of Ryan's usual car, a sleek black limo sat at the end of my driveway, and although it didn't stretch out all that long, it still seemed a tad too much for just the two of us.

"What, no horse drawn carriage?" I asked teasingly, walking beside him as we headed for the car.

The chauffeur stood out on the curb, opening the door for us as we approached. "Maybe next year," he winked jokingly, making me laugh as we shuffled into our seats.

Driving downtown on one of the busiest nights of the year was sure to be a pain, with more than half the city out and celebrating, and as we sat stuck in traffic, the stereo system played out a smooth mix of music.

"So, are you excited to only have one more semester left of school?" Ryan asked, his fingers intertwined with mine.

I shifted my head from where it had rested on his shoulder. "More like terrified," I admitted, ducking my head as my gaze landed on the seam of my dress. "There are only a few months left until I'm no longer sitting in a class everyday learning about the world, instead I'll be out there living it. I'll have to find a full-time job, which will be hard enough to come by, but on top of that, I still have to look for an 8-week placement for the end of the term to even be eligible for my degree."

"Hey," Ryan said, his hand coming up to cup my chin as he turned my gaze back to him, "It might seem scary now, but it'll all work out in the end." A soft smile appeared on my lips at his encouraging words. "Plus, if you ever need a recommendation letter I'd be happy to write one. I'm sure a lot of magazines would love to hire you if they knew how close you were to one of Hollywood's finest celebrities."

I laughed and shook my head, grateful for the mood change as he grinned. "No thanks," I replied, pecking his lips, "I think I'd rather fight this battle on my own."

"And that's what makes you so admirable," he said softly, making my forehead ripple in confusion. "You could easily use me to better your career as a journalist," he added, his eyes scanning my face, almost as though he was trying to commit this moment to memory, "But you aren't. You're completely content with taking your fate into your own hands and just letting me sit beside you through it all as your biggest supporter."

"You might be my second biggest supporter though," I counter-acted, trying not to think about how raw and true his words truly were, "Abbie's got you beat by just a bit."

He smiled. "Second biggest supporter then."

"And thank you, for saying that," I continued, "You know I'd never use your job to further mine."

"I know you wouldn't, which makes this", he paused, squeezing my hand for emphasis, "All the more real to me."

And he kissed me then, showing me in one simple movement the truth that laid behind all the words he did and didn't say.

I was taken by surprise as the car lurched to a stop at what looked to be a dead-end road, but as the chauffeur appeared to open the door and Ryan climbed out, it seemed as though it wasn't a mistake. This was our stop.

"So," I started, climbing out the limo as Ryan offered me his hand, "Where exactly are we?"

"We're at the club," Ryan replied, gesturing vaguely to the one story building across the street.

Eyeing the building in front of us, I was skeptical. If it wasn't for the people walking through the entrance, all dressed to the nines and ready to impress, I would've never guessed that a nightclub laid just a few steps through the front doors.

Intertwining his fingers with my own, I allowed him to lead me across the street, and after giving our names to the guard at the door, we were led inside where the night seemed to just be getting started, despite it being just shy of nine 'o'clock. While the crowd wasn't all that large yet, the music had already started to blast from the speakers.

As I took in the space, I realized that there were two levels to the clubs. The top level, and the one we were on, seemed to have booths and other seating options spread out over the area while two bars, one on either side, served drinks to paying customers. The bottom level however, which was built into the basement of the club, could be over looked from where we were standing. There was a dance floor that spread across the entirety of the level, as well as a DJ booth at the front where two men were currently spinning their tracks.

"How is this place not more popular?" I asked, raising my voice to be heard above the music as I followed Ryan towards the nearest bar.

"My friend was pretty selective when he opened this place a while back," Ryan started, nodding towards a pair of empty stools at the end of the bar. "He didn't want just anyone coming in and causing trouble, so he left it pretty low key. The place isn't advertised much, and the only ways to get your name put on the list are to know the owner, have connections, or be willing to pay quite a lot of money for a good time. Unless you're here with someone, if your name isn't on the list outside, the bouncers won't let you through."

I raised my eyebrows. "Seriously?"

"Seriously," he nodded before flagging down the man behind the bar. "Do you want a drink?"

"Sure," I replied, eyeing the menu behind the board, "I'll have a strawberry daiquiri."

"You like the fruity drinks, huh?" Ryan commented with a smile as I shrugged in response. He turned to the bartender, relaying him my order. "And I'll have a jack and coke," he added, sliding a twenty dollar bill across the bar.

"The drinks are expensive," I muttered as I grabbed my drink, low enough so that nobody but Ryan would be able to hear me.

He laughed in return, taking a sip of his drink before resting it down on the counter. "Yeah," he agreed. "When my friend started to get a lot of repeat business he started jacking up the prices, knowing that the people who came here could afford to spend a few extra bucks on a drink."

"Telling lies about me again Ryan?" a new voice added teasingly, his hand clamping down on Ryan's shoulder as he hovered behind him.

Ryan rolled his eyes. "But where was the lie David?" he shot back with a grin before waving his hand between the two of us. "David, this is Zoe. Zoe, this is David, the owner of this place." I set my drink down next to Ryan's, waving hello with a smile on my face.

David nodded down at me in return, a smile on his lips. "So, you're the girl that this one can never stop going on about."

"I guess I am," I answered, laughing lightly as I saw the tips of Ryan's ears tinge a dark shade of pink. "Anyways, how do you two know each other?"

"I was friends with one of his cousins when we were younger," David started to explain, "But we ended up going to the same high school so we hung out a lot as we got older."

"He also failed to mention how I helped him design and build this place when I was looking for a way to pass the time between auditions," Ryan added on. I raised an eyebrow, more than a little impressed by that.

"It slipped my mind," David smirked as a crowd of men called his name from across the floor. "Well it looks like I'm needed elsewhere. You two have a good night, and just tell the bartender that I said your next few drinks are on me."

"Thanks man," Ryan said before David turned and walked away.

I grabbed my drink from the bar, taking a sip of the sweet and tangy liquid. "He seems nice."

"Mhm," Ryan agreed, "It feels like I've known him forever." And from there our conversation took a turn, varying from stories of our adolescence to random tidbits about our lives that we had yet to share.

When both our drinks sat empty on the bar top, Ryan turned to me. "Do you want to dance?" Ryan asked. He nodded down to the bottom level, where a fair few more people had migrated to the dance floor since we'd arrived.

Biting my lip, I nodded, accepting his hand as we headed down the stairs and onto the dance floor. Pushing our way through the growing crowd, we came to a rather secluded spot and stopped.

"If you feel uncomfortable at any point or want to leave, just let me know and we'll head out," he said over the music, leaning his head closer to me as to be heard.

Nodding in understanding, I smiled up at him as the song changed and we started to dance. Unlike some of the other couples that were surrounding us, the two of us danced a little more modestly than those looking as if they were about to strip each other naked on the dance floor, if not a little awkwardly at first. I'd danced with him before, sure, but never like this.

As the songs began to blend together and the bass became more prominent, I felt myself gaining a bit more confidence. The people around us were strangers that I'd probably never see again, and with the lights dimmed low, I decided to let go.

Moving closer to Ryan, I trailed my arms up his chest until they rested loosely around his neck and began to sway my hips more prominently to the beat of the music. As my eyes caught Ryan's, his lips turned upwards and his hands grasped my hips tighter, sending shivers of heat up my spine as he pulled me impossibly close.

It surprised me somehow, how good of a dancer he was, and yet, as the music surrounded us and the time passed, I'd managed to get swept away, engrossed in the electricity that was crackling between us.

But everybody needed a break sometime.

"I'm going to go and get another drink," I said, stepping back from him, "Did you want anything?"

He shook his head. "No, I just have to head to the bathroom," he replied, "I'll meet you up there in a few minutes.

Nodding, the two of us parted ways. It took me longer than expected to make my way across the, now packed, dance floor as I weaved my way through the gyrating bodies. Making it up the stairs, I found an empty space at the bar, managing to get the bartenders attention rather quickly as I placed my order.

Pulling my cell phone out of my clutch while I waited for my drink, I shook my head as I saw a single, suggestive text come through from Emily. Typing out a quick and witty reply, I tucked my phone away just as an unfamiliar man sided up to me at the bar. "Hey gorgeous," he started, speaking low and sultry as though he thought I'd find it more attractive, "I've never seen you here before."

Turning my head towards him, I saw that the guy was probably around Ryan's age. His dirty blonde hair was spiked upwards and the look in his eyes told me his intentions were not so friendly. "Yeah," I said slowly, wishing Ryan would hurry up, "It's my first time here."

"Well, did you need anyone to show you around?" he asked smoothly.

"Uh, no sorry," I said, pulling the front of my dress up slightly as I noticed his eyes flicker down towards my chest more than once, "I'm actually here with someone."

"They won't need to know," he said, his voice lowering as he leaned closer to me. "Now why don't you just come downstairs with me? I'm sure we can find a dark, secluded corner..."

"How about no?" I replied forcefully, pushing myself away from him as the shot of vodka I'd ordered, along with the orange juice, was passed towards me.

"Oh come on..."

Ryan cut off whatever pleads the sleaze was about to make as he appeared next to me, pulling me safely into his chest. "She said no," he said menacingly, "Now leave." He looked as though he wanted nothing more than to land one solid punch to the guy's face.

"Whoa, sorry man," the douche replied, his hands up in mock surrender as he began to back away from me, "I didn't know she was taken."

"Yes you did," I pointed out smartly, feeling smug as he shot me an irritated scowl before turning on his heel and walking away.

"I knew I shouldn't have left you alone," Ryan grumbled under his breath, a frown creasing his forehead as he turned to me with an apologetic look on his face.

Bringing my hand up to cup his face, I shook my head. "Don't worry about it," I said dismissively, "I can take care of myself."

"But you shouldn't have to."

"Like I said, I was fine," I continued, planting a soft kiss against his cheek, "But thanks for stepping in."

I knew I'd gotten through to him when a soft smile appeared on his face that mirrored my own. Turning to grab the shot I'd ordered, I brought the small glass up to my lips, downing the sharp liquid in one smooth gulp before grabbing my juice to sip as a chaser.

"Feeling better?" Ryan asked teasingly, his eyes sparkling with amusement as he pulled me closer to him.

"A little bit," I admitted sheepishly, and although my glass was only half empty, I left it abandoned on the bar as I grabbed his hand, "But I want to dance some more."

He didn't seem to protest as he laced his fingers through mine, leading me down to the dance floor once more. The space was almost packed now as the time ticked closer to midnight, but we were still able to cozy up with enough space that we weren't hitting against the people around us.

Ryan brought our intertwined hands above my head, twirling me quickly and unexpectedly before pulling my body close to his. A warm smile grew on my face before I turned away from him, pushing my back against his chest as I moved my body. His hands, which had previously hovered around my hips, trailed up and down the top of my thighs as we danced, one occasionally moving up to graze my stomach lightly over the fabric of my dress.

Our bodies felt as though they were molding into one as we swayed to the music, the hum of the music keeping us alive as the bass ricocheted off the walls. My eyes eventually slipped shut as I took in every movement the two of us made together, only cementing the fact that the heat between us was slowly driving me crazy.

It was intoxicating, it was passionate, and it was exhilarating.

"TEN!"

We must have been dancing for longer than I thought, as I opened my eyes to see everyone around us counting down along with the DJ.

"Nine, eight, seven, six."

Turning around, my eyes met Ryan's to see that they were shining with happiness, fire, and hunger. He wanted me, I thought, and for a moment, I wondered if my eyes looked similar to his.

"Five, four, three, two."

Everyone around us seemed to fade away as his hands trailed further up my body, leaving a trail of heat as they went, before stopping just below my jaw.

"One!"

His lips clamped down on mine before the cheers even began. His tongue quickly made his way inside my mouth, coaxing an embarrassing moan from deep within me, but in the heat of the moment, I couldn't care less. I kissed him back with just as much hunger and passion, but as the kiss continued, both of us let go slightly. Our hurried movements moved down a notch as the kiss turned sensual and slow, giving light and fire to every nerve ending in my body.

Pulling back slightly, my eyes were still partially closed as I felt his breath fanning my face. One of his hands had managed to dip down to my waist, his thumb rubbing dangerously slow circles just above my backside. I opened my eyes then to see him scanning my face ever so carefully.

"I think we should get out of here."

The words were out of my mouth before I could give them any thought, though I didn't take them back as Ryan's eyes snapped quickly to meet mine. Standing my ground, he seemed to understand what I was suggesting, what was written in between the lines.

He nodded wordlessly, joining our hands together as he pushed his way through a gap in the crowd. I noticed him briefly pull his phone out, tapping something out quickly before shoving it back into his pocket. "Come on," he murmured lowly, his voice thick with lust as we exited the building, nodding towards the limo that seemed to be parked in the same place we'd left it.

Following closely behind him, my head was spinning with nerves as we got in the back of the car. Not because I was unsure, but because I was, and I didn't have a lot of experience. Besides the one time that had brought Abbie into this world, I hadn't had the urge to be with anyone so intimately again. I'd learned my lesson on one-night stands, but that wasn't what this was.

This was Ryan, and I knew he wouldn't hurt me.

The ride back to his house was silent and as each minute passed, there seemed to be a greater chance of my beating heart exploding out my chest. My nerves were heightened but my senses were also alight, as Ryan's hand never left mine, his fingers locked tightly with my own as his thumb drew mindless patterns atop my skin.

When the limo came to a stop, the two of us stumbled out of the car, sending a quick thanks to the driver before heading straight for the door.

The energy around us had sparked once again and it seemed, as Ryan struggled with his keys, that he couldn't open the door fast enough. Once inside, there was a split second of space between us as he closed and locked the door, but before either of us could say a word, he was backing me up against the wall, pushing his entire body into mine as his lips caught mine in a searing kiss. It only took a few accelerated heartbeats for his lips to trail slowly down my jaw, moving swiftly and purposely against my skin.

My arms wrapped around his neck, grasping at a few strands of hair at the back of his head as he continued his treacherous assault on my neck. The scent of his cologne hit my nose, and as I breathed him in, I couldn't stop the light moan that escaped through my lips.

"Bedroom, now."

Ryan didn't need any more instruction as his hands slid down and under my butt, lifting me in one swift movement, his lips never leaving my neck. My legs wrapped around his waist tightly on their own accord as we moved up the stairs, my heels slipping off in the process, landing on the floor with a small thud.

Before I knew it I was pressed up against a wall once again, except this time it was a door, and the contact didn't last long as Ryan pushed it open to reveal his room. He used his foot to close the door behind us, leading me towards his bed as he laid me down first before crawling on top of me.

Our lips met once again in a fiery haze, my hand reaching out to grab the front of his shirt, pulling him down so that his solid body was pressed firmly against mine. His hands were travelling up and down my body, but when they began skimming just underneath the hem of my dress, he pulled back.

"Zoe," he breathed, leaving just a sliver of space between our mouths.

"Ryan," I returned, my voice airy and soft as my hands travelled up to his hair on their own accord.

His eyes met mine, flicking down to my lips briefly. "Are you sure?"

Figuring it was enough of a reply, I pulled his head back down so that our lips mashed together. Taking this as the go-ahead, his hands slowly started to push the fabric of my dress up, massaging the skin of my thighs as he went. When his hands reached just below my hips, I wiggled slightly, not breaking the kiss as he slipped my dress further up my body. When his rough hands gently graced my breasts over the thin lacy fabric of my bra, I sat up slightly, bringing Ryan with me. In one swift movement I placed my hands on top of his and pulled the dress clean off, throwing it down onto the floor.

Left sitting there in nothing more than my bra and underwear, I watched as Ryan's hands graced my skin, moving wherever they could reach as his eyes drank me in.

"Beautiful," he all but growled as his lips dipped down towards my collarbones.

My hands shakily started to work on the buttons of his shirt, and when they were all undone, I pushed the fabric down over his shoulders, marveling at the sight that greeted me. I knew my boyfriend wasn't extremely athletic, but saying he wasn't fit was a blatant lie. His chest and arms were sculpted from numerous hours spent at the gym, and in that moment, as the tips of my fingers traced along his abs, I couldn't be more thankful.

A groan escaped his lips before he pushed me down onto my back, falling on top of me so that we were skin to skin. Our kisses were a mix of moans and sensual coaxing as our tongues danced to a whole new beat.

Soon enough his pants had joined the ever-growing pile on the floor and his lips had trailed down to the swell of my breasts as the clip of my bra popped opened. I was all but panting when the last layers of clothes that kept us separated were stripped minutes later. My breathing had sped up and the muscles in my stomach were clenched together tighter than they'd ever been before.

He leaned back for a second, grabbing protection from his bedside table before gently hovering me, his eyes trained on my own. Ryan's hands came up to cup my chin softly, kissing me so delicately that I was afraid that I might burst from what was building deep inside me.

And in that moment, without any regrets, I gave myself over to the man I was fast falling for, wholly and completely.

CHAPTER 18

"Caramel macchiato with soy milk."

I called out the order, the last one after an extremely exhausting shift, and handed the woman waiting patiently on the other side of the counter her cup. "Have a great night."

Through the glass windows at the front of the café, I could see that the sun had long since set, leaving the sidewalks of Los Angeles relatively empty. The dinner rush, which usually only lasted for an hour, had started in the late hours of the afternoon, and had just ended with the small hand of the clock resting at the eight. The line had been non-stop for hours, and after forgoing my break, I was about ready to fall asleep on my feet.

Once the woman exited the shop, Colette turned to me, leaning up against the counter. "Please tell me it's over," she muttered tiredly, wiping her hands on the underside of her apron. She'd started her shift early this morning when her parents had asked her to come in to help, and if I was feeling tired, I couldn't imagine how she was feeling.

I chuckled at her lack of enthusiasm, but just by my laugh you could tell that exhaustion was slowly washing over me. "I think it's over," I replied safely, knowing that we were only open for another hour. Even now, only two people remained in the café and they looked to be on a date, cuddling up to one another in one of the back booths.

"Thank god." She turned, grabbing a clean rag from beneath the counter to start the clean up. "Do you mind staying a few extra minutes to help cleaning?"

Although I'd been due to clock out a few minutes previous, it was hard to say no to the hopeful look she wore. The sides of my lips tilted upwards as I nodded. "Sure."

Her shoulders sagged in relief. "Thank you," she said gratefully, tossing a rag my way. "I'll punch you in a red-velvet cupcake."

I rolled my eyes at her bribery but didn't refuse, because truthfully, there wasn't anything I was craving more in that moment.

Setting to work, I made my way around the counter and began wiping down the empty tables, and by the time I was done, the couple in the back had decided it was time to leave. By the time I'd swept the floor and rearranged a few of the chairs it was quarter after eight, and I made my way to the back of the café, signaling to Colette that I was heading home.

Clocking out, I let the ties of my apron fall around my waist, finding it somewhat freeing as I shed the dirty uniform. Spinning the dial on my locker, I popped open the door, hanging my apron on a hook before reaching into my bag for my phone.

3 missed calls from Ryan.

Curious as to what he had wanted, I punched in his number, leaning my shoulder against the cold metal lockers as I heard the line ringing. It didn't take long for him to answer, perhaps two or three rings, before I heard his voice through the phone.

"Zoe?"

I knew, as my insides fluttered happily, that if we'd been face to face, I wouldn't of been able to resist the urge to kiss him at the sound of his velvety smooth voice. It was warm, welcoming, and something that I was quickly becoming addicted to.

"Hey," I replied softly, smiling to myself.

"How are you?"

"I'm good," I replied, his voice alone succeeding at pulling me from exhaustion. "I just finished work, but how are you? I saw that you called."

"Yeah sorry." I could imagine him running his hand messily through his hair as he spoke. "I forgot you were working tonight. I had to text Emily to make sure I hadn't done anything worth ignoring me."

"Oh, no." I started shaking my head before I realized he couldn't see it. "No you didn't. Was there, I mean, did you want to talk about something?"

"No, I just missed you."

Spoken confidently, those words sent a shiver down my spine, as I was caught somewhat off guard by his honesty. "Oh," I managed to squeak out.

His laughter suddenly filled the phone. "What? No 'I miss you too Ryan'?"

"Of course I miss you," I mumbled embarrassedly, wondering how, after almost three months, he still managed to make my cheeks heat up and my tongue to get tied up. "How were your interviews today?"

It was the first week of February, and with the release of Ryan's latest film just a few short days away, he'd been whisked out to New York City for a press tour. Radio interviews, television appearances - the whole shebang.

"They went alright I guess," Ryan started, "But they weren't really unique. Most of the time when we have a string of interviews like this, a lot of the interviewers end up asking us the same questions.

I'm pretty sure at least three radio broadcasters today asked me and the others how we all got along while shooting and if there were any fights behind the scenes."

"Well were there?" I asked teasingly, causing Ryan to chuckle.

"No, at least none that I was involved in," he quipped.

As I continued asking him how his trip was going, I found myself zoning out, invaded by my own thoughts as he began to explain further about his day.

Over the days he'd been gone I'd been supportive, wishing him luck and calling him every night to talk, but I was getting restless. I wanted him home already, because while he was out exploring the big apple with his cast mates and management, I felt like I was being pushed to the sidelines.

It had only been a week, but it felt like forever.

"When are you coming home?"

The sentence sprouted from my mouth before I had time to think about it, cutting off whatever Ryan had been talking about. I bit my lip, realizing my mistake as silence greeted the line. Worry filled my mind until I heard him sigh.

"My flight only leaves JFK tomorrow afternoon around two, so I probably won't be back in LA until nine," he said softly.

"I just wish you were here now."

"I know babe, I do too," Ryan replied, "But it's only another 24 hours or so, and then I'll be home. It's not that long.'

"Okay," I said, feeling a smile tug at my lips, "I..."

I stopped abruptly as I realized what three words had almost slipped from my lips. I wasn't ready for those three words – at least I thought I wasn't.

"Zoe?" Ryan's voice rang through the other end of the phone, urging me to continue.

"Yeah sorry," I said, shaking my head, trying my best to clear my thoughts, "I was just going to say that I really miss you and I can't wait to see you." My voice started to soften at the tail end of the sentence. "But I actually should be heading home."

"Why, where are you?"

"Still at work," I answered sheepishly.

"Damn, I'm sorry," Ryan apologized, "I'll let you go so you can get home. You drove to work right?"

"You don't need to apologize, it's just been a long day and I'm pretty much ready for bed," I explained, my exhaustion falling over me once again as I yawned. "And yeah, I drove today."

"Good, because you shouldn't be walking home this late all alone."

My insides warmed once again as his sweet side shone through, knowing all he was thinking about was whether or not I was safe. "I won't be," I reassured him. "I'll see you tomorrow. Goodnight."

"Goodnight."

With a smile, I pulled the phone away from my ear, ending the call. Turning around, I jumped, not expecting Colette to be leaning against the break room's door, listening in on the conversation.

"Well that was just adorable," she said teasingly.

"How long have you been standing there?" I asked embarrassedly, my head ducked as I gathered the rest of my things together from my locker.

A grin formed on her face. "Long enough to know that tomorrow will be a good night for you, what with your boyfriend back in town."

My cheeks were ablaze at her words and what they were insinuating. I wasn't the type of girl to advertise the moments that I spent alone with my boyfriend, and although it was all in good fun, her teasing still made me slightly uncomfortable.

"Oh shut up," I mumbled under my breath, causing her to laugh as I shut my locker. I brushed passed her, my hair falling down to cover the side of my face. "I'll see you later."

The amusement was still clear in her voice as she shouted after me, "Goodnight."

Pushing the front door of the café, I held it open as a lone customer passed through before heading out back to the parking lot, jumping into my car as I headed for home.

I wish it had been the sun that woke me up hours later, but sadly, that wasn't the case.

An incessant buzzing was pulling me from my slumber, and I wasn't the least bit thrilled, as my eyelids were forced open to see my room was still pitch black. My vision was blurred, but through my hazy state, I was still able to make out the numbers on my alarm clock.

It was only three in the morning.

Rolling over with a groan, I tried to pull the covers higher up, grabbing my pillow to cover my ears. All I had was hope; hope that the buzzing would stop soon. I sighed when, seconds later, the buzzing ceased. Releasing my pillow, I snuggled back into the comfort of my bed, only to be rudely interrupted when the buzzing returned with a vengeance a minute later. Pushing the blankets off of me, I reached out grabbing my phone to see that there was an incoming call.

Ryan.

Confusion filled my head as I swiped against the screen, bringing the phone up to my ear. "Hello?"

"Hey." His voice was much less groggy than mine was at this early hour. "How's it going?"

I yawned. "It would be a whole lot better if I was still asleep," I mumbled, letting my head fall back against the pillows. "Why are you calling so early? Isn't it like six in the morning over there?"

For a few seconds, all I received as a response was the sound of his warm laugh traveling through the phone line, but as the laughter faded, he replied, "Come open your front door."

My ears must have been tricks on me, as I could've sworn I heard him ask me to go downstairs. "Come again?" I asked, willing him to repeat himself as I pushed myself up into a sitting position.

"I said you should come and open your front door," he repeated. I could almost feel him smiling through the phone. "You don't want anyone to see me standing out here like a stalker, do you?"

My legs were swinging out from underneath the covers before he was finished talking. I didn't drop my phone as I ran, my body fully awake in that moment, heading down the stairs. The path felt longer than usual in the dark and I was surprised that, as I skidded into the entryway, I hadn't mistakenly bumped into anything. Flipping the latch on the door and pulling it open, my eyes widened as I saw Ryan standing there.

His hand was still holding his phone up to his ear, but his gaze had shifted when I opened the door, eyes gleaming as he gazed down at me with amusement.

I blinked my eyes a few times, trying to make sure that this wasn't a dream. It was reality. My boyfriend was actually here.

His eyebrows lifted as a grin stretched across his lips. "What, no hello?"

I couldn't speak; the words were lodged in the back of my throat. Instead, I shook myself out of my shocked state, stepping forward to swiftly close the space between us. His arms wound around my body gently, although his grip was strong, as though he didn't want to let me go. I shut my eyes and enjoyed the moment, just breathing him in as my face tucked into chest.

Nothing but silence surrounded us for a few moments, letting me just sink into his embrace and savor the moment. This was what I'd been missing. The closeness. The support. Knowing that if I needed him, he'd be here in a heartbeat.

Unfortunately, the moment couldn't last forever. He was the first to pull back, but he kept an arm around me as he stepped further into the house, closing the door behind him. It left us with no light; solely the darkness keeping us company.

"How are you here?" I whispered, breaking the silence between us.

The hand that wasn't hovering around my waist came up to cup my cheek, the pads of his thumb gently brushing against my skin. "I was at the airport when you called me," he explained, a faint smile on his lips. "I booked an early flight home so that I could surprise you."

"At three in the morning?"

He shrugged sheepishly. "Whatever works."

A feeling of euphoria washed over me as my gaze dropped to his lips for a brief period of time. "And your manager or costars didn't mind that you left before them?"

As my eyes drifted back up to meet his, I was able to tell right away that he'd no doubt been aware of my wavering gaze. "No," he said slowly. A satisfied smirk played on his lips as he shook his head. "We were finished with the interviews, so nobody had any reasons to stick around. My manager and I were able to find early flights out and everybody else is on the flight back tomorrow."

My heart was fluttering like it never had before and I didn't have a reply for him. Instead, I reached up, letting my arms rest around his shoulders as I brought my lips to his.

The caress was soft, the fire alight, and the passion infinite.

However, as a yawn crept up on me just a few seconds after our lips connected, I was reminded that it was, indeed, still the middle of the night.

"Tired?" Ryan chuckled as I pulled back, covering my mouth as I yawned.

"Aren't you?" I threw back sleepily, "It's three in the morning."

"I slept on the plane," he replied matter-of-factly, shaking his head. "Did you want me to leave so you can get some rest?"

My heart lurched forward at the thought of him leaving so soon. He'd just got here, and I didn't want to let him leave. "Or, if you're still tired, you can come upstairs and keep me company," I suggested. "To sleep, just sleep," I clarified as I saw a familiar twinkle appear in his eyes.

"I think," he smiled, intertwining his hand with my own, "That's just what I need."

Waking up the next morning next to Ryan was pure, serene bliss.

I didn't know what time it was, but the sunlight was streaming into the room through the curtains, slowly but surely waking me up. In my, very revealing, pajamas, I was all too aware that Ryan had slung his arm around my waist sometime during the night, pulling me in closer to his chest. Our bare legs were tangled together underneath the covers, and the feeling of my bare skin touching his was enough to make goose bumps rise and my insides quiver with excitement.

Closing my eyes to savor the moment, I sighed, cuddling closer to him, my face tucking in to the hollow of his neck.

He stayed still for a while, but soon enough the spell was broken. His arm tightened around me, pulling me impossibly close as he drifted into consciousness.

A groan escaped his lips as I pulled back slightly, titling my head upwards on the pillow. His eyes blinked open, adjusting to the light that had fallen into the room before zeroing in on me. His hair was disheveled, the remnants of a short and impromptu make-out session that had taken place early in the morning, and it only made him look more appealing at this hour.

"Good morning," I whispered, the side of my lips tipping upwards.

"Mmm, it sure is," he returned, his voice deep and velvety smooth, sending chills down my spine. His hand had inched below the fabric of my camisole, rubbing slow patterns against the exposed skin. "What time is it?"

Just as I was about to turn over to take a quick peek at the clock on my bedside table, the sound of footsteps hit my ears. The pitter-patter didn't stop, but instead grew louder and louder until I heard the doorknob of my room jiggling.

Biting my lip in anticipation, I watched as the door pushed open to reveal Abbie. She trotted into the room happily, still clad in her pajamas, her bed head messily tied up in two pigtails. As she walked closer to the bed, only to realize I wasn't alone, her eyes widened.

"Ryan," she squealed, jumping up onto the bed and wiggling her body in between the two of us.

He laughed, his arms moving away from me as we were separated. "Hey Abbie," he said with a smile, pulling himself into a sitting position, "I've missed you."

"I missed you too," she said, a toothy grin splitting her face. "When did you get here?"

"Last night when you were sleeping. I didn't want to wake you up."

As their conversation drifted to where he'd been and why he'd been gone for so long, I simply laid back and admired the two of them. Abbie had crawled up onto his lap and was now sitting there comfortably as Ryan smiled down at her.

The scene made my heart clench. There, in front of me, were the two most important people in my life at that moment and I wanted, no, needed, them to get along.

Abbie's eyes widened suddenly, cutting off her own train of thought as though she'd just remembered something. "Are you staying for bweakfast?" she asked, cocking her head to the side as her eyes flitted between the two of us. "Aunty Emily is making pancakes."

Ryan's head twisted towards me, raising an eyebrow.

"He's staying," I nodded, causing a smile to emerge on both of their faces.

"But we'll be down in a few minutes," Ryan added, "Okay Abbie?"

She nodded, muttering something about going back down to the kitchen to help, before she edged herself off the bed and scurried out of the room.

"So," Ryan began, a smirk slowly appearing on his face, "How much time do you think we have before we have to be downstairs?"

His eyes were sparkling wickedly while a flush crept onto my face at what I thought he was insinuating. "I don't... I... I mean..." I stammered, not knowing how to respond.

Luckily, Ryan pulled me out of my misery as he dropped his façade, laughing at my reaction. "Don't worry babe, I just want to talk."

"Oh."

"Yeah, so," he started, his grin depleting into a small smile as he pulled me closer, "You know how Valentine's Day is next Friday?"

My heart skipped a beat.

That was something I was increasingly aware of, as it had taken me ages to figure out a gift for him. "Yeah..." I trailed, urging him to continue.

His eyes roamed my face as he struggled to find the right words. "And how I've been doing a lot of press interviews and appearances for the movie that's coming out soon?" I nodded, now curious to where he was going. "Well," he said sheepishly, "The premiere is actually on Valentine's Day."

And with those few short words, any thoughts of a quiet, intimate Valentine's Day suddenly crashed around me. "Umm, okay," I mumbled, "Did you want to do something the day after then, or?"

As his head began to shake, my heart dropped even deeper into my chest.

The expression on my face must've given away how I was feeling. Ryan leaned closer; letting his lips caress mine for a brief moment before pulling back. "You didn't let me finish." His hand was holding my chin still as his thumb ran slowly across my bottom lip. "I want you to come with me."

"To the premiere?" I asked, lying there stunned.

He chuckled. "Yes, if you're all right with that."

My head was spinning. "But..." I paused, trying to find the right words, "I've never been on a red carpet."

"And neither had I before my first movie," he commented, flashing a grin before his smile softened. "There's nothing to be nervous about," he said reassuringly, "I'd be right next to you the whole time, but if you're still not up for it..."

"It's not that," I spoke slowly, closing my eyes for a few seconds before I reopened them, meeting Ryan's curious gaze. "I do want to be there to support you. It's just, are you sure?"

"I think it's about time the world meets the girl I'm completely crazy about."

That was all it took for every piece of the puzzle to fall into place. It just felt right. "Well in that case," I said, "How could I say no?"

His smile grew as he inched closer, my arms tightening around his neck. "Did I mention that we're also going away for the weekend after the premiere?" My eyes widened at the news, but as I opened my mouth to reply, he shook his head. "Emily's already promised to look after Abbie, and Dean's coming over Friday while her and Dustin go out."

It was almost overwhelming, the emotions that were floating between my head and my heart. There were no words to describe how wild the butterflies in my stomach seemed to be swarming. "You just thought of everything, didn't you?" I breathed out, a smile gracing my face to match his.

There was no time for a response before our lips met, and in that moment, I didn't see how it was possible for things to get any better.

CHAPTER 19

 My steps faltered and my heart stopped as my eyes stayed glued to my phone screen. More specifically, the single message that had just appeared in my inbox, sitting unread as my mind began to jumble with nerves.

This was it.

Holding my breath, I tapped the screen and opened the e-mail.

Zoe Hamilton,

During our interview with you earlier this week, I was pleased to see that you were well prepared and enthusiastic about working for our journal. My team and I have reviewed the sample articles that you left, and I must say, for such a young mind, you do have a way of making history come alive. I especially enjoyed reading your take on life after war, the piece you centered on war veterans.

It is because of this, and more, that I am happy to extend an offer to work with us here at The Historical Press during your upcoming placement. We will also be considering you for a full-time position upon your graduation if the next few months run smoothly.

Please contact me with your decision as soon as possible so we can work out a few minor details. I can be reached by this e-mail address or by the phone number listed below during our regular work hours.

Sincerely,

Caroline Harley

Head Editor, The Historical Press

I skimmed over the e-mail once more, making sure that my eyes weren't playing tricks on me. As it slowly started to sink in that I'd landed the job, a smile bloomed on my face. Barely able to contain the thrill of excitement that spread through me, I took a screenshot of the e-mail and sent it out to Emily and Ryan.

Seeing the time at the top of my screen, I realized that, by reading my e-mail, I'd accidentally made myself late for my last class of the day. Pocketing my phone, I sped up my pace until the building I was heading towards come into view.

The classroom for my Social History course was small, as less than 50 people were registered for the class. I was very much aware that several of my classmate's eyes were veering away from the professor as I opened the door at the back of the class, slipping in five minutes late. Ducking my head, I avoided the amused look my professor was giving me as I quickly spotted a free seat near the back of the classroom. Walking down the row, I avoided the backpacks that had been carelessly left in the aisle, pulling out the empty chair before beginning to tune in to the lecture.

An hour later, I had three pages full of notes focusing on immigration into America in the early 19th century. Tuning out the professor for a moment, I uncapped a highlighter and went over the important dates that I figured I would have to memorize.

"Zoe Hamilton?"

Startled, my hand jolted across the page, causing a frown to develop on my features as I noticed the bright yellow line that trailed halfway across my page.

When I realized that I'd once again heard my name, my head popped up curiously, letting my gaze travel around the room before it landed on a woman standing by the door. She looked to be in her mid-30s, but I couldn't remember a time when I'd ever met her.

"Yes?" I spoke up hesitantly, suddenly conscious of my classmates looking back at me.

It was after I replied that I realized the reason she was there. More so, what she was holding in her hands. It was a beautiful bouquet comprised of red and pink roses, and the sight of it made my heart catch in my throat.

Standing up, I made my way to the front of the room, embarrassed as I felt everyone's attention on my back.

"These were left for you at the undergrad office," the woman stated, a sweet smile on her face. She passed the bouquet over to me, nodding to the card that was placed amongst the flowers. "Someone surely couldn't wait until tonight."

A flush spread across the apples of my cheeks as I took the flowers, nodding at the woman before returning to my seat. "Now, back to what I was saying," the professor started, scanning the room before her entertained eyes landed on me. I sent back a sheepish smile, sinking lower in my seat as my classmates turned their attention back to the front of the room.

I found it difficult to concentrate during the second half of the lecture, my mind still racing from receiving a bouquet during class. Yes, it was Valentine's Day, but I hadn't expected it. When there were only about five minutes left in the scheduled lecture, my professor turned her back to list the readings we were meant to study on the board. It seemed as though I was the only one not paying attention, my eyes flitting curiously to the card that sat, unread, on the bouquet I'd tucked beneath my seat.

Glancing back and forth, I realized no one was watching me as I hastily plucked the card from the bouquet, ducking lower in my seat as I read the handwritten note that rested inside.

Happy Valentines Day!

I could have waited until I saw you tonight to give these to you, but then I thought that you deserved to know you're loved every second of the day, even if you're not sitting right beside me. We haven't even known each other for six months yet, and we've been together for less than three, but you've somehow managed to become the person that I think about as soon as I wake up and the person I want to be next to as I fall asleep. You've invaded my heart, my mind, my body, and my soul.

I can't wait to have you all to myself for the whole weekend because I know, with you by my side, it's going to be amazing.

Yours truly,

Ryan

Seeing the trail of hugs and kisses running after his name made my heart flip backwards within my chest and a smile grow. In that moment, the war that my mind and my heart had been having ceased, my heart claiming victory.

After just a few short months, I had fallen in love with him.

The sudden realization was frightening, nerve-wracking, and exhilarating all at once. My mind was a mix of emotions. Every little thing that Ryan had done for me over the time we'd known each other began to appear so much more significant than it had before. From the way he didn't judge me on my past to the way he spoke about our future. Piece by piece they all fit together, sending a rush of yearning and devotion through my blood.

No matter how unfamiliar the feeling was to me, now that I'd grasped onto it, I didn't ever want to let go.

I'd unknowingly made my way towards the end of a rigid cliff, ready to make a fateful leap into the abyss below. My feet were dangling over the edge, and the only thing that I could hope for was that Ryan would be at the bottom, ready to catch me.

My voice was shy and timid as I found Emily in the living room later that afternoon. "Emily?"

I'd been shook from my thoughts back in class as the professor dismissed us, leaving us with readings and an assignment to be completed in time for the next lecture. Rummaging for a pen, I'd swiftly jotted down the notes on the board before following my fellow classmates out the door.

Walking into Abbie's daycare had been awkward, considering I had been holding a bouquet of flowers that seemed to have caught most people's attention. Maybe I had just been over-analyzing everything, but in my head, everyone who turned my way had a look of admiration on their face.

Abbie, of course, had been thrilled to see the flowers in my hands, saying that Ryan must have really loved me if he had sent them to my school. However, all her comment had done was add fuel to the fire that was consuming my soul.

Now, as I waited for Ryan to pick me up for the weekend, I stood nervously, waiting for Emily to acknowledge me. She twisted her head towards me, a curious expression on her face, while I figured out how to phrase the question hovering on the tip of my tongue. "Yeah?" she replied, encouraging me to continue.

"I was wondering," I trailed, my hands fidgeting, "How did, umm, when did you know you were in love with Dustin?"

I had ended up sputtering out the remainder of my question, but as Emily's eyebrows rose in surprise, a grin quickly following, I knew that she'd understood. "Why do you want to know?" she replied teasingly.

Shrugging, I attempted to play it cool; paying no mind to the heat I felt slowly spreading across my cheeks. "Oh, just wondering," I said, walking over to sit next to her on the couch.

"It wouldn't happen to be because you finally realized you're in love with Ryan, would it?" I stayed silent, my blush growing even more prominent, and her grin stretched wider. She shook her head. "Fine, you really want to know?" I nodded, biting my lip. I realized that, even though we had talked frequently before I moved here, her relationship with Dustin was rarely a topic we discussed.

"When I met him I wasn't ready for a relationship," she started. "We partnered up for a project at the end of my first year of college since neither of us really knew anybody in the class, but we ended up getting on well. Once exams started that term, the two of us met up constantly and studied together, even if it wasn't for the class that we shared. It was like we just clicked."

"He asked me out once exams were over, but I really wasn't sure about it because of how badly things had ended with the guy I'd been seeing before him. In the end, he'd done a lot to convince me to take a chance on him, and I did. That summer was one of the best I've ever had, and when we grew closer, the nights we spent together were amazing. When the next year of school rolled around, I thought we'd go our separate ways, you know, a summer romance that would eventually fizzle out when we couldn't be around each other every hour of the day."

The smile on my sister's face as she recounted the early days of her relationship managed to cause a drop of envy to flow in my veins. She was so happy. So in love.

"But it didn't," she continued. "One night, when he had his arms wrapped around me, I started to realize how everything had changed. I was happier than I had been in years, the guys that I'd see on campus no longer caught my eye, and the warmth that I felt, just lying there with him, was like nothing I'd ever felt before. So before I could process what I was saying, I blurted out that I loved him." She laughed, a look of pure affection gleaming in her eyes. "I remember being terrified as he moved away from me, thinking that he was going to want me to leave. He just looked at me for what felt like forever, and when I tried to leave in embarrassment, he just pulled me back in. A smile was on his face as he told me he loved me too, and I finally felt like I could breathe again."

"But that's what love is. It's terrifying and it's breathtaking. It's like sinking into a giant wave of emotions, and when everything falls into place and the water settles, your vision is clear and you can breathe easy again."

Every word she spoke seemed to strengthen the feeling inside my chest. I was in love with Ryan. I knew it, I just wasn't sure if I would actually be able to tell him.

"Aren't I supposed to be the one giving you love advice?" I joked.

"But I'm not the one who needs it," she replied slyly. I was left with no time to reply as the doorbell went and a smirk settled onto her lips. "Now go," she nodded towards the door. "Go and live your fairytale."

I quickly got up, a thank-you slipping through my lips as I made my way towards the front door, only to be greeted by a small stuffed bear. The bear itself was grey and fluffy, but in its hands was a star that read 'congratulations'.

"Umm, hey?" I offered in confusion, looking up to meet the eyes of my boyfriend, who was still holding the bear out towards me.

His lips turned up into a smile. "Hey."

I raised an eyebrow, nodding down at the stuffed animal. "Is that for me?"

His smile grew and he stepped inside, letting the door close behind him as his arms slowly wound around my waist. "I would've got you flowers to celebrate, but I kind of already sent you some today," he said, pulling me impossibly close. "Congratulations on getting your placement."

A grin grew on my face to mirror Ryan's. "Thank you," I said softly, "And thank you for the flowers too. They were gorgeous."

"Gorgeous flowers for my gorgeous girl," he said, his voice just above a whisper as he leaned closer, his lips slanting over mine. My heart sped up and my arms wove their way up his chest to rest atop his shoulders.

The moment was interrupted, however, when Abbie rounded the corner, a hopeful expression on her face. "Momma," she said. Ryan and I pulled apart at the sound of her voice, and my face flushed due to the fact that my three-year-old daughter had caught me making out with my boyfriend.

"Yes sweetie?" I asked, clearing my throat as I laid my head against Ryan's shoulder.

"Are you leaving now?"

I nodded, pulling away from Ryan completely to crouch in front of her. "In a few minutes we are," I replied with a smile.

Her tiny arms reached out and I pulled her closer into a tight hug. "I'll miss you," she mumbled into my shoulder.

"I'll miss you too." My heart squeezed as I realized that, for the first time since she'd been born, I would be away from her for an entire weekend. "But you'll have a fun weekend with Emily, and Dean will be over soon to take care of you tonight."

Mentioning Dean's name quickly put a grin on her face. Ever since Christmas, every time that the two of them would see each other, they'd spend hours playing around. She looked up to him.

"And until he gets here," I started, turning around to take the bear from Ryan's hands, "I think this little guy will keep you company."

Squeezing the stuffed animal tightly to her chest, her grin widened and her eyes flickered happily between Ryan and I. "Thank you."

Ryan chuckled behind me. "Not a problem," he mused, not at all upset that I'd given his gift to her, "But your mom and I better get going. We don't want to be late."

Picking up the duffel bag I'd thrown together when I'd got home, Ryan quickly took it off my hands, his lips quirking upwards as he went to wait in the car. After a final round of goodbyes, I grabbed my purse and headed out the door.

Tonight I was taking a giant leap in our relationship. Whether I was ready for it or not, I didn't know, but buckling myself into Ryan's passenger seat, I knew that with him by my side, I'd be able to face even the toughest of challenges.

My eyes were closed as Ryan's stylist put the finishing touches on my makeup for the night. My fingers felt like they were tearing away at the fabric of the chair as I tried my hardest to stay still and ignore the pit of ever-growing nerves that had sprung to life inside me.

Upon arrival at Ryan's house, it had taken him only seconds to introduce me to Yvette, as I'd entered the living room to see her sifting through a rack of clothing and countless boxes of accessories. She'd led me upstairs shortly after, and for the past hour and a half I'd been stuck in one spot, letting her work her magic.

"There," Yvette said after what felt like forever, pulling back to examine her work, "Take a look."

Opening my eyes, a handheld mirror was immediately thrust towards me, allowing me to examine her handiwork. My hair had been tamed of frizz and was now curled, the strands falling softly past my shoulders. As far as makeup goes, she'd been so precise that, if you weren't looking closely enough, you'd barely be able to tell that I was wearing any. There was now a subtle glow to my cheeks and a glimmer to my eyes that made me look refreshed. Her final touch had been a nude lipstick, blending it together with a coral lip-gloss to make my lips the most beautiful shade of pink.

"So, what do you think?"

Placing the mirror down on her makeshift makeup counter, I smiled. "I love it," I said, "Thank you."

"Don't thank me yet." She shook her head, walking away for a minute before returning with a gorgeous gown in her hands. "You still have one more thing to do before you're ready."

I'd been hesitant when Ryan had first informed me that he would take care of my dress for the night. It appeared that I really didn't have anything to worry about. Biting my lip, I took the baby pink dress into my hands before being ushered into the bathroom. After mistakenly slipping a foot into an armhole, I managed to figure out how the dress was supposed to fit. Holding the front up against my chest, I walked out of the bathroom to see Yvette waiting for me patiently.

"Can you zip me up?" I asked, turning my back towards her.

Without a reply, she pulled the zipper slowly up my back, making sure not to catch my skin before smoothing out the fabric. "There, now you're done."

Sending her a gracious smile, I ran my hands down the sides, shifting my gaze to the closest mirror, and what I saw was enough to make my breath catch in the back of my throat. The long pink gown had a high neckline, the fabric resting tightly against my skin until it synched at my waist. From there the fabric flowed out freely, most of it disappearing just below my knees, however, a few layers continued to fall until they grazed the ground. One shoulder had a small strap holding it up while the other had a sleeve that draped down to cover the length of my arm.

"Now did I do a good job, or what?"

Laughing at Yvette's confident smile, I nodded in agreement. "You really did," I said.

She grinned excitedly. "Now let's go see what your boyfriend thinks, shall we?"

Heading downstairs, I spotted Ryan before he saw me. He was facing the opposite direction, fiddling with his suit jacket when I called out, "Has anyone ever told you that you look incredibly handsome in a suit?"

His head turned towards me, his eyes widening a fraction as they trailed down my body, admiring Yvette's handiwork. "Zoe," he breathed out huskily. Stepping towards me, he drew me closer, his hands resting just above my waist, his gaze piercing right through me. "You look..."

"Amazing," Yvette offered, cutting into our conversation. It had slipped my mind that she was still here, and when both our gazes snapped towards her, we saw her grinning in awe from where she stood at the bottom of the staircase.

Ryan rolled his eyes. "I wasn't going to say that," he said, causing me to raise an eyebrow teasingly. Realizing his mistake, he back-tracked. "Not that you don't look amazing," he said in a rush, his hand leaving my waist as he reached into his pocket, "But I was going to say that there seems to be something missing." Staring at him in confusion, it all clicked together when, out from his pocket came a golden chain with a small pink heart hanging from it. He grinned as my eyes widened. "You didn't think flowers were all you were getting today, did you?"

I stood there frozen, not moving and not saying a word. He'd uttered me speechless as my mind subconsciously tried to count how many jewels were embedded in the pendant. As Ryan's hands reached across my shoulders, clasping the necklace in place at the back of my neck, a shiver shot down my spine in reaction to the cold metal.

When he pulled back, admiring his gift that now hung from my neck, I was snapped out of my shocked state. Picking up the small heart, I smiled softly. "You really need to stop buying me jewelry," I said jokingly.

His lips quirked upwards and he nodded his head, prompting me to follow him into the living room. Bending behind the couch, he pulled out a rectangular black box, handing it over to me. "I promise you that there's no jewelry in there," he teased, urging me silently to open it.

Lifting the lid, I gasped. Inside sat an absolutely gorgeous pair of heels. They were gold with specks of pink surrounding the peep toe, and they looked to be exactly my size.

"How did you know what size I am?" I asked, taking the shoes out of the box before stepping into them.

He shrugged. "I asked Emily."

My chest warmed at the thought of him going through the trouble of asking my sister for help just to get me a gift. "You know," I said, my voice just above a whisper, "I would say thank you, but I don't think that's enough."

My gaze trained on his, I was able to see the happiness gleaming in his eyes. "Well, I suppose a kiss will have to do."

Having slipped on the heels, our mouths were almost level, separated by a hair-width of space. Without any hesitation, I leaned in, planting my lips on top of his softly, quickly letting him take control of the kiss, his hand maneuvering beneath my hair to cup the back of my neck.

"You guys do know that the premiere starts in just over an hour, right?" Yvette said from somewhere behind us, snapping the two of us back into reality.

"Yeah," Ryan breathed out as he pulled himself away from me, an airy undertone to his voice, "We should get going."

I smiled, nodding towards the front entryway. "Lead the way."

It turned out that Ryan hadn't gone completely overboard, having rented a sleek black car instead of a stretch limo for the night, which I was grateful for. I figured that I'd already be looked at strangely tonight, suddenly appearing as the girlfriend of the star of the film, and I didn't want to draw any more unnecessary attention to myself.

The premiere was about 40 minutes away from Ryan's house, and while I'd done a decent job keeping calm for the majority of the ride, as we got closer and closer, I could feel my nerves threatening to take over. My hands began to fidget and my leg started to shake underneath my dress.

None of this went unnoticed by Ryan, his hand sliding in to grasp my own while he cast a curious look my way. "Are you okay?"

His voice was soft and caring, causing me to release a breath that I hadn't realized I'd been holding. "Yeah," I said slowly. Glancing towards the tinted windows, I was able to see that we were approaching the event, suddenly puling up behind a line of cars that looked similar to our own. "I'm just a little nervous I guess."

Ryan leaned closer, his lips brushing against my temple. It caused a rush of warmth to run down my spine, and sinking into the feeling, I felt like I could conquer the world.

"I'll be right next to you the entire time," he promised, "You're going to be fine."

Despite my apprehension, his soothing words were enough to lift my lips into a smile.

I'd zoned out and the world outside the backseat of the car ceased to exist for a few moments. Ryan and I were the only two that mattered. I was brought out of the clouds however, when the car made one final stop.

"Ready?" Ryan asked, encouragement radiating off of him.

Nodding, I was saved from replying as someone opened the door and signaled for the two of us to step out onto the carpet. Not many people could see us yet, but the sounds of screaming fans and flashing cameras were loud enough to evade my senses.

Ryan stepped out first, causing an influx of noise as reporters and fans screamed his name. He paid no attention to them, turning back towards the car to offer me a hand. Gripping his palm tightly, I slid out of the car, biting my lip before a smile overtook my features.

This was insane.

The sun was slipping down over the horizon, but as the sky turned dark, the red carpet was bright as could be. Lights illuminated the pathway from every which way as we made our way onto the carpet, joining numerous celebrities and guests that had helped to make this movie. A voice sounded over multiple speakers to announce Ryan's arrival, and suddenly, all cameras turned towards us.

The flashes blinded me while my eyes tried to adjust. There were so many cameras and whichever way I looked, one of them would catch my gaze. Leaning closer to Ryan, I laughed, "This is crazy."

He turned to me, his eyes gleaming. He was in his element right now; the wide smile on his face proof that while he enjoyed living a relatively private life, events like these had managed to capture a special place in his heart. "You get used to it," he replied happily, squeezing my hip to pull me closer to him.

Our exchange didn't go unnoticed by the paparazzi, many of them calling out to us from behind microphones or video cameras. An organizer that Ryan seemed to know led us towards the section where other celebrities were currently getting interviewed.

"They'll ask you a few questions each, so just be patient with them," he reminded Ryan, who simply nodded, familiar with what was to come. An encouraging smile was sent my way before the man disappeared to help out elsewhere.

I stayed supportive by his side as the first few reporters stayed focus on Ryan, ignoring my presence while they tried to delve deeper beneath the skin of the actor who played the lead. He answered each question with confidence, speaking nothing but praise when asked about the film, Knights of Fury, or his co-stars.

Once the fifth interview had begun I was expecting to be left out once again, but when the woman had gotten a few replies out of Ryan, her gaze shifted towards me.

"And who's your date tonight Ryan?" she asked.

Ryan's smile widened as he chuckled at the question, tugging me closer to his side as he replied, "This is my girlfriend Zoe."

I smiled politely at the reporter, but was caught off guard when her next question was directed towards me. "Well, you're certainly a lucky girl Zoe," she commented. "Ryan here plays a rather dashing knight in this film, but how do you feel knowing that you're the one girl he plays a knight in shining armour for in real life?"

Quickly racking my brain for a reply, I decided to just be honest. "I don't see him as a knight in shining armour," I shook my head, causing the reporters facial features to crinkle with confusion. "I never saw myself as someone in need of saving, but while he may not be a knight, he definitely swooped into my life to make everyday a fairytale. He's more of a prince that makes an average girl like me feel as though she's worthy of the world."

There was awe in the reporter's eyes when I finished speaking. Turning to Ryan to make sure I hadn't said the wrong thing, I was greeted with a kiss to my cheek that warmed the skin where his lips touched.

"I'll let you two get on with your night," the reporter said, wishing us well before her attention shifted to another actor.

Shaking my head, I said, "Well that was unexpected."

It was then that I also realized that we'd reached the end of the red carpet. Prior to heading inside, the two of us posed for a final few photographs, smiling at the cameras. Ryan guided me towards the edge of the carpet so that he was able to sign autographs for a few lucky fans before the security intervened.

The noise from the streets died down when the door of the building closed behind us. "And yet, you gave a perfect answer," Ryan replied happily, referencing my earlier comment.

His hand squeezed mine affectionately. "Really?" I asked, worried that the reporter or other people wouldn't see it that way.

He nodded quickly, shaking away my doubt. "Absolutely."

Feeling relatively good after my first red carpet experience, I acknowledged the bubble of excitement that was growing in anticipation to seeing Ryan on the big screen. He'd be amazing, there was no doubt, but I couldn't wait to see the movie.

Although a number of people were hovering in the lobby of the building, Ryan wrapped his arm around my shoulder, guiding us towards the screening room. Guests and celebrities filled the room as well, and it seemed like a lot of people, not just me, were antsy to see the movie.

When we found two free seats near the center of the theatre, a man, who I quickly recognized as the director of the movie, from when Ryan had pointed him out to me, came over to grab Ryan. Apparently the stars of the movie had to introduce the film before it would play, and with not much time before the showing started, he was rounding up the main cast to the front of the room.

"I'll be right up there," he promised, nodding to where a microphone stand was being set up beneath the viewing screen, "Don't worry."

I nodded, telling myself that I'd be fine on my own for a few minutes. With one last fleeting smile, he was off. I watched him go, leaving me alone as the seats surrounding ours started to fill up with people I didn't recognize. Whether they were guests, other celebrities, or supporting actors, a majority of them sent me strange looks, whispering to their friends words that I couldn't quite pick up on.

I knew I was out of my element, but that didn't give them any reason to ridicule me underneath their breaths.

Ducking my head, I closed my eyes. Slowing my breaths, I replayed any encouraging words Ryan had told me so far tonight, and soon enough, I felt my spirits lifting back up.

The room suddenly erupted in applause and my eyes popped open in bewilderment. Most of the lights in the room had dimmed; the only ones still shining fully were the ones at the front of the room. Ryan stood alongside his fellow cast members while the director and writer of the film gave a short speech. They were passionate and excited, hyping up the film to the audience.

By the time the room went black and Ryan returned to his seat beside me, my expectations for the film were high.

And all those expectations were met.

Knights of Fury followed the life of a young knight, played by Ryan, and his three friends as they embarked on a quest to save his childhood friend, a woman named Rosalina, who was also Ryan's love interest in the movie. She'd been kidnapped while working alongside the princess of the city, and while not many people saw her as a significant loss, the tribe that had kidnapped her knew the truth. It was she, not the crown princess, who was next in line for the throne, and the evidence had been covered up since Rosalina's birth. Ryan's character fought long and hard to save his friend while trying to prove to the citizens what had been kept from them.

It was an adventure, it was a romance, and it was a journey.

When the end credits began to roll, many guests rose to their feet with applause, including me as I looked to Ryan in amazement. He stood proudly; clapping along with me while the director took to the front of the room once more, thanking everyone who'd played a part in the creation of the movie.

"You never explained the movie like that," I said jokingly as we walked out of the theatre hand in hand.

"I didn't want to spoil it for you," he replied cheekily, confusing me when he began pulling me in the opposite direction that the crowd was moving.

"Where are we going?"

"The driver is picking us up at the back of the building so we can head straight to the airport without any delays."

"But my bag is..."

"It's fine," he said reassuringly, placing his hands on my shoulders. "Yvette took care of everything once we left and she texted me during the movie telling me that it was all good to go."

Having no reason not to trust him, I nodded, my mind reeling back to the movie I'd just seen. "You were amazing in the movie by the way," I said, a cheeky smile growing on my face as I remembered the scenes where his armour had been shed, "And your costumes weren't too bad either."

A wicked grin spread across his face at the tail end of my sentence, his arm wrapping tightly around my waist. "Is the image of me dressed up as a knight slipping its way into your fantasies Zoe?" he asked. My cheeks burned at his teasing. Laughing, his hand reached up to move a few stray hairs back into place behind my ear. "You're adorable."

"You're not too bad yourself," I said, mustering up the courage to speak over my embarrassment.

His facial expression changed suddenly, a look of uncertainty taking over his wide smile. "You weren't angry, you know, when you saw me kissing another girl?" he asked, his voice carrying an air of uncertainty.

"I mean, it's not like you were actually doing it in front of me. You filmed it months before you even knew me," I replied with a shrug. "Why? Did you want me to be?"

He shook his head fiercely. "No, it's just..."

"It's your job," I cut him off. Weaving my fingers through his, I offered him an encouraging smile. "I get it. Sometimes you need to do things that you wouldn't normally do to make a great film. Whether it's creating a believable romance with a co-star or something dangerous for an intense scene, either way I'll support you because, in the long run, I know you love what you do." And I love you, I added silently.

Any worry present on his face quickly faded at my reassurance. His mouth opened to reply, only to close when his phone beeped, alerting him of a new message. Without even checking it, he pulled me out the back door of the building. "Come on," he said, leading me towards the same car that we'd taken on our way here.

Once we'd left the craziness of the premiere behind, the ride to the airport was smooth. I spent the majority of the ride with my head resting on Ryan's shoulder, exhaustion slowly taking over.

When I could see airplanes taking off in the distance through the window, I realized that we weren't on the usual route to the airport entrance. "Where are we going?" I asked, looking around to try and figure out where we were.

"The airport," Ryan said mischievously.

I raised my eyebrow. "Are you sure?"

He nodded, not saying another word as the car continued to drive through the streets that surrounded the airport. Finally, the driver pulled off on a side road, stopping at a security gate before slowly driving through when the officer gave the all clear.

Curiosity was swirling in my head as the car rolled to a stop, but when I realized that we were pulling up on the airplane platform, I sat became still.

"Told you we were heading to the airport," Ryan laughed, pulling my hand as the driver opened the door to the backseats, letting to onto the runway.

"How is this even possible?" I asked in astonishment, my eyes wide as they stared at the giant airplane next to us.

"There are a few perks to being a celebrity," Ryan replied, a smirk on his face, "Especially when the head of security here has a daughter that's a huge fan."

Shaking my head in amazement, I watched as Ryan rounded the back of the car, pulling both mine and his bags from the trunk, as well as an extra bag that he handed off to me. "Yvette packed some things in there from her collection of clothes. You can change out of your dress once we get settled on the plane."

I smiled, following Ryan when an airport worker guided us onto the plane, showing us to our relatively private first class seats. Once our bags were settled into the overhead compartments, I headed to the bathroom, needed to change out of my outfit into something more comfortable. Slipping off my heels and my dress, I tossed them carefully into the bottom of the bag before folding the dress up and placing it on top. Yvette had packed me a pair of black yoga pants with a design down the leg, as well as a loose white t-shirt and a bright pink zip-up hoodie that I threw on.

Returning to my seat, I saw that Ryan had also changed, now decked out in a pair of black sweat pants, a long sleeve t-shirt and a beanie.

"Hey," Ryan said, noticing me approaching. He stood up from the aisle seat, taking the bag form my hands to store it up above with our other luggage. Nodding down towards the pair of seats, he said, "I saved you the window seat."

"Thanks," I smiled. Crouching to make sure I didn't hit my head on the compartments above, I found myself getting comfortable in my seat, Ryan's arm winding around my shoulder once he sat down beside me.

I'd had an amazing night tonight, and although I knew things would start to change now that people knew I was dating Ryan Adams, I was optimistic that the two of us would be able to make it through.

As the plane made its accent into the sky, I let myself relax into Ryan arms, and soon enough, I found my eyes closing on their own accord as I drifted to sleep.

CHAPTER 20

The only bits of information that Ryan had given me regarding our trip had been that we were boarding an airplane after the premiere and it would be taking us to a relaxing weekend away. Other than that, I had no idea what our getaway would entail, and in all honestly, I didn't have a clue where we were headed. I figured we were at least staying within the country, as my passport hadn't left the bottom of my handbag since I'd carelessly thrown it in there while packing.

Having fallen asleep almost as soon as the plane set flight, I wasn't able to coax our destination out of him, and before I knew it, I was being jostled awake by Ryan hours later.

"Zoe, wake up."

I'd been partially aware of him calling my name a few times now, but finally, the words were starting to register in my head as I hazily slipped into consciousness. I battled against my better judgment to force my eyes open to realize that my head was rested against Ryan's shoulder. Blinking my eyes into focus, I lifted my gaze to meet his. "What time is it?" I asked groggily, realizing that the only light around us came from the light that had been switched on above our seats.

"You look cute when you're confused," he mused, causing a flush to spread down my neck, "And it's just past three. We've just landed."

No wonder I was so tired. I'd gotten less than three hours of sleep, all of which I'd been hunched over in an airplane seat, and now I was being forced awake. "In the morning?"

Ryan smiled, nodding. "Yeah," he said, "Now come on, we have to meet the driver out front. It's a little bit of a drive to get to where we're going."

"And you're still not going to tell me exactly where that is?"

"I'll give you a hint," Ryan said, standing up from his seat once most of the first class passengers had left the plane. He tugged our bags from the overhead compartments. "We're at the Seattle airport."

"Seattle?"

He nodded in response, a knowing grin playing on his lips. "Yes, Seattle."

"And what exactly is in Seattle that's worthy of a weekend getaway?" I asked, yawning in the middle of my sentence. I lifted a hand to rub my eyes, trying to awaken my body a bit more as I stood up and shuffled my way into the aisle. We were the only ones still left on the plane and the flight attendants were watching us impatiently.

"You'll just have to wait and see."

The airport was, surprisingly, more packed than I'd expected for such an early hour of the morning. The workers didn't look too happy to be there and the customers arriving with us looked unmistakably tired. While most people surrounding us headed off towards the baggage claim, Ryan pulled me to his side, making sure to keep his head down while steering us towards the pick-up parking lot. With everyone otherwise preoccupied, we were able to make our way outside without being noticed.

"I expected a quiet town, not a big city," I said as we stepped through the doors of the airport. The night air was chilly and although my hoodie did a sufficient job in blocking the wind, I was itching to route through my bag for my jacket.

"Just because we're in the city now, that doesn't mean we're staying here."

"What?"

He shot me a mischievous smile; thoroughly amused at the way my eyebrows drew together in confusion. "I told you that you'd be relaxed this weekend, and I'm keeping my promise," he said. "We still have a bit of a car ride until we get there though."

I nodded, hearing the familiar beep of his phone. "Right, what time is it now?" I asked as he pulled his phone out to read the new message.

"Three-thirty."

"And how long until we actually get there?"

He gave a sheepish smile. "That depends on traffic."

I rolled my eyes. It was too early for him to avoid these questions. I needed to know when I'd be able to collapse onto a real bed instead of an airplane seat or the back seat of a car. "It's the middle of the night," I said flatly, "There is no traffic."

"Probably about an hour then." I sighed, dropping my head against his chest. He shifted our bags so that they were both hanging from one arm, the other wrapping around my torso. "Sorry about all this," he apologized, and seconds later I felt the softness of his lips touching my forehead. "This was the only flight I could get so that we'd have the whole weekend together and fly back Monday morning. If you want to sleep in the car you can, I'll carry you up once we get there."

I pulled my head back slightly, seeing a sea of worry swirling in his eyes. If he thought that he'd ruined this weekend in any way, he was mistaken. Somehow, we'd managed to fall under the radar thus far, and I could only hope that the rest of the weekend would be like this.

Just the two of us.

My lips tilted upwards. "Maybe I'll stay awake if you tell me what our mysterious destination is," I said teasingly, trying to ease the tension.

It appeared to work; his shoulders relaxing as though a weight had just been lifted off. "If you want to find out, you'll just have to stay up for another hour."

"I don't think that's possible," I said, yawning mid-sentence, "And I don't understand how you're so awake right now. Shouldn't you be just as tired as I am?"

"I slept for a bit on the plane," he replied, shrugging his shoulders. "I'm used to having a weird sleep schedule."

I nodded, cut off from responding when a white car pulled up to the curb. It was sleek, it looked expensive, and I figured it was the one we were waiting for considering the majority of people surrounding us were waving down cabs. Confirming my suspicions, Ryan's arm fell from around my waist, as he led me towards the car.

When the car rolled to a stop, a man that looked to be in his early forties climbed out of the driver's side, greeting Ryan with a polite smile before popping open the trunk and asking for our bags. Ryan moved towards him, shaking his hand and exchanging pleasantries while helping him fit the luggage into the cramped space of the trunk. When the bags were safely tucked away, the driver returned to his spot up front while Ryan rounded the back of the car, pulling open the back side door.

"After you."

The backseat wasn't the largest, in fact, it was quite cramped, but after buckling up I simply pulled my legs up to rest beneath me so that they weren't squished up against the seat in front of me. Watching Ryan squeeze in beside me had me chuckling underneath my breath. His legs were bent at the knee, though his knees were nearing his stomach with the lack of room he had, and his back was hunched so that his head didn't squash against the roof. Turning to see the amusement on my face, Ryan rolled his eyes, extending his arm along the top of the back seat.

After voicing my thoughts regarding the size of the car, I'd learned that Ryan hadn't actually rented this car for the weekend; it was simply a shuttle service that the place we were headed provided. The name of our destination, however, had not been slipped into Ryan's reply. I'd tried to ask the driver where we were headed, but after receiving a signal from Ryan in the mirror, he'd opted to keep his mouth shut for the entirety of the ride.

Turning my gaze to the window, I realized we were driving through the main streets of Seattle. It seemed as though all the buildings were lit up, bringing life to the quiet streets at the early hour. There were several skyscrapers that caught my attention, but before long all of the lights simply blurred together.

The reason: my eyes were slowly drooping.

I hadn't even noticed the transition I was experiencing, but before I knew it, all I could hear was the buzzing from the engine as the sounds and sights of the city disappeared. The last thing I remembered before slipping completely from consciousness was the feeling of lips against my scalp, a soft whisper of jumbled words causing me to drift to sleep.

I didn't wake again until the morning.

The sun was flooding into the room as I blinked my eyes opened, adjusting to the bright light. Pulling myself into a sitting position, I stretched my arms above my head, realizing only then that I was sitting in an enormous bed, centered in the middle of an unfamiliar room. Furring my eyebrows, I tried to recall a moment when I'd woken up last night, but I couldn't clasp onto a single memory after falling asleep in the car.

Looking around the room, my eyes widened. Everything in the room looked rustic, though the elegance of it all gave clue to its expensive design. The lights were dimmed low, the furniture was wooden, and the sliding doors that led outside showed a small deck looking out onto a vast array of forest. There were two plush chairs placed in front of a large brick fireplace, a small dinner table wedged in between them. Other than that, all I could see was two small hallways at the end of the room, one presumably leading to the bathroom while the other led to the door.

I shifted in the bed, throwing my legs over the side, but was immediately hit with a gush of cold air. My gaze shifted downwards to see that sometime in the night I'd lost the clothes I'd changed into on the airplane, and was instead wearing nothing more than my underwear and a large white t-shirt of Ryan's.

Rolling my eyes, I lifted my gaze back up as a squeak hit my ears. Pushing a cart of room service around the corner, Ryan was dressed in a pair of jeans and a t-shirt, his eyes widening as he noticed I was awake.

A cheesy grin overtook his features, taking in my sad excuse of an outfit as he wheeled our food towards me. His hair hadn't been touched since he'd woken up, still disheveled and strewn on top of his head, and the happiness radiating off of him gave him a childlike aura, which I found strangely appealing.

"Good morning," he said cheerfully, leaning in for a quick peck on the lips. "How did you sleep?"

The sides of my lips pulled upwards. "Good, though I could've done without the new pajamas," I teased, raising an eyebrow as I saw a red hue dust the apples of his cheeks.

"I figured you would've been too hot in what you were wearing," he said with a small shrug.

"Sure," I drawled, though a laugh made it's way through my lips. Pecking him on the cheek, I leaned back and eyed the various plates that were scattered a top the food cart. "So," I said, lifting the lid off one to reveal a delicious looking omelet, "What's for breakfast?"

"You mean lunch?" Ryan laughed, wheeling the cart towards the fireplace before transferring the plates onto the table.

"What do you mean?" I asked, glancing around to see if there was a clock in plain sight. There wasn't. "What time is it?"

"It's almost noon," he replied, sending me a smile as he nodded at me to sit down. "You were out like a light last night that, even when I carried you up and tucked you in, you didn't open your eyes. I actually thought I'd have to wake you up myself this morning using whatever means necessary."

"And I bet that would've been a big inconvenience to you, wouldn't it have been?" I asked shaking my head in amusement.

I quickly noted the grin that spread across his face as he plated a few of the dishes for me. "The biggest."

Laughing, I dug into my food. It was delicious, as to be expected, but it suddenly registered in my mind that, having not stayed awake the night before, I hadn't found out where we were staying.

"So, am I finally allowed to know where, exactly, we are?"

"I'm surprised it's taken you so long to ask," he commented, a smile on his face. "We're at Willows Lodge, a small resort just outside Seattle."

From what I could gather by just looking at the view through the glass doors, this place was definitely private, located off the map and away from the public. "How did you find this place?" I asked. "Have you been here before, or...?"

He shook his head, swallowing the food in his mouth before responding. "My mom mentioned it to me when I asked her if she knew anywhere I could take you for Valentine's Day," he said. "She tried to suggest simply taking you out to dinner, but when she realized I wanted to be hidden away from prying eyes, she said this place was amazing."

My heart clenched, love and warmth taking hold of it. Not only did he take me somewhere quiet and romantic, he'd asked his mother for advice.

The words I love you were on the tip of my tongue, I just didn't have the confidence to let them free. "What's so amazing about it?" I asked instead.

"All she said was that this was where her and my dad spent their first anniversary," he said. The fact that he'd taken me somewhere that held significance to his family was endearing, causing a soft smile to hover on my lips. "When I called, the people I talked to said that they had an award-winning restaurant and a relaxing spa. They said that not many people take the drive out from the city to explore up here, so the gardens and trails around are relatively private. I just thought it'd be a nice surprise." A smirk appeared on his face as he continued, "Plus, the rooms have really big beds. Comfy too."

He winked in my direction, causing me to laugh, realizing where his train of thought had landed. "Well that must've been the selling point," I said teasingly.

He grinned, laughing along with me. "You know it."

Letting the laughter fade, the two of us kept up light conversation as we finished off our food.

An hour later I had thrown on a few layers of clothing from my suitcase, keeping warm with a jacket and scarf as the two of us headed outside to explore the resort grounds. Forgoing a pair of gloves, I tucked one hand into my pocket, the other intertwining with Ryan's naturally.

Leaving our room, we headed down the staircase at the end of the hall, trying to steer clear of our neighbours, and pushed through a door that led to the back of the building. A chilly wind nipped at my exposed skin, reminding me that we weren't in California anymore.

Not knowing which direction to go, we took a guess. Following a trail that split through the trees, we eventually began to see signs that set out a path for us to follow. Not many other guests had chosen to look around like us, and though I could see the appeal a day at the spa held, I couldn't lie and say I wasn't enjoying myself. Once I'd become accustomed to the colder air, the walk became peaceful and serene.

It felt strange to be so tucked away from the world for a while, and I welcomed the breath of fresh air.

I was all too aware that I'd stepped out from the shadows the night before, publically appearing next to Ryan on the red carpet, and that I'd willingly thrown myself into a world so different from my own. While my world revolved around a three year old bundle of joy and a self-inflicted expectation to finish my degree, his was a whole different kind of chaotic. Ryan had people all across the world wanting to know what he was doing at every moment of the day. Whether it was filming a scene for an upcoming movie or tying his shoelaces to go out for a run, they wanted to know. There were some who wanted to see him fail and some who looked up to him.

His life was a rollercoaster. There were good days and bad ones, but as an entirety, it was wild and unpredictable.

I wasn't sure how the news that he was dating a college student with a daughter would come across to the public, if they would be supportive or try to tear us apart. I didn't know if I'd be thrust into the spotlight or slowly sink back into the shadows when new gossip crossed the headlines. There was so much uncertainty laid out on the path before me, but with Ryan by my side, I hoped that, together, we would be able to conquer what was ahead.

Suddenly, quite literally pulling me from my thoughts, Ryan yanked me sideways. Stumbling over my own two feet, I felt my back press up against a tree. Our shoes were sinking into the slushed mud, having veered off of the path, and my eyes widened. "Is someone coming?" I asked quietly. When I turned my head, struggling to see or hear anyone around us, I looked back to Ryan with confusion.

He shook his head, though I did notice how he'd taken another step closer to me, pushing his body up against mine. "No," he replied, his eyes twinkling with amusement as he gazed down at me.

His lips were on mine in an instant. This kiss was not sweet and it was not innocent. It was passionate, needy, and full of yearning. There was no space between the two of us as he frantically moved his lips in sync with my own. His fingers were tangling themselves in my hair as I grabbed the front of his jacket, desperate for more of the warmth that was spreading to every corner of my body. I felt a new thrill surge through me, remembering that while we'd yet to see a single soul, that didn't mean there wasn't a chance of us getting caught against a tree in the middle of a forest, our hormones taking the lead.

He pulled back, his breath still mingling with mine. Opening my eyes slowly, I felt a lazy smile tug on my lips. "What was that for?" I asked, my voice sounding airy and light after being left breathless by his kiss.

"I just felt like it," he smirked, shrugging. I rolled my eyes. "Plus, I thought it'd be a way to lead in to me telling you that we have to be back at the resort in about half an hour."

Curiosity filled my eyes, my forehead crinkling with confusion. "Why, what's in half an hour?"

"I may have booked us both a private hour at the spa," he admitted. His hands, having never fallen from where they'd been woven into my hair, cupped my chin and tilted it upwards. The feeling of him brushing a feather light kiss against my lips before he continued speaking was enough to get my heartbreak back to a racing speed. "I wanted us to be able to relax for a bit. Not that this isn't relaxing, I just thought you'd enjoy a massage or something to brush off a bit of stress."

"You thought right." An impish grin formed on my face, while my grip on his jacket tightened once more. Calculating how long we'd been exploring, I'd guess that we were about twenty minutes away from the resort. "So you said we have thirty minutes right?" He nodded. "Then how about we make use of the next ten before heading back?"

Happiness radiated off of him when he understood what I was suggesting. I'd re-ignited the fire within him, and he didn't falter once, his lips attacking mine with yet another earth shattering kiss.

Half an hour later the two of us were running hand in hand through the back door of the resort, hurrying our way through the halls with laughter. Not having time to head back to our room and change, we pushed through the glass door of the spa. The worker's sent us a strange look as we stopped at the front desk, trying to calm ourselves and catch our breaths, although when their eyes landed on Ryan, those looks disappeared in an instant.

"Sorry we're a bit late," Ryan said, although the smile on his face was attesting to how apologetic he really was. Turning to face me, his eyes were glinting with the memory of what we've been doing to loose track of time. "I booked a private hour here for my girlfriend and I over the phone."

"Sure," the employee stammered, clearly aware of whom she was talking to. "I'll just go make sure everything's ready for you two." She offered us a nervous smile before scurrying off and out of our sight, returning minutes later with two white dressing gowns. Directing us to the changing rooms, she informed us that our masseuses would be with us when we were ready.

True to her words, when I slipped off my clothes and pulled on the fluffy white robe to cover myself, I walked out to see Ryan talking quietly to one of the women waiting for us. Hearing me approach, his gaze turned to me, his irises sparkling with a secret. No words were said to curb my curiosity, and before I could open my mouth, the two women directed us to lie down on the bare massage tables.

Lotions and oils were used to make the experience more relaxing, and although the pressure was borderline painful at points, I breathed through it, knowing it would be worth it in the long run. The woman, who was currently digging deep into the knotted tissues of my shoulders, was working magic. I could physically feel any worries I'd built up over the past few weeks fleeing from my body, and it felt amazing.

When her hands disappeared after only half an hour, I turned my head to see her signaling me to sit up. Pulling the tie on my robe tightly, I followed her instructions, but was confused as to what was going on when I saw Ryan still enjoying his own massage.

His eyes opened slowly at the sound of my feet hitting the floor and, noticing my puzzled expression, his lips curved into a soft grin. "Just go with it," he said quietly and encouragingly.

Not knowing what was going on, but trusting my boyfriend's wishes, I followed the masseuse into the next room. Lining the walls were hundreds of nail polishes, as well as several chairs set up in front of footbaths. Realizing what was going on, I picked out a baby pink colour from the shelves, keeping in theme with the holiday, and took a seat in one of the chairs. The next half hour was spent sitting back and unwinding as one of the employees worked on perfecting my manicure and pedicure, while another women came into the room to give me a soothing facial.

I'd never had the luxury of spending time at a professional spa before, and after spending just an hour with these women, I knew that I would definitely look into treating myself more often.

The spa experience was short though, the time for our privacy expiring all too soon. Feeling awakened and refreshed, I headed back to our room with Ryan, only to be given another surprise.

Without my knowledge, Ryan had been able to slip a black cocktail dress into my luggage. It was one that I'd seen hanging on Yvette's clothing rack the night before and it was gorgeous. The arms were intricately stitched with lace, attaching to an otherwise simple dress that fell to the middle of my thigh. Uttered speechless, Ryan took the opportunity to inform me of the dinner reservations he'd made at the restaurant downstairs.

It didn't take me long to get ready once I'd been shaken from my state of wonder. I simply pulled my hair up into a sleek pony-tail and shimmied into the dress, choosing to only enhance my make-up the slightest bit. Rummaging quickly for the pair of heels Ryan had gifted me the night before, I slipped into them, smiling when I saw Ryan rolling up the sleeves of one of the dress shirts I'd bought him for Christmas.

The restaurant was fancier than I expected, five stars to be exact. Not even a minute after we were seated, an expensive bottle of red wine was brought out and poured into two glasses in front of us. The menu was one single sheet of laminated paper with seven complex dinner options to choose from, ranging from oven-roasted lamb chops to a vegetarian stir fry served over wild rice. It was a nice meal, and we were lucky enough not to be bothered by anyone as we ate, but it just wasn't my style. It was too elegant, too lavish, and too refined

When I had escaped to the bathroom for a few minutes to escape the dim lighting and cultivated environment, Ryan had paid the bill, sensing that I wasn't entirely comfortable in this setting.

It wasn't until we were strolling down the hallway towards our suite that he spoke to me. "Did you not like dinner?" Ryan asked nervously, a crease of worry slipping into his expression.

I shook my head as he unlocked our door, ushering me inside ahead of him. "I did," I insisted, continuing as his eyes turned skep-tical. "Everything that you've done for me over the past two days has been absolutely incredible. It's been like I've been thrown into a fairytale, living in an unimaginable dream, and I've loved every second of it. I just, I don't know," I sighed, "I wanted something a little more relaxed and easygoing tonight."

He stepped closer to me; one hand grasping my hip while one hand cupped my chin, tilting my head upwards. Our eyes met and his eyes were thoughtful, almost searching, but it was clear that he wasn't mad. "Why didn't you just tell me?" he asked, rubbing his thumb in circles just above my waist. "I've would've just cancelled the reservations and ordered something to the room."

"I didn't want to ruin your plans."

He shook his head. "My plan was to spend time with you this weekend. It doesn't matter what we're doing, as long as we're together."

A smile pulled at my lips. "So you don't mind relaxing in the room for the rest of the night? Maybe watch a movie?"

"I think that sounds like the perfect excuse to hold you close to me," he replied cheekily, pulling me closer to his chest.

I laughed, planting my hands on his firm chest before pushing away. "I just have to get changed," I said lightly, "And then I promise I won't leave your side."

"I'm counting on it."

Shaking my head in amusement, I retreated to my suitcase. Tossing a few articles of clothing to the side, I searched for my pajamas before hitting a cardboard box that I'd completely forgotten about. Snatching it from the bottom of my bag, I grabbed the first pair of pajamas that I could spot before turning back to Ryan.

The air left my lungs at the sight of Ryan shirtless. He had stripped off his shirt and was working on the belt of his dress pants as his eyes trailed up to meet mine. I was aware of the amusement in his eyes as he nodded down to the box in my hands. "What's that?"

"Umm it's just something I bought you for Valentine's Day," I managed to breathe out, a nervous smile surfacing. "I wasn't sure what to get you, but I remembered you mentioned that you used to like building them, so, yeah." I extended my arms, pushing the present in his direction.

He was curious and intrigued, stepping forward to take the box from my hands. I hadn't wrapped it due to a considerable lack of tissue paper lying around my house, and watching him stare at the box in silence was making my hands jitter.

"Do you like it?" I asked quietly, biting my lip.

I saw the exact moment that it sunk in for him, the exact moment he realized that I remembered the conversation we'd had a while back about his past, and that I'd based his present on a hope that his past hobby hadn't died.

I had bought him a model plane kit, like the ones he had built when he was a kid, and as Ryan looked down at it, his eyes were wide with astonishment and disbelief.

I wasn't sure what I was expecting him to say, but the words that fell from his lips were a complete surprise.

"I love you."

"W... Wh... What?" I stammered out, eyes bulging.

I don't think he truly realized what three words he had uttered, his eyes widening in realization, but when a few moments of silence ran between us, his gaze softened. "I never thought I'd see another one of these kits again until I had my own kids, and with my busy schedule, I don't even know if I'd ever have time to sit down and build it with them. And then I met you. The first time I bumped into you, you intrigued me. I wasn't wearing much of a disguise, but you didn't recognize me." He smiled at the memory as he moved closer to me, discarding the gift on the table next to us. "Then we got closer and I met Abbie and you agreed to be my girlfriend. I hadn't thought about having a normal life again since my first premiere, and when you two suddenly became such a big part of my life, it felt like everything I believed in was turned on its axis. I found myself thinking about what it would be like to wake up next to you every day and hear Abbie playing downstairs with the toys that my family would no doubt buy her, just because she's too adorable to not love. She takes after her mother like that." His voice was tender and my eyes were filling with tears of happiness, though I kept the floodgates closed, not allowing them to fall. "I love you Zoe Hamilton, and I promise you I'll do anything possible to have you stay around for a long, long time."

My mouth was quivering now, but I was eventually able to find the courage I needed. There was no falter in my voice as I said, "I love you too Ryan."

His pupils brightened. "You do?"

I laughed, feeling one tear escape as I nodded. "Yes," I managed to force out.

Before I knew it, our mouths were locked in a fiery, passionate kiss. His tongue teased my bottom lip and I was unable to stifle the moan that it evoked, causing him to grin against my lips. My hands trailed up his bare chest effortlessly. I was conscious of my feet taking steps backwards. When the back of my knees hit the edge of the bed, I fell back against the soft sheets, knowing a movie was now the last thing on the either of our minds.

It was safe to say that we didn't leave the hotel room again until the next morning.

Our night was spent exploring the love we harbored, finally giving in to the feelings that had been circling us from the first moment we'd bumped into each other in Corner Café all those months ago.

It was late in the morning when the two of us awoke. His arms were wrapped securely around my shoulders when my eyes fluttered open after the most amazing dream, and I couldn't of asked for a more perfect morning.

Knowing that our flight left early the next morning, Ryan asked me over breakfast if I wanted to head into the city for a few hours, in disguise of course, to sight see and act as run-of-the-mill tourists. I'd nodded excitedly, the thrill of wandering the streets of an unfamiliar city building in my stomach.

Seattle's streets were lively for a Sunday afternoon. There were cars whizzing past us and other people surrounding us on the sidewalk, but with the small disguises we'd both adorned at the resort, not a single passerby glanced our way.

There were shops lining each side of the road. With each step we took, the window displays seemed to change from expensive couture to books displays to freshly baked desserts. Spotting a pizza place at the next street corner, I pulled Ryan's hand, crossing the street to join the short line of customers. The food was greasy, unhealthy, and overall bad for us, but I didn't care one bit as I stuffed the food into my mouth once we'd found a vacant bench to sit down.

The food was only the first thing that we stopped for however, as the stores we spotted throughout the city began to draw our attention and spark curiosity. Ryan had managed to wrangle me into a science store for kids, in which I laughed as he stood with a wide smile on his face, watching an employee help a group of kids make their very own silly putty. I, on the other hand, coerced Ryan into stepping into a used bookstore. It wasn't the most organized or the biggest of places, but the inside held character, the books slightly worn and battered from years of love from past owners.

"I can't believe you bought five books," Ryan said, shaking his head as we walked out of the shop, a bell ringing over our heads. "When are you going to have time to read them?"

"I'll find time," I replied, swinging our intertwined hands back and forth, "And I tend to go overboard in books stores sometimes."

"That's not to hard to believe," he teased.

Shoving myself into his side half-heartedly, I wasn't surprised when his hand left mine, seeking out a resting spot on my shoulder.

The streets became busier as the afternoon began to disappear. We must've spent hours exploring the downtown, and when we reached an area that slowly started to disperse into high rises and company buildings, we figured that we'd spent all the time possible in the city. With an intersection up ahead, I prayed that finding a taxi back to the resort wouldn't be too difficult.

What happened next was unforeseeable.

It may have been due to the fact the two of us were too focused on hailing down a taxi, or it could've been fate playing a cruel joke on me, but as we reached the street corner, the two of us bumped into another person coming around the corner.

There body collided mostly with mine, Ryan taking it upon himself to steady my feet as I toppled backwards from the collision, having not seen anyone in my path.

"Sorry, I didn't mean to..."

The voice trailed off in disbelief when they realized whom exactly they had bumped into. My spine stiffened and my eyes snapped up in urgency, needing to see if this was really happening. It couldn't be, not now. Yet here we were, standing face to face as though not a day had passed since we'd last spoken.

"What are you doing here?"

CHAPTER 21

The woman's eyes widened, her skin paling to a ghostly white. "Zoe," she stammered, unable to form a coherent response.

"Mom? What are you doing here?" I repeated.

Seattle was the last place I'd expect to bump into my mother, considering the last time I'd seen her and my dad was months ago; a few days before I moved out of the old house in Arizona. They hadn't called, they hadn't texted, they hadn't checked in with Emily, Abbie, or I at all.

And now, a weekend meant for relaxation had been tainted because of this untimely run-in.

My mom cleared her throat, standing up straighter to appear calm and collected. Her eyes flicked to Ryan for a quick moment before landing back on me. "Your father and I flew out yesterday morning to meet with a few witnesses for an upcoming case," she explained. "We're here for the next couple of days, though we certainly didn't expect to see you here."

"I'm sure you didn't," I mumbled, only then catching on that she'd mentioned my father. "Dad's here too?"

"Of course he is," my mom replied. "We need to put up a united front when dealing with clients, and..."

Before she could finish her explanation, the man in question rounded the corner in a hurry, stopping in his tracks as he bumped into his wife. "There you are," he said, having not noticed me yet, "I thought we were meeting at Fiore."

When she didn't reply immediately, his eyebrows furred in confusion, his gaze shifting in my direction. His green eyes widened with recognition, an unreadable look sweeping across his features. Where as my mom's hair had grown longer and healthier since I'd last seen her, my dad's had become shorter, grey patches beginning to take over his once dark hair. In fact, pressure and work seemed to be taking a toll on both of them, as I could pinpoint wrinkles and stress marks that hadn't been there before.

"Zoe."

My lips pulled into a dry smile. "Hey dad."

He picked up on my tone immediately, his eyes narrowing as he spoke in a bitter voice. "What are you doing all the way out in Seattle?"

I wanted to laugh. I wanted to tell him that I could've traveled across an ocean without him knowing, and yet, with the words on the tip of my tongue, I couldn't muster up the courage to let the free.

He was trying to be civil, and so the least I could do was try.

"Ryan surprised me with a weekend out here," I replied, taking a deep breath to calm myself as I intertwined my hand with Ryan's. I could feel him tense beside me, realizing he'd been brought into the conversation. Having skimmed over the details of my home life with him, I was sure that he'd caught on that this was not a reunion I was thrilled about. "Mom. Dad. This is Ryan Adams, my boyfriend."

My tight-lipped smile was enough to show the two of them how I truly felt introducing them to him, but as I turned to Ryan, my features softened ever so slightly. Although I hadn't thought that meeting with my parents was even a possibility this weekend, I was glad that I was getting it over with.

Ryan held out his free hand, shaking my dad's hand with a firm grip. "Nice to meet you," he greeted, addressing both my parents with a nod. Though, having known him for a while, I could hear the tight edge to his voice.

My dad however, didn't pick up on the undertone to Ryan's voice. Or if he did, he didn't show it. "You too," he replied, seemingly friendly, as if he was being introduced to a new client. Though after taking a better look at him, I could tell he was concentrating a bit too hard on Ryan's appearance. "You look very familiar son. Have we met somewhere before?"

As the word son fell from his lips, a hostile feeling surged through my veins. The word was a term of endearment, and after neglecting my sister and I for the better part of our childhood, he was using it to greet a man that he'd met just short of five minutes previous.

Ryan's gaze shifted to me, silently asking if I was okay with them knowing of his fame, but before either of us could get the words out, my mother's voice cut into the conversation.

"You're in the movie that's coming out soon," my mom began quietly, having figured it out all on her own. Turning towards my dad, she explained further, "He's on the billboard across the street from our firm; that's where you've seen him before."

"Is he now?" my dad asked, racing an eyebrow curiously before the recognition sunk in. I gulped, hesitantly shifting my attention between my parents and Ryan. A gut feeling bubbled in the pit of my stomach, and not a pleasant one either. "Then I'm sure you've been busy recently. So tell me, when did you find the time to start seeing our daughter?"

Meeting Ryan's gaze, I could sense that he was uncomfortable with the situation, his hand tightening around my own. He wanted to say something, anything to my father, but he also wasn't wired that way. Ryan was too nice and caring to explode on someone he'd just met.

So it was me who responded after the lull of silence. "We met a few months ago dad," I replied, not holding back my irritation, "Not that it's any of your business though."

"It most certainly is my business," he countered authoritatively, clenching his teeth in an effort not to raise his voice. "I think I deserve to know if my daughter is suddenly going to be paraded around on the arm of some. What am I supposed to say if someone recognizes you? That I knew nothing about it?"

"Exactly, because then they'll know what kind of parent you really are."

Seeing a vein pulse in my father's neck should've been a warning sign for me. I knew I should've regretted the words that slipped past my lips, but in the heat of the moment, I couldn't stop them from tumbling out. And I wasn't sorry.

"Alright you two, break it up," my mother intervened, sensing the tension that was starting to build between my father and I. Stepping outside the bubble the four of us had been entrapped in, I noticed that people around us were casting their gazes in our direction, and it wasn't because there was a celebrity in the mix. "Why don't we go somewhere else to talk?" she asked, looking between us with a nervous look before her eyes stopped on me. "Your father and I were going to meet at Fiore; it's a quiet café a few blocks up. We can go there if you want."

I was about to decline, not wanting to spend any more time than needed in my parent's company, when I felt a subtle movement on my hand. Ryan had began running his thumb over mine gently, soothing the mess of feelings fighting in my stomach and clearing my thoughts. It was a small gesture, but it was also a silent conversation. He wanted me to talk to them, to clear the air between us.

Inhaling slowly, I closed my eyes. "Okay," I breathed out, "Okay."

"Then let's go, before we make a scene," she said, also having noticed the attention we'd been attracting. Her gaze turned to Ryan and she cleared her throat. "Will you be joining us?"

Ryan seemed hesitant at first, but when he glanced my way, his eyes apologetic, I already knew his answer. He shook his head as he faced my parents again, confirming my suspicions. "I think I'll just head back to the resort on my own," he replied, slipping his hand from mine as it reached out and took the shopping bag I'd been holding. He bent his head to kiss my cheek, whispering quietly in my ear as he pulled back. "Give me a call when you're heading back, and try not to kill them."

I snorted under my breath. "No promises."

Ryan laughed as well, sobering up as he stepped back from me, bidding farewell to my parents. I watched him retreat down the sidewalk, his hand out to hail a taxi, and all I wanted to do was yell at him to come back. He was a safety blanket that I'd gladly wear while dealing with my parents. He was a source of fire beneath my feet, but as he took one final glance back before sliding into the back seat of a car, my silence was all that could be heard.

This was something I had to do on my own.

"So," I gulped, turning back towards my parents, "Shall we?"

Fiore wasn't exactly what I was expecting for a café, but with my parent's expensive taste, I should've anticipated it.

Stepping through the front door, there were no jingling bells above our heads that sent feel-good vibes through my body. The usual feeling of comfort that came with a hole-in-the-wall café was missing, as this was not a place of comfort. The interior looked to have one belonged to a small five-star restaurant, having only been converted into a café in recent years, and the prices made my eyes widen, seeing as they were almost triple what Colette's family charged back home.

The menus were sleek and sophisticated, printed onto boards five feet above the front counter, and the two workers behind the counter both wore black dress shirts with the café's name embroidered just above their hearts.

It was quiet though, which meant there would be less of an audience if this conversation escalated as quickly as it had on the street.

Approaching the front counter, I saw one of the workers cower in her stance at the sight of my parents. They looked intimidating, I'd give them that, but there mere presence shouldn't frighten an innocent worker. Though I'd assumed they'd visit this place previously, having not once glanced at the menu before ordering.

Requesting two coffees for themselves, I butted in and ordered a frozen lemonade. If I was going to make it through the next hour or so, I needed a lot more than coffee to keep me sane. I'd caught sight of freshly baked muffins in the display cases, however, with an unsettled stomach, I didn't think I was capable of stomaching more than a small drink.

After being handed our drinks, I followed my parents to a table near the back of the café. Even though there were no other customers, they seemed to be keen on keeping our conversation private.

"So, are you guys actually here on business?" I asked, breaking the silence after taking a sip of my drink.

My mother's hands curled around her coffee mug. "Yes," she replied, clipped and quietly. "Why? Did you think I was lying?"

I shrugged. "How would I know? I just find it a bit weird that, after not talking to you guys for the past six months, you just happen to bump into me in downtown Seattle."

"We didn't plan to bump into you," my father responded gruffly. "Your mother and I are in the middle of an important lawsuit, and some of the key witnesses in our case live in the downtown area."

"Yeah, mom already told me."

"Don't interrupt me young lady," he said sharply, taking a deep breath before continuing. "And if your mother already mentioned it, then why ask? We're here because our job needs us to be, yet you seem to be here gallivanting your time away with some boy that we didn't even know existed."

My blood was beginning to boil at how he was speaking down to me, as though disappointment and shock were emotions too mediocre for him, and I was trying exceptionally hard to keep my temper under control.

"And how would you know he existed, or anything about my life for that matter? Do you know what I'm taking in school, or do you know that Emily's been in a relationship for the past two years?" I asked. "No, you don't, but that's because we don't feel the need to tell you the significant details of our lives any more. We moved out for a reason."

I could see the fury light up in my dad's eyes, though my mother spoke before he could. "To be more independent, we know," she said, her eyes casting down to study the hardwood glaze of the table. There was a pause in conversation as she struggled to figure out her next words. "And where is Abbie? Have you left her alone somewhere?"

A sardonic laugh escaped my lips. "Oh, such a great grandparent you are, noticing after more than half an hour that Abbie's not here. Bravo," I said, not giving any thought to the fact that the filter between my brain and my mouth was fading by the second. "And that's rich coming from you, considering that once your careers began to take off, you more or less abandoned Emily and I."

"That's not fair."

"It's completely fair," I continued, my voice rising to a higher volume before I brought it back down. "When Abbie and I lived back in Arizona, you guys never took the time to care about her, so why start now? And if you must know, she's staying with Emily for the weekend."

"So what?" my dad started, "You suddenly catch a guy's attention and then you forget all about your daughter?"

"Just like you suddenly got invested in your work and forgot about yours," I threw back, angry that he'd even suggest such a thing. "Ryan may not be a father to Abbie, but he sure as hell cares about her. He's never looked down on me for being a single mother, and never once expected me to give up plans with her to spend time with him. Abbie comes first, she always will, and he knows that."

"And if you really believe that he'll be okay being your second priority for much longer, you're more naïve than I thought."

My father had been treading a dangerous line, but with that comment, he fell face first over it. My anger was in full throttle, and there was no reigning it back in.

"Ryan isn't you dad. He isn't just going to forget about other responsibilities when things get hard."

"I never forgot about you."

"You're right, you kept such a watchful eye on me that I ended up getting pregnant and your other daughter ended up arrested. Well done." It was tough throwing my own mistakes back in their face, but it needed to be done. "You let Greta practically raise Emily and I. She was the one that ate with us, that helped us with our homework, and who we went to talk to when times got hard. You two were always at work or locked away in your office, and when we were old enough to finally recognize what was happening, we didn't need you anymore."

"This conversation isn't about us," my father replied, grinding his teeth as he spat out his next words, "This is about you and that boy."

"You don't suddenly get to step back into my life." I spat out. "What? Are you scared that I'm suddenly going to be thrust into the spotlight and spill all your dirty little secrets? If so, don't worry. I don't plan on wasting my breath on people who don't matter to me."

"Ryan's only going to hurt you Zoe," my mother chimed in, appearing concerned as she took my father's side in this argument.

"How would you know? You met him for less than ten minutes, and during that time, he barely said a word to either of you."

"He's famous," my dad replied, as though the words spoke for themselves, "He'll get bored with you soon enough."

"What, did you want me to end up with someone like you? An up and coming lawyer with a solid job and a massive trust fund to match his high-class attitude?"

"We want you to end up with someone who has a promising future, yes," my mom replied. She seemed to have a better hold on her temper than my father and I. "An actor's career doesn't always last, and once his fame goes away, what more does he have?"

"Are you kidding me right now?" I asked. My eyes were hooded with rage and disbelief. "He's a good person! Which is more than I can say for you two. When was the last time you guys held a conversation that didn't revolve around your firm or a client? You guys have a partnership, not a relationship, and I don't want that."

"He's not good enough for you..."

I couldn't stand hearing them belittle Ryan any longer, and if we were anywhere but a public place, I would've considered throwing something to calm my anger. Pushing myself up from my seat, I was seething, my eyes glinting dangerously. "That's something for me to decide, no you," I said resentfully, "And trust me, he's more than good enough."

I didn't wait around to hear what else they had to say, turning on my heel and making my way to the front of the café. Yanking the door, I stomped onto the sidewalk, stopping when the fresh air hit me. Once I'd made my way around the closest corner, I rested my back against the brick, trying to calm my ragged breaths.

It had been a long time since my parents and I had gotten along. There were years of resent, anger, and distance separating us, and one conversation wasn't going to change that.

Only when I shook my head, trying to clear my thoughts, did I become aware of the newsstand that I'd stopped beside. And of course, as if a fight with my parents wasn't enough drama for the day, the front cover of one of the most popular magazines had a picture of Ryan and his female co-star from Knights of Fury plastered across the front page.

The headline read, Just Co-Stars, Or Something More?

I caught the date of the magazine and saw that it was more than a week old, meaning the picture had more than likely been taken on the press tour in New York.

I trusted Ryan, I really did, and although I hadn't wanted it to happen, I realized that my parents words had gotten underneath my skin. I knew in my heart that there was nothing to this article, but that didn't stop me from second-guessing myself.

Clenching my eyes shut, I forced my racing mind to slow right down, stopping the thoughts that began to develop. Pulling myself together, I waved my hand, seeking out a taxi.

Giving the name of the resort to the driver, as I didn't know the address, I was lucky enough to learn he knew the way. Resting my head back against the seat, I let the events of the past hour replay in my head. The collision, the shock, the spitfire accusations, and the hostility. It was a lot, and I was surprised I was holding myself together.

It only clicked that I hadn't called Ryan when the taxi pulled up to the front of the resort, dropping me off once I handed him a few bills to pay the fare. Stopping at the front desk, I got directions to my suite, as I hadn't thought to check which one we were staying in, before heading up to meet Ryan.

"Please tell me you didn't somehow know that my parents had work in Seattle this weekend," I said, slamming the door of the room in a huff.

Shedding my coat and my shoes, I turned to see Ryan sitting in the middle of the bed, where he'd been scrolling through his phone before I'd taken him by surprise. His eyes were wide with alarm and hurt. Pushing himself off the bed in a hurry, he quickly made his way across the room. "No, of course I didn't," he rushed out. His hands sought out my shoulders as he crouched down, making our eyes level as his gaze seared into mine. "I had no idea your parents would be here, or that we'd bump into them. I wanted to plan a relaxing getaway for you to give us some alone time, but this, you being upset, was never my intention."

I sighed, collapsing against his chest while his arms circled my waist. "I believe you," I mumbled quietly. I felt the burning ache of tears welling up in the corners of my eyes as I pressed my face closer to his skin. "It's just been a rough day."

One of his hands trailed up my back, rubbing slow circles at the top of my spine. "I'm guessing the conversation with your parents didn't go too well?"

Sniffling a bit, I felt a few tears escape as I replied, "Not even in the slightest."

He let the silence linger for a few moments, just holding me. I accepted the comfort because, as I stood in his arms, it was easy to forget about the guilt that was gnawing at my stomach. It was what I needed; reassurance that he wasn't going anywhere.

"You don't need to explain," Ryan said softly, pulling back only as my breathing leveled out and my tears ceased to fall. One hand stayed wrapped securely around my waist, while the other trailed up my body, pushing stray wisps of hair away from my face. "Just know that if you want to, I'm here to listen."

A smile managed to tug at the corner of my lips. Without answering, I didn't take my eyes off him, grabbing his hand and guiding him towards the bed. He looked as though he was getting the wrong idea when his eyes widened and he sat stiffly on top of the covers.

"I don't... we shouldn't... you're not..."

I shook my head, silencing his protests with a strong pull on his arm. He laid down beside me, hesitant at first, but when I made no moves towards him, his legs intertwined with mine and his hands sought out my waist.

"I want to tell you what happened," I sighed, moving further into his touch, "I just don't know where to start."

"Well," he said softly, "You can start at the beginning, or the middle, or even the end if that helps."

It was a wonder how his teasing was able to resonate through my blurred thoughts, but never the less, a light laugh escaped my lips before I dove head first into the explanation. I skipped the unimportant bits, like what I'd ordered and where we'd gone, and jumped right into the memories that had my teeth grinding as I recounted them.

Not once did he interrupt, though when his jaw clenched and his hold on me tightened, I knew he was listening to every word. It hurt to repeat the cruel and disgusting things my parents had said, but he needed to know. He needed to know that, while their words and advances had played with my mind, I still trusted him.

I still loved him.

When I reached the end of the tale, my gaze locked with his, my hand running over the delicate features of his complexion, committing them to memory. "I know it's a lot, but please understand that, even though they think they have control over me, they don't," I said, my voice just above a whisper. "They haven't since Abbie was born, maybe even before that, and there is no way that they'll ever come between our relationship."

The wheels were turning in his head, and when he finally sank into my touch, I was able to breathe easier.

"Why couldn't your parents be like mine?" he asked. "What's so wrong with welcoming someone into your family with open arms?"

My chest tightened as I heard the agony he was attempting to mask. "My parents aren't wired that way," I said, trying and failing to find the bright side to the situation. "Don't worry, considering how much I love you, I'm voiding their opinions."

I moved closer to him when there was nothing else I could say. My head fell perfectly in the crook of his neck as my lips met a small patch of skin, underneath of which laid a beating vein flowing towards his heart. His arms tightened around me in an instant, pulling me so that my soft curves were aligned with his hard physique. A shiver rang through my spine when the soft outlines of his lips left a ghost of a kiss against my forehead.

A day that had started out adventurous had taken a turn, leaving the two of us in shambles, wondering when we'd feel complete again.

"So, how were mom and dad?"

It was Emily's first question when I'd arrived home the following afternoon. Our plane had touched down less than an hour before, and knowing I had to work at four, Ryan had dropped me off before heading off to a meeting with his manager.

The night before had been rough, and while Ryan had confessed he had planned to take me out to a local diner, we ended up ordering room service for dinner, neither of us wanting to escape the sanctuary of our room. It was a quiet evening, eventually filled with miscellaneous small talk and subsidiary gestures, but the events of the day still loomed around us, casting an eerie shadow over the remainder of our trip.

I had sent Emily a text before I'd fallen asleep, summing up the talk with our parents, but was left with no energy to explain anything further.

Letting my luggage drop to the floor, I moved to collapse against my sister, my body sinking deep into the sofa as I pulled my legs up to my chest. It was a reflex when I was scared, a position where I felt like nothing could hurt me.

"Horrible," I said simply, sensing the feelings of hate and despair working their way back into my head. "They haven't been an active part of our lives for months, years even, so what made them think that, after one short run in, they had the authority to say things like that and get away with it?"

Emily had dealt all too often with my parents harsh and frivolous words before she'd moved away, and while I'd been the one to comfort her then, it was now her turn to ease away my stress.

"It's just the way their minds work," Emily reasoned, moving a supportive hand across my shoulder. "They think now that we're mature enough to step into the real world, they can all of a sudden reign us back in to follow their unrealistic expectations."

"They said that I shouldn't be wasting my time with Ryan because he's only going to hurt me," I forced out, sounding weak and worried as a hiccup of tears followed suit. "And they tried to say I wasn't a good enough mother."

"Assholes."

I laughed through my sadness, bringing a hand up to my eyes to soak up the tears. "You can say that again."

"Zoe," she started, shaking her head, "You can't let them get to you, because if you do, you'll end up ruining your own happiness. Ryan is one of the most genuine guys I've ever met, and what you two have is something special. If it doesn't end up working out, it's because you both put everything you had into the relationship, but wanted different things in the end. That's just what love is, sometimes even your best isn't good enough, but you two are so in sync and supportive of one another, that if you can't make it work, then there's no hope for the rest of us." I couldn't help the tiny smile that quirked upon my lips. "And they haven't been around to know that you're a damn good mother. Abbie adores you, and I know that there isn't anything you wouldn't do to see her smile."

Those were the words that carried me forward the rest of the day. They replayed on a loop in the back of my mind as I played with my daughter for the first time in days, as I texted Ryan letting him know I was headed to work, and when I stepped foot into Corner Café, ready for my shift.

I was distracted, momentarily, by the fresh aroma and the undertones of burnt coffee grounds, that I hadn't realized the room was uncharacteristically busy.

People old and young were littering around the front of the café, casting their gazes towards me with a drop of curiosity. Their eyes were bright with excitement, which only had me more confused. I could see Colette struggling behind the counter with the mad rush, and when I slipped into work mode quicker than I'd expected, a coo from customers alerted her of my presence.

"Zoe," Colette said, stumbling with wide eyes, as though caught off guard, "I didn't think you'd be coming in today."

My forehead creased together with concern. "Why wouldn't I?"

She sent me a sympathetic gaze, wiping her sugarcoated hands off on a spare tea towel before pulling a load of newspaper out from under the register. Casting my curiosity towards the crumbled papers, my eyes were drawn to the front page, of not one, but several of them, that read:

Ryan Adam's Mystery Girl – The Inside Scoop on Zoe Hamilton

CHAPTER 22

I didn't know what to do. I didn't know what to think. All I could do was stare, wide eyed and daunted, at the pages laid out before me.

While all the headlines were similar, every paper seemed to have their own source for photos. There were snapshots of us from the red carpet, which were to be expected, however, the photos of us from the past couple of months had the hair on the back of my neck standing on end. I gulped, my eyes scanning the various pictures. One was of us walking down the street hand in hand, another of us talking as I worked the counter at the café, and one picture had been submitted by someone at the basketball game when we'd had our first kiss.

One paper, however, had managed to capture the two of us at the resort in Seattle over the weekend. The blown up spread showed us joking around in the trails, including a rather embarrassing picture of Ryan pushing me up against the trunk of a tree, his hands on my ass as we clung to each other in a private moment of passion.

It was mortifying to say the least.

I knew that there was a possibility of me being a topic of interest following the premiere of Knights of Fury, but I never thought it would escalate to this extent.

I wasn't important. I wasn't newsworthy. I was normal, and now my life was plastered across the pages of a paper for everyone to see.

My mind was whirling a mile a minute and I felt like hyperventilating when my heart began to contract at a faster pace.

When Colette's hand touched my shoulder gently, I realized that I had zoned out of my surroundings, having been solely focused on the tabloids. I came back to, only to realize that the line of customers had tripled in just a few minutes. The newcomers at the back were whispering amongst one another, casting their gazes through the swarm of people in front of them, who all seemed to be recording the scene with their phones.

I was the center of attention, and I didn't know what to do.

"I think you should head home until this all dies down," Colette said quietly, casting me a sympathetic gaze as I turned to face her. Apprehension masked my face, as I didn't want to leave her to deal with the crowd alone, but she saw right through it. "I can take care of this, and my parents are on their way to help out. Now go."

Watching as the crowd slowly began to scrutinize me, I gulped, nodding my head before retreating to the back room. Sinking back against the wall, I waited to make sure that no one had followed me, and was able to finally release the breath that I'd been holding. The hazy storm in my mind was beginning to clear, leaving me alone with my thoughts.

Those stories had cut their way through the tougher skin that I'd believed to build, and I hadn't even been able to read the articles, simply browse the headlines.

Before I could stop myself, I found myself pulling my phone from my pocket and dialing a familiar number.

He picked up on the second ring.

"Zoe?"

"Ryan," I said shakily, "Can you pick me up?"

"Pick you up? Where are you?" he asked, his voice laced with concern and curiosity. "I thought you had to work this afternoon."

"I'm at work. I just, I didn't think that it'd be this bad, and there are so many people," I rambled, not able to form a full sentence. I clenched my eyes shut. "Have you seen any of the papers today?"

I heard him cuss under his breath, and I figured that he'd worked out what was going on. "My manager mentioned a few stories, but I didn't think it was that big of a deal since the premiere was on Friday," he admitted. Even through the phone line, I could make out his stress and frustration. "How many people are there?"

"A lot," I replied meekly.

"Okay, okay," he repeated, as though he was pacing, trying to formulate a plan. "Here's what to do," he said, having had a few moments to collect his thoughts, "Just stay at the café. I'll be there to pick you up as soon as I can, and hopefully we'll be able to get away without too many people noticing."

I could tell his words were serious, and I nodded, only to stop seconds later when I realized he couldn't see me. "Okay, I'll be waiting."

"I love you Zoe," he whispered, causing a smile to appear amongst the chaos. "This will all blow over soon."

The line clicked dead, and within the same instant, Colette startled me, pushing open the doors to the back as she breezed into the room.

"I'm really sorry about all this Zoe," she apologized. "I honestly thought that you'd have seen the articles already, or else I would've called you myself to tell you not to come in."

"It's okay," I said, forcing a small smile on my face as I accepted a hug, "Really."

"It's not," Colette disagreed, shaking her head, "But my parents are out there right now trying to get rid of everyone who's only here to see you. Hopefully everything will calm down soon."

Colette's parents were miracle workers, because just a few minutes later, the buzz of excitement that had been humming from the front of the café lowered significantly. By the time my phone beeped with a text from Ryan, notifying me that he'd pulled up at the front, I was able to walk through the café with my hood up and my head down. Once I reached Ryan's car, pulling open the passenger's door, I breathed a sigh of relief.

Ryan cast a worried gaze my way. "Are you okay?" he asked, his eyes trailing my face to try and pinpoint any kind of physical harm.

"I'm fine," I said, beckoning him to start the car. When his foot hit the gas, shifting the car into motion, I rested my head back against the seat. "I just wasn't expecting it, that's all."

Concern flitted across his features while his gaze shifted frequently between the road ahead and me. "Are you sure?"

I'd never thought that I'd be in a situation like this, and if I was being completely honest, it was frightening to know that, on my own, I might not be strong enough to deal with the repercussions. Whether it was because I knew he had experience with the press, or simply because of my feelings for him, when Ryan was around, I felt the pressure lessen and I was able to make sense of everything.

"Yes." His hand sought out my own, intertwining our fingers with a gentle squeeze, and I realized that he was veering us away from my house, as well as his own. "Where are we going?"

"When I left my house there was a swarm of reporters parked on my street," he said. His grip on the steering wheel tightened, turning the knuckles on his hand white, while his tone was clipped and full of anger. "It took me a while to loose them."

I squeezed his hand in an effort to comfort him. "You didn't have to..."

My protests fell on deaf ears as he continued without much more than a pause. "And I don't want them finding out where you live, if they don't already know," he added, sending a shiver of uncertainty down my spine. "So I thought we'd head to my parents for a while and wait for some of the commotion to die down." His gaze finally swiveled from the road as he took a deep breath, his eyes swimming with apprehension. "Is that okay with you?"

While I would have preferred to curl up in my bed, the familiarity and company keeping me levelheaded, I was aware of the risks, and nodded.

The drive took a bit longer than expected, and Ryan spent every few seconds glancing in his rearview mirror to make sure that there was nobody tailing us. He was anxious and on edge, but he had every reason to be.

By the time we pulled up at his parent's house, the tension had only eased marginally. I had called Emily when we'd hit the congested afternoon traffic, and it was clear how uncomfortable and guilty Ryan felt while listening to me explain the situation to her.

It felt wrong to me, walking unannounced into a home that wasn't my own, but crossing the porch, Ryan reached in front of me and pushed the front door open. His hand rested on the small of my back, ushering me inside, while he raised his voice to let his family know we were here.

I'd barely had time to hang my jacket on the coat rack and kick off my boots before Sophie had rounded the corner into the entryway, pulling me into her arms. It was surprising, but not unwelcome, as she closed the gap between us. I hesitated at first before I hugging her back, falling into the comfort that she offered me.

She was treating me like a daughter, something that I'd not felt like in ages.

After a moment or two, she pulled away. "Oh honey, what happened?" she asked, keeping me at arms length while her eyes flitted between Ryan and I. "Ryan said that you guys were in the paper and that there was a riot at your work. Are you okay?"

I managed a small smile as I nodded. "Still in one piece, and I'm dealing."

"That's good then," she replied, her optimism beginning to shine through, "And know that you're always welcome here if anything ever gets too hectic. Just call and come on over whenever you need."

"Thanks."

Looking back at Ryan, who had stayed silent through our whole exchange, I could see that his worry lines were starting to disappear, and a ghost of a smile was playing on his lips. The light in his eyes dimmed however, when his phone beeped with an incoming call, a tight expression masking his face as he accepted the call.

"Let's leave him alone for a few minutes," Sophie suggested, seeing him run a stressed hand through his hair.

Ryan forced a smile, hearing his mother's suggestion, and nodded, mouthing for me to follow her.

Stepping into the living room, Ryan's dad was nowhere to be seen, but Dean was sitting with his feet up on the couch, relaxing as a basketball game aired on the television.

"Hey," he said in greeting as he noticed me, turning down the volume of the game, "What are you doing here?"

I smiled apprehensively and returned his greeting, taking a seat on one of the spare chairs. "I went into work an hour ago, only to learn that there were several papers printed today with Ryan and I on the cover of them."

"At least next to you, my brother might actually look decent," Dean replied with a smirk, winking in my direction.

I was tempted to laugh, but with an unsettling feeling still brewing in the pit of my stomach, all I could manage was an eye roll. "Always the charmer," I said sarcastically. Ducking my head, I could feel a flush of heat work it's way up my neck when I remembered some of the pictures that had been printed. "And not all the pictures were from the premiere," I admitted.

His eyes were quick to notice the blush I was trying to keep at bay, and a smirk stretched across his lips. "Then what were they of?" he asked, teasing undertones surfacing as he wiggled his eyebrows suggestively.

My blush intensified, a surge of embarrassment flowing through me. Before I could sputter out a reply, Sophie rounded the back of the sofa and hit him over the head flippantly. "Oh hush boy," she scolded. The unexpectedness of the contact caused his eyes to widen in surprise, and he brought his hand up to rub the spot that had been hit. Dean grumbled under his breath in a huff, causing a small smile to tug at my lips when his mother rolled her eyes. "Don't mind this little brat," she said, jutting her thumb in Dean's direction, her voice now directed towards me. "And don't worry about the papers; the tabloids always find a way to blow things out of proportion and make you want to go into hiding."

Her words didn't make me feel any more at ease.

"In fact," she continued, "I remember when Ryan first got into the industry. He was about twenty when an article about him surfaced. I think he'd gone out with a couple of friends, and somehow, they had all ended up wrestling in a public park." Her smile was encouraging, if not a bit comical. "I'm not sure exactly what went on, but a few days later a picture of him lying on top of one of his friends in the park was plastered across thousands of tabloids, insinuating that he was hiding his sexuality. Now I knew that Ryan wasn't gay, as he'd had brief girlfriends before, but he was so embarrassed after that."

Dean let out a loud laugh, joining his mother on the walk down memory lane. "That was hilarious," he guffawed. "He locked himself up in his room for a week and didn't want to talk to anyone."

A giggle escaped my lips, finding the tale highly amusing. "And I bet you really enjoyed teasing him about that."

Dean grinned. "You know it."

"My point, darling, is that most of the time there's nothing you can do to stop reporters from fabricating stories for money and their own entertainment," Sophie said. "You just have to roll with the punches, and try to keep yourself from falling down."

Letting the weight of her words sink in, my gaze dropped to my hands, fidgeting around with the bottom of my sweater. "So you don't care what gets written about your son?" I asked faintly.

"Of course I care," she explained softly, "I just choose not to believe it unless I know that it's true."

The smile that tugged at my lips was crooked. I'd never paid attention to magazine spreads before meeting Ryan, figuring they were all drawn up to cause a rift between celebrities and their fans. And I'd been right on most accounts. Sitting there as the conversation dropped, I was glad that there were people in my life that I could rely on to know me better than what the papers made me out to be.

"Now I know you're not telling my girlfriend stories about me when I was younger," Ryan commented casually, raising an eyebrow as he stepped into the room, pocketing his cell phone.

"No," Sophie grinned, "Why would I ever do such a thing?"

He chuckled in response, shaking his head. There was a split second when a wry smile was visible on his lips before it disappeared, replaced with a tight expression that made him look like he'd aged five years in just five seconds.

"Can I talk to Zoe for a moment," he said. The words were void of emotion and caught me off guard. "Alone."

I was buzzing with curiosity, trying to work out the reason his mood had changed so suddenly. When I did however, it felt like a punch to the gut.

The phonecall.

"Sure," his mom shrugged, standing up from the edge of the couch she'd been leaning against, "I'll be in the kitchen if you need me. Are you two staying for dinner?"

With a glance in my direction, I shrugged, and he nodded before his mom turned and left. Dean, however, laid back against the sofa, turning the volume of the television back up, and Ryan raised an eyebrow.

"What?" Dean asked, his lips quirking up into an amused smile, "You have your own room upstairs. No one will bother you there."

Ryan shut his eyes briefly and shook his head, dimming his frustration before locking his gaze with my own. I faltered when he nodded his head up the stairs, a gesture aiding me to follow him, but stood up slowly, trailing behind him until he closed the door behind us.

I had never seen his childhood room before, and while the floor and walls were spotless, and a queen size bed lay in the middle of the room, there were still a few personal touches that littered the space. Three sweaters with the name of his high school embroidered across the front hung in the open closet, along with other miscellaneous items, and a few remaining science awards were scattered sparsely with old-style model planes on the shelves.

"So," I began cautiously, fiddling with a single photo frame on the bedside table. Ryan was young in the picture, perhaps twelve or thirteen, and was proudly holding up a first place ribbon for his science project in the background. "Does this conversation have anything to do with the phone call you just took?"

I glanced back at Ryan, who was still hovering near the door. His eyes were blank and looking straight through me before he shook himself free of his daze. "Sorry, what did you say?"

I bit my lip nervously, placing the frame back down as I rested on the edge of the bed. "I asked if you wanted to talk because of the phone call."

A fleeting rush of anger burned in his green eyes, but it was gone just as quickly. He dragged a hand through his hair stressfully, taking slow steps towards me until he lowered himself down next to me. One hand lifted up, sliding gently across my cheek with a gesture I wanted to sink into.

But I knew that I couldn't. I needed to know what was going on, the weight of the unknown too heavy to bear on my shoulders.

"Zoe," he swallowed, at a loss for words with a look that made my heart clench with pain.

My back straightened as I met his gaze straight on. "Tell me."

His eyes widened at my forwardness, sighing when he knew he could no longer prolong the inevitable. "Have you," he cleared this throat, "Have read the articles that were printed today?"

"No, why?" I prompted, my eyebrows furring together in confusion.

He sighed and I tried not to panic when he weaved one hand through mine for support. "Some of the articles that were printed only talked about us at the premiere. They skimmed over the movie and then focused on the two of us, speculating how long we've been together and how serious we are."

"Okay," I gulped, knowing that there had to be more for him to look so troubled, "And what about the others?"

Ryan's eyes clenched. "They went digging into your past, wanting to know more about you," he revealed remorsefully. "They know you got pregnant at a young age and kept the child, that your parents are Mr. and Mrs. Hamilton, two of the best lawyers in the south, and that you're studying at UCLA for journalism."

He continued when I urged him to, wanting to know exactly what people were saying about me and what was now out in the world as common knowledge. With the best intentions, he tried to gloss over the negatives, only mentioning briefly that articles were surfacing about me trying to get money out of him to help with child care, or that I was only dating him to further my career, but I knew he was sugarcoating it. Not many cared that Ryan Adams had finally found love with an unexpected, bright-eyed girl.

They just wanted a story, and one that would make their readers to want to know more.

Reporters were ruthless. I'd had two or three professors over the course of my degree that believed that anything should be done to uncover a story, no matter how morally or ethically wrong it may be. It was frightening, knowing that somehow, these reporters had been able to dig up such extensive knowledge about my life.

I shook my head vehemently. "No," I said, refusing to believe what he was saying, "How could this happen? How are people able to find all of this out so quickly?"

"The press works in mysterious ways," he said dejectedly. "Sometimes they're able to find everything online with just a few clicks, and other times people sell them insider information." He paused for a moment. "And I would ask if you thought your parents had something to do with this, but..."

"They didn't even know about you until yesterday," I said weakly, finishing his thought.

He nodded reluctantly. "These stories starting forming Friday night, Saturday at the latest in time to get printed," he explained, "And after what your parents had to say to you, I'm not exactly sure they'd want these articles printed in the first place."

"Yeah, well, I'm sure they'll have something to say when they get wind of them," I grumbled, leaning my head on Ryan's shoulder. His hold on me tightened as his arm came up to hook around my shoulder. I could feel the pressure of everything building inside of me, and sooner or later, without warning, I knew it would explode. "I don't know what to do."

"Right now, just relax, and tomorrow figure out what you want to do," Ryan replied, running his fingers through the ends of my hair. "It'll die down eventually, and the best thing you can do is to just keep a level head and continue on with your life."

I couldn't think of a reply, and found myself comforted by the silence that surrounded us. Over the course of the minutes that followed we managed to shift positions on the bed, and were now lying next to each other. My arms were slotted around his back, my head tucked into the crook of his neck, and his hands were securing me against him, one hand in my hair and one on the base of my back.

"There's nothing I wouldn't do for you, you know that right?" he asked softly, pulling back slightly to scan the expression on my face. His fingers on my back were slowly beginning to move in a soothing pattern, sending small shocks of electricity through my nerves. "Even if that means suing every reporter who publishes false and unwanted stories about you."

A faint smile grew on my lips. "I know," I replied, my voice just above a whisper.

Tilting my head upwards, I felt his breath hitch right before I slanted my lips over top of his. It was a soft, slow kiss. It wasn't rushed, but fleeting, lasting only long enough for me to reacquaint myself with the feeling of being safe, protected, and wanted. When I pulled away, his warm breath fanned my skin, and I prayed that the two of us would make it through this mess relatively unscathed.

It was well past midnight when Ryan dropped me home, having lost track of time once dinner had finished. His whole family and I had sat in the living room, just talking, trying to forget about what loathsome beasts the press could be.

With the federal holiday falling on Monday, my classes resumed the following day, forcing me to jump right back into my normal routine after a weekend full of love, surprises, and chaos.

I was nervous when I arrived on campus that morning, thinking that everyone would immediately have eyes for me. Luckily, I was able to blend into the crowd for a majority of the day, not drawing attention to myself.

It was only when I sat down in my afternoon classes that I began to notice my classmates turning their gazes towards me. My hopes of a quiet day were diminishing, but then again, in lectures that housed less than twenty students, I was bound to be noticed. Focusing on my professors turned into a struggle, and by the time my last class was let out, I threw my books quickly into my bag and rushed out of the building.

I felt as though my whereabouts had spread like wildfire. Every way I looked I saw groups of people looking at me with wide eyes and tight lips, making me feel small and inferior. It was like I was under the observation of a microscope and I couldn't escape. None of them approached me, simply judging me from afar, and I wasn't sure if I preferred it that way or not.

In that moment I would've given anything to be able to shrink back into the shadows.

To make matters worse, when I spotted Ryan's car parked just outside the student parking lot, the whispers and hushed conversations grew louder. He was standing on the curb waiting for me, in plain sight of everyone, with not even a pair of sunglasses to disguise his appearance.

"Hey," he greeted, offering me a smile as I approached him.

"What are you doing here?" I asked him nervously, not being able to stop my eyes from flitting back to the curious crowd that was beginning to move towards us.

A brief glimpse of happiness flickered across his face, before it was replaced with worry. "I thought, well, maybe you'd want to a ride today," he offered, though his words were strangled with uncertainty. "With everything that happened yesterday, I didn't know if you wanted to be alone or not, and you weren't answering my texts, so..."

I hadn't even realized that he had texted me. In light of the articles that continued to appear, I had turned off my cell earlier that morning, cutting off the temptation to scroll through the links and read the comments.

"So what? You didn't think I was capable of dealing with this on my own? That I wasn't strong enough?"

His eyes widened, flashing with hurt as he rushed to correct himself. "No," he shook his head. "You're one of the strongest people I know, I just thought that maybe you'd like the support today."

"I'm just trying to get out of here," I mumbled, speaking loud enough for him to hear as I cast my gaze towards the ground.

"Then let's go," Ryan said in a rush, moving to open the passenger's door of his car, but I shook my head.

"Alone."

"What are you saying?" he asked, realization dawning on him as I took a step backwards. He moved forward before I could say a word, frantically pulling me into his arm as if it was the last time he'd ever hold me like this. "Please don't say what I think you're about to," he murmured with fear. "Please tell me you're not about to leave when I can finally tell you I love you."

"No, I just, I don't know," I sighed, unable to find the right words to explain how I was feeling as I pulled myself from his hold. "I'll call you tonight okay."

This time, when he reached out to grasp my arm as I went to walk away, I was expecting it. I maneuvered around him quickly, moving out of his reach in just a few steps. "I'm sorry," I said quietly. I wasn't sure whether I was apologizing to him or to myself, because as I caused him pain, I was also tearing my own heartstrings apart.

By the time I was far enough away that I couldn't see the devastation plastered across his features, I looked back to see him getting swarmed by fans. All of them were requesting pictures or autographs, and although the guilt was eating away at my insides, I mustered all the strength I could to turn away and keep walking. I knew that I needed the space to get my thoughts settled, and I wanted to prove to myself I could handle the stress on my own.

When I reached the daycare, I breathed a sigh of relief walking through the doors. There were a few others parents picking up their own children, but when nobody looked at me strangely, I figured they hadn't seen the articles, and I was thankful.

Walking home with Abbie, I was given a distraction as she told me all about her day. She'd eaten her entire lunch, which she was extremely proud of, and explained how her and another girl had joined a group of boys at playtime to build a castle out of wooden bricks. Her day had been so simple, so carefree, and the exact opposite of mine.

"Momma, is Ryan at our house?" Abbie asked as we turned onto our street.

I flinched at her question, knowing that because of me, he was probably still stuck in the middle of a hoard of fans. "No baby, why?"

She lifted her hand and pointed down our street. "There are cameras over there."

Freezing, my shoulders were rigid as I lifted my gaze in panic. Parked just two doors down from our house, there were two large vans, as well as ten reporters with microphones and cameras set up, waiting to start rolling.

Someone must have noticed us, as the shouting began just seconds later, flashing lights and reporters flooding my vision, blocking out everything else. They were calling my name, trying to get a response, but as I felt small nails gripping into my palm, I remembered that I wasn't the only one under fire this time. Abbie did not need to be a part of this chaos, and I didn't want her anywhere near these people.

Grasping at her hand tightly, I tried and failed to push my way through the crowd. I'd get past one person just to be greeted by another, and it felt as though the reporters were multiplying the more I struggled to escape.

"Just move!" I yelled in frustration, elbowing my way between two cameramen.

I didn't care if I appeared crazy on the cameras; I needed to get Abbie safely into the house before dealing with them.

Amongst the chaos, I quickened my pace, realizing that we were in front of our neighbours house now, and there weren't many more feet separating us from our front door.

The surge of energy that coursed through me was short lived. I went to step forward, pulling Abbie along with me, when I felt her hand slip from my own. Turning around in horror, my eyes scanned the surroundings for my daughter.

The reporters were closing in on me, not giving me any room to breathe, and in that moment, I felt as though the world was crumbling quickly beneath my feet.

CHAPTER 23

"Abbie!"

My eyes darted out frantically, scanning through the mass of people. Frustration bubbled up inside of me when the reporter's pursuits failed to cease. They were acting as though everything was fine, as if this was normal.

This wasn't normal.

My daughter had slipped from my grasp and these strangers hadn't noticed; they didn't even seem to care.

Through the panic and the crowd, I hadn't noticed another, more familiar car pull onto the street, whipping quickly into the driveway before Emily and Dustin stumbled out.

"Are you people out of your god damn mind?" Emily yelled.

Pushing her way through the hoard of cameras until she reached me, she wrapped her arms safely around me, giving me the much-needed support.

"And who are you?" one of the reporters asked curiously.

"I'm her fucking sister, that's who, and if you and your group of paid minions don't move back so she can find her daughter, there will be hell to pay."

A commotion began at Emily's open-ended threat, though the words simply went in one ear and out the other. The screaming and the fighting was all too much, and just when I thought the weight of the situation would crush me, a soft whimper caught my attention. I didn't know how it was possible to hear it over the crowd, but when I did, my head snapped down, my heart breaking when I saw my daughter clutching her leg in pain. She was resting on the sidewalk, squished between the masses of people. Her eyes were red and rimmed with tears while her chin trembled, a frightened expression masking her face.

Shaking myself free from Emily's arms, I dropped to my knees immediately, pushing everyone away until I had my baby in my arms again.

"It's okay, it's okay," I cooed in her ear, running my hand over the top of her hair to smooth it down.

I was trying to be reassuring and put on a brave face, but on the inside I was trembling.

"I'm scared," she mumbled into my shoulder.

The words were like a punch to the gut, and knowing that I was part of the reason this had happened was painstakingly horrible. Though, due to my actions, everyone finally seemed to realize what had happened, taking a few steps back from Abbie and I to give us room to breathe.

The shutter of cameras was enough to notice that, while they had backed away, they were still looking for a story, and would stop at nothing to get it.

Anger coursing through my veins, I opened my mouth to give them all a piece of my mind, but was stopped when Dustin voice rang through the crowd.

"If all of you aren't off this street in less than a minute, I'm calling the police," he announced, loud and authoritatively. He held his cell phone up as well, letting the press know that he wasn't kidding around. "You're all trespassing on this property, not caring that you're creating a nuisance and a hazard for us, as well as the neighbours, and on top of all that, you've managed to injure a sweet and innocent young girl. I'm sure all of your bosses will be thrilled when you go into work tomorrow with a restraining order taped to your backs."

I wasn't able to tell how much of his threat was exaggerated to get his point across, but it worked. Many eyes widened as they realized that, amongst the chaos, my daughter had gotten hurt, and they knew that if word got out, they'd be the ones under siege.

I was too focused on calming Abbie down to pay attention to the group of reporters, but when Abbie's breathing finally started to level out, I lifted my head to see that the crowd had disappeared, the last of them piling into their van and rushing off down the street.

"Zoe," Emily said, her voice filled with worry as she regarded me with glazed eyes, "That doesn't look so good."

Abbie whimpered again at Emily's observation, having nodded down to her leg, where the bottom of her pant leg had rolled up. The skin near her ankle was swollen, progressively getting worse the further down you looked.

"You should get her to a hospital," Emily continued, biting her lip anxiously. "We can drive if you need it."

My mind was frantic but my movements were slow. One arm wound its way around Abbie's back, while one slipped under her bent knees, carefully lifting her off the ground. Her eyes stung with tears as I jostled her into a more comfortable position, and her arms let go of her leg as they wrapped tightly around my neck.

"It hurts momma."

"We're going to get you to a doctor Abbie, don't worry," I said quietly, kissing the side of her head while it lay on my shoulder. Looking back up at Emily, I nodded solemnly. "Let's go."

The hospital wasn't where I'd envisioned spending my evening.

Most of the ride was spent with Abbie clutching tightly at my arm, the two of us in the back seat of Dustin's car as he drove as quickly as possible. We got stuck in rush hour traffic, and after struggling to find a parking spot, we walked through the sliding doors of the hospital, only to be hit with the faint smell of antiseptic and the somber environment of the waiting room.

Dustin and Emily found a set of free seats while I brought Abbie up with me to the front desk.

The nurse behind the counter looked like she was at the end of a long and exhausting shift, and her eyes veered towards us as we approached.

"What can I do for you?" she asked, grabbing a clipboard from a shelf beside her.

"Umm, my daughter fell over on the sidewalk and she wasn't able to stand up," I explained, tweaking the story a bit. "She was scraped up pretty badly and even though I don't think it's broken, there's something wrong with her ankle."

The nurse nodded, writing down a brief description of what I'd just told her on the top of the form, and I gulped when my eyes caught her checking off a 'possible fracture' box.

"Here," she said, sliding the clipboard over to me, "Just take a seat and fill out what you can of this. Bring it back up when you're done, but just so you know, there may be a bit of a wait until a doctor can see her."

I nodded with understanding, having already figured that the wait times at the LA hospital were abysmal. Balancing the clipboard in one hand and supporting Abbie in the other, I headed over to where Emily and Dustin were seated.

While waiting, I was unable to stop my eyes from taking in the other patients in the room. There was an elderly couple that had fallen asleep on the other side of the room, a few teenagers that looked to have been in a fight, and a handful of worried parents, stressing just as much as I was while their children sat beside them.

The longer I sat in the hard plastic chair, the more I seemed to let my anxiety take a hold of me. Abbie had managed to overcome some of her pain and fall asleep for an hour or two, but I was stuck waiting, watching as one by one, the room emptied out, only to be replaced with newer guests that sauntered through the doors.

Finally, hours later, after Dustin had gone out to pick up some food, and Abbie was shaken awake, a doctor stepped out from behind the double doors near the back of the room with a clipboard and called Abbie back, ready to take a look at her.

"Sorry, for the wait Ms. Hamilton," he started. He was young, maybe in his early thirties, but I could see that his hair was starting to grey in places from the high-stress that came with his job. "Now can you tell me what happened?"

"But I already told the nurse," I said, shifting nervously, "We were walking home this afternoon and she tripped on the sidewalk."

His eyes glanced my way for a brief moment, though he kept the majority of his attention on cleaning the cuts and scrapes on Abbie's legs. "I know, that's what I read on your file," he replied, nodding to the clipboard that I'd filled out, now lying on the table next to the hospital bed. "But, there are bruises on her shoulders, the top of her arms, and her back, and if what you're telling me is the truth, I'm forced to believe that the bruises were given to her some other way."

An eyebrow of his raised, and I shrunk back, ducking my head. He knew that it hadn't just been a simple fall, but that someone, or something, had also badgered her around, and right now, he was assuming that person was me.

"It wasn't me," I spoke quietly, my voice raw with emotion, knowing that I would never be able to lay a hand on my little girl.

"I know it wasn't you," he said, "But if you won't tell me who it was, I can't be of any help to you."

"I don't know if you could be of any help anyways," I muttered.

"What do you mean?"

I sighed. "Do you know who Ryan Adams is?"

The doctor, who's name tag read Phillip, nodded. "He's been a few good movies I've seen recently," he replied, though he looked confused as to where this conversation was headed. "But what does he have anything to do with these injuries?"

"Umm... well, he's my boyfriend."

He looked at me skeptically. "So, you're telling me that Ryan Adams was the one who hurt your daughter?"

"NO! God no," I shook my head venomously, "Ryan's my boyfriend yes, but he'd never hurt Abbie." I ran a hand stressfully through my hair, making it a bigger mess than it already was. "The two of us decided to make our relationship public a few days ago, and somehow the press found out everything there is to know about me. I thought I could just shrug it all off, but then I was walking home with Abbie and our street was packed with news vans and paparazzi. They ambushed us, and Abbie ended up getting stuck in the crossfire."

"And I just didn't know what to do," I continued in a panic. "There were so many of them, and none of them were listening to me, and I wasn't strong enough to push them back." I finally took in a deep breath, quenching the fire in my lungs with a heap of oxygen. "Sorry, I just, I couldn't do anything to help her until my sister and her boyfriend got there."

"It's quite alright," he smiled, though there was pity in his eyes, "But if being in a relationship with him is putting your daughter in danger, than you might want to think a bit harder about what's more important to you. It's important to be with someone who makes not only you, but also your daughter, feel safe. You need to be careful with who you give the key to your life to, because if it's the wrong person, you can end up falling in a downwards spiral that's difficult to come back from."

I breathed out slowly, watching as the doctor slowly undid Abbie's shoe, touching and prodding at her ankle carefully. "I didn't think you were a therapist too," I replied lightly, though his words had made an imprint in the back of my mind.

You need to be careful.

The sides of his lips tugged upwards, the corners crinkling. "I have a soft spot for children," he admitted, "So if it makes their lives easier, I sometimes have to be the one to tell parents exactly what they don't want to hear." I nodded, biting my lip as he turned to face me. "I do have some good news for you though. Abbie's ankle isn't broken."

"Oh, thank god."

"It is however, badly bruised, as well as twisted," he explained. "She's going to have to stay off of it for a few days, and I'm going to wrap it so she doesn't put any unnecessary pressure on it. If you don't have any pain medicine at home for her, I suggested stopping by the hospital's pharmacy on your way home to pick up a children's dosage, because she might experience stunts of pain on and off tonight and tomorrow."

"Thank you, thank you so much," I said, leaning back against the wall in relief.

"Not a problem, it's my job," he replied, "And once I'm finished wrapping the gauze I'll go and get the discharge papers. She's not required to stay for observation, but if you find anything worsening, please come back so I can take another look."

I felt worthless, knowing there was nothing I could do as I waited beside the bed, holding Abbie's hand while the doctor carefully wrapped her ankle. Every so often, as he moved the gauze around to tighten it, I'd catch her wince with pain, and a dull pick would poke at my heart each time.

It didn't take long for him to finish, and when the gauze was secured, he instructed us to sit tight while he collected the discharge papers.

Less than a minute after he'd turned and left the room, the door swung back open. Emily rushed into the room, Dustin right behind her, and crouched down on the opposite side of the bed. "Please tell me she's okay," she begged.

I took a deep breath, trying to fight the claustrophobic feeling that sitting in this hospital room gave me, but all I could feel were my lungs and throat tightening up. "She's fine," I croaked, coughing for a moment before standing up. "I need some fresh air. Are you guys okay to watch her until the doctor comes back?" I asked with pleading eyes.

Emily was too busy fussing over her niece, explaining to her all the up sides that came with getting injured, like eating all the ice cream you wanted and laying down during the day, but Dustin nodded. He was standing back from the bed, hovering around the doorway as he motioned towards the exit.

"We'll be fine," he replied, the ghost of a smile pulling at his lips, "Go."

Mouthing a quick thank you, I rushed out of the room. Everything seemed to be building up at once, only for reality to come crashing down, leaving me gasping for air. I no longer had a hold on my normal life. Between my published past, the horrid reporters, and my daughters current predicament, I suddenly realized that I didn't have a clue what was happening.

I knew where the problem was though.

It had all been my fault. I had chosen to fall in love with a wonderful, sweet, and caring guy, only to be slapped in the face when things began to fall out of place. He was the perfect person, but the doctor had been right, I couldn't ignore the fact that while his life remained in the eyes of the public, mine might never be safe again.

There was a reason I never really dated before Ryan, and that had been because Abbie was always what was most important to me, and it was as if falling in love made me forget that. She wasn't someone I could put up for gamble, and it broke my heart to know that, while keeping her safe, I was loosing another.

Amidst my self-pity, I was mindlessly wandering through the halls of the hospital, catching my breath and allowing my mind to run wild. What I didn't expect was to be pulled from my thoughts as I neared the waiting room, walking straight into the arms of the person that made my thoughts all the more real.

"Zoe," Ryan whispered, his lips pressing softly against my forehead, the imprint searing into my skin, "Thank god you're alright."

For a brief moment, I let myself sink into his embrace, cloaking myself with the warmth and the comfort that he offered. His arms drew me in, and I felt like I had broken through the surface, finally able to breathe again. Though the next wave hit me all too soon, my instinct kicking in as I pulled myself back, letting my arms fall to my side while his hands hovered loosely on my hips.

"Ryan, what are you doing here?" I asked slowly, having not expected to see him here.

"Emily called me," he replied easily, almost as though our fight this afternoon hadn't happened.

I sighed, closing my eyes. He hadn't noticed the deadpan tone my words had been asked in, too hyped up on the situation at hand to grasp the obvious.

"Is Abbie okay?" Ryan continued worriedly, his eyes darting around as though the answer would suddenly appear. He dragged a hand through his hair stressfully, shaking his head. "I should have never let you go this afternoon; I just knew something like this would happen. If I ever find out who leaked your address, or figure out who was involved with this, I swear I'll go straight to the police."

His anger was rising, his jaw clenched, and while I knew the words were meant to be reassuring, they were anything but.

"Ryan," I said, cutting him off. His posture stiffened, facial expression rigid, as I looked up at him. The exact moment when he looked into my eyes, I saw a flash of sadness and understanding wash over him, his taut expression becoming more prominent. "I thought, this afternoon when I," I said shakily, trying to get the words out. I closed my eyes, breathing in before the words flowed out of me, cold and detached. "I told you I needed space."

"But..."

"And this is exactly why," I continued, knowing that my resolve would weaken if I let him speak. I couldn't change my mind again, not right know, not in this situation, and not with what was at stake. Taking a few steps back, I continued, "Look what happened to Abbie this afternoon, and that was just by accident. What if someone actually tried to hurt her or me because we were close to you? I don't know if I want to take the chance with something like that. Taking a few steps back is what I need right now, because I don't think I can live my life under constant scrutiny."

"I understand that," he replied weakly, his hand trembling as it reached out for me, "But if you'd just let me..."

"Please!" I interrupted him, my voice rising louder than I'd intended.

I felt the air leave my lungs when I saw his eyes widen in shock. He was the one that was trying to fix this, he wanted to stay, but I was the one unwilling to risk it.

Sometimes true love required a sacrifice; one that was for the best intentions, but succeeded in breaking both hearts at once.

I clenched my eyes shut. "Please," I repeated, just above a whisper as I slowly began to step backwards, "Just go."

Without saying another word, I didn't look back as I traced my path back to Abbie's room. Pushing the door open, I saw that the doctor was there now, and as I sank back down into a seat beside the bed, I saw Emily's gaze flit to meet mine. There was no hiding how I was feeling, the emotionless mask having dropped as I left Ryan standing alone in the middle of a hospital. Her eyes turned sympathetic, but I shook my head slightly, indicating I didn't want to talk about it.

Listening to Abbie speak with the doctor, a small smile on her face, I was more than a little relieved that she would be okay, but after what had just transpired, I didn't know if I would be.

After all, a broken heart takes the longest to heal.

The night that followed was a hard one.

Not only did Abbie have trouble sleeping, a side effect of having her ankle throb with pain every hour or so, jolting her awake, but my phone just didn't seem to want to shut up.

Texts, calls, and e-mails were coming through constantly. While a fair few of them were from Ryan, wanting to talk or simply wishing me a goodnight, a majority of them were from strangers, or from people I'd met briefly back in Arizona. They'd caught wind that I'd moved to Los Angeles, and suddenly, now that I was in a relationship with Ryan Adams, they wanted to re-connect and catch up.

When the clock on my bedside table read well after three in the morning, I finally took the initiative and shut my phone off, tucking it safely into the bottom of a dresser drawer so that I knew I wouldn't be disturbed.

Waking up the next morning was difficult, and when my alarm went off, I knew that I didn't have a choice in the matter. My daughter needed me today, and although I had a full day of class, I didn't trust anyone else with her right now.

I just wanted to be with her, to make sure she was okay.

The day started off uneventful at best, with a simple breakfast after Emily had left for work and carefully getting Abbie ready for the day. A few of her bruises and cuts were still quite raw, causing her to flinch when I helped her pull her loose fitting dress over her head, but overall, she looked better than she had the night before.

Knowing that she had to keep her ankle elevated for a better part of the day, I set her up with a little play area in the living room. She could see the television from where she sat with a box of toys I'd brought down for her, and her leg was propped up on a pillow, relieving some of the pain that came with the injury.

While she played, I brought my notes and textbooks down to the living room, wanting to keep an eye on her while I tried to go over the topics I figured would be covered in the classes I was skipping. There wasn't much to memorize, but a few new concepts and ideas that were outlined for me to go over and address.

Learning from home felt like a good decision on my behalf, until the doorbell rang just after lunch.

My hand stilled on top of my notebook, my grip on my pen tightening as Abbie looked up to me with curiously wide eyes.

When the bell rang once more, thoughts began to rush through my head. Maybe it was more reporters, looking to see if I was home, or maybe it was Ryan, wanting to talk after the dust had settled. Either way, I didn't have the energy or the desire to talk, so I stayed seated.

After one more ring, the bell finally stopped, and I was able to shrug off the interruption once Abbie asked me to help her put in a movie she wanted to watch. The moment flew from my mind, but when Emily came home hours later, talking with someone that I couldn't quite pinpoint, my eyebrows scrunched up in confusion, only to rise in surprise when her and another rounded the corner.

"Greta?"

The woman that had raised me and taught me almost everything I knew was standing in my living room. The same woman I hadn't seen in almost six months and was the one person from home I missed everyday.

"Greta!" Abbie exclaimed loudly, struggling to get up from her spot on the floor with her injury. She wiggled around for a moment, against my protests, before Greta finally realized that she'd been hurt.

"Oh honey," Greta said gently, moving towards Abbie to save her the struggle. "How are you? You've grown so much!"

After a quick conversation and catch up with Abbie, where Greta noticeably didn't say a thing about the obvious injury, I started up a movie, pressing play as Greta, Emily and I retreated to the kitchen.

"Not that I'm not happy to see you, but what are you doing here?" I asked, disbelief still clouding my brain. I could only come up with one reason as to why she wouldn't be back in Arizona, and it sent a jolt of anger through my blood. "Our parents didn't fire you, did they?"

Emily's head snapped up immediately at my accusation, her eyes widening at the possibility.

The tension simmered quickly though, as Greta shook her head with a smile, a hint of a laugh escaping her lips. "Heavens no," she replied, "I quit."

The tail end of her reply was what had the both of us looking at her in bewilderment. "You quit?"

Her smile softened as she beckoned us towards her. "Come here," she said, wrapping an arm around either of us. "The only reason that I stayed with your parents for so long was because of you two. I would've never worked for people like them if I hadn't gotten to raise two smart, beautiful, and kind-hearted girls from the get-go. But you're both grown up now, and there's no need for me to stay in a house all alone, working for those tyrants."

My eyes grew in shock before I burst into laughter, Emily joining me soon after.

"What?" Greta asked, a smirk crinkling her mouth, "It's true."

The conversation took a turn, ranging from how we'd been to what she'd been up to since I'd left, and through it all, we were happy to invite her to stay with us for as long as she wanted.

Later that night, once everyone had gone to bed, I was tackled by a moment of weakness. Opening up my dresser drawer, I pulled out my phone, turning the power back on as I headed down to the living room. Once it shot to life, a mass of missed messages and calls began to pour through. They were similar to the few I'd seen the night before, and were the very ones that I'd wanted to avoid, but my curiosity overpowered my logical sense of thought.

Scrolling through the messages, most of them were too upbeat, all wanting one thing or another from me, but there was the odd spiteful one. Those ones were from blocked numbers or unsolicited phones, simply sending me messages or voicemails acknowledging me as nothing but scum on the bottom of the ocean floor.

The tears began to build as I went through those messages in particular, not able to help myself, and I froze, stopping mid sniffle as footsteps battered down the stairs. Turning my head to the right, I saw Greta's face appear through the darkness, the only light around us was the small beams shining from my phone.

"Sorry," I said quietly, my face apologetic, "I didn't realize you were still awake."

"It's alright dear," she waved me off, "Now do you want to talk about what's got you up so late and close to tears?"

She was too perceptive for her own good, and as I brought my hand up to wipe away the water from my eyes, she moved closer, flicking on a lamp so that I couldn't hide in the shadows. "It's nothing," I said unconvincingly.

"Oh?" she raised an eyebrow, "So it has nothing to do with this famous boyfriend of yours?"

"If you could even call him that anymore," I muttered, ducking my head as I switched off my phone once more.

Greta's eyes were soft and sympathetic as she placed her hand on my shoulder, still hovering behind the couch. "How about we have a talk?" she offered, "I'll even make some hot chocolate if you want?"

The prospect of a warm cup of chocolaty goodness was too good to pass up, and I found myself nodding, the corner of my lips twitching upwards.

A few minutes later, the two of us were settling into the couch, mugs in hand, and I was brought back to the first night I'd spent in this house. They were less confusing times, and all I remembered

Emily telling me was that I'd meet a guy out here that would make me feel like his first priority.

And I had, but Ryan wasn't the type of guy I had envisioned myself falling for.

"Well, I saw some of the articles about you," Greta started, causing my skin to flush. "They were actually one of the reasons I came down here."

"What? You weren't just missing us?" I asked teasingly, trying to lighten the mood.

She rolled her eyes and cracked a smile. "Of course I was," Greta replied, "But I also wanted to make sure you were okay."

The smile that graced my face was sad, as I relayed wordlessly exactly what she already knew; I wasn't okay.

"Are you going to tell me what's wrong sweetie, or are you going to make me guess?"

I sighed. "It's just," I paused, struggling to find the right words, "Most of my childhood was spent trying to appease my parents and make them proud of me. I felt like I was under a microscope, being watched by everyone around me until I stepped out of line or messed up in some way. Leaving home, it was a weight off my shoulders, knowing that I wouldn't have to act like someone I wasn't in public, but dating Ryan, I feel like I'm right back where I started. People are looking at me, and I'm not sure I want to be someone in the spotlight."

She didn't say a word as I sat there and explained, just nodding understandingly and waiting until I was finished to reply. "Do you love him?"

It was such a simple question, with such a simple answer.

"I do."

"Then do you want to know what I think?" I nodded. "I think thank you need to take some time for yourself, and really figure out what you want, and what you're willing to give," she replied, her words heavy with her own beliefs. "Love is a tricky thing to navigate, and it's never easy. A person can fall in love one hundred times and never find the spark that exists between two people after just a simple hello. Others though, they're lucky. They may feel their heartbeat accelerate and their whole world shift when they meet that one special person, but one of the most important things that people tend to forget is that you can't let the love you have for one person consume you. You need to be able to see clearly, to know when you're falling too quickly or when you're moving in a direction you're uncomfortable with."

"If you need some space, it means you're thinking clearly," she continued. "If Ryan is able to see that, he shouldn't judge you for it. When all of this is over and you come to a decision, if he truly cares about you, he'll be there waiting, and if not, you know that you're love story wasn't meant to last forever."

The tears were growing again, and although it was hard to hear, it was the truth.

I wasn't doing anything wrong. I was forcing myself to see if there was a light at the end of this dull tunnel I had slipped into, and I needed to lead this venture on my own.

"Thanks Greta," I replied, my voice raspy and quiet. Resting my head against her shoulder, I felt her arm come up around my shoulder, pulling me in to her comfort. "You always know what to say."

"Anytime darling," she said, "Anytime."

CHAPTER 24

G reta stayed with us for just under a week. It was long enough for us to show her around town once Abbie had started to feel better, and it helped remind me why I missed having her around.

She wasn't my blood, but she was a far better mother than mine would ever be.

Having her around had also proved a much-needed distraction from all the chaos in my life, but once she left, everything was still there, right where I'd abandoned it.

In the days that followed, the countless messages my phone was receiving began to gradually subside when people realized that I wasn't going to reply.

Ryan, however, didn't give up that easy.

While the first few days were hard, reading and ignoring his frequent pleas to see me, I knew it was for the best. I struggled with grasping just how much he had come to mean to me in just a short period of time, but I knew that, no matter how difficult it was, I needed to put aside my feelings and see the bigger picture.

After almost a week of one-sided communication, I finally plucked up the courage to send a single message in reply.

Ryan, there is no doubt in my mind that I love you - please understand that. You are on my mind constantly, and I find myself missing you when everyone has fallen asleep and I'm left all alone with my thoughts. You are one of the best things that has ever happened to me, but you're also one of the most terrifying.

The life you live is extravagant and public, and while I know we can try to fade behind the rest of Hollywood's drama, I want to make sure that, whatever I decide, is best for me and Abbie. I don't know what I'd do if something else happened to her, and she's the most important person in my life.

I've told you I need space, and I mean it. I want to figure this all out on my own terms, and I'm sorry. I promise you, that when a path clears, you'll be the first one to know.

The message was sent, and nearly a day later, a simple reply came through from Ryan.

I understand. Just know that I love you Zoe.

Those simple words were almost enough to have me drive the distance between our houses. They were short, self-explanatory, and what I'd wanted to hear, but they also tore my heart apart. I was putting him through so much unnecessary pain, by loving me, and I felt like the most horrid person.

That night, once I'd tucked an almost-healed Abbie into bed, I crawled into my own bed, noticing that while the scent was no longer prominent, the remains of Ryan's woodsy aftershave still lingered on his side of my bed. Settling my head onto his pillow, I breathed in the scent, drowning in it as it embraced every nerve in my body until I felt drops of water streaming down my cheeks.

I cried for us, for what could've been and what may never be again.

I fell asleep with tearstains etched onto my face, and when I forced my tired eyes open the next morning, there wasn't a single message on my phone. The communication between Ryan and I had come to a standstill, and maybe it was for the best, at least for the time being.

And so life went on.

Colette and I agreed that it was apt to I cut my hours at the café while things continued to die down. I still worked a few shifts here and there when the business was slower and the possibilities of being bombarded by the public were at a low, but as March approached, I was more concentrated on my placement at The Historical Press.

A majority of my classes had finished up with a final test after only two months, letting me and my classmates focus solely on gaining the experience we needed to propel our careers forward, though we still had a few assignments due through online submissions.

It was intimidating and overwhelming, standing in front of the journal's headquarters on the first Monday of March. The building was fairly large for a lesser-known company, but they had done quite well for themselves, having started writing and publishing from the basement of a small two-story house. Now, with a five level building in the heart of downtown, they were thriving with their exposes on the importance of remembering the past, stating that the more we understand about our beginnings, the greater our future will become.

Hitching my workbag higher on my shoulder, I took a deep breath, smoothing out my blouse before stepping through the glass doors and into the lobby. There were quite a few people who glanced my way as they stepped onto the elevator while I nervously made my way to the front desk.

After talking to the receptionist, I slowly began to relax when my boss, Caroline, came down to meet me and show me around.

Unlike some supervisors, who were driven and professional, she was incredibly friendly and somewhat laid-back. The atmosphere of the journal was surprisingly casual, though everyone was still focused on writing the best content for their readers and worked their hardest while in the office.

Once the tour and brief introductions to some of the other staff were done with, Caroline led me to a small alcove on the third floor. There was a sleek black desk, accompanied by an armchair and a few new bits of stationary for my use.

It wasn't much, considering the extensive layouts that other employees around me had, but I was grateful for the opportunity. Everyone had to start somewhere, and it just so happened that my somewhere was here.

The days spent working at The Historical Press were hard, with several responsibilities being thrown my way right off the bat, but it was also eye-opening. My co-workers and supervisors were putting their trust in me, and I felt obliged to give them my best work.

Plus, the experience proved to be an excellent distraction from letting my thoughts drift to Ryan.

I quickly developed a new routine. I'd wake up and start my day, dropping Abbie off at daycare before braving the downtown traffic, picking up a coffee on the way to work. A few of my co-workers had invited me out to lunch once or twice, though I'd usually object in favour of packing my lunch and saving a few dollars that could be of use down the road. When I'd find free time between researching and drafting article ideas, I would make way on some of my final projects for my degree, e-mailing my former professors for advice and clarity on what they expected of me.

Before I knew it, three weeks had passed.

Packing up my things after a particularly busy Friday afternoon, replying to an influx of messages and reviewing a few too many ideas I'd written down, Caroline stopped me before I could step onto the elevator.

Turning to face her as the doors sealed shut, my expression was curious as I asked, "Is there anything wrong?"

"Oh no," she shook her head in reply, a smile blooming on her face, "In fact, quite the opposite. The piece you submitted on Monday showed great potential, and while I did make a few notes for you to go over next week, I just wanted to tell you that I think there's a spot in our next issue for it."

My eyes grew wide in surprise. It was clear, after the helpful guidance of Caroline, that my work did need a lot of work, and I certainly hadn't expected to be published in such a short amount of time. "Really?"

She nodded, amused by my excitement. "Really," she affirmed. "You've improved immensely in these past weeks, and your article is on track with the theme of our next issue. If it's alright with you, I'd like you to sit in on our meeting Monday morning to get a taste of how the publishing process works and what will be expected of you."

The words were like music to my ears, and I found myself nodding before she even finished her explanation. "Of course, I'll be there."

"Glad to hear it," she said, bidding me farewell as the elevator doors slid open again, "Have a good weekend Zoe."

"You too," I said in response as I stepped into the lift, letting the doors close before a wide smile burst across my face.

Riding the elevator down to the ground floor, accomplishment floored my mind, and there was nothing that could be done to dampen the high that I'd begun to ride.

The feeling of euphoria was still flowing readily through my veins when I arrived home that night, excited to tell Emily the news, and well on until I was shaken awake the following morning.

Being pulled from my dreams, my eyes fluttered open to see my daughter climbing up on top of the covers. She seemed extremely excited, and she had the right to be. Not only was it a Saturday, which meant that we'd no doubt be spending the day together, today was also her fourth birthday.

"G'morning momma," she chirped, lisping her words together while a splitting grin formed on her lips.

She was wearing a pair of pink pajamas and her blond curly hair had yet to be tamed of frizz, which meant that she'd only just rolled out of bed before waking me up.

"Good morning sweetie," I replied, hugging her closer to me as I decided to tease her a tiny bit. "What's got you so happy this morning?"

Abbie giggled when my fingers poked at her side, her eyes shining bright with happiness. "You know it's my birthday," she said through numerous fits of laughter.

"Oh, that's right," I said jokingly, pretending to have suddenly remembered, "You're four today, aren't you? Practically a grown up."

Abbie nodded, proud at the notion of being another year older. She'd grown up so much right under my nose that it seemed like yesterday when I was holding her in my arms as a newborn baby. Looking at her now, it was startling to realize that she was growing up, and would be off to school in just a few short months.

"When are people coming over?" Abbie asked, pulling me from my thoughts.

Sparing a quick glance to the clock resting near my bed, I rolled my eyes, seeing that it was only just after seven, and she was already excited for her party.

Deciding to celebrate a little more than a simple dinner in and a small birthday cake, I'd taken the liberty to organize a small party for her later that afternoon. It wouldn't be anything big or extravagant, but Colette and Dustin were joining the three of us for dinner, and I'd ordered an ice cream cake that Emily would pick up just before the party.

Abbie was aware of all of this, but what she didn't know was that I'd stayed up a few hours after she'd gone to sleep, blowing up balloons, hanging streamers, and decorating the downstairs so that she'd receive the entire thrill of having a birthday party.

I smiled, pulling myself up into a sitting position in the bed, maneuvering Abbie so that she sat on my lap. "Nobody's coming over until this afternoon sweetie," I said, rushing to continue as I saw her expression veer sad in response, "But, if we head downstairs now, I'm sure I can work some magic and get a special breakfast made for the birthday girl."

Her mood lifted instantly, grabbing my hand in a hurry to drag me out from underneath the covers. I followed her downstairs, letting her take the lead as I watched her happy expression turn to one of awe, taking in the decorations I'd scattered over the entirety of the downstairs. Abbie didn't have just one favourite colour, she liked them all, and with that in mind, I'd stuck to a rainbow theme for her special day.

She stayed quiet while she took it all in, her mouth agape with wonder.

"And there's the birthday girl," Emily exclaimed as the two of us turned into the kitchen.

She was standing in front of the stove, spatula in hand, as she made Abbie's favourite breakfast — chocolate chip pancakes. Abbie's hand fell from mine as she rushed up closer to the counter, standing on her tiptoes next to Emily to get a better look at the pancakes as they cooked.

Emily placed her hand on Abbie's shoulder, leaning down to kiss the top of her head. "Happy birthday Abbie."

The lights in Abbie's eyes were shining bright as her head swiveled towards me. She was elated, without a care in the world, and I wanted to do anything I could to make this day one to remember.

Hours later, after rounds of food, laughter, and letting her open a few small presents early, Abbie's small birthday party had begun. To her, it didn't matter that the only people there to celebrate her birthday were people that were years older than her. She was the center of attention, and she loved it.

Dustin and Colette had both arrived around three 'o'clock, both of them carrying a present for the birthday girl.

"Is it time for cake yet?" Abbie asked with wide-eyes, turning to me as everyone cast me a look of amusement.

When Emily had brought home her birthday cake hours before, it had taken me quite a bit of persuasion to stop Abbie from digging into it right then and there.

I shook my head, a smile curving on my face. "The pizza's not even here yet Abbie," I said, smoothing down her hair as I shifted closer to her on the couch. "The cake is for dessert."

"But can't we have dessert before dinner?"

"I don't think that's how it works," Emily replied, and when the doorbell suddenly rang, she stood up from her seat beside Dustin, "I'll get it."

"See," I said, poking Abbie's side gently, "I'm sure that's the pizza, and once we're done eating you can have as much cake as you want."

Her grin spread wide in excitement, and I found a vast amount of amusement in my daughter's craving for sugar, laughing along with Colette and Dustin until Emily reentered the living room with another guest behind her.

"So..." Emily spoke carefully, causing a shift in the atmosphere, "It wasn't the pizza guy."

My lungs tightened up and I stopped breathing for a moment. At first glance, everything I'd tried so hard to sort through and all the feelings I'd pushed to the back of my mind came flooding back in a rocky wave. It was hard to see him standing there, knowing that when I had pushed away his brother, I pushed away him as well.

Abbie was oblivious to the tensely charged air as she wiggled out from my hold and scurried her way towards him. "Dean!" she greeted eagerly, throwing herself into his arms as he bent down to hug her, "Are you here for the party?"

"I didn't even know there was a party going on," he replied, his expression not wavering as he cast a glance in my direction, meeting my eyes with a jolting familiarity. "I Just wanted to come by a wish you a happy birthday."

"Well you can stay, can't you?" Abbie asked, her tone begging, "Can't he momma?"

I let the air out of my lungs, clearing my throat as I nodded slowly. "Sure," I said, trying my best to keep my voice level, "You can stay if you want."

He seemed to sense my apprehension, as did most of the others in the room, but when Abbie let out a cheer of delight, he was stuck, just as I was. Neither of us could say no to her, especially not today.

So he moved further into the room, bringing Abbie with him as he took a seat next to Dustin, starting up a conversation with him. I noticed him shoot a surreptitious gaze my way as Emily settled down next to me, sending me a worried gaze herself.

My mind was reeling, and I knew that wishing Abbie a happy birthday wasn't the only reason Dean had shown up here, but that it had just as much to do with mine and his brother's broken relationship.

"Are you sure this is alright?" Emily asked in a hushed whisper.

Moving my head to the side in a subtle gesture, I bit my lip and stayed quiet. We both knew that, since the night at the hospital over a month ago, I'd spent countless hours thinking of ways that I could make my relationship with Ryan work without the eyes of the public. I'd reluctantly fallen flat with ideas, and had resorted to pushing all the good memories we shared to the back of my heart, hoping that time would be a good enough cure for a broken heart.

The truth was that time wasn't helping; I was simply avoiding the truth, and with Dean here, everything I was pushing down was starting to splash to the surface.

When the doorbell sounded again, I was the one who stood from my seat, mumbling that I'd get it. Luckily, it wasn't another Adams brother, because I didn't know what I'd do if Ryan had shown up here. Would I have pushed him away again, or let him back into my life? The pizza guy wasn't looking for those sorts of answers however, just a simple cash tip and friendly business before he was back on his way.

Setting the pizza down on the coffee table, I let my mind drift away from Ryan as Colette pulled me into a conversation about my placement. It reignited a spark of happiness, explaining to her what my boss had told me the day before.

Throughout dinner and well on until the six of us finished off the ice cream cake, I could feel Dean's gaze flick towards me on occasion. It wasn't often, but was frequent enough for me to take notice, considering his appearance had put me on high alert.

My suspicions were confirmed when Abbie finished opening her presents, a wide grin stuck on her face as her eyes casted over the pile of opened gifts in front of her. Colette had bought her an easy bake oven, which had boosted her spirits as she opened it, seeing the small packages of treats that she could now create, while Emily and Dustin had gone splits on a cute little gift basket. It had a few treats, a new pair of slippers, and stuffed rabbit that talked when you squeezed its stomach.

Having opened a few of my smaller gifts earlier, when I handed her a giant gift bag, she unwrapped several new items of clothing that would serve her well as the weather started to warm up, as well as a new doll that she'd had her eye on the last time we'd gone to the mall.

"Thank you," Abbie said cheerfully, going around to give us all hugs.

When she reached Dean, who hadn't given her anything, he gave her a tentative smile. "You seem to have forgotten a few presents Abbie," he said, reaching down next to him. He grabbed a pink gift bag that had been tucked behind his chair. One I hadn't noticed was there up until now.

Handing her a handful of unwrapped sweets and chocolates that had been tied together with a piece of ribbon, she readily accepted them in excitement. "These are from me," he said slowly, before continuing as he handed her the rest of the bag, "But this is from someone else who wanted you to have a great birthday."

"Ryan?" she asked, beaming as she sat cross-legged on the floor and begun to tear the tissue paper apart.

Dean's eyes lifted to mine for a moment, as I sat still in my seat, nodding in confirmation before watching her unwrap the present. It felt like a punch to the stomach when she pulled out the present with joy, resting the kid's science kit on her lap. Ryan had told me that, along with the model planes that he would build, those kits were something he could spend hours doing as a kid, and now he'd given one to Abbie.

Desperately in need of a moment alone, I retreated to the kitchen while Abbie turned to show the box to Emily, asking her to help with opening it.

I needed to clear my head, which was racing with a thousand thoughts at once.

With me eyes closed and my senses unfocused while I evened out my breathing, I braced my hands against the kitchen counter, not noticing that someone had followed me.

"He drove me here you know." My shoulders stiffened and my head propped up as he spoke, his voice low and void of emotion. "He wanted to come in, but I had to be the one to tell him it probably wasn't the best idea."

"Dean..." I whispered achingly, turning around slowly to meet his eyes. They were the same piercing green as his brother's, sending a sharp pain directly to my chest.

He shook his head. "I'm not here to get an apology out of you or to make you feel bad," he said, siding up next to me, leaning back against the counter with just a few inches of space separating us. He was more than four years younger than me, but the conviction in his voice and the look on his face had me wary of what he had to say. "I'm here because I knew that you wouldn't listen to my brother, so I want you to listen to me."

I swallowed as Dean paused, though I kept my eyes focused on the tiled floor. "I'm listening."

"Ryan doesn't get close to a lot of people," he started with. "He has friends from when he was younger, but ever since he started acting he feels like he can't trust that many people. He'll be friendly with his co-stars, since they're in a similar situation as him, but normal people like you don't catch his eye often. In all honesty, he should've been leery of you when he met you, but he wasn't. He saw something in you that he liked and just rolled with it."

"He told me about you after he brought you to the wedding, and I knew that he was starting to fall for you. It was obvious. He spoke about you like you were a breath of fresh air, like someone who he'd known forever instead of just a few weeks." He wavered for a minute, his shoulders relaxing. "The night of my basketball game, after he'd asked you out, he was on the phone with our mom for almost an hour, nervously asking her where he should take you that wasn't too flashy and would be hidden away from the press."

"I'd never seen my brother as happy as he was when he was with you. He was focused on his career a lot before you walked into his life, and I don't know what you did, but you brought him back to normality. Ryan was starting to forget what it was like to just be a normal guy in love with a normal girl, and you want to know what the worst part about this is?"

I shook my head, feeling my throat lodge up and water spring to my eyes.

"You broke his heart over something that was out of his control," he said earnestly, "And even if he wanted to fix everything, he can't, because none of this was his fault."

It felt as though he'd just dumped a bucket of ice water over me. The oxygen was dragged from my lungs as my perception shifted on its axis. My body was hollow as my jumbled thoughts aligned, letting me see what had always been right in front of me.

Everything that had happened was enough to scare me into believing the first thing that came to mind, causing me to put all the blame on Ryan. Truthfully, nothing had been his fault. My parents were at fault for putting the idea in my head that Ryan may not be good for me, the press and Ryan's curious fans were to blame for the news articles and comments that had surfaced about our relationship, and the relentless paparazzi were to blame for the ambush that had put Abbie in the hospital.

Ryan had been there for me through everything, right up until I foolishly pushed him away.

"What happened to the little brother that laughed at his brother's pain?" I choked out, chuckling softly as I wiped away the tears that had begun to fall from my eyes. "I didn't think it'd matter to you if I left."

His expression cracked, the sides of his lips pulling upwards. "Abbie's grown on me," he shrugged, "Plus, I wouldn't mind having you as a sister some day."

My cheeks flushed a soft shade of pink as I ducked my head, leaning my head on his shoulder. I felt his arm wrapped around the base of my back, and while it didn't provide the same warmth that Ryan's hold did, it brought comfort to me.

"Do what you need to do Zoe," Dean whispered sincerely, "Just know that my brother won't wait around forever."

Tucking Abbie into bed later that night, Dean's words were playing constantly in my head, like an echo that just didn't want to stop.

"Did you have a good birthday sweetie?" I asked, pulling the covers up and over her body.

She nodded sleepily, yawning as she snuggled further into her blankets. "Why didn't Ryan come momma?"

The question surprised me; I hadn't expected it, and with everything cluttering my mind, I didn't know how to explain it to her. She'd asked about him over the past month, when he'd been visibly absent, and I'd managed to dodge the questions with short replies. This time, however, I couldn't find it in my heart to lie.

"Because love is complicated, and sometimes, it makes a mess of us."

Her eyebrows scrunched up, not fully understanding. "Do you love him?"

There was no question as to whether or not my feelings had changed, because my heart still beat faster at the mention of him. "Of course I do."

Leaning down, I could see her eyes falling shut when I pressed my lips against her forehead. "Then tell him momma," she said tiredly. "I miss him."

"I miss him too," I said quietly, my words scattering into the silence that surrounded us.

Abbie was asleep not long after, and shutting the door to her room, I sunk back against the wall. The day had been chaotic and eye-opening, Dean's appearance making me understand the errors I'd made when dealing with the situation. All I had wanted to do was clear my head, but I'd somehow succeeded in creating an even bigger mess.

Before I lost the courage that was giving me a clear mindset, I headed down the stairs, grabbing my keys on the way to the front door.

"Hey," I said, hovering in the entrance of the living room, waiting as both Emily and Dustin's heads turned to face me, "Would you guys mind watching Abbie if she wakes up?"

My hands were fidgeting as Emily's eye scanned my face curiously, before landing on the keys in my left hand. Understanding flowed through her, a soft smile pulling at her lips. "Sure," she said encouragingly, "Just don't mess this up."

There was only one place that she knew I could be headed, and I bit my lip before turning towards the door. "I'll try not to."

It wasn't all that late in the evening, though the sun had already set. The stars were beginning to appear in the darkness above, and as I drove down the familiar route to my destination, my shaky fingers were gripping the steering wheel tightly.

I hadn't rehearsed what I was going to say, but I knew that I had to do something to fix this, before it was too late.

Pulling into the driveway, it took a few seconds for my heartbeat to level out. Taking a deep breath, I pushed the driver's door open, walking slowly up to the front door. Bringing my hand up to knock, I was sent reeling backwards when the door opened before my hand could even meet the wood.

And just like that, as a woman's face greeted me, fragments of my heart began to chip away, falling down to join the pool of panic in my stomach.

CHAPTER 25

T he woman looked to be in her early thirties, though she was an unfamiliar face, and seeing her leaving Ryan's house at this time of the evening did nothing but send a skittish shiver down my spine.

She had been laughing when she opened the door, stopping short at the sight of me. Her hair was pulled back from her face, sitting neatly at the top of her head, while her black coat was left unzipped, revealing a sophisticated ensemble of a ruffled blouse and a high waisted skirt. The woman seemed to embody professionalism, though the laughter lines surrounding her mouth gave reason to believe she wasn't as strict as she appeared.

Never the less, her intimidation factor was high as I steadied myself from the shock, taking a few hesitant steps backwards.

"I'm sorry," I stuttered, clearing my throat as I rung my hands behind my back, "I was looking for Ryan..."

There was a moment where she paused, a calculating look on her face before she smiled, moving the strap of her bag higher up on her arm. "Don't worry about it," she said smoothly, her voice calm as she turned her face away from me. "Ryan, someone's here to see you."

"Oh no," I said hastily, second guessing my decision on coming here tonight, "If you guys are busy – "

"Nonsense," she cut me off, shaking her head, "I was just leaving."

I opened my mouth to reply, seconds away from turning and running from my spot altogether, when Ryan rounded the corner. "What do you mean? Who's at the door?" he asked, pausing as his curious gaze landed on me

He stopped short, his green eyes as striking as they'd always been as they widened in surprise. It was apparent that he hadn't expected to see me, especially not today of all days, but when the curiosity and shock faded from his features they were left blank, giving me no clue as to what he was thinking.

I'd almost forgotten that the two of us were not alone at the moment until the woman, whose name I had yet to catch, cleared her throat while flitting her eyes between the two of us in amusement. "Well, I'd best be off then," she said, catching onto the tension between Ryan and I as she stepped out onto the porch. She turned to face Ryan. "Remember to call me when you have everything sorted out."

As Ryan nodded with compliance, she seemed satisfied, lifting her hand in a short wave before heading off towards the car that had been parked across the street.

Her statement did nothing but heighten the feeling of uneasiness, but after voluntarily forcing myself out of Ryan's life the past month, I didn't think I was in any place to question him about it.

When her engine started and she peeled off down the road, I let out a breath that I hadn't realized I'd been holding. Her departure lifted an unpleasant amount of weight from my shoulders, but as I turned back to face Ryan, it was abundantly clear that it was just the two of us.

I was at a loss for words, standing there in front of him. He hadn't changed much in the time we'd spent apart, but his hair had grown longer, now messily coiffed on top of his head, and he hadn't shaved the past couple of days, his stubble growing out in a gruffer look than I was accustomed to.

It felt like we were two strangers meeting for the first time; the air awkward and charged with uncertainty.

"Zoe," he started hoarsely, digging his hands deep into his pockets as his shoulders tensed. Getting rid of the tickle in his throat, he continued, "What are you doing here?"

I gulped, forcing myself to get the words out. "I wanted to talk."

When he didn't responded right away, the weight of my heart became noticeable as it sunk to the pit of my stomach. He reached out with one hand to grab the door, and just as I thought he'd close it, wanting nothing more to do with me, he pulled it open wider, stepping aside to motion me in.

The door closed behind me and I found myself holding my breath in anticipation for what was to come. I didn't know how he'd react – whether he'd be happy to see me or angry with me for leaving. It was the unpredictability that had my nerves shaking as I followed him silently into the lounge.

With a simple nod of the head, he gestured at me to sit down. When he took a seat on the other end of the couch however, the short distance behind us felt like a palpable attempt at space – a defense mechanism to shield himself from me.

"So," I said, shifting uneasily, "Abbie loved your birthday present."

"That's good," he replied, his voice void of emotion, "I wanted her to enjoy it."

I brought my hand up, running my fingers through my hair in a nervous manner. "Yeah, and it got me thinking about what you were talking about on Christmas; about enjoying the days when everything was simple," I started to babble. "Then it was just you in my head, and I just, I wanted to come and see you and – "

"Zoe."

I hadn't realized I was letting my eyes wander around the room until he cut me off, effectively snapping my gaze back to his.

There was a sharpness to his look that had appeared all of a sudden, apprehension swirling in his irises before he spoke again. "What did you really want?" he asked, "Because I know you didn't drive all the way here after cutting me out of your life just to thank me for sending a birthday present to Abbie."

I sighed. "I said I wanted to talk," I said quietly, "But what I really wanted to do was apologize."

"For what?"

I raised an eyebrow incredulously. "For what?" I asked, wondering if he had suddenly lost all recollection of the past few weeks. "You said it yourself, I cut you out of my life – "

"Which was understandable – "

"Don't," I said fiercely, shaking my head. "Don't try and justify what I did. I had you wanting to help me through everything. Hell, I even had your family there for me, but I pushed you all away because I was scared."

"It was sort of my fault though," he countered, continuing on even when I tried to interrupt. "I should've known better. The paparazzi have been following me around for years, and even though I don't like it, I don't always notice it. I forget that they have their ways of finding out even the best-kept secrets. I let you walk away from me that day in the parking lot... and I let them interfere with your normal life."

"My life has never been completely normal Ryan," I said, my voice relatively calm. "I grew up with my parents not really in the picture and then I got pregnant as a teenager. Meeting you was one of the most normal things that has happened to me. And don't blame yourself for something that was out of your hands. I knew the risks of getting involved with you, and I was aware of the articles that were circulating online. I should've been more careful and understanding when you tried to help me."

"But you couldn't have known that they would show up at your house."

"And neither could you!" I yelled stressfully, causing him to flinch back at my force. I let out a slow breath, giving myself time to work out the mess in my mind before I spoke again. "I had the choice to leave you at any point. I could've walked away before any of this even started, but I didn't. I went to that premiere with you, I chose not to hide our relationship, and I fell in love with you."

His expression softened marginally at my words, and maybe, just maybe, I thought I might be getting through to him.

"I think I sort of just freaked out. Everything came crashing down around the same time and I wasn't ready for it. I was afraid to talk to you because I didn't know how you'd react, and in that whole mess, I ended up losing you."

He sighed, inching a smidge closer to me, his arm reaching out across the back of the couch to twirl the ends of my hair. "You haven't lost me."

While his actions were distracting, I had enough control over myself to send him a flat look. "You haven't tried to talk to me for weeks," I pointed out, "Not that I blame you for wanting nothing to do with me."

I could feel his gaze on me, even when I cast my head downwards to avoid it. I felt my breath hitch as his hand moved to grip my wrist, pulling me closer to him in an act of surprise. He was close now, with little room to separate us, and his focus was solely on me. Shock surged through me as his hand slowly trailed up my arm, his touch searing through my skin before his fingers splayed gently and hesitantly across my cheek.

"The only reason I haven't tried to reach out to you is because I didn't know how you'd react if I did," he reasoned quietly. "My job already had you running away, and I couldn't take it if you ended up lashing out at me again. So I kept my distance, no matter how hard it was."

"I must've put you through hell."

He nodded. "You did."

I let myself lean into his touch, closing my eyes to savor the moment. "I don't understand," I admitted. "You shouldn't be okay with this; you shouldn't be forgiving me so easily."

"Did you want me to yell and make a scene?" he asked, his eyebrows rising with hilarity, "Because I could. If that's what it takes to get you to put this whole thing behind us and keep moving forward then I'll do it."

I shook my head, the corner of my lip quirking upwards. "No, it's just," I sighed, meeting his gaze, "I'm sorry. I'm sorry for not giving you a chance to try and help. I'm sorry for being an idiot and letting my fear consume me so heavily that I took my anger out on you. And I'm sorry for not realizing all of this sooner; I just wanted some space, but I think I took too many steps back."

"Not too many," he countered, "Or else I wouldn't still be in love with you."

I paused for a moment, figuring out how to ask the question that was on the tip of my tongue. "Then who was leaving when I got here?" I asked meekly, my voice wavering.

His eyes sparkled with vague amusement. "Why? Jealous?"

I bit my lip – an action that didn't go unnoticed by Ryan. "Do I have a reason to be?"

He pushed a few stray hairs back behind my ear. "Not at all," he said sincerely. "She's the director of a film I was just cast in, and she was here going over some things in my contract."

"So nothing's going on between you two?"

"Nothing."

I let out a breath I hadn't realized I'd been holding, feeling my heart race as I lunged forward, wrapping my arms around his neck in a hug that was a month overdue. It was an action that was so simple, so effortless, that sometimes I forgot how comforting it was having someone wrap his or her arms around you and hold you close.

With my head on his shoulder, I could feel his heart beating through his shirt as his palm rubbed gentle patterns on my back. "Maybe we needed the time apart," he said, pulling back slightly so that our faces were a hair's breadth away from one another.

There was relief and promise swirling deep within his eyes. "And now?"

"Now," he replied lowly, his eyes flicking down to my lips, "I think we've spent enough time avoiding our problems."

"What about the paparazzi? And your fans?" I asked, fighting off the urge to lean in and close the distance between us. "Just because I haven't seen them lately, it doesn't mean they aren't always going to be around."

"It's like you said – they're always going to be there as long as I'm still famous."

My eyes narrowed. "You're not quitting your job," I said tenaciously.

"No," he chuckled lightly, pressing his lips to my cheek. His lips were warm and soothing, sending a spark of electricity through my veins as they skimmed the corner of my mouth. "If my fans are really my fans then they'll be supportive, and maybe you'll get recognized a few times when you're out with Abbie. The paparazzi on the other hand, will get bored when another story breaks, but if they don't, I promise that there will never be a time that I intentionally leave you to deal with them yourself. I'll always be there for you."

I cracked a smile. "Always, huh?"

He didn't falter once as he leaned in again, his breath fanning my lips. "If that's alright with you," he replied.

"It's more than alright," I said softly, before trailing my hands up his chest and pulling his head down so that our lips met.

Even though the action was based on impulse, I found myself hesitant in the aftermath. My lips were slow against his, trying my best to savor every flick of the tongue and the way our breaths mingled as one.

I'd known all this time that Ryan had stolen my heart, and it was pointless of me to try and live without it. The fear of jumping back into this relationship was still there, but I wanted to be with him, and in the end I knew that it would be worth it – craziness and all.

Ryan pulled back, meeting my gaze evenly. A flicker of concern crossed his features. "Are you sure about this?" he asked huskily, as though reading my thoughts.

"With all my heart."

He was the one to claim my lips next, kissing me thoroughly, causing my toes to curl in delight and a gasp to escape me. It was rough, sensual, and demanding. My body was burning as his hands fell down to grip my hips, and I moaned when his lips left mine, only to trail down my neck and deeper along the collar of my shirt.

It wasn't long before he had pushed me backwards on the couch, climbing on top of me so that the space between us disappeared in oblivion. I wound my legs around his waist, pulling him so that our lips met once more with a delicious passion that I could feel all the way down in my core.

My mind was clouded, but every part of my body was screaming for him.

His fingertips grazed underneath my shirt, sneaking upwards as I melted into his touch. He took up all my senses – I breathed in the scent of his aftershave, relished the sweet taste that lingered on his tongue, felt his stubble scratching softly on my skin, and heard his satisfaction as I brought him to the same level of bliss that I was soaring on. The friction of our bodies moving against each other was maddening, and something that I had gone all too long without.

When he picked me up after I'd been kissed breathless, I laughed, seeing the sly grin on his face as he pulled back while keeping his hold on me. His eyes glimmered with excitement and desire, more than likely a mirror image of my own, and his tongue darted out to trace along his lips.

I dragged myself back to him swiftly, putting my own mark on him as he guided us upstairs – desperate to reunite in a crazy, amorous, passionate explosion.

"You know," I said absentmindedly, "Your brother really knows how to guilt trip someone."

He looked at me, a smirk on his face as he contained his laughter. "You're thinking about my brother right now?"

It was more than an hour later and the two of us were tucked underneath the covers of Ryan's bed, cuddling after reconnecting in an exhausting and exhilarating passion.

I rolled my eyes, shoving his shoulder playfully when he chuckled at my reaction. "Laugh all you want," I mused, "But I might not have shown up tonight if Dean hadn't talked to me today."

His hand trailed up my sides under the covers, a path of sparks lighting up along bare skin. Cupping my cheek and tracing his thumb against my bottom lip, his irises darkened. "Then I guess I should thank him... eventually."

As much as his touch lit an interest in me, I knew that I couldn't spend the night here in his arms, no matter how much I wanted to. I had Abbie at home, and I knew she would be looking for me early in the morning. I'd said all that I needed to, and more, and I knew that I would have to leave soon enough.

"So, tell me more about this movie that you signed onto," I requested, trying to steer the conversation away from anything that would tempt me to abandon my responsibilities.

Tucking my hands underneath the pillow that my head rested on, I waited, interested to hear about what he'd done over the past few weeks. I wanted to catch up, to just talk, but he stilled, giving me the impression that I'd said something wrong.

I just didn't know what it was.

"Ryan?" I started, lifting my head hesitantly, "What's wrong?"

He shook himself out of it, though his eyes betrayed him when he met my gaze. The teasing and happiness had disappeared, replaced with vulnerability, fear, and guilt. "I didn't... I didn't know that you'd take me back, and the movie..."

His voice was barely audible as he spoke and his low rambles were lost on me as confusion fueled my curiosity. "What?"

"The movie is an adaptation of a popular thriller and romance novel," he began slowly, regarding me warily. "I auditioned to play the leading actor months ago and hadn't heard back, but the guy who did get cast ended up having filming conflicts, so they called a few weeks back."

"That's great," I said happily, not seeing the problem.

He barely acknowledged my words as he continued to speak, as though waiting for the moment where he had to drop a bomb.

"I went in and read lines through with the female lead, and I guess the director thought that we had good chemistry in front of the camera. After a few more takes they'd offered me the role."

"And how is that a bad thing?" I asked, my next comment teasing as the sides of my lips lifted upwards. "Does the person cast as your love interest have a crush on you or something? Did you think I'd get mad now that we've sorted everything out between us?"

"It's not that," he gulped, not catching onto the joking tone I'd used, "But I wish it was that simple."

Aggravation bubbled in the pit of my stomach as I sat up in bed, using my arm to keep a sheet up against my chest. "Then what?"

His green eyes locked onto mine, and while they were able to ease the tension that was beginning to build, his next words crushed my heart.

"It starts filming next week... in Europe."

I was silent as it sunk in, but when my gaze drifted around the room, I noticed the suitcases that were half full of his belongings. They took up a large amount of space, barricading the front of his closet, but because I'd been preoccupied when Ryan brought me in here, they'd been glossed over.

"Oh."

"Yeah."

"So what?" My voice was raw with emotion as I felt tears building in my eyes. "Were you just going to leave the country without even saying goodbye? Did Dean know? Is that why he told me that you wouldn't wait around forever?"

"No." He shook his head quickly, reaching out for me as I pushed myself up off the bed. Grabbing my clothes off of the floor, I hastily threw them on. "My family doesn't know about it yet, because until tonight, I didn't know if I was going to take it."

"Why not?" I asked, my irrational and erratic train of thought coming to a halt. My clothes were on, and as Ryan pulled on a pair of pants over his boxers, I found myself able to think more clearly.

"Because of you," he stressed.

His words struck me, my eyes widening as he brought a hand up and shakily dragged it through his hair. "Me?" I said quietly, the word slipping from my lips in shock.

We were treading in fragile waters, having just sorted out one obstacle only to be faced with another.

"Yes you," he said, taking a step forward as I stayed rooted in place, "Because I didn't know if I could leave without at least talking to you first." He was less than a foot away from me now, pausing in his motions. His face outlined his frustration with the situation, with me, and with himself. "But Dean mentioned that he talked to you and said everything he could've said to get you to see reason, and I thought that if you didn't reach out to me, then maybe you didn't want to."

"I'd hardly had time to think about what he said before I came over here," I defended myself, though my voice was relatively level as I interrupted.

In a desperate need of strength, Ryan took one more step forward, running his hands down my arms until they intertwined with my own. "It wasn't planned for the director to drop by tonight, but she wanted me to take the job," he explained. "We went over the filming schedule, discussed what she had planned for me if I took the role, and by the time she was finished, I'd signed the contract. I figured that you needed more time, and with me completely out of the picture, you'd get the space you wanted and I could use the time to regain focus on my career."

Ryan exhaled as he finished, releasing the pent up energy in his lungs. I understood where he was coming from, about me needing time, because if Dean hadn't shown up at Abbie's birthday, I might've kept all thoughts about resolving my problems in the back of my head. He had always been free to make his own choices, and a month after a mistake on my behalf, that wasn't going to change.

"So you would've ended it?" I asked bravely, holding my breath as I awaited the answer, "Our relationship – you wanted out?"

He lent his forehead against mine, closing his eyes. "Not in the slightest," he breathed out, "But if that's what you would've wanted, I didn't think I was capable of moving on while being so close to you."

He was instilling in me the confidence he had with his feelings for me, but that didn't change the fact that I had no idea what I was going to do. It was just minutes ago that I believed I had regained my footing with Ryan, knowing that we were both willing to work for our relationship in whichever ways we needed to – and I still knew that. The problem was that the grasp on us being together wasn't as tight; it had loosened, and was wobbling with uncertainty.

I knew that I wanted him close, that I wanted him to stay, but it would also be unfair of me to ask that of him.

This was his career. It was something that he loved to do and had been given the privilege to experience, and I wasn't going to be the one to take that away from him.

Standing there in front of him, letting myself get lost in his eyes as they pulled me in, I saw the plea of emotion cross his features, begging me for a response.

I had been weak, pushing Ryan away because of my insecurities and faults, but now, I needed to be strong, or else I'd risk the relationship we were both so invested in.

I loved him, but I couldn't be selfish.

Mustering up all the courage I had, I closed the distance between us, my fingers gliding gently over the skin beside his lips. "I love you," I spoke softly, a certain conviction behind my words that made their meaning solid, "And distance isn't going to change that."

I kissed him then. He inhaled sharply at the first brush of our lips; mine moving on top of his slowly and smoothly. With every movement I was trying to convey the thoughts that were consuming me, as I couldn't find the words to explain. The kiss was short, but it left the both of us breathless when I pulled back, my eyes still closed in an attempt not to loose our connection.

"Go."

I forced my eyes open to see his reaction, and for the first time, I saw the faint trace of tears building in his eyes.

"Go to Europe," I continued, choking back the sobs that I wanted to release at the thought of him leaving. "Film the movie and make memories that you'll never forget. When all is said and done, if you still want to come home, I'll be here waiting for you."

A shiver, so inviting, trailed down my spine when his arms tightened around me. "You shouldn't have to wait for me Zoe," he said, "There will always be times when my job forces me to be apart from you."

"Sometimes, you have to make sacrifices for the people you love, and just hope that it'll all be worth it in the end."

While his lips lifted up into a soft smile, sadness pooled in his eyes. "I love you Zoe," he breathed, angling his head so that our breaths mingled and ours mouths aligned perfectly, "And no amount of time apart will change that."

I fell into his kiss immediately, knowing that it signified a new beginning for us.

That didn't mean I wasn't absolutely terrified of what was to come, because the future was never a sure thing, but I was ready to take a step forward in our lives – no matter how bittersweet the feeling was.

EPILOGUE

My gaze wandered nervously around the courtyard, darting through the masses of people. Ryan had promised that he'd be here, but after a few short texts yesterday morning, I hadn't heard from him and I was starting to get worried.

"He'll be here," Emily said, shaking her head as she watched me jitter.

I bit my lip. "How do you know?" I asked exasperatedly as possible scenarios began to race through my mind. "Maybe his plane was delayed, or his filming schedule changed. Or maybe he just changed his mind and wanted a clean break."

She rolled her eyes.

The night after Abbie's birthday, I had returned home conflicted. There was no question as to whether I wanted to make the relationship between Ryan and I work, but I was hesitant about doing it at a distance.

When morning came I was forced to tell Abbie, and Emily as she listened in, what the situation with Ryan was. I told her he was leaving, and I remembered the stab of pain I felt when I saw the frown gloss onto her features and sadness flood her eyes, but

I also explained to her that I did love him. That even though he'd be thousands of miles away, we would still stay in contact.

With the little time Ryan had left in Los Angeles, the three of us – Abbie, Ryan, and I – tried to spend every moment together. He insisted on driving me to work every morning the following week, dropping off Abbie at day care on the way, and would be waiting in the parking lot after I finished. Some days we would go out for ice cream or an early dinner, with Emily, Dustin, and Dean tagging along near the end of the week, but other days we just wanted to spend time together relaxing.

It was a temporary routine, and the knowledge of his departure loomed over our heads until our time together reached its expiration date.

The following Saturday, just one week after we'd reconnected, his family and I gathered at the airport to send him off. Abbie had already said her goodbye and had stayed at home with Emily, and as I watched Dean and his dad wish Ryan well, his mom and I standing back as we held our tears at bay, I was relieved I'd chosen to come on my own.

His family took their time, but when they were done with their goodbyes, I stepped forward, taking my turn.

"Have fun in Europe," I had said tentatively, ignoring the tears that choked back my words, "And come back in one piece."

Trailing his hand up my arm, leaving goose bumps as he went, it weaved into my hair as his eyes memorized every inch of my face. "It's only a few months," he said, his voice was deep and quiet, a faint smile gracing his lips, "And then I'll be home."

"Until you get another job."

A startling heat flashed in his eyes. "We'll make it work," he had insisted before pulling me close and kissing me breathless. He hadn't cared that his whole family was watching our exchange, solely focused on giving me a proper and thorough goodbye.

And for the most part, we had made it work over the last three months. While the two of us had been optimistic about him having a few free weeks throughout filming, his schedule had been hectic, and he'd only managed to make it back for a quick two-day trip at the end of April. It was difficult, there was no denying that, and some times I wished that he was there to hold me as I fell asleep, but we both fought through.

The one good thing that had come out of our time apart was that the paparazzi had come to the conclusion that we had broken up, and had decided to let go of using me for a story. Once the news of Ryan's departure to Europe had spread, the spotlight only lingered on me for a few days before dimming until it was out, leaving me to live my life privately once again.

The months had passed, and after finishing up my classes and the allotted time for my internship, I'd been given the opportunity to write for the Historical Press full-time, giving me something to enjoy as I waited for today.

Because today, after all of my hard work, I was finally graduating.

When I'd told Ryan the date of my convocation, he had immediately talked to the director and his manager to arrange the week off. He had called yesterday morning, confirming that he would be here, but now, with the ceremony set to start in just a few minutes, Ryan was nowhere to be seen.

I had already seen Dean and his parents, after they had insisted on being here today, and found myself thoroughly amused when Abbie managed to wrangle Dean into looking after her as the four of them went looking for a few spare seats.

"Zoe," Emily said, pulling me out of my own head as she grasped my shoulders, "Stop worrying. This day is all about you, and you don't want to think back on today and remember that you were tense and nervous the whole time, do you?"

I released any stress that had pent up in a long, relieving breath. "No," I replied softly, "I don't."

"Then smile," she encouraged teasingly. "You don't want me getting any embarrassing pictures of you walking across the stage with a frown on your face."

I laughed, wrapping my arms around her and hugging her close as the Dean stood up at the front, calling for everyone to take their seats.

"I guess I have to go see where everyone else got to," Emily stated as she pulled back with a smile, "Go rock that stage."

Thanking her once more, I turned my back on her as she headed into the crowd of guests and I took my spot amongst the sea of fellow graduates. Everyone was wearing the black graduation gown and caps, and while I had thought ahead and worn a thin summer dress underneath, the hot, afternoon sun did nothing but make me hope that this would be quick.

Contrary to my wishes, the graduation ceremony dragged on; a whirlwind of guest speakers, various professors, and select student taking up time in the sweltering heat. More than an hour had already passed when the degrees started to be handed out, but with hundreds of graduates waiting to be called upon, there was no doubt that the day would drag on.

I sat through it all though, trying to keep my mind from drifting to Ryan as I clapped politely for every person who walked across the stage.

When it was my turn however, I felt my palms sweating and my mind racing, knowing that once I had the degree in my hands, I'd officially be a journalist.

"Zoe Hamilton: Bachelor of Arts – Journalism."

Hearing my name be called, I stepped forward, climbing the few stairs as I made sure not to trip, and made my way to the center of the stage. Accepting my degree with a wide smile, I cast my gaze out onto the crowd where I could clearly make out the cheers and applause. Dean and Emily were on their feet in excitement, the latter with a camera in her hand as she snapped several pictures of me, and Abbie was grinning in Dean's arms, hands clapping with a proud grin on her face.

I ignored the small prick to my heart when I didn't see Ryan cheering along with them, but I shook out of it, focusing as I shook a few more hands on stage before returning to my seat.

Eventually every graduate had crossed the stage, and in a moment that brought an end to the ceremony, we stood up as the class of 2016, throwing our caps into the air in celebration.

Laughter and excitement had filled the courtyard as people dispersed to see their friends and family, and I followed suit, maneuvering my way through the crowd.

I stopped short when the people around me simultaneously began to step back from me, clearing a path ahead of me. Confusion circled my head, but when my gaze landed on who was standing just a few feet in front of me, my breath caught in the back of my throat.

A surge of relief and joy passed through me as I saw Ryan standing there, bare of a disguise, his eyes gleaming with something that resembled the look of a groom on his wedding day. He didn't care that there were people around him whispering and turning to us with wide eyes – and honestly, neither did I.

Smiling, I rushed forward, closing the distance between us before throwing my arms around his neck and holding on. Any coherent thought in my mind quickly dissipated as his arms wrapped securely around my waist and he brought his lips down to meet mine with an intensity that shot through me like lightning.

My fingers latched onto the front of his shirt as I felt a pressure at the base of my back, forcing me closer towards him in a mix of heat and excitement. Our lips were hot, heavy, and needy as they moved against each other, not paying any mind to the onlookers.

We were both breathless when we pulled apart, our breaths mingling in short pants.

"I missed you," I said, catching my breath as I brought a hand up to cup his face.

His smile softened as his arms stayed wrapped around me. "I've missed you too," he replied, "So much."

"I thought you'd changed your mind," I admitted quietly. "I couldn't find you before the ceremony, and I thought – "

I was effective cut off as he peppered a few light kisses against my lips. "The plane was delayed, and I didn't want to text you in case I did miss it, but I managed to sneak in to see you walk across the stage," he explained. "Congratulations by the way."

"Thanks," I smiled.

"So... are you still in love with me?" he asked teasingly, though there was a hint of nerves and uncertainty laced in his voice. As though he thought I'd changed my mind.

I lifted myself up on my tiptoes, pressing a gentle kiss on the under side of his jaw, feeling him shiver against me. "I never stopped."

A rush of air flowed out of his lungs at my words before a grin grew on his lips. "I guess it's kind of hard to forget about someone when you're calling or skyping them a few times a week," he said cheekily.

I scowled playfully, pinching his sides. "Hey, you didn't seem to mind."

"Why would I?" he asked sincerely, "In case it wasn't obvious, I'm sort of in love with you."

"I mean, it was kind of hard to tell," I replied jokingly.

He laughed lightly. "God I missed you," he said, leaning so that is lips rested against my forehead. "You have no idea how hard it was to hear your voice and see you through a webcam, and not be able to hold you or kiss you the last few weeks."

"Well hopefully that won't be a problem much longer."

"One more month," he said. "One more month and I'll be home for good."

Pulling back, I cast him a curious expression as seeds of hope began to grow in my veins. "For good?"

He smiled, hiding a secret, but before he could respond, a cheery four-year-olds voice cut through the crowd.

"Ryan!"

Turning in his arms, I saw Emily and Abbie lingering back with Ryan's family before Abbie wiggled her hand out of my sister's to come racing towards us.

Ryan chuckled as he crouched down just in time for her to fly straight into his arms. "Hey Abbie," he said as he hugged her, standing as he balanced her on his hip, "Did you miss me?"

"Of course I did," she chirped happily, looking between him and I with a wide smile. "Are you here to stay?"

He shook his head. "I still have to head back to Europe to finish filming," he explained, rushing to continue when he saw the beginnings of a frown tip her lips downwards, "But it'll only be a few weeks. Then I'll be back for the summer." I smiled, aware that he'd arranged to have the summer off to spend time back in LA.

"And since I just signed on for a movie in the fall, I'll be here a lot longer."

My eyes widened at his confession, gasping in surprise. "You're filming here?"

He nodded happily, wrapping the arm that wasn't supporting Abbie around my waist. "It's got a solid script so far, and they've started to book studios around the area," he said.

"So once you come back, you're here long-term?" I asked, needing confirmation before my heart burst from an overload of emotion.

"I'm with you two long-term," he nodded, leaning down peck my lips with a promise.

I'd moved to Los Angeles for a fresh start, wanting to finish my degree and spend more time with the people that meant the most to me, but I had gained so much more.

The three of us were together, and while we had a long way to go before making it permanent, in that moment, I was well and truly happy.

www.ingramcontent.com/pod-product-compliance
Lightning Source LLC
Chambersburg PA
CBHW071433190726
48292CB00001B/220